The Unexpected

Inlander

Kellyn Thompson

The Unexpected Inlander
Published independently by Kellyn Thompson
Copyright © 2018 by Kellyn Thompson

First Published as *The Final Robertson* by K. E. Thompson 2016

This revised edition published 2020

Paperback ISBN 9781087889856
Ebook ISBN 9781087889870

For Tim

1

When he arrived in Washington, D.C., upon returning from the small town on the northernmost part of the Florida coast, Chris did not even stop by his house before going to the hotel where the ball was to be held and where Talon Robertson Jr. was already checked in.

Unlike the civilians in line before him at the hotel reception, he did not have to provide travel documentation. Upon seeing the note in his reservation that he worked for government, the hotel clerk knew not to ask any questions and simply smiled at him as she welcomed him to the hotel and slid his key across the counter. He thanked her with a warm smile that he knew made others feel comfortable and at ease. As he expected, her smile deepened and she relaxed in response.

"Enjoy your stay," she said.

"Thank you, I will," he told her, though he had not yet decided if he would spend the night.

As he made his way to his room in the grand Coastal hotel, Chris politely greeted others in the hallways and elevator, as was the social custom on the Coasts. He was not insincere, but it was his habit to blend perfectly and invisibly into his immediate environment. It made it so that, in the retrospect of the memories of those he encountered, he was never remembered. It was one of the reasons he was the best at what he did.

When he got to the room, he checked it for microphones and other tools of espionage, along with anything else that might look suspicious or out of place. He made sure the curtains completely covered the window. He opened the closet and, as expected, there was a tuxedo ready for him that was made to fit his measurements, which he had sent to the tailor that morning. And on the table was an invitation to the ball that evening.

He set his duffel bag on the bed and checked his watch. He had an hour and a half to kill. In general, he did not like to have downtime in the middle of a project. When he started a mission, he liked to work through the whole job until it was over. The agency would assign him to a case, give him a target, and let him handle it. A mission for him, from assignment to completion, typically took no more than a day or two. But this case was different.

Though Chris was not sure if he would carry out this portion of the mission that particular evening, he wanted to be ready if the conditions were right. He stretched and performed various exercises to warm his body up after traveling and to loosen his muscles to prepare them for anything that might happen that evening. As he did so, he began reviewing the mission in his mind, beginning with the first meeting with his boss regarding the Robertsons, through his time in Florida, all the way to the people he had just passed in the hallways and the details of his hotel room. It was another reason why he was considered the best and why he had been chosen for this job: he was continually vigilant and constantly reviewing the details of a case—but he was so subtle about it that those around him never knew his mind was so active. The people he encountered would never consider he was anything beyond a typical citizen, let alone what he really was.

After finishing his exercises and stretches, he went to the bathroom, turned on the shower, and tested the water with his fingertips. When the water was lukewarm, he took his clothes off and stepped inside.

Still reviewing the case in this mind, he scrubbed his skin, though he had already thoroughly washed himself earlier that day. Now, he washed again not only to look fresh and thus better blend in with the other attendees but also as a precaution, just in case there were any traces of blood he may have missed before. There wasn't any blood, of course; he was sure of it. But he was cautious about these things and always took extra measures to cover any traces. It was yet another reason why he was the best in his profession.

He was not where he thought he would be at twenty-eight. As a boy, and even as a teen in training with the agency, Chris had thought that by now he would be married and even have a family of his own, or at least be in the preparation stages. His brother already had a wife and kids. And his best friend, Zaire, was married. But Zaire did not have kids—at least Chris was not completely alone on that front.

Instead, life happened, and circumstances changed, and opportunities arose. Chris had, years ago, accepted the life of solitude of the position his strengths and abilities had placed him in. This was a life he was not only good at but one where he could best contribute to society and make the world a better place. And with the way this mission was going, along with his flawless record, he had hopes that he would one day be promoted to boss, the highest position in the agency, working directly under and answering only to the twelve Presidents that ruled over The Sectors.

As he finished getting ready, he checked himself in the mirror, making sure all the knives he was carrying were completely concealed. He did not think he would use any of them that evening, but he liked to be prepared.

Once Chris was fully dressed and ready, he decided to go to the hotel bar and wait there, hoping he might run into Talon Jr. early or gather more information if other Pure Star members were there. According to the information the agency was able to obtain, Talon Jr. was the only known Pure Star member attending the ball. But Chris had done enough stalking and observing to be able to recognize members of the anarchist organization, should any be in the vicinity, even if not attending the event themselves.

Purebred extremist groups began to form shortly after The Ban on Pure Breeding was implemented forty years beforehand. However, it was only in the last five years that they really gained any traction. Pure Star, though not the largest, was the most notorious anarchist organization. The group had started out simply as a club, where membership consisted of citizens who refused to obey the rules of genetic modifications. But within the past five years, they had started acting on their beliefs, destroying buildings or systems, hacking databases, and even killing people. As they made their presence known, the government started watching them more closely, and the agency began investigating them.

It was discovered that the Robertson family was at the top of Pure Star and ran the organization. They had spearheaded and coordinated all the attacks. When the agency decided the best way to defeat Pure Star was to get rid of its top tier, Chris was chosen as the one who could most likely pull it off in a way that would not alert the rest of the group—at least, in a way whereby the group would not figure it out until it was too late. Each member of the family had to be taken care of discretely and each in a way that would not bring forth any suspicion of government involvement. It was a tall order, even for him, but with his training and extensive experience, his superiors were confident in his ability to eliminate the targets without the risk of eliciting any backlash from their followers.

As he exited the elevator, Chris wiped the serious expression off his face, relaxed his muscles, and assumed a softened look, ready to act like one of the many guests.

There were others at the hotel lobby bar before the ball, including a few politicians and officials whom he recognized. He ordered a soda and watched the news playing on the television above the bar, while continuing to observe the people in his periphery. A special report was streaming on the rise of attacks on government in the last five years. Statistics were being shown of how the number of attacks had risen steadily, but they failed to report that the number of attacks had fallen within the last year, most sharply in the past six months. Good news was never worth reporting to broadcasters, who were alarmists by nature and dramatically stretched everything to get higher ratings. The rise of anarchy was no light matter, especially to Chris, who found their meaningless chatter about it offensive. To the broadcasters, however, it was just the nightly conversation topic, quick to change if a more lucrative one arose. If he spent more time with people, he would have had to watch the news regularly so he could know what the general public knew versus the real information he knew from the agency. But for him, not having to keep up with the discrepancies was just another benefit of the solitary lifestyle that came with his job.

A Purebred woman sat in the chair next to him. Without looking at her, he recognized her as Clara Fontanne, daughter of two of the wealthiest attorneys held on retainer for politicians and a rising attorney herself. She was wearing a short, bright formal dress, cut low in the neckline, not entirely inappropriate for a woman in her early twenties. With his eyes still on the news, he wondered if her parents kept their high positions for the sake of their own careers or for the sake of her status in society. Chris would not have called himself a Purebred sympathizer by any means, but he was much more tolerant than most of the people of his generation. Being a government agent, it was definitely not an opinion he would share with his peers. Though opting out of the genetic modifications was not technically against the law, it was certainly not seen as being obedient to The Order.

Chris had planned on entering the ball alone, slipping in without notice, but as he saw in his peripheral vision the number of couples going into the ballroom, he reconsidered. Walking in alone might look odd at this event and therefore might make him stand out, but walking in with someone like Clara might help him stay invisible. Being a Coastal Purebred, she was obviously wealthy and of high status, so walking in with her would help him fit in and look like he belonged there, too. But because she was a Purebred, people would not pay too much attention to her, so walking in with her would not draw attention to himself.

He glanced down at his beverage and then made eye contact with her, being sure not to show recognition in his gaze. She laughed flirtatiously in response and glanced down at her own beverage. She looked back at him, but before she could speak, he started to walk away. She put her drink down and quickly followed him to catch up.

"Now with a grin like that, you can't possibly expect me to wait on you to make the first move," she said as she slid her arm into his. "Are you staying here tonight?" Though she thought she met him for the first time in that moment, she had actually hit on him more than a year earlier.

Chris played along, not letting on that he knew who she was or that they had ever previously met. "I'm not sure yet," he said as they approached the door to the ballroom.

"Maybe I can convince you," Clara said, squeezing his bicep. As she did so, she leaned in closer to him, and he could smell the citrus notes of her perfume.

"You're alone?" Chris asked as he looked around, pretending to make sure her partner was not nearby and would not be angry at him for stealing her. He needed her to think it was her idea for him to escort her inside.

"I am right now, and right now is when I want to go in." She released her grip on him to retrieve her invitation from her purse. "If my date wants to make me wait, he can find me inside."

Chris reached into his pocket and pulled out his own invitation, as well. He held his arm out for her to take, which she did, this time lightly placing her hand on his forearm, as was the custom.

They showed their invitations to the officers at the entrance and proceeded through the narrow doorway. An officer in the small entryway on the other side looked over Clara. It was a quick assessment that the officers on the Coasts were trained to do imperceptibly when dealing with Coastal Purebreds. Chris noticed it because he noticed everything, and he could tell Clara also noticed it, probably because she was so used to it, which Chris assumed was also the reason she did not react to it.

When they entered the ballroom, people glanced at her—her dress drew much attention—but once they saw she was a Purebred, they looked away, unimpressed. As he had planned, they did not bother to look at him at all. No one cared whose arm she was holding.

"Wow," Clara said under her breath at the sight of the decor and finery.

Chris quickly scanned the large ballroom. The mixture of aromas from perfumes and colognes worn by the guests and bouquets of flowers and foods of all flavors gave the room an instant sensation of richness and depth. Most of the people were standing around talking, as it was still too early for dancing. Anybody who was anybody in government would be there. A few Purebreds were scattered throughout; a setting such as this was probably the only place to see so many well-to-do Purebreds in one room.

A quartet was on a small stage in one corner, playing soft notes that could be heard but which were not so loud as to interfere with conversation. Chandeliers and extravagant flower arrangements set the tone and enhanced the different colors and textures of evening gowns and tuxedoes worn by the guests. Several tables lined one wall, displaying food in exquisite culinary sculptures. Servers circulated with hors d'oeuvres and drinks. An open bar stood on the opposite wall, and Talon Jr. stood halfway to it. He was wearing a sharp white tuxedo with gold undertones and carried with him the air of inherited arrogance that Chris had come to recognize in his observations of the Robertsons.

Clara began talking to a friend. Before she could include Chris in the conversation, he released her and stated, "I'll get us something to drink." The room was already crowded, and she quickly lost sight of him. She turned back to her friend and carried on her conversation.

His boss was not entirely convinced that this was the best timing—and, honestly, Chris was not convinced, either—but he wanted this next one to be done outside of the target's home, since the last three had been done in their private residences.

He had started with the patriarch, Talon Robertson Sr., seven months earlier. The Robertsons had hosted a party at a rented venue on Louisiana's coast. Chris had been flawless that evening, acting as the charming bartender, and he had quickly gained favor with his target. Since the party consisted of a mixed population of both Modifieds and Purebreds, it really could have been anybody who put methanol in the drinks served to Mr. Robertson, who died in his sleep that night. There was no toxicology test performed, and the paramedics, after interviewing witnesses from the party and learning of how many drinks Talon Robertson Sr. had consumed, labeled it simply as death by too much alcohol.

After an appropriate time had passed, he went after Mrs. Robertson, the matriarch who had no problem running the organization without her husband and who had not missed a beat after his death. If she had suspected foul play, she never revealed it. When he thought of how the family had so quickly taken over running the organization without Talon Sr., Chris knew the Robertsons had expected the law to catch up with them at some point. The actual perpetrators who had carried out the acts had already been arrested, but the Robertsons had to have known it was only a matter of time before they were linked to the crimes, as well. They had been prepared for it.

After staging her death, Chris had searched the house for anything that could give him more information about the family and the Pure Star anarchist organization they ran. The

Robertsons owned much of the surrounding land and had added onto the old family house so that it was complete with an indoor swimming pool, a movie theater, a gymnasium with an indoor basketball court, and two large ballrooms where they hosted parties for high connections. The whole house was full of contraband, items that dated back to a disordered society before The War That Brought Order and that were supposed to have been destroyed at The War's end. But it was not his job to pay attention to illegal possessions. Instead, he just wanted to gather information that could tell him more about the targets so he could complete his mission, and none of the pre-War artifacts could tell him anything useful.

It was only in the three private living rooms on the third floor where any useful items, such as personal family pictures or keepsakes, were found. From there, he learned of Mr. and Mrs. Robertson's four children—Karen, Talon Jr., Adele, and Adam. From what he found, he was able to profile their personalities, hobbies, interests, education, and achievements. From their possessions and the things they chose to display, he could tell each member of the family was brilliantly manipulative in a unique way. Each family member contributed to running the organization.

Karen and Talon Jr. were born before The Ban on Pure Breeding. That their genomes were not Modified was never an issue for them. But Adele and Adam were born in the first few years after The War's end and thus after The Ban on Pure Breeding. As post-War non-Modifieds, they were classified as "Purebreds" and were therefore hardly considered legitimate citizens of The Sectors. Their family's wealth and social standing saved them from the Purebred Community System they should have otherwise been subjected to.

He remembered looking at all the family photos and artifacts and thinking of how Karen and Adam both had families of their own and how they had each opted out of the genetic modifications for their children, in keeping with Pure Star's code. Chris had not wanted the children, Purebreds though they were, to be involved and had decided to take this into consideration when planning how he would take care of Karen and Adam. For they, not their children, were the targets.

He left the house after his thorough search, having exhausted all the leads available there. When the police found Mrs. Robertson, their report concluded that in a fatal accident she had slipped and hit her head on the porcelain tub after taking a bath.

Chris had waited a month and a half before targeting the older sister, Karen. She had a consistent schedule, but she also had many people constantly around her. Anybody who would have gotten to her alone would have to have either been a trained stalker like himself or someone on the inside. He had to make it look like someone on the inside, like a disgruntled group member the family did not trust. From his observations of the group, he knew there were several key members the family did not trust but kept close so they could monitor them.

Karen was too cautious and slick to have accidents and too levelheaded for suicide, so he made it a straightforward burglary-turned-murder, but well timed so no one, especially the children, would see. When she walked in on him robbing her house, he shot her three times with the gun he found in her nightstand, accurate enough to do the job, but not accurate enough to be from a trained professional. He had timed it perfectly, and her husband came home alone to find her, for on Tuesdays, their children spent the evening with their aunt Adele.

Chris had waited another three months before going after Adele. He had rented a house near her and made himself inconspicuous, studying her and her associates to plan the most logical and coincidental death. Unlike her sister Karen, who had been strong with a dominating presence, Adele had operated on a natural look of vulnerable innocence to make people want to help her. She was in her late thirties, had been widowed several years earlier, lived alone, and kept to herself.

In his few months in Florida, Chris had already seen the effects of the assassinations. Three of the greatest masterminds in anarchy history were gone, and operations for the gang were no longer smooth. Their plans were sloppy and uncoordinated, and they were miserably bad at covering their tracks. But Adele had tried to keep it alive. Her legacy as a Robertson had given her the connections her parents had made, but it was a lot of work for one person, especially for her. She had never been integral in planning. Her brothers, Talon Jr. and Adam, lived on the South Coast in Texas and ran divisions of the organization from there.

Following the deaths of his parents, Talon Jr. had returned to Florida for a week to tie up loose ends. After Karen's death, he had returned to Florida for a longer period to help Adele learn how to lead and to establish a new system for their communications. The three remaining siblings—Talon Jr., Adele, and Adam—were the new leaders, and dynamics and responsibilities had to change. But before a new structure could be finalized, Talon Jr. was invited to the ball in Washington, D.C., full of government officials and politicians. It was the opportunity of a lifetime, and he was not one to pass up the chance to infiltrate government himself. One of the older Pure Star members, born before The War, had infiltrated as a government official, worked his way up, and managed to get

Talon Jr. an invitation. Talon Jr. had asked his sister Adele to join him, but she had declined, so Talon Jr. left Adele alone in Florida to prepare for this important evening.

That was two weeks ago. Though Talon Jr. had, the previous evening, called his sister and again asked her to accompany him, she had again declined, saying she would be ready to act after he told her what to do next.

But in a terrible and fatal accident, Adele slipped while chopping fresh fruit for her breakfast, and the large knife had stabbed her thigh, through the femoral artery—at least that was what the police would conclude with the way Chris had left her that morning. It was unlikely that her body had been discovered, yet, and Talon Jr. probably did not know about her death.

Chris made his way through the groups of people and made conversation with someone near his target. When he heard Talon Jr. mention that he was going to the bar, Chris turned around to do the same. He brushed against Talon Jr. and casually picked up the man's cell phone out of his pocket.

They both apologized to each other, and Chris introduced himself as Charles, an art collector from New York. They walked together toward the bar for drinks.

Talon Jr. took an immediate interest. "I'm Talon, but please call me Hawk," he said, shaking Chris's hand. "What sort of art? I'm something of a collector myself." They ordered their drinks and stepped off to the side to talk.

In preparation for this conversation, Chris had familiarized himself with where certain pieces were and what his new friend Hawk might be interested in. He mentioned pieces he knew were privately owned and well known but was careful not to say he had pieces that would make Hawk suspicious.

By now the family had probably caught on, and he had to balance the timing so that the two remaining targets were eliminated as soon as possible but still in a way that would not indicate direct government involvement. With how sloppy the group had become, there was no longer any risk of backlash that would result in any serious damage. As for Talon Jr., Chris was still not sure if he would take care of him that evening or follow him back to Texas. At this point, he decided he would just see how everything played out and take the first opportunity that presented itself. As for Adam, he had disappeared more than a week before the event. Chris hoped he could get information from Talon Jr. regarding the location of his brother, but he would not push it, lest he tip him off as to what his true motives were. Though he was eager to finish the mission, Chris could not mess up now. He had to remain as steady and smooth as he had been in the seven months that he had been working on this case.

"Very impressive. I'd love to borrow some pieces for my museums—on loan, of course." Hawk had taken the bait and saw Chris as a potential ally.

"You have museums?" Chris was a good actor and sounded genuinely as if he had not already known this information.

"I have two private museums in Arkansas and a public gallery in Oklahoma City. It's kind of a personal mission to bring sophistication to the Inland, but it also serves as a place for Coastals to go when they have downtime on business trips. I think it helps them feel more at home. There's a fairly decent market for it, actually."

"I can imagine," Chris said.

"Well, it gives them a comfortable place to be so they don't have to be around Inlanders. And I'm always on the lookout to give my galleries a better reputation." He started to pat his pockets with his free hand. "Let me get some information from you, and we'll set up a time for me to look at what you have." He walked to a nearby table, set down his drink, and started searching more frantically with both hands. "I'm sorry. I can't seem to find my phone." He looked around the room as if trying to remember where he might have left it. Then, he looked back at Chris and said, "I hate to be rude and run off, but I'm afraid I'll have to touch base with you later. I'm expecting a call." He started to walk away.

"Actually," Chris started.

Hawk stopped and turned back to Chris.

"If it's urgent, you can use my phone to change your voicemail so people call your hotel room instead." Chris pulled out a phone and held it, along with a business card, out to Hawk.

Hawk looked at the phone, the business card, and then back at Chris.

"In fact, take it for the evening," Chris said, encouraging him to take the phone, using the tone in his voice and expression on his face that he always used when he needed someone to trust him completely. "I don't need it tonight, come to think of it. People can leave me a message if they need to. It will be a nice break, actually."

With a tilt of his head and slight suspicion in his eye, Talon Jr. took the phone from him. "Thank you," he said, looking at the business card. Hawk looked toward the door, and Chris could tell he was considering going back to his room to look for his phone. But then Hawk looked around the room, and Chris could tell he did not want to waste a single moment or possible opportunity to make a name for himself among government officials.

Chris waited patiently with that same rational yet trusting look on his face, knowing if he said anything now it would come off as pushy and therefore suspicious.

Hawk glanced at Chris and then at the business card once more and relaxed, releasing any residual suspicion. He looked back up at Chris. "I'll return it in the morning when I buy you breakfast. We can discuss a deal for the loans and set up a time for me to visit New York." His devilish smile made Chris realize how he had formed so many close connections. He was genuinely interested in everybody because each person he came into contact with was a potential connection, cover-up, or alibi.

Chris knew that Talon Jr. had gotten every investment backing he had ever asked for—though the investors did not know that a portion of their investments were used to supply illegal means, the profits of which they never saw. But always happy with their returns, his investors never questioned if the numbers were true.

"Actually, I have to catch an early flight back, so I'm afraid I have to leave the hotel before six," Chris said. He looked around with conceit. "I would suggest meeting later this evening, but I'll be"—he turned as he checked out a woman who was walking by—"busy." He looked back at Hawk, who gave Chris an approving look.

"But I believe you'll be busy with someone else," Hawk said and nodded toward someone behind Chris.

Chris turned around and saw Clara, who winked at him when their eyes met.

"I'll trade you for anyone in this room," Hawk said in a low voice.

Chris turned back to him. "Anyone?"

"For a Purebred like that, I'll get you two of whatever you want."

"She's worth a bit more than that, wouldn't you say?" Chris suggested, playing along. He was grateful for Clara, now, for his supposed connection with a Purebred was giving him more rapport with his target.

Hawk chuckled with an air of mutual defeat. "I'll leave your phone at the front desk, then," he said decidedly.

"No, I don't trust this place," Chris said quickly and leaned in as if to relate something of the strictest confidence.

Hawk brightened in interest and prepared himself for secrecy.

"Last time I stayed here," Chris started in a low voice, "a watch went missing from my room, and they denied they had anything to do with it." He clasped his fingers around his watch, and Hawk took note of it.

"I hope you got compensation if it was like the piece you wear now," Hawk said and lifted his sleeve over his wrist as the two men compared timepieces. "Mine's not as nice as yours, but the style suits me more."

Chris nodded in agreement and waited calmly for Hawk to come around. He had Hawk's full trust, now.

"I'll tell you what. This is the key to my suite," Hawk said as he pulled out a hotel key and told Chris his room number. "I'll leave the phone on the table at the entrance. Just replace the phone with the key."

"Are you sure?" Chris asked him, convincingly surprised by the man's trust.

"Of course. You gave me your phone. The least I can do is give you my key." The two men laughed at the joke, and then Hawk said with a devious smirk, "Just try to be quiet and do not disturb, if you know what I mean."

Chris took the key and looked down at it as he laughed with Hawk.

"Well, I'm going to go change my voicemail," Hawk said. "We'll arrange an appointment when I return?"

Chris agreed, and his target went outside, dialing as he left.

Chris pulled out his personal phone and quickly sent a message that the temporary phone was in use. In an office nearby, Chris's friend and colleague, Zaire, was monitoring the temporary phone. Chris put his personal phone away and made small talk with other guests while he waited.

Hawk returned, and they set a date for the following month. Hawk wrote the date and time of the appointment on the business card Chris had given him. After polite conversation, they parted to continue the evening making new connections.

When Chris turned around, Clara faced him. "Is this my drink?" she asked, taking the untouched bourbon from his hands.

"You wanted to talk to me?"

"I was hoping to do more than talk, but we can wait until another time, if your mind is elsewhere. I've taken an interest in you."

"Have you, now?"

Clara looked beyond Chris and smiled wryly to someone behind him. "Your friend looks at me like I'm a piece of meat."

Chris turned around to see Hawk, who raised his eyebrows and gave a nod. Chris turned back to Clara and whispered in her ear, "You might steer clear of that one."

She whispered back, "I know."

He looked at her, hiding his surprise that she was able to spot a villain among her own, and instead grinned at her like they shared an inside joke.

She waved to someone across the room and turned back to Chris. She put her hand on his arm, indicating she was about to take her leave, and said, "Don't worry about me. I can handle myself. I have all my life." She raised her glass and thanked him before walking away.

Shortly after their separation, when he was certain he could gain nothing further from observing Talon Jr. in that setting, Chris slipped away from the party, unnoticed. He went to his hotel room and changed into a black silent outfit, gloves, and silent shoes. He then let himself into Talon Jr.'s suite.

The suite was on the top floor of the hotel and was complete with a living room, dining room, kitchen, two bedrooms and a coat closet at the entrance. Chris checked the coat closet and saw that it was empty. He safely assumed Hawk would not use it that evening and stepped inside. As he waited, he again reviewed the details of the case in his mind.

Chris stood focused, silent and motionless in the closet for more than three hours before he heard the door open. Talon Jr., with more than a few drinks inside of him, brought a loud and clumsy woman to his suite. Chris listened intently, hoping the woman would leave. If she did not, he would have to wait until another time to get to Hawk. He should have known Hawk would not return to his room alone. But he waited, nonetheless, just in case she did decide to leave. He heard the couple go to the back bedroom. Almost five minutes later, he heard the woman getting a glass of water and announce she was about to take a shower. He heard Hawk tell her he was going out on the balcony to smoke. After Chris heard the staggering woman hit every surface and corner on her way to the bathroom, the shower was turned on, and she was inside it. He stepped outside of the closet, got his phone from the table, and went to the balcony.

"I got the phone," Chris said, holding it up as he stood in the doorway.

Chris was careful not to step out onto the balcony immediately. The bedroom behind him was dark, and the bright light from the balcony sconce masked him so his face could not be seen next to it. He glanced at his watch and looked around the outside. Most of the snipers on the tops of the surrounding buildings knew of him from training, but they did not keep track of his missions. But, really, it did not matter if they did see him. Any mistakes he made would have easily been fixed with false alibis and retractions of statements by witnesses. But one of the reasons he was the best agent in the agency's history was because in the eight years he had been doing this, nobody had ever had to cover for him. He quickly calculated which positions on the balcony would not give him away.

Talon Jr., who had been looking away from the room, was startled and turned around suddenly. In the contrast of the light from the streets and balcony, his light skin carried a pinkish undertone, making the light freckles on his shoulders and arms apparent. He had a five o'clock shadow that was lighter than the hair on his head, which was dark red. In the night, his dark blue eyes could have been mistaken as brown. He held his hand up to shield his eyes from the light next to the doorway where Chris was standing and gave Chris a confused look as he stared at his clothes. He tried to play it off, remembering that he was shirtless and had also changed into more casual pants. He smiled and said, "Oh, yes. You didn't have to come in and say hi. You're lucky you didn't come in within the last hour." He laughed and gestured toward the bedroom, which caused him to sway, but he caught himself before falling.

Glancing at a sniper turning to walk away from them, Chris slyly walked out onto the balcony and asked, "Is your family in on the art gallery? I have been known to give discounts on loans to family businesses."

Chris was nonchalant, and Hawk suspected nothing. Instead, he nodded his head in understanding that Chris wanted to discuss business, a topic Hawk never turned down. He turned away again as the August heat caused beads of sweat to form on his muscular back. Chris smiled to himself when he saw the glass of whiskey in Hawk's grip. It would be a useful prop for his purpose.

Hawk looked grave and deep in thought. "My family is…" He trailed off and did not finish. He put a hand on the balcony wall to steady himself. "My brother is straying from the family values." Hawk was being serious and reflective. "He's changed his aspirations, changed his views and teaches his kids different ways than what we were taught. He's becoming quite estranged." He laughed and waved the hand with the glass, like he was flinging his brother's new image to a distant world.

"That's too bad, to see families split apart," Chris responded.

Chris stepped out of a sniper's view and into the shadow of the back corner farthest from the door to the room. The humid night air was a thick blanket of heat around him, but his heart and lungs were steady. He heard people walking on the street below. The shower was still going, and the woman was still inside it. Chris was running out of time, but he wanted to first try to get information about Adam.

"Where is your brother?" he asked Hawk, like he was just curious to get to know him a little more.

"Oh, he lives on the South Coast in Texas, but he's in Iowa right now." Hawk chuckled loudly and drunkenly as he leaned against the wall to face Chris. "Yep, says he's going to get our sister." His tone made it apparent he thought his brother was foolish. "Thinks he can help her hide," he said with sarcasm and laughed again. But then a flash of guilt crossed his face as he realized he was getting too personal and had said too much. "Anyway," he continued and turned away from Chris. "This is a beautiful city. I always love visiting." He took a drink.

As a sniper turned around, Chris shifted positions once more, moving closer to the edge of the balcony. "You can see the new monument from here," Chris said and pointed down the street running alongside the hotel. Then, he added, "Not really well, I guess." He leaned over the edge and said, "Oh, yeah, you can see it really well from this angle." He looked down and saw that the people he had heard earlier were nearly out of sight. He casually made sure nobody else was coming. He quickly glanced down and measured the distance and geometry required for the concrete base of a streetlamp to ensure the death would be instant.

"Really?" Talon Jr. asked as he staggered closer to Chris, bumping against the balcony wall for support, and leaned over. "I can barely see it."

"You have to lean out a little bit more," Chris said as he took a step back in time for a sniper across the way to turn around and miss seeing him as he retreated back into the shadows. The sniper scanned the horizon, saw Talon Jr. leaning over the railing on the balcony, and continued to scan her surroundings. "Your brother searches in vain," Chris told Hawk, his voice low and ominous.

"I know. She's hopeless," Hawk said as he leaned out farther, squinting his eyes to near closure, determined to see the monument despite his intoxicated, blurry vision.

The sniper turned back around, facing away from them, and continued pacing the top of her building. Chris stepped up behind Hawk and said, "She's dead."

Talon Jr. barely had time to register what Chris had said before Chris, in one swift motion, lifted him up by the waist of his pants and gave him a slight push over the edge.

Before he could be seen or the thud of the body down below be heard, Chris was in the bedroom, retrieving the business card he had given Talon Jr. at the party. He heard the whiskey glass shatter on the sidewalk, glanced at the balcony to be sure no trace was left, and was out of the suite before the woman got out of the shower.

Chris silently shut the door to the suite behind him as he left, satisfied that one more piece of the mission was a success and only one target remained. But as he headed back to his hotel room, Chris searched his memory for any indicators that Adele had been planning a trip to Iowa. He knew there was nothing he overlooked. He had not stalked Adam or Talon Jr. as much, since they had been in Texas, but he had stalked the rest of the family for months in Florida. There was never any mention of Iowa. And in the past days in particular, when he was closest to Adele, hiding in the shadows of her house, observing her every move, listening to her every word, there was absolutely no intention of leaving on her part. Nor could he think of any reasons as to why she would meet Adam in Iowa of all places. It was possible that Talon Jr. had lied, having caught on to who Chris was and what he was about to do and so gave false information to help his brother hide. But if Talon Jr. had wanted to give Chris a false lead, he would have made up a more believable lie. It just didn't make sense. And he did not like when things did not add up, especially when a mission was so close to completion.

2

Around six o'clock the next morning, Chris woke up and checked his phone for messages. There was one from his boss, telling Chris and Zaire to be at his office by eight o'clock.

As he was setting his phone back on the nightstand, another message came through, this one from Zaire. It read: "Breakfast at 7?"

Chris smiled when he saw it. It felt good to be back home and to return to the normalcy of life before this unusually long mission. Breakfast with Zaire was a habit they had started back in training.

Citizens were chosen for their Societal Roles in a three-round recruiting process, where the first, second, and third rounds occurred at ages thirteen, fifteen, and eighteen, respectively. At each round, a citizen was evaluated and appointed a role in society, after which they were sent to specialized schools for further training in their assigned fields. Those who were not recruited remained in the mainstream school system for talents to surface. If they were not recruited in their first round, they were retested at age fifteen. At eighteen, any students left in the mainstream school system took generalized tests and were placed in jobs or colleges and redistributed throughout The Sectors as needed.

Chris had been recruited to work in government at age thirteen, during his first round of testing. To his family and anyone else who knew he worked in government, that could have meant anything; as a government employee, he was required to never reveal his specific job. Only public officials and officers were allowed to reveal their titles. But specifically, Chris had been recruited to train to be an agent. The agency Chris worked for was the official law enforcement of the Sector government system, concerned largely with keeping order on a Sector level, as opposed to the officers who walked the streets.

It was on the first day of training that he met Zaire, who was fifteen at the time, having been recruited during his second round. Over that first year in the academy, the two became best friends. One thing they shared in common was their eagerness to get started early in the day, so they often ate breakfast together. Upon completing his training at the age of eighteen, Zaire was redistributed to Washington, D.C. When Chris completed his training two years later and was also sent to D.C., they continued the tradition by meeting for breakfast at the restaurant in the basement of one of the agency's buildings.

After replying, "See you then," Chris set his phone on the nightstand and got out of bed. When he finished exercising, he put on his gear and grabbed his duffel bag. Before he left, he checked the hotel room to make sure it was the same as he had found it. On his way to the agency, he walked on the street where Talon Jr.'s body had fallen. It had been cleared, and everything was back to normal. If the people walking around knew about it, they did not care enough to look.

As Chris approached the restaurant, Zaire came from the opposite direction. "Hey, man, what's up," Chris said.

"It's good to see you," Zaire said, hugging Chris. "It's been a while, hasn't it?" The entire seven months Chris was in Florida, he had been in contact with Zaire and their boss, Xiao, but they had not seen each other in person. "I've got to hand it to you, Chris," Zaire said as he opened the door, "you've definitely outdone yourself with this one. How are you doing?"

"I'll be glad when it's over," Chris said as they walked toward a table. As they sat down, Chris looked over his coworker and snorted. "By the way, nice suit."

Zaire pretended to adjust his suit jacket. "Yes, I'm changing departments soon and being moved to Public Relations. Once we put this one in the vault, I'm officially on the front end of the public eye. This afternoon, I'm shadowing a press meeting."

It was customary in the agency that agents were moved to a new department every two years. It was instigated to keep everything fresh with new ideas and constant evolution. Zaire's intelligence made him a great analyst in the Department of Anarchy Prevention, but his genuine and friendly disposition was ideal for dealing with the media. People trusted him, and he contributed to the agency's positive image. He had been in the Department of Public Relations once before, so it would not be a rough transition for him.

But unlike Zaire—and the other agents—Chris had not changed departments for eight years. He was technically still in his second Department Assignment, while Zaire was on his sixth and transitioning into his seventh.

Custom teams were assembled for each new case, varying member associations to ensure secrecy and prevent corruption. An agent's file consisted of their current Department Assignment and availability, their grades and performance records from the academy, and notes on their work and experience in the agency since graduating. Boss's would search the database of available agents within their department and request their service for a specific position in a mission, matching the skills of the agent with what was needed for the case. Agents were not supposed to be chosen for the same position for consecutive missions, but Chris was almost always assigned the position of assassin on missions, even though an agent holding the same position for so many missions in a row was frowned upon by the agency. It was Xiao who continually convinced the twelve Presidents who ruled over The Sectors that Chris should remain in the Department of Anarchy Prevention. He was good at his job. He was valuable.

Furthermore, agents were not supposed to work with each other or bosses for consecutive missions. But when they were all in the same department—that is, when Zaire was also in the Department of Anarchy Prevention—Xiao convinced the Presidents to let him choose Chris and Zaire for his cases more often than what was technically allowed. The three of them— Chris as the field agent, Zaire as the analyst, and Xiao as their boss—were so brilliant with their tactics and maneuvers that the Presidents let them work together more often than was usually permitted.

Though Chris could be equally as friendly as Zaire, a Public Relations job was one Chris would never want. "You're a good fit for it," he told Zaire.

"It's not so bad so far. I actually watch the news on a regular basis now."

Chris glanced down at his menu. It had not changed since the last time he was there. "I haven't followed the news since we started training. Fifteen years of disconnection." Chris closed his menu and put it at the edge of the table. "What's it like?"

"The news is the same as it was before—not just when I was in Public Relations last time, but even when we were kids." Zaire put his menu on top of Chris's.

They both fell silent as their waitress approached the table. "Well, hello there," she said flirtatiously to Chris. "Welcome back. I haven't seen you in a few months at least."

Like many of the agents, Zaire and Chris ate at the agency restaurant every morning, beginning each day brainstorming suspects and crimes without being heard or bothered. It was ideal for agents because it was full of small alcoves for privacy, and there was abundant space between the tables. Though located in an agency building, there was an expectation that people kept to themselves there, free to take a break or hold private meetings.

"I was out of town," Chris said as he smiled at her, avoiding Zaire's eyes.

"Oh, well, then I can't be mad at you anymore. I was afraid you were cheating on us." She poured water into the glasses on the table. "The usual, gentlemen?"

They nodded, and she took their menus. As she walked away, Chris unfolded his napkin, put it on his lap, and finally looked back up at Zaire, who was suppressing a smile.

"Well, she didn't remember that I haven't been here in a month," Zaire said, delighted that someone had noticed Chris. "How are you holding up?" he asked Chris more seriously.

"I'm all right. Glad to be home. Looking forward to the end of this mission."

"Seven months is a long time," Zaire agreed. "But eight years is also too long."

"Really?"

"You've changed," Zaire said. "Your reports have become dry, and I can tell you're settling into a comfortable life where you are."

"It's probably just this case. Once it's over, I'll be back to the usual pace." Most cases, for Chris's part, took no more than a few days. Other team members would assemble the intel.

When they were ready, they would call in Chris and brief him on what he needed to know for the case. Then, he would finish the job swiftly and quietly.

"Maybe. But I have a more selfish reason for wanting you to switch departments and settle down," Zaire said seriously.

"If your wife is trying to set me up with one of her friends again, tell her she had her chance and blew it."

"Oh come on, that was two years ago."

"It doesn't matter. I haven't changed that much."

"Well, that's not the news I wanted to tell you."

Chris leaned in closer, realizing his friend had been waiting until they were in person to tell him his news. "Okay," he said.

Their waitress came back and put hot tea in front of them both. They thanked her and remained silent until she was out of earshot.

"We both got a clean bill of health." Zaire could not hide the excitement in his eyes.

Chris's heart sank, despite being happy for his friend. He knew this day would come, when Zaire would progress through life's milestones without him. But he had long ago accepted his current lifestyle and convinced himself that he was satisfied.

"We're on to stage two," Zaire continued, referring to the Child License.

The Child License had been instigated immediately after The War That Brought Order, forty years beforehand: stage one was the physical screening, mostly a genetic analysis performed by a computer algorithm that ensured seventy percent genetic diversity on at least three nodes; stage two was the psychological screening, mostly a common core template of criteria to ensure applicants were in harmony with The Order and society; and stage three consisted of financial and life planning, mostly a process to prepare files, systems, and databases for a new member of society. Once completed, the

License was officially given to the applicants, and they had government approval to reproduce. Once a child was conceived, genotyping commenced, and the embryo's entire genome was mapped. If there were any known problems, such as mutations that would result in disease, the genome would be properly edited for a healthier, crisper version of the embryo to develop into a Modified human being. In addition, the latest advances in genome editing were also prescribed to make the Modified human less susceptible to viruses and bacterial infections. Since introducing the Modified Human Genome and The Ban on Pure Breeding, most of the world's previously known genetic, viral, and bacterial diseases had been eliminated in The Sectors. The rare cases of disease that remained were contained in the Purebred Communities that were located in the Inland.

The Right to Bear Children was a result of the original post-War Ban on Illegal Breeding, which had introduced the Child License and made it illegal to have children without it. Those who had broken the law had their children taken from them and were made sterile. As a result, a messy black market of babies and surrogates and reproductive organs had ensued. That original Ban on Illegal Breeding was quickly replaced with The Ban on Pure Breeding, which made it so that children of parents who earned a Child License and had the embryos Modified had government privileges made available to them. Those who did not comply and chose not to have their children Modified—"Purebreds," as they were called—did not receive government privileges. If they could not afford to take care of them on their own, their non-Modified offspring were forced to live in Purebred Communities, where limited resources were made available to them in exchange for work. Thus, only the wealthy could afford to break this law.

"You don't think they'll realize you're psycho? Those counselors are highly trained." There was sarcasm in Chris's tone. It was commonly known that the psychologists who screened Child License applicants had flunked out of higher level jobs for the government, so they screened married couples to see if they were fit to raise children.

"*I've* had training. I can pass any psychological exam thrown at me," Zaire said with a smirk. "It's my wife I'm worried about."

"Well, congratulations, man," Chris said, standing up to give Zaire a congratulatory hug.

Zaire laughed as he also stood up and hugged Chris, no longer hiding his excitement, even for the sake of his friend. "Thanks, man."

As they sat back down, Chris said, "You'll have to keep me updated on the process."

"Oh, I will. It will be a nice change from our normal topic of conversation."

"Yeah, great timing." Agents were not allowed to discuss their work unless they had been assigned to the same mission. Now that Zaire would be in a different department, they would have to keep all thoughts of work to themselves.

"Anyway," Zaire started, "all this thinking about kids got me thinking about you. You know, it would be nice if you had kids, too, so they could be friends."

"You just want me to find someone, have kids, and change my life completely. Easy."

"Well, don't you?"

"No, I like my life," Chris said, a little too defensively.

"Oh, I'm certain you think you do," Zaire said. "But I was thinking about the old days. I remember in training, you were the best one in the class, a silent stalker with quick, clean motions—and you loved it, but I also remember you said you only wanted to be a field agent for a few years, and then you wanted to be in stationary departments so you could have a family. What changed?"

"Nothing changed. I'm still the best."

Zaire laughed lightly but said, "You know what I mean."

Their waitress returned with their omelets. They thanked her and started eating, remaining silent until she left.

"Well, that was years ago. And I'm good at this. And that's no life for a kid, to have an assassin for a father."

"See, most would not have that concern. You are wasting your personality by not having a family. There are millions of people out there who want children but don't pass the exams. You owe it to them to have kids of your own."

"I'll work on it. I've got time," Chris said as he continued eating. "Maybe when I'm a boss. I think I have a good shot at it. Xiao has all but said so."

"It's not a guarantee. Plus, most bosses don't have families."

"True," Chris agreed. "It's hard to build a career and a family."

"And you'll probably be too old by that time," Zaire pointed out.

All the bosses in the agency were of the older, pre-War generation. But age was another reason Chris had given up the idea of having a family someday. The genetic modifications worked best on couples in their late teens and early twenties, which was the age most people were when they got approval to procreate. Plus, there was a strict age cap for earning the Child License: it was not given to couples if one of the partners was older than thirty-five.

Chris thought for a moment about Zaire being a father, and he could not help but contrast it to Talon Sr. Though he had never given modifications a second thought, he could not help but be intrigued by a family with such strong convictions. And Clara Fontanne, whose parents had also chosen to opt out of the modifications, with only their status and wealth to save her from the Purebred Community System.

"Have you two discussed cosmetic modifications, yet?" Chris asked. Though the mandatory modifications were provided at the expense of the government, couples could pay extra for additional modifications if they wanted to. And typically, wealthy Coastals wanted to.

"Not yet, but I know Melinda has some ideas," Zaire replied. Then, he set his fork down and said, "You know, each time we go over the application and every time we do some step in the process, I can't help but think of people like the Robertsons. They're all just so lazy. It's not *that* much work, and it's a much better chance in society, not to mention those Communities are a waste of resources and a complete health hazard."

"I never understood why the ones who were licensed to live received all the funding and government support," Chris said. "Don't their genetics already give them the advantage? It's the children whose parents refuse to modify them that need the most help."

"But it was cruel for their parents to bring them into the world," Zaire argued.

"Exactly. It's not their fault," Chris said, unconcerned about voicing such an opinion to Zaire.

Though Zaire did not always hold the same opinions, he always respected Chris's views and right to have them. But he knew better than to ever tell anyone else in the government about such a conversation.

"No," Zaire agreed. Then, he added, "But they wouldn't have survived anyway. They are already a lost cause. It's foolish to waste resources on them."

Zaire looked at Chris, wondering if this case was getting to him. "If anything," Zaire continued, "they are a constant threat to our society and survival. As potential hosts for diseases we've fought so hard to eliminate, they provide a breeding ground for a virus or bacteria to mutate into a strain we're not genetically vaccinated against, and then we would have another pandemic on our hands." He took a drink of his tea before adding, "In fact, I'd argue that just by having so many still in The Sectors, even if confined to the Communities, we already have an epidemic on our hands. We can't just risk all our lives and society because the parents wouldn't comply."

Chris shook his head. "I don't get why they opt out, either. You'd think parents would want the best for their kids. I know I would."

"That's because you're a responsible human being. See, you're already thinking of your kids. Now, you just need a mate. It can happen quickly, you know. It did for me and my wife."

"I don't want to go through a matching service," said Chris.

"You're the only one."

"I know, but I like the idea of just meeting someone."

"Nobody just meets the person they end up with. The odds of you getting approved for the Marriage License with someone you randomly meet are very slim. You're better off going with a service, like the rest of us. You get matched with someone, and you are already preapproved for the Marriage License and the Child License."

Chris looked at Zaire seriously, seeing how his friend was moving on in his life, while Chris was stagnant in a position he was just well suited for. Then, he relaxed and shrugged. "Maybe it is time for a change."

"Really?" Zaire asked, a little too excitedly.

"Yeah. In fact, I'll make a deal with you," Chris said optimistically as he leaned in closer. "If I fall in love today and find some woman who wants to have my kids just so your kids won't be lonely losers on the playground, this will be my last mission as an assassin."

Zaire laughed out loud and leaned back, putting his hands up in defeat. "Okay. But," he said, pointing at Chris, "I'm going to hold you to that, my friend."

Chris smiled and said, "In all seriousness, I have to finish this case before I can think of anything else."

"You could at least go on a date or two—with anyone—just so you're not so pathetic when you finally do decide to get a personal life...if you ever allow yourself to see someone as anything other than an element of a case." Zaire was annoyed, but he knew not to push it too much. Chris would come around eventually, and if he didn't, they were still best friends.

Chris had no intention of meeting anyone anytime soon, at least not until the case was over. There was no room in his mind for anything except the Robertsons. But he knew after this case, there would be another case. There always was.

"True, but you know there's only one type of woman for me."

"Oh? And what is your type?" Zaire asked.

"These past few months, these three women, in particular, you know?" Dramatically, as though truly in cheesy love, Chris said, "I just can't get them off my mind."

Zaire snorted as he put his tea down, shaking his head with annoyance. "Agent Rockford, always thinking about the case."

Chris said with sarcasm, "Karen, strong and in control, Adele, vulnerable and fulfilling my need to care for someone. But of course, their mother was so demanding. I appreciate a woman who knows exactly what she wants."

"So it's a Robertson woman you want, is it? That's your type?" Zaire asked, trying to take Chris's mind off the case.

"Didn't think I would go for the Purebreds, did you?"

"Don't even joke about that."

"Oh, come on, they're desperate and eager. I thought you'd be in favor of the fastest track."

"Seriously, man."

Chris put his napkin on his plate and said, "All right, seriously: Why was Adele going to meet Adam *in Iowa?*"

Zaire did not answer his question. Instead, he said, "You know, I think you'll find your Ms. Robertson sooner than you think." He wiped his mouth with his napkin and stood up to leave.

Chris stood up, too. "No, I won't. Women like the Robertsons just don't exist anymore."

"Thanks to you."

*   *   *

When Chris and Zaire arrived at their boss's office, there were already two other team members there. They were both young women, likely in their second Assignments and probably new to the Department of Anarchy Prevention, since Chris did not recognize them.

The agency operated on a three-tiered system: at the top were the twelve Presidents; the second tier consisted of the bosses that reported to them; and everyone else was an agent. A team was assembled for each case, and regardless of the size of the team, each was commanded by only one boss. Moreover, a boss could be in charge of multiple teams and cases at any one time; similarly, agents could work on multiple cases and be on multiple teams, depending on their positions in missions. But it was customary for assassins to work only on a single case at a time, due the time commitment required for the task and because assassins operated in the field and were therefore rarely at the headquarters long enough to work on anything else.

Having been assigned to the position of assassin for almost every case since he was placed in the Department of Anarchy Prevention for his second Assignment, Chris was rarely on more than one case at a time.

Xiao, their boss for this case, and the two new agents were discussing possible locations of Adam Robertson.

"Come on in," Xiao said to Chris and Zaire as they approached the door. "Chris, I want you in Iowa this afternoon. Flying will be faster than driving. We'll need you to search out the final target in person." His boss projected the map that was on his desk up onto the wall.

"Ooooh. Iowa," Zaire said with mock enthusiasm. His sarcasm, however, was not without merit.

For over forty years, since the end of The War That Brought Order, the entire world's society was contained in an orderly structure across the Eastern, Central, and Western Sectors—minus the inhabitants of Mexico. Mexico had refused to sign the Treaty of The Sectors to serve The Order and thus remained the only other country in the world and had their own system of government. As part of the restructuring of the world and the people that remained after The War, the Great Redistribution was a program that randomly assigned all Sector citizens to new locations to vary the population and meet the steep demands of rebuilding the world after the devastation of the pandemic and destruction from The War. Citizens were assessed, categorized, and redistributed from their native homes to wherever they would be most useful. Additionally, jobs, social status, and wealth were distributed to specific physical locations. All Inland areas across The Sectors were less desirable. The Coasts were beaming with wealth and upper class. In the Inland, people had the menial jobs, usually working in factories for people who lived on the Coasts they had never seen. The country's middle and lower classes were placed in the

Inland. As such, it was a breeding ground for discontent and heightened law enforcement. Where the Coasts had a ratio of officers to civilians at one-to-twenty, the Inland had a ratio of four-to-one.

Zaire walked over to the map and zoomed in on Iowa. "She probably planned to hide in Des Moines. It's the only city in that region that has government buildings with dead rooms. I wouldn't put it past the Robertsons to gain access to those buildings, and I can't see how she would hide anywhere else."

Zaire and Chris had spent two years—Chris's first Assignment—in the Department of Surveillance working on the Surveillance Project, which had been initiated shortly after they completed general training. The Surveillance Project installed retina scanners, biometric sensors, and cameras in doorways and on every street and mile marker on highways, in addition to internet and phone activity monitors for every square mile and microphones in cars. Data points from each device were recorded but could also be viewed in real time via satellite. Dead rooms were constructed with walls that blocked any incoming or outgoing signals and served as a place where government officials could hold discussions or interrogations without the Department of Surveillance watching.

"But there are only three zones left to be completed for the Surveillance Project, and they're all on the West Coast," Zaire continued. "I can't figure out how she planned to get there incognito." All new programs of surveillance, society, and technology were first implemented in the Inland, so surveillance was nearly perfect in and around the route to Iowa.

Zaire pulled out his notebook and started programming it. He projected a map of Texas from his notebook onto the wall next to the map from his boss's desk. On the map were timestamps of Adam's signatures, identifying his movements. "Adam's signal disappeared here." Zaire pointed to the most recent timestamp on the map. "He didn't even bother setting up a decoy signal. But maybe we can try something old school and search for him by looking for material signatures or fingerprints."

"If he can make his signal disappear, he will cover any other signatures," Chris pointed out. "He must have been in a hurry not to set up a decoy."

Zaire continued focusing on something on his notebook. "Communications between Adam and Adele were so limited. Even if they were speaking in code, nothing points to Iowa or going into hiding. Maybe it was a predetermined meetup location. Maybe they decided years ago that if they were ever in jeopardy, that's where they would go, and one of them gave the signal."

"But Talon Jr. sounded like he did not approve," one of the new agents said.

"That could be for anything," said Xiao. "Maybe that's why he went to the ball instead of the meeting location."

"Adele didn't look like she was planning on going anywhere," said Chris.

"Maybe she was waiting for someone to help her travel under the radar," the other new agent suggested.

Zaire projected a third map, showing the Florida Coastal city where the Robertsons had lived and the timestamps and locations of Adele's signatures in the days leading up to her death. They all stared at the maps and thought in silence for a few moments. Chris could feel the eyes of the two young agents watching the three of them work together. They were legends in the agency, and Chris knew the new agents were trying to learn as much from them as they could.

"Their patterns are too inconsistent to show they were planning anything," Chris finally concluded. "It doesn't make sense that she would hide in Des Moines unless they had a branch of their group there and she planned to carry out something more permanent. If she thought the deaths of her parents and sister were murders and that she was next on the list, she would have gone to Texas and asked Adam's drug-trafficking connections to get her to Mexico."

"Alleged connections," Xiao corrected him. Though they knew Adam had to be involved in the illegal trade, they did not have sufficient evidence for an arrest, nor could they be certain he had connections with Mexico that would have helped Adele go into hiding.

"Talon Jr. said something about going into hiding, but we should also look into any plans Adele may have had there," said Chris.

"Right," Zaire agreed. "We know the three of them were figuring out how to lead Pure Star without their parents and Karen. Maybe she was going to start a new group in Iowa and leave the home base to someone else, Karen's husband perhaps. And to get it going, she would hide for a while before it was on its feet."

"Talon Jr. mentioned Adam was straying from family values," Chris added contemplatively. "But Adele definitely was not."

They thought a few minutes more, and then Xiao finally said, "Well, it's just Adam now. Zaire, draft up a petition for Surveillance to hack any block on Adam's signatures, and bring it to me within an hour."

"Rockford," Xiao said to Chris, "you'll go to Des Moines and wait for us to give further direction. Keep a lookout for him, but also be prepared to get a car or take a flight if we find out he's somewhere else. Erasing him is our priority, regardless of what we find out about plans he and Adele had."

"You two," Xiao said, turning to the two new agents, "book a flight and accommodations for Chris in Des Moines, and continue searching for any leads on what Adele's plans were. Find out if there are any associations between Pure Star and Iowa."

They all agreed and started to leave.

"Rockford," his boss called to him. "Stick around for a second."

As the others left the room, Chris sat down across from Xiao.

Xiao and Chris were exceptionally close for any two people in the agency, especially for a relationship between a boss and an agent. Xiao had been one of the founders of the agency following The War, and he had recognized Chris's gifts and potential early on. Chris had long wondered if Xiao was the one who put him in general training in the first place. After two years into training, when Chris was fifteen, Xiao took him on, almost as an apprentice, and did extra training exercises with him outside of the typical program. Though there were several older agents in line before him, it would surprise no one if when a position for boss opened up—that is, when one of the current bosses died—Chris would move up in the agency.

"If she was planning on hiding," Xiao started, "they must at least suspect the murders, if not suspect government involvement."

"Do you think any of the other Pure Star members suspect us?" Chris asked him.

Xiao did not respond right away but, after a few moments, shook his head. "Not that we can tell. And with all the chaos that seems to have come about, it may not matter. They can't launch any more attacks on the government without us knowing about it. But we still don't want to give them a reason to try." Even when Chris's work was consistently flawless, Xiao never let up on pushing him further.

"They won't find anything. Each death has had a reasonable cause: a poisoning by an enemy, a robbery gone wrong, and three accidents, all sufficiently timed to be just that. And I have been invisible the entire time."

"Your stunt last night seemed to work well. The woman he was with told the police he was very drunk and must have fallen off the balcony while she was in the shower. But I'm not sure their followers will see the timing as being as random and coincidental as we would like."

"I'm not sure the more paranoid members would have ever believed the deaths were not planned and on purpose, anyway. But there is enough reasonable doubt at this point to make most of the members question if it is really a conspiracy. It will at least divide the group and make them weaker." Then, Chris asked, "Do you think I should wait on Adam?"

"No," said Xiao. "But Chris, there is a lot of pressure on this case, not just for the safety of society but for you, as well. This is the biggest case of your career. You have worked on this mission for seven months, and you have continually exceeded expectations. You have done everything right, not just for this mission but for all the ones you have been assigned to. I want you to know that your work has not been overlooked, nor has it been taken for granted."

Chris knew Xiao was alluding to Chris moving up in the agency and becoming a boss. They had talked about it on several occasions in the last year. That Xiao kept mentioning it gave Chris the impression that he was somehow aware of an opening becoming available soon. It was a position Chris had wanted ever since he learned about it when he was recruited to work in government when he was thirteen. For fifteen years, he worked tirelessly, pushing himself to be the absolute best that he could be and striving to constantly grow and get even better and reach previously unattainable goals—all for this opportunity, which Xiao was all but telling him was at the end of this mission.

"Thank you, sir," said Chris.

"But this is not just the biggest case of your career, Rockford. This is the biggest case in anarchy history. If you mess it up now, none of your successes up to this point will matter."

"I understand, sir," Chris said, unconcerned. He had trained and continued to grow in strength, stealth, stamina, and intellect for fifteen years. He was more than qualified for this. "I will find him and complete the mission with the excellence expected of me."

"Make sure you do," Xiao said. But he was confident in Chris's ability to conclude the mission with perfection. When Chris was fixated on a target, nothing could stand in his way.

3

Chris arrived in Des Moines that afternoon and went directly to his hotel, which was located in the Coastal District. As usual, he did whatever he needed to do to blend into the environment around him. In this instance, it meant being a Coastal businessman in an Inland city for work. Coastals did visit the Inland for reasons not related to work, such as vacationing in the mountains or at the best lakes, which had Coastal-like resorts to cater to their guests; but the only reason a Coastal would visit an Inland city would be for business. As such, all Inland cities had a Coastal District, a designated area for visiting Coastals. The few blocks of the Coastal District were not *truly* Coastal in terms of quality or luxury, but they were as Coastal in appearance as any place in the Inland could be. To even better serve visiting Coastals, some places within Coastal Districts of Inland cities were exclusive, meaning Inlanders were not allowed inside, unless they worked there. Working at such a place was the highest level of social status an Inlander could achieve; the next step in promotion would be redistribution to the Coasts and becoming a Coastal citizen.

After his meeting with his boss that morning, he had gone to his house to pack and get ready for this last phase of the mission. Only once had he thought of the conversation with Zaire at breakfast that morning. Zaire had not brought up Chris's marital status since he himself had married his wife shortly after meeting her through a matching service two years earlier. That he brought it up now, when his life was about to undergo another major change, was not surprising; Chris understood that Zaire did not want to go through these events alone.

Yet, Chris knew it was more than that. Zaire was a brilliant analyst, probably the best in the agency, aside from the bosses. Even if he did not want to treat his personal relationships like part of the job, Chris knew from experience that sometimes it was too difficult to separate the two. As a profiler, Zaire could not help but analyze someone, just as Chris could not. So if Zaire voiced concerns that Chris was gradually sinking and stagnating, he was probably right. Though Chris did not feel like he was unhappy or incomplete or dissatisfied with his life, he knew an outsider's perspective provided a vantage point of things an individual was blind to. If Zaire brought it up, then it should not be ignored. But he had no room in his mind for that kind of introspection and self-analysis right now, so he resolved to deal with it after the mission was completed.

Chris went to his hotel room and performed his usual ritual of inspecting the room and doing exercises and stretches to prepare his body for anything that might happen, reviewing the case in his mind as he did so. When he was done with his checks and stretches and exercises, he decided to go to the hotel's restaurant. It had been several hours since he had eaten, and he was eager to get to public areas and search for his target. Though Adam was a Coastal, it was not guaranteed that he would be in the Coastal District—they had profiled him as being more than capable of blending into Inland society—but the hotel where Chris was staying was the most logical place to start the search for the final target.

The hotel was attached to a convention center and was busy with Coastals visiting from all over the Western Sector. It was not Coastal-exclusive, so there was a mixed population of upper-middle-class Inlanders and upper-class Coastals. As he walked through the hallways and the lobby, Chris smiled at and greeted fellow Coastals, per Coastal social custom, and ignored the Inlanders, per Inland social custom—all the while remaining alert to the possibility of running into Adam Robertson.

The restaurant was packed: only two seats at the bar remained open for immediate seating. The bartender had just given him his soda, utensils, and a menu when she sat down next to him, and at first he hardly noticed. For years, he had learned how to most effectively take advantage of his heightened sense of surroundings, glancing about the room when no one was looking and making use of his peripheral vision and hearing. It was easy for him to take in every movement in the room equally, without surprise or suspicion.

"Is someone sitting here?" she asked, putting her clear plastic purse on the back of the chair and taking off her jacket. The question, though it had been a mere formality, was much more polite than one would expect from an Inlander. Being at a hotel in the Coastal District, he wanted to assume she was a visiting Coastal, like himself, but instinctively he knew she lived in Des Moines.

"No, not at all. Go ahead." He did not look at her directly, only at the menu.

"Oh…ma'am, you dropped this." Out of the corner of his eye, he saw her pick up a Coastal woman's purse and return it to the owner. She sat down and turned back to him. "This place is crowded tonight. I'm glad I found a seat." She did not look at him as she said it, but he could feel all of her attention on him.

"Yeah, do you know what's going on?" It was rare that he talked to strangers, but she did not treat him like one. He looked at her then, and a surprising comfort settled within him as their eyes met.

"Well, you're in the best steakhouse in Mid-Inland." She spoke to him like they were old friends.

He searched all his memory for her, but her mannerisms did not match anybody he knew. "No, I'm not. I've been to the best steakhouse in Mid-Inland. It's on the false coast in Chicago." He had been calm and unsurprised all his life, but a wave of serenity passed over him in her presence that both excited and chilled him. Who was this person who could affect him this way? Nobody could move him, per his training, which was the best in the world.

She looked confused that he had somehow made the comment without the slightest hint of arrogance—he was a Coastal in an Inland city, after all—but she accepted the challenge. "Nope." With a small smile, she pointed over at the wall where a framed cover of a magazine featured the restaurant. "Just came in last month. This one is officially the best…at least according to the writer of that article." She smiled playfully at him. It was as if since childhood they had bickered over meaningless trivialities and now she added another victory to her tally.

He looked at the framed cover of the local magazine and let out a breath of laughter. There was no way the small, local publication could have afforded to send the judges to anywhere outside of Des Moines. As hard as it was for Inlanders to get travel permits, it was nearly impossible for Inland-based businesses to obtain the permits for their employees.

He turned back to her, and her smile caught him off guard, and she imprisoned him in a paralyzing gaze. She lacked the scar of a Modified, a dimple and discoloration of the skin that marked one of the cheeks, a side effect of the *in utero* genetic modification surgery. Nearly everyone younger than forty had it. Had he not spent the past seven months watching, stalking, and studying a Purebred anarchist organization, he might have been surprised to see an unscarred face.

Though natural, her smile was absolutely stunning. She was beautiful, but only in a genuine way. And she did look familiar to him. It was obvious she'd had a nose job and minor facial cosmetic surgery sometime in the past that was not drastic. At least, it was obvious to someone who was trained to notice these physical changes people make—just like it was obvious to him that her long brown hair was dyed and her soft brown eyes were colored contacts, for neither her brown hair nor her brown eyes matched faithfully with her skin color, not for a Purebred anyway. He imagined she would have used tinted skin toner, as many Coastals did, had it not been so hard to obtain in the Inland. But what he noticed most of all was his surprise at his own reaction to her. No, he had never seen her before. And looking her in the eyes, he could see no recognition in her gaze, either. Instead, she was truly in the moment, not distracted or spacey like most people he encountered. She looked back at him as if he were the only other person in the entire world.

All of this was noticed in only an instant, but he felt like he had been staring for a full moment and quickly turned away, embarrassed for the first time in his life. Already he realized he had never met anybody like her. But he could not shake the feeling that he knew her from somewhere. *Could she make someone feel so at home in her presence that she tricked that person into thinking they already knew each other?* he thought to himself. People were friendly all the time, but she was already familiar to him.

But even if he had never seen her before and would never see her again, he would remember her clearly as the one person in the entire world who had ever made him feel embarrassed. "Well, I guess that explains the crowd," he said and looked down at his menu again but was unable to read it.

"Well, that and the storm outside, and everybody in here is probably staying here," she said.

"Are you?" he asked.

"No, I'm waiting out the rain. I walk to work—can't be bothered to get pulled over every day." She laughed at her own joke. "I don't usually work Saturdays, but I didn't get everything done this week that I needed to. I thought I'd see if it lets up before I get a ride. Plus, it's a good excuse to eat here." She looked around for the bartender.

Instinctively, he did the same. "Well, now that it's so hyped up, I'm eager to order." He pointed to his menu. "What's good?"

"Well," she said softly, putting her thick hair behind her ear as she leaned toward him to look at his menu.

He saw light freckles under her makeup—another feature of the Purebreds, for moles and freckles and other skin-damaging effects from the sun were genetically prevented in Modifieds. She also had no wrinkles, save a single laugh line around her mouth and the beginning of a small frown line between her eyebrows. Thus, he surmised that she was probably in her early-twenties, worked indoors, and spent a great deal of her time studying with her eyes.

"Steak, obviously," she continued, "but the East Asian fillet is my favorite. I know it sounds weird, but it's actually really good."

He looked at the ginger-orange glaze description. "Sounds sweet." He acted like he was disgusted by the description but was trying to be polite by hiding it.

"It is." She looked at other things on the menu, trying to find something else for him.

She had not reacted to his pretend disgust as he had expected her to, giggling flirtatiously or acknowledging his opinion...almost as though she knew it was not genuine. *A fellow agent, maybe?* he thought.

She wore upper-middle-class Inland attire, upscale for the Inland, but still plain, ill-fitting fabric that lacked pockets and had haphazard stitching showing at the seams. Time, quality, and effort were reserved for making Coastal clothing. But still, to have access to what she wore, it was likely she interacted with Coastals for her job. And that she was a Purebred living in the Inland with a job outside of a Purebred Community already set her apart. She was also wearing a perfume he had never smelled before, something subtle and soothing, like a small stream in a forest. It took all his strength not to look at her.

"The basic New York strip is classic," she said as she pointed to it, not ashamed to invade his personal space, though they had not officially met.

"Maybe I'll start with that and branch out tomorrow at breakfast."

"You're staying here, then?" She looked back at him, giving him an excuse to meet her gaze.

"You're the one who called it." He flashed a grin he had used many times to draw reactions from women in missions.

But she was not affected by it. "Are you here for the convention?" she asked.

"No, what is it?" He tried to relax and become more natural.

"It's a car show that's held annually. Actually, it's only two years old, but some famous people have brought their cars, so I think that's why there's such a big turnout. The price is only what it was last year, but I think they're beginning to realize they should have raised it. It's good for the city, I think."

"What famous people?" he asked, probing her for her interests.

"Beats me."

So she was not one to be starstruck.

The door to the kitchen opened, and Chris nodded to the bartender, a tall man who could be tough or jolly, depending on a generous tipper's preference. He came over and apologized to Chris for taking so long. Chris accepted his apology and turned toward the Purebred woman next to him, allowing her to order first. The bartender stared blankly at him a moment and then made a show of turning to her and waiting for her to order. She ordered a tea and the East Asian fillet, rare, and then she turned to Chris as if to tell the bartender he was ready to order as well. He ordered the New York strip, also rare.

He noticed that she treated the bartender and himself the same way she had talked to the woman who had dropped her purse: she looked at people as though her full and complete attention were directed solely to them, as though there were no stranger to her in the world, no unfamiliar territory, almost as if nothing were new to her. And she did this without any regard for how they were treating her.

"You're the only person I've ever met who also likes to eat steak rare," she said after the bartender left. She sat back in her seat, and they were back to normal conversation, just between the two of them.

"The bloodier the better," he said and then instantly regretted it. "But cooked, of course," he added quickly. He had never felt stupid or self-conscious before *in his life*.

"So, what brings you to Des Moines?" she asked.

"I'm here on business."

"What business are you in?" she asked the million-dollar question.

Before he could answer, the bartender came back with her tea and said he had forgotten to ask what sides they wanted with their steaks, no doubt because he had been so shocked by a Coastal insisting that a Purebred Inlander order first.

After they answered, Chris changed the subject. "I'm sorry, I didn't catch your name."

"Oh, my name is Jenna Macklemore. But please, call me Jenna." She stuck her hand out for a handshake, another sign she regularly interacted with Coastals.

He took her hand. Her Purebred skin was unexpectedly soft, and her grip was firm and confident. "I'm Christopher Rockford. Call me Chris." He was grateful for the excuse to look into her eyes again. Despite the contacts, he felt like she had no false pretense. Nearly everybody he met maintained an appearance that was different from who they really were underneath. It was his job to see through it. But there was nothing to see through here. Yet, instinctively, he knew she was holding something back, something she had been hiding for so long that it no longer affected how she carried herself. *Perhaps she just has regrets she has learned to live with*, he thought.

"It's nice to meet you," she said, seemingly oblivious to his fascination with her.

"Same to you. What do you do downtown?"

"I work at the art museum."

"Oh," he said.

"Yes, we have an art museum here. It's not fancy like where you come from, but it's enough." She paused, but before he could protest she added, "I'm not the curator or anything. I just help manage what we put on the walls sometimes. I mainly help with planning special events and catering to Coastal clients."

That made more sense to him. He surmised that her job had trained her in Coastal manners and wondered why they had hired a Purebred. But the way she made those around her feel comfortable made her a good fit for such a position, and he could see why she would have been chosen for it. He wondered if she had been specifically pulled from a Purebred Community for such a Societal Role. From what he understood, Purebreds in the Communities did not undergo the rounds of testing that citizens in mainstream society underwent, mainly because Purebreds in the Communities remained within the Purebred Community System. If they were redistributed, it was usually to another Community. Practically the only way for Purebreds to get out of the System was to get married and get approved for the Child License and have Modified children, at which time they would be assigned a place in the Inland. But he did not profile her as a mother.

She continued, "It's not super prestigious or anything."

"No, I didn't mean to—" he started.

"I know," she said, interrupting him. "Actually, I just didn't want to sound snobby or artsy or whatever. This is your first time in Iowa, isn't it?"

"Yeah," he said. Well, he *had* been to Iowa before, but the job had only lasted an hour, and he was on the next flight out before the body had been discovered. "Maybe I'll drop by this terribly not fancy museum and compare it to the artsy snobs I'm used to back home." Curious, he asked, "Where do you think I'm from?"

She took a moment to think of her answer. "Well, obviously a big Coastal city."

Before she could finish her guess, an officer approached them and asked for her citizenship card. With retina scanners at each doorway and entrance, Purebreds were certain to set off alarm signals that would be followed up by security checks.

They lacked the Modified genes that gave rise to the unique and personalized proteins read by the retina scanners that identified individuals. Hence, they typically had to check in wherever they went to register themselves as being allowed outside the Purebred Communities. In the Coastal cities, they rarely checked Purebreds unless they did not fit the appearance of upper-class Coastal status. In the Inland cities, random spot checks for vehicles and pedestrians were frequent, especially for "suspicious" persons—namely Purebreds outside of Purebred Communities. Though he knew about the security checks, it was the first time Chris saw the procedure in action.

She showed the officer her government-issued ID card and smiled as Chris pulled his wallet out of his pocket to show his, too, though he had not been asked. The officer examined her ID closely, looked at her, then back at the card, looked at Chris, looked at her again, and handed the card back to her. He did not even glance at Chris's card.

Chris had never been carded before, and technically still had not since the officer did not ask for it then, but she had gone through it with such ease that Chris realized this was common for her. When the officer left, Chris turned to her and felt a guard he never realized he had was slowly lowering. He liked this Purebred and decided to shamelessly allow himself to be drawn in.

Continuing their conversation, he said, "So I don't look like I'm from around here. Takes one to know one."

"You're correct that I'm not from here, but I'm actually from a small town, and Des Moines is the largest city I've ever lived in. It's been good to me though, and I think I wouldn't mind a bigger city when I move." As soon as she said it, she tensed up, but only very slightly.

Had he not been trained to notice such subtle physiological changes, he would have never caught it. He supposed she tensed up from having referenced moving. Relocation was decided by the government, so she had either already been alerted that she would be redistributed, or she was expecting it. Either way, she felt like she had said too much.

"Where are you from?" he asked.

Before she could answer, a server came with their meals. She asked for utensils and more tea. He asked for steak sauce.

"Try it without, first," she said. "You may not need it." She lifted her eyebrows and shook her head, as if reprimanding him for insulting the meat.

He cut off a bite, careful not to break the plastic fork and knife as he sawed off a chunk of meat, and ate it. "Okay, this is the best steakhouse I've been to…in Iowa."

"It's awful, isn't it?" She giggled as she asked the question, as if knowing it was nothing close to the quality of food served on the Coasts.

"No," he said defensively. "It's not bad. It even tastes like real meat."

She burst into laughter. "I assure you, for a Coastal, it's real. They would never hold back on their Coastal customers."

Without meaning to, he smiled in satisfaction at having made her laugh. Then, seeing that she had nothing to eat with, he asked, "Would you like to have a bite? Sorry, I didn't mean to eat in front of you."

"No, no, no, don't worry about it," she insisted. "I told you to do it."

The bartender returned and gave her utensils and more tea. After seeing Chris watching him, he apologized to her for not giving her a menu or utensils when she first sat down. She told him not to worry about it, truly unaffected.

She turned back to Chris and asked, "Would you like to try some of mine?"

He shrugged and nodded, his mouth full of another bite. He had not realized how hungry he was and secretly chastised himself for not paying more attention to his appetite.

She opened the packet of the orange-ginger glaze and spread it on the steak. Chris involuntarily tensed up at the gesture, knowing the cook would have prepared the glaze on the fillet if it had been served to a Coastal, or at least a Modified. Some of the powder was not completely mixed into the glaze, and she tried to spread it evenly. She cut off a chunk that was big enough for three bites, even by his standards, and offered it to him.

"Oh, no, just a bite is fine," he protested, covering his mouth with his napkin and trying not to talk with his mouth full.

"I can never finish it, anyway," she said. "You'd be doing me a favor not letting it go to waste."

He tried it, and this time she took a bite of her steak, too, turning to him to catch his response. "That's actually a lot better than I expected it to be. It's not as sweet as it sounds in the description."

"I think it's the ginger flavoring. They put in enough to give it a bite, and the orange flavoring gives it the zing."

He could tell she was trying not to laugh at the glaze. He would have expected an Inlander to be either proud of such a sophisticated food creation or embarrassed that it was not anywhere close to the high standards of the Coasts, where actual ginger and orange would have been used instead of artificial flavors. He considered the possibility that she had not been trained to interact with Coastals but had instead grown up as one. Though rare, Coastals did sometimes get demoted to Inlander status and were redistributed to the Inland.

"Do you cook?" he asked. "You seem to know a lot about flavors and taste," he added, unsure of why he was justifying his question.

"Yes, I like to try new things and experiment a lot. It's a hobby for me."

"I cook, too, but I don't think I'm any good at it," he confessed.

"We'll have to have a cook-off," she said, as if they saw each other regularly.

"I'd like that, but I don't want you to have to eat my food, so I'll just bring something from a restaurant."

"Well, now I *have* to try something you make." Hesitantly, she asked, "How long are you here?"

"Maybe only until Monday. I'm not really sure, yet."

"Monday, as in the day after tomorrow?"

As a profiler, he knew from the way her lips had just tightened that she probably used to bite her lower lip when she was nervous but had stopped the habit. He also knew, though she was quick and subtle about it, that she was assessing him in that moment, or, rather, the potential danger of him.

He said, "Yeah, maybe. It depends on how things go." As he said it, he completely relaxed all his muscles, even slouching his shoulders slightly, as he put his utensils down. Then, he looked away from her as he took a drink of his soda. The maneuver worked, and she seemed to relax. He wondered what he had done to alarm her and committed himself to being as unthreatening as he could make himself from then on.

"Do you have to work tomorrow?" she asked.

"No, I thought I'd see a bit of Des Moines, so I came a day early."

She opened her mouth as if to say something but then quickly closed it and instead picked up her tea and took a drink.

Chris continued eating, hoping the silence would draw out whatever it was she was going to say.

Cautiously, she said, "You know, I don't normally do this sort of thing, but if you're interested in getting a tour from a local, I'd love to show you around."

"What don't you normally do?"

She blushed, and he felt his heart glow. He had never made anyone blush before, at least not in a good way, not without intimidation.

Then she laughed nervously and glanced away as she replied, "Well, I don't normally ask total strangers out."

"We're not *total* strangers. You know my name. That's more than anybody else in here, along with the other billion people in the world."

Sharing his sentiment, she sat up straighter, and with an agreeing smile, she looked him in the eyes and said, "All right, friend."

And that was when it began. They had taken an immediate interest in each other, and now they both knew it. With one look, all gaps between them began to close, and a ceaseless string of conversation began. They talked about their interests and Des Moines, the car show, stories of their youth, and any other topics they could find in common. Neither said where they had grown up or went into details about their lives. They respected each other's subtle hints about staying away from certain topics, which was a Coastal social custom. Despite an instant connection, they were still acquaintances getting to know each other.

He hoped he did not look as pathetic as he felt, and he thought of Zaire's comment and wished he had taken the advice to date much earlier in his life, if not just for practice so he could have been prepared for this encounter. For all his training and work history, he had absolutely no experience with actually feeling these emotions firsthand, even though he had flawlessly portrayed them in many of his missions.

But he could tell this was also new territory for her, though not as new as it was for him. Yet, he could also tell it had been a while since she had allowed herself to consider a man the way she considered him then. Something about her mannerisms— the slight hesitations, the lack of flirting—indicated to him that she felt like she was breaking a rule or at least doing something someone had told her not to do or that she had forbidden herself to do. *Maybe she's married?* he thought to himself. Maybe that was the solution to her mysterious effect on him. But he had profiled enough of her personality by this point to know that she acted like this not because she was deceitful but because she was cautious. It was not a personality trait; something had happened in her life to make her this way.

At eight o'clock, a band started playing, and their conversation turned into comments made between songs, comments that often resulted in both of them laughing. At one point, he made a joke, and she playfully pushed him away. He tried to focus on the band playing the next song after that, but all he could think about was that spot on his arm where she had touched him and forced himself not to stare at her directly. Despite the interruption of the loud music, it felt as though they were in constant communication.

It was still storming outside, and around midnight he asked her if she needed to go home. She hesitated again, and he was afraid their evening together had come to an end. She looked down at her phone, considering leaving, but then she put her phone back in her clear plastic purse and said she would take a taxi later.

The band quit playing around two o'clock in the morning, and most of the people left. It had become even more crowded, with standing room only while the band was playing, turning into more of a saloon than a restaurant. They stayed and continued talking. Neither had ever talked so much in their lives, and their throats were dry. They drank many cups of water and cheerfully agreed to watch the other's seat for many trips to the restroom. Their voices were hoarse and raspy, and their faces hurt from smiling for so long.

At three o'clock, the bartender alerted them that it was last call, though neither had been drinking alcohol. When they did not order anything else, he brought them their bill on a single check. From the moment she sat down, the bartender had assumed they already knew each other.

"I got it," they both said at the same time.

Chris handed the bartender his card before she could even unzip her purse. "This one's on me," he told her.

She thanked him and promised that she would get it next time, causing a satisfying rush to surge throughout his core at the thought of her wanting to see him again.

At four o'clock, the restaurant was closing, and a new staff came in to start preparing for when the restaurant would reopen at six o'clock for breakfast. They and two other couples were the only ones remaining. The bartender did not have to say anything to Jenna and Chris, but he had to go to the other couples and persuade them to leave. Chris watched, making sure the inebriated patrons did not give the bartender trouble.

When he looked back at her, Jenna was watching him. "Well," he said as he stood up. He took her jacket off the back of her chair and held it up to help her put it on.

"Thank you," she said as she slid her arms into the sleeves. "You know, I'm not really that tired, and neither of us has to work tomorrow."

"Yeah?" he said quickly. Then, he immediately felt stupid for sounding so excited, wondering to himself why he was so unreserved. He cleared his throat, resetting himself back to calm.

"Well, there's a 24-hour diner not far from here. It's terrible for your health, and the coffee always tastes several days old, but it's open, and—" She paused, and he gave her a questioning look. "Is it bad if I'm embarrassed to say I'm hungry again?"

"I've been famished since midnight. Sounds perfect." He asked the bartender to call a cab for them and led her to the hotel lobby. They had a mutual understanding that neither wanted to leave public areas.

Shortly after they sat down in the diner, a Mexican man sat at a table alone, almost out of view. Almost immediately, an officer approached him and asked for his citizenship card, just as the officer had asked Jenna for hers when they first arrived. It was not an odd occurrence, except that Chris had seen him at the hotel restaurant, where he had also been carded, and where, like now, he seemed to check out as a legitimate citizen of The Western Sector. He had presumably come only to hear the band, having stood by the far side wall, and left promptly when the band left the stage. *Where would one go in Des Moines between the hours of two and four in the morning?* Chris thought.

They talked over greasy eggs and potatoes, alongside drunken Inlanders that filled the dining area and made for amusing entertainment. As she had been throughout the entire evening, he noted that she was very polite and well mannered, another indication she had either grown up privileged, though her genetics should have forbidden it, or she was well trained to interact with Coastals.

On the television in the diner, the news was giving a brief update on the status of anarchist activity across The Sectors. All the drunken Inlanders were too loud for the television to be heard, but on the screen there was a graph showing the rise in attacks over the last five years and the slight decline in the last year leading up to six months ago.

"I'm so tired of hearing about anarchy. If it's so bad, why don't they do something about it?" She was sitting plainly and relaxed, with her arms crossed and her elbows on the table.

"*If* it's so bad?" Chris asked.

"Well, it seems to have died down a bit in the past year or so, but they keep talking about it like there's a worldwide panic."

As she said this, Chris realized that the general public rarely saw the effects of the attacks. He wondered if they had ever broadcasted the attacks at all when they happened or if they were only doing it now because the threat was on the decline.

She continued, "If it's five years old, why are they just now talking about it?" She paused, a little embarrassed for the rant. "I mean, don't get me wrong, thank you to those protecting us, but I'd appreciate news stories that are more relevant to me." She said it with such ease that he realized this was how non-government citizens talked about news stories.

He laughed it off, satisfied that she did not trust the media. And to be honest with himself, he knew he was also satisfied that he had a hand in her security. But the irony of her words stung him because this news story *was* relevant to her, for he was there to catch such an anarchist in her city.

"Oh my, it's already six o'clock," she said. "I'm so sorry to keep you out so late. You're probably tired after traveling."

"Not at all. I've been running on adrenaline all night, actually."

She gave him a small smile as she said, "Me, too."

"I have to say, I've never met someone at a bar and talked to them until six the next morning. I don't think I've talked so much in my entire life." He started massaging his jaw with his fingertips.

She laughed at his gesture. "You pull it off well. I've never done this much talking either, actually."

"Do you go to bars often?" he asked.

"No, I don't really do the whole bar scene. I don't drink, actually."

"I noticed. I don't drink either."

"May I ask why?" she asked.

"I don't like feeling out of control, and I think people"—without averting his gaze from hers, he nodded his head toward the table next to them, where a group of college students were challenging each other to balance pickles on their noses—"look stupid when they're under the influence...of any drug." He shrugged at the last addition to his statement, noting its irony to himself, for he felt he looked quite stupid under her influence.

"Yes, I agree. That's why I don't drink." She also shrugged. "I'm also just afraid of what I might say. I've never gotten drunk because I'm terrified I'll start telling people things I shouldn't. Obviously, I talk a lot without the effects of alcohol."

He did not press her on details, though things one "shouldn't say" could have been anything from rude comments about the listener to specific secrets about the speaker.

"Would it be weird if I asked what you're doing later this evening?" she asked suddenly.

"I thought you already knew."

She looked at him, startled and embarrassed that she did not remember.

"You're showing me around Des Moines, right?"

She sighed in relief. "If you're still up for it." She took a deep breath. "Actually, I have two free tickets to a theater tonight. I wasn't going to go, and I'm sure it's nothing like you've seen on the Coast, but—"

"I've actually never been to the theater." He cut her off, destroying her assumption that he was more sophisticated than she.

"Oh," she said, surprised.

"I guess I've just never had the opportunity."

"Oh, well, I'm sure it will be really boring for you, and it's terrible for me to even ask, so don't say yes just to be polite."

"I'm saying yes so I get to see you again."

His comment made her smile, and she pulled out her phone. She passed it across the table so they could exchange numbers.

When he gave it back to her, she looked at it. "I thought you said you lived in Washington, D.C. What area code is this?"

"Virginia," he answered. He had never given anyone his personal cell phone number, but he thought it was too suspicious to give her the number of the temporary phone he had gotten before coming to Iowa, which had a Des Moines area code. Furthermore, he had made a decision to pursue this, just to see where it would go. He did not have high expectations because years of experience forbade it. But even if it did not work out, he wanted to tell her anything true about himself that he could, which, being a government employee, was not much.

They walked back to his hotel, and he asked the front desk to call a taxi for her. He fought the urge to follow her cab to make sure she made it home safely. There was a reason she, as part of the general public, had no idea how dangerous a simple car ride home could be. Instead, when the cab driver held out his hand for a card to swipe to pay for the fare, Chris insisted on handing the man his card and told her to send him a message when she got home.

He went to his hotel room, put the "Do Not Disturb" sign on the door, and got ready for sleep. Before pulling back the covers, he got her message: "Home safe. Thanks again for dinner and breakfast and the ride. See you this evening."

He got into bed and put his phone on the nightstand. After a minute, he looked at the text again. It was not until about the fifth time he read her message that he realized it was rude of him not to respond.

It had been ten minutes since she sent the text, plenty of time for her to fall asleep. If he sent a message now, there was a possibility it would wake her, which he did not want to do.

But if he did not send anything at all, she might wonder why—maybe he accidentally gave her the wrong number or maybe something had happened to him in the time it took her to get home. Maybe he had fallen asleep or simply did not care. He definitely did not want her to think that.

So, he sent, "Thanks for letting me know. Looking forward to seeing you later," and waited for a response. After a few minutes, he decided she was probably asleep and that he needed to sleep, too. He put his phone back on the nightstand. Then, he checked it again and read her message one last time.

He lay in bed, feeling more content than he had ever been in his entire life, and he wondered how he could have ever thought he had felt content before.

4

Chris woke up six hours later, and the memories of the previous evening flooded his mind, sending a wave of excitement throughout him. He had to push all thoughts of Jenna out of his mind so he could get ready for the day, according to his morning routine: quickly recounting the major events of the case leading up to the present while checking his belongings and the room for signs of disturbance and performing a series of stretches and exercises. He checked his phone, but there were no updates. On his way to the hotel's gym, he told his team he would stand by, acting like a tourist while awaiting orders. He knew Zaire would be immediately suspicious, but there was no way, nor reason, to hide what he would do that day.

At the gym, he thought about the case, starting at the beginning, focusing now more on the details than the major events. He thought of Mr. Robertson's hand holding the drink that would kill him, the same way Talon Jr. held his drink on the balcony: thumb, index finger, and middle finger around the glass that rested on the ring and pinky fingers under the base.

He thought of Adele chopping fruit with a knife as big as her forearm. He saw her left hand holding the fruit steady while her right hand clenched the knife's handle, knuckles tight and white. He remembered Mrs. Robertson's hand as she reached for the gun on the table when she saw him. He remembered Jenna blushing, trying to hide her smile.

He set the weight down. He knew if he were truly indifferent to her, she would not have been the first thing on his mind that morning. Every morning, he woke up with the current case on his mind. He picked the weight back up, willing himself to focus.

But he wanted to know everything about her. He wanted her to want to know everything about him. He loved that he felt vulnerable around her, that he felt embarrassed about saying certain things, and that he cared about what she thought of him. It was all addicting and exhilarating, a drug he had never had that made him high throughout the evening, emotions he had acted out many times before but had never truly felt for himself.

Over the course of the previous evening, he realized that how he felt was what Zaire had described to him when Zaire told him about the woman he would later marry. At the time, they had been working together on a case with Xiao. At one of their breakfast brainstorming sessions, instead of discussing the case, Zaire could not contain himself and told his best friend that he had met someone. They had been trained so well to never lose control, to never let their guards down, to never have a moment when they were not vigilant. But Zaire had said that when he was with this woman, he loved that he could not control his heartbeat around her. He loved that he felt vulnerable around her. He couldn't keep his guard up around her, and he *liked* it.

At the time, Chris had called him soft, unable to understand how anyone would love not having control of their thoughts, physiology, and feelings. But this Jenna Macklemore had changed everything in the course of a single evening. He had been trained too well not to be vigilant, not to notice every subtle change that happened in the room with the staff or the drunken college students or the Mexican man, or the fact that she knew the area code for Washington, D.C., off the top of her head. For the first time, he wished he could turn his mind off so he could focus all of his attention on her.

Focus, he told himself, *only one target left, and then it's done.* He finished his workout and his account of the case in his head, Jenna-free, and went back to his hotel room to shower and dress.

He went to the concierge and asked her where he could get a suit. She told him of a tailor shop with Coastal fabric that would make a suit on the spot for Coastals. He went to the shop, only two blocks away, and before being allowed to enter, he was required to show his ID to an officer at the door to prove his Coastal citizenship.

The shop, though still in the confines of the Coastal District, was small. The front room only had one chair for waiting, but a tailor came out to meet him before he had time to sit down. The man was cheerful and overly delighted to have a customer.

He greeted Chris immediately, saying, "Hello, sir. Thank you so much for coming in today. Please, follow me to the back room, and I will assist you." He nodded his head enthusiastically and bowed several times as he said it.

Chris followed him to another small room in the back and told the man his measurements, not wanting to waste any time.

"Certainly, certainly," said the man, and he left Chris in the room alone. The room was big enough to fit the two of them, and some clothes, but nothing else. There was no dressing room, no curtain, no chair, and no wet bar or other accommodations one would have found at a tailor on the Coasts. The walls were white, and the mirror had no frame. As Chris looked at himself in the mirror, he saw it was slightly bent in the bottom right corner, giving one of his legs a distorted appearance.

The tailor returned with some pre-made suits for Chris to try on. In the past, it had taken no time to find a suit. Shopping was a waste of time and at the top of his list of least favorite activities. If he had needed a suit, he would go to the tailor, pick out fabrics that went well together and were fit for the occasion and purpose, and then it was done. This time, however, he could not be satisfied. So used to choosing a look that would help him sink into the background, he had never actually *looked* at clothes before, not on himself or anybody else. He had only used them as a tool to assess someone, to collect data and analyze them for his own purpose in pursuing a case. Now, he noticed the smallest difference in two shades of the same color, seeing how they actually changed the whole outfit's appearance. The textures and materials were different, not only in how they felt but also in how they looked. He had always used these details as data to perceive the message the wearer was sending, but he had always taken for granted that the tailor put together his own message for him. Now, he was quite aware of how his clothes presented him, and he found he had grossly underestimated the amount of time it would take to get a suit. For this reason, he was happy that in the Inland the custom was to just alter a previously made suit rather than making one from scratch.

After an hour, despite the best efforts of the tailor who was helping him, he felt like nothing was right on him. Perhaps, he realized, it was because it was the first time he had ever truly looked at himself in the mirror and judged himself as an outsider would—as a person he wanted to impress would. As

Jenna would. Despite his effort to keep the thoughts out of his mind, he kept replaying the events of the previous night and morning. That he spent more than an hour looking for something to wear for that evening was entirely Jenna's doing.

After making his decision, the tailor took his card and swiped it for payment.

"Please, sir," the man said, "if you liked your experience today, would you mind adding a little extra to the charge?" The man's voice wavered a little bit as he said it. Though he must have made such a request hundreds of times, Chris could only imagine some of the responses the man must have received in his experience with Coastals. Tipping was purely an Inland custom.

Chris told him how much to add on top of the bill, and said, "This is a great business you have here."

With relief, the tailor beamed with pride and bowed to Chris again, saying, "Thank you. Thank you very much. And thank you for your business. Would you like to wait, or would you like me to deliver your suit to your hotel?"

"I'll wait on it," said Chris.

The man led him back to the entrance room, where Chris waited while the suit was altered. The room, though it looked nice at first glance, had a musty smell to it, and the carpet must have looked new when it was installed many years ago. There were a few water stains on the walls and ceiling that had been painted over, and the plastic chair—which had the appearance of a sturdy wood frame and a comfortable cushion—squeaked when he sat down, and the legs wobbled if he moved at all, causing more noise. He decided to stand.

As he was leaving the store, tailored suit in hand, Jenna called to tell him she would meet him at his hotel in an hour. He was in the lobby fifteen minutes before she arrived. Sitting naturally, off in the corner waiting, he spotted her before she saw him. She walked confidently into the lobby, vaguely giving a glance to objects around her. She wore a tan knee-length raincoat and dark heels. Her hair was not straight, as it had been the night before. It was styled so that rolls of hair fell just below her shoulders. She had two small black umbrellas in one hand. He stood up to greet her, and when she saw him, she smiled warmly and walked toward him.

"Hello," she said cheerfully. "I didn't bring my car. Everywhere we're going is in walking distance. You look nice."

"Not as nice as you, I'm afraid," he said.

"Oh," she said, and then she quickly added, "I styled my hair," as if explaining how it could be that she looked nice. Then, she immediately added, "I mean, thank you."

He noted her embarrassment for the excuse. "It looks nice."

"Thanks," she said and looked down. "Well, we have a reservation at a steakhouse down the street. I know nobody told you we have steakhouses here, but Iowa loves its meat, or at least the Coastals who visit do."

She started walking toward the door, and he followed.

"I don't mind eating steak two nights in a row," he said.

"Well, in my opinion, the place where we're going is much better than the place where we met."

As he opened the door for her, he said, "I would assume so if it needs reservations."

She thanked him as she walked through the doorway and added, "Well, I don't know if it actually does or not. I've never eaten there on a Sunday night."

"You only take your dates there on weeknights? What special place do you reserve for the weekends?"

She laughed bashfully. "There are no dates." They were walking down the street. It was not raining, but the clouds above promised a downpour at any moment. They quickened their pace to avoid it. "I guess you noticed how cautious I was last night, but we had just met, and I want to thank you for not inviting me up to your room."

"I didn't know I was supposed to."

Still walking, she turned to him and gave him a disbelieving look.

"I just don't date much either." He shrugged. "And I thought last night was perfect."

"But," she started, confused, and then shook her head in apology. "I'm sorry, I shouldn't make assumptions. Maybe it's an Inland thing, but—"

"It's not," he said. "I just got the feeling we were having a good time but not ready for that."

"Well," she said hesitantly, "I'll be honest with you and say it's been a long time for me."

"It's been never for me," he confessed indifferently.

She stopped walking and then tried to hide her confusion. She looked at him again with this new information in mind. He was young and extremely attractive and obviously a wealthy Coastal. He could tell that now she wondered what was wrong with him, what she had missed.

"You've *never*…?" She trailed off and did not finish the question. "I'm sorry," she added quickly. "It's none of my business."

He laughed and put his arm around her shoulder to turn her forward so they could continue walking. "Let's just say I work a lot and don't have time to get into relationships."

"I'm not sure that matters to most people," she said.

"Does it matter to you?" he asked.

"Yes, but—well—I mean, you know most people don't really do the relationship thing unless they want kids."

"I know. But I don't like the idea of using people like that and being so casual in that way. It's too weird."

"So, then you've never been in a relationship?" she ventured to ask. Then, she stopped walking and looked at him with astonishment. "Wait, is this your *first* date?"

Someone nearby overheard her ask it and looked at them.

They both laughed, each embarrassed—she for the outburst, he for the lack of experience.

She said, "I'm sorry. We don't have to talk about this. I just wanted to throw it out there in case you were planning on that for this evening."

"I have been on a few dates," he assured her as they started walking again, but then he added, "I'm just not good at this. What about you, if you don't mind me asking?"

"No, I don't mind. It's a fair question. I've gone on many dates and have been in a few exclusive relationships, but I don't go to bed with just anyone." She paused and then confessed, "And, truthfully, it's been over three years since I've even gone on a date."

"You work a lot, too?" he asked.

She shrugged as she said, "More like I've become a lot more cautious than I used to be."

He wanted to know what triggered her caution, but he did not press the matter, knowing this was already too personal of a conversation for them both, despite the ease with which their society so openly discussed intimacy and relationships. "Well, then," he said, "I'm not so odd, am I?"

"You're very odd," she said, "like me."

They had arrived at the restaurant, and as she approached the door, he beat her to it and opened it for her.

"Thank you," she said with an upbeat tone. She told the host their reservation number, and they were led to a table. He pulled out her chair for her, took her raincoat, and handed it the host. She was wearing a sleeveless fitted knee-length silk dress, charcoal black with light purple designs that accentuated her creamy skin. It was an older dress, not in the current season's style, but Coastal nonetheless. He wondered how she was able to get Coastal clothing and then thought maybe it was provided to her for her job for when she met with Coastal clients. He stood, dumbfounded, and then laughed at himself in his mind. She sat down, oblivious to him staring at her.

"Can I bring you a wine list?" their server asked, pouring water into their clear plastic cups.

Chris snapped back into reality and sat down. "No, thanks, we don't drink."

When the server left, he saw that she was studying him, looking at him in a different way than she had the night before. The previous night, she had looked at him as though he were something fun to try. Now she looked at him as if maybe this could actually go somewhere, as if she may actually dare to think this could be anything more than a single date with a stranger.

"It was pointless to tell him," he said.

His words broke her trance. "What was?"

"He'll come back with samples for us to try, probably a Riesling for you and a Merlot for me."

"A what?"

"He'll bring us wine to try."

"Oh. Why?"

"Probably to get us to buy a bottle so our bill will be more and he'll get a larger tip." It seemed perfectly logical to him. Such tricks were common in the Inland.

"How do you know?"

"He just seems like the type."

"Oh." She looked down at her menu, dismissing his comment.

He let it go. "What do you recommend?"

"Well, to be honest, I've only been here twice. It's a little expensive, which is fine if you're with someone, but to dine alone, it's a little odd."

He understood that what she meant was that it was odd for *her* to dine alone at an expensive restaurant. Since most Purebreds had no government privileges and were thus usually unemployed and therefore placed in Purebred Communities, it looked suspicious for one to dine out at such a place, let alone to pay. And though they did not get carded when they entered, he did not see any other Inlanders in the dining area.

"I'd rather just go some place simple where I don't stand out so much," she added.

He wondered if that was why she dyed her hair and wore contacts. He wondered if doing so somehow helped her blend in. With that thought came a feeling that had lasted only an instant the night before. It troubled him that she was alone so much, yet he could not reconcile this feeling, for he much preferred his own company to that of others. And with this troublesome feeling came that suspicion again that he had known her from somewhere else, elementary or middle school, perhaps. It was possible, since he did not know where she had grown up. Perhaps he was wrong when he decided she did not also work for government. Maybe he had seen her through that channel.

"I agree, it's a little odd to come to a place like this by yourself for no special reason." Playfully, he asked, "Is this the only restaurant of its kind here?"

She shot him a flirtatious look. "*No*, we have other nice restaurants in Des Moines, thank you very much."

"I didn't mean to offend. I just didn't realize it was such a happening city."

He focused on her, but his peripheral attention rested on the Mexican man at the bar. An opaque partition separated the dining area from the bar area, just transparent enough for silhouettes to be seen. He had seen the Mexican man when they arrived, though his back was to them. He was careful never to look directly at him, but he noted the Mexican man watching as they were taken to their table. He had seen one of the servers the night before, too, but he marveled that this Mexican man would eat at all the same places as himself: first the hotel restaurant last night, the diner this morning, and now here.

"Nice restaurants don't make a place happening, but it's not a dump, you know," she said, continuing their conversation.

"Okay, okay, I'll quit with the Inland jokes."

"It's a city, you know, not some little farm town."

He laughed. "And what do you know of little farm towns?"

"I grew up in a small town."

"I remember you said that. But was it a farm town?"

"Well, no, not exactly. But what do you know of small towns, Mr. Washington, D.C.?"

"I grew up in a small town, too, actually. Idaho, if you can believe it."

"You're not from the Coasts?"

"No, but I rarely spend time in the Inland, except for Idaho and Arizona. My parents were redistributed to Arizona a few years ago, but they were allowed to keep their house in Idaho. My brother and I check on it every month or so."

"I'd like to see it sometime," she said. "I've never been to Idaho, but I've seen pictures of the mountains."

The server returned with two plastic wine glasses, each with a sample of wine. "I know you said you could do without wine tonight, but the chef strongly recommends these to complement his dishes. For you, sir, a Merlot," he said as he set the plastic wine glass down in front of Chris. "It's a tame red with subtle hints of vanilla and cherry." Jenna stared at Chris, impressed, and he gave her a secret, sly smile. Their inside joke was undetected by the server. "And for you, ma'am, a Riesling." He set another plastic wine glass down in front of Jenna. "It's a white wine that is just a little sweet and dry with a citrus finish." The server went on to explain the specials of the evening to Chris and then left them to look over their menus.

Like an unbeliever who had finally been converted, Jenna asked, "So, what's his type?"

"Male, most likely, probably in the restaurant business."

She let out a laugh. "You know what I mean. How did you know he would bring these? This didn't happen to me last time. Is there a sign saying they serve a complimentary tasting?" She looked around for some sort of clue he may have seen that would have tipped him off.

"He's the type to try to sell us alcohol so the bill will cost more so we'll be forced to give a bigger tip."

She nodded her head, acknowledging she remembered he said that already but wanted more.

"Rieslings and Merlots are like the baby food of wine, especially the Inland versions. They don't have strong tastes, so even if you don't like wine, you could tolerate these. He's hoping you'll taste it and decide it's not so bad."

She seemed suspicious of his knowledge. "Well, I'll have to keep that in mind. You dine out often?"

"For business, and eventually you just kind of pick up that knowledge, I guess." In fact, he had picked up that knowledge in training, when his class was learning about all the different wines they might encounter at dinner parties while on missions and how to convince others of their knowledge, or lack thereof if the case called for it.

She looked down at her menu and changed the subject. "I'm having the duck."

His eyes stayed on her. "No steak?"

"I'm not really feeling like it tonight. And I love the duck they serve here."

"Have you ever had it at home?" After he said it, he realized it was an odd thing to ask. But being himself was new to him. He did not want to use the conversation tricks on her that he had learned in training. He did not want to use any sort of tricks on her at all.

"What do you mean?" She closed her menu and looked back at him.

"Does anyone in your family hunt?"

"No." She shook her head. She did not offer any more information, and he took the hint to close the conversation. He wondered if he should not bring up the topic of family again, as this was the fifth time since they met that she shrugged it off. Yet, years of experience told him not only exactly how to draw it out of her, but also that he must. In his profession, you knew everything about the company you kept.

He closed his menu. "I'll have the New York strip again," he said, and then he added scientifically, "to compare it to the other place."

They sat in silence for a few moments. She glanced around the restaurant, enjoying the atmosphere. The room was dimly lit with soft lights on the walls and candles on the tables. The walls were a soft yellow color, and the vinyl floors had the appearance of rich, dark, brown wood. Each table was a different neutral color, and candlelight flickered about the room. A Coastal gentleman who looked nearly seventy, sat alone at a table on the opposite wall. He smiled warmly to her and gave a single nod. She smiled back, recognizing him, and waved. He was a regular visitor of the museum and was one of the most prominent donors. He was always polite and friendly, but he had a dark presence about him, not like he was dangerous but like he was up to so much more than he seemed.

Something about him had always indicated to her that he had mysterious, unexplainable depth that she could relate to, even though she did not know anything about him at all. She had never asked, but she had always suspected that he had played a role in her being hired at the museum. Not many places would hire a Purebred, even with her extensive knowledge of art. But the museum hired her, and he always seemed particularly encouraging, going out of his way each time he visited to make sure he talked with her.

Her eyes settled on the print of a famous painting above his table. It had been a favorite since childhood, but she had never seen the original. Rumor had it that the original was not in one of the exquisite museums on the Coasts, as one would expect, but was instead on loan to a small, privately owned museum in the Inland. She thought about how the government-owned museum where she worked would never be able to land such a deal.

"So, what are your favorite art museums?" Chris asked after following her gaze to the print on the wall.

"Oh, I haven't really been to many. My job is more on the receiving end than the scouting end." Her look softened, and he realized she loved art but did not see it as often as she would have liked.

He did not hide his surprise. "Why not? Aren't there pieces you want to see?"

She took a deep breath. For starters, it was not the easiest thing in the world for a single Purebred in Des Moines to get a travel permit, but she was not one to bring up that sort of topic at the dinner table. "Well, I don't really have anywhere to go, and we actually get a few good exhibits that come through each year. I think there are just enough Coastal citizens that visit often enough for our museum to be on the map."

He nodded his head and said "All right" and took a sip of water. He decided to avoid further job questions for fear she might turn them around and ask about his job.

"Do you travel a lot for your job?" It was as though she had read his mind.

"I do, actually, quite a bit."

"Is that why you don't get into relationships?"

"That's the easiest reason." He steered the conversation away from his work. "I'm also terribly awkward and self-conscious." He wasn't, at least not until he met her. But it was a discussion he could handle.

She straightened in surprise. "You don't come off that way."

"It's a front. I'm good at pretending."

"You seem confident," she said, trying to assure him.

"Oh, I'm very confident. I just haven't had much practice in the way of women," he said with a flirtatious smirk.

She snorted at his wording, closing her mouth in an attempt to hold back her laughter and not embarrass him. Their server returned and took their orders, and when he left, they resumed conversation.

"Well, let me give you some pointers so you don't ruin yourself in the future. You already have good manners and put people at ease, so I won't give you advice there. Most women will want to go home with you on the first date, so you should prepare a way to not hurt their feelings if it's your wish to stay alone—I won't ask why." She gave him a sly smile. "Your family should only be involved if you're serious about someone. There's no need to introduce them beforehand. Politics generally don't come until the third or fourth date. And—"

"Why's that?"

"Because political issues are based in beliefs, and anything you say in opposition to their beliefs after you know what they are is perceived as an attack on them personally. But, if you've already established that you like each other because you've been on several dates, then it will be perceived as simply a difference in opinion instead of an attack."

"Do you know this out of experience as the attacker or the attacked?" he asked.

"I know it from stupid business meetings," she answered.

"Well, let's skip to it then, to be safe. If this should end over political beliefs, we'll end it now."

Liking his directness, she sat up straighter and said, "Okay, on what topics do you want my opinion?"

"The heavy ones: marriage, abortion, sterilization, capital punishment…" He already knew her answers would not affect his opinion of her. He liked her, regardless of what she would say. But he purposefully gave a list to hide the last one, which was the only one he really cared about. And he purposefully left out The Ban on Pure Breeding.

"All right, then," she said with a smile. She took a deep breath, thinking of her answers. "Well, I like that getting the Marriage License is very difficult, and I like that people must be married to apply for the Child License. A couple should think about their relationship to each other as much as they have to think about children and how they would be as parents." She paused, and he nodded in approval. "It surprises me that abortion still exists for non-married couples, given that everyone, except for maybe you"—she gave him a flirtatious smile—"is on the pill. But I am, overall, against it. And birth defects shouldn't matter." She added that last part quickly, knowing it was against dating protocol to say such a thing. But there was no risk in voicing that opinion. It had been years since babies with birth defects were not euthanized, if not aborted before birth.

He swallowed hard at this bold point of view. He had never heard of anyone having that opinion.

"Of course," she continued, "I'm referring to the situation where conceiving the child in the first place was consensual. That brings me to sterilization, which I think is a good thing. Sex offenders should definitely be made sterile."

He lifted his eyebrows, still nodding in approval.

"And capital punishment is a good thing, I think," she finished.

He had read her correctly, assuming she would say all these answers she told him, minus the opinion on birth defects, which he had not thought of. But with her last stance on capital punishment, he acted surprised, daring to dive deeper into her opinion. "You do?"

"Yes, I do, as long as there is a trial," she said.

He breathed calmly, not revealing any of himself, for it was his job to carry out capital punishment without a trial. "And what about the law enforcement that does away with those criminals?" he dared to ask.

"I wouldn't want that job, but I understand that someone has to push the button to make it happen."

She missed his probe, so he tried again. "But what about the ones who do away with the criminals who don't deserve a trial?"

She shrugged. "Those are just rumors."

As if the question were just a fun hypothetical, he asked, "What if they weren't?"

"Hmm," she hummed, playing along as she looked away from him to think about it.

Chris could feel his heartbeat begin to quicken in anticipation of her answer, and he silently took in a slow, deep breath to hide his anxiety.

Finally, she looked back at him and shook her head slightly. "I can't see how that would ever be okay."

With the way she said it, it was like a hand reached into his gut, grabbed his insides in a clenched fist, and then twisted.

She continued, "I mean, that's why they're just rumors, right? As controlling as The Order is, even they wouldn't go that far. And can you imagine what kind of person would take on that job? And what that kind of lifestyle and mentality would do to someone?"

"No," he replied lightly.

"What about you? What are your controversial political beliefs?" she asked.

"I can't imagine ever wanting to get rid of your child."

"Do you like children?"

"I do. My brother has three, and I love them more than anything in the world. He hates it, but they get whatever they want when they're with me."

She smiled as she imagined him as an uncle. "Do you want some of your own someday?"

"I do," he said matter-of-factly, leaving out that he did not think it would actually happen. "Family is something I could never live without."

She nodded but did not volunteer any of her own thoughts on the matter. Again, avoiding family. *That makes six times*, he thought to himself. "Do you want children?" he asked her.

She smiled sweetly and nodded. "I've always dreamed of having a big family." Something in her eyes gave away sorrow, a loss she felt. He did not know if she was unable to have children or if she had grown up as a lonely child, set aside by society for her genes, or if she had once had a big family that she lost. In any case, she missed something now.

He did not press her on the subject and, wanting to keep her happy, changed the topic to something more optimistic. "So, where are we going tonight?"

"Oh, you'll probably never want to see me again after it," she said.

"It can't be that bad."

"It's a musical."

"I've never been to a musical. It will be perfect."

"Then there's a reason you've never been to one. Your friends know you well enough to not invite you, and you've never gone out of your way to seek out the experience."

"Well, we'll see if I like it. I probably will. Which musical is it? I may have heard of it."

"Green is the Forest."

"I have heard of it, but I know nothing about it."

She gave him a short synopsis and assured him that he should not expect too much because it was a local theater group, not anything like he would see on the Coasts.

"Why do you assume I would know the difference? You always act like I come from a high-class area of a huge city where I am acquainted with all things sophisticated."

"Well, I don't mean to imply that. Just keep in mind that you're not likely to run into hotshots or government officials here."

"I appreciate that you do not put government officials and hotshots in the same category."

He noted her self-consciousness of Des Moines and wondered why she was there in the first place. She did not seem like a small-town girl from Iowa that was redistributed to the big city of Des Moines. Nor did she show any history of typical Purebreds, poor and ignored. No, she was delicate, educated, well mannered, and comfortable in the presence of Coastals.

Though she worked and lived as an upper-middle-class Inlander, she was most decidedly a southeastern Coastal.

Their entrées came, and as they ate, they continued talking about lighter subjects than politics, laughing and flirting with ease. They talked about the art that was hanging on the walls and the music that was playing in the restaurant. After they finished eating, she went to the restroom, and he checked a text message he had received during the meal on his personal phone. It was from Zaire, alerting him that he had news, stating cryptically, "My brother-in-law is in town. If I tell you where he is, will you go entertain him so I don't have to deal with him?" He put his phone away as their server walked by, and when Chris tried to pay the bill, the man told him Jenna had already taken care of it. When she returned, she had her raincoat, and he helped her put it on.

"Thank you for dinner," he said.

She looked victoriously at him, knowing she had successfully fooled him with her trick. "I told you I'd get it next time."

When they arrived at the theater early, he left her at their seats to call Zaire. When Zaire answered, Chris simply said, "Hey, I'm at the theater—where are you?" as though he were talking to someone who would be meeting him there.

"I'll address this theater business later." His tone was serious, but Zaire, no doubt, looked forward to asking Chris about his new suit and fancy dinner plans. "He's using the identity of 'Jay Whittaker,' and he's staying in a hotel not too far from you, but it's not in the Coastal District, nor is it downtown. We've decided to keep you at your hotel while we try to figure out why he's in Iowa. As far as we know, there is no official deal set. Find out what you can, but don't do anything until we know what his plan is. We've decided to check it out in case he leads us to other anarchists. I'll send the details to your notebook. Call me tomorrow. I'm dying to know about 'Green is the Forest.' I'd assume Adam is there, but you would have told me if you already found him, and I happen to know from his signature patterns that he is not particularly a theatergoer."

"All right, I'll put your ticket at will-call. See you soon." Chris hung up and returned to his seat next to Jenna. She still had her raincoat on, her legs were crossed, and she was flipping through the program.

"Have you ever been here?" he asked her when he sat down.

"I came here with coworkers one time."

The lights dimmed, and the musical started. She glanced at him a few times during the performance, as though trying to figure out if he was bored. "We can leave anytime," she whispered to him.

"Don't worry, I'm enjoying it. Just enjoy it yourself," he responded in a whisper.

A little embarrassed, she leaned back in her chair and returned to watching the stage.

After a pause, he leaned in toward her and whispered, "I can be more expressive if you'd like, but it might look odd, as I am not accustomed to reacting to musicals."

She laughed quietly at his comment but did not avert her eyes from the stage. She patted his hand and said, "It's okay."

When she started to pull her hand back to return it to its place on her lap, he grabbed it and intertwined their fingers.

She did not glance at him again and allowed herself to be fully immersed in the art.

His eyes watched the performers, but his attention was on her. She did not watch the stage as one who watched for entertainment. She studied it. She listened to the words and heard the way the performers delivered their lines. She followed the actors' movements and the way they used the props. She watched the stage crew work in the shadows.

Her hand rested in his, unmoving and relaxed. He kept his hand still, fighting the urge to feel her soft Purebred skin under his fingertips.

During intermission, they stayed in their seats and talked. As people left, she removed her raincoat and folded it on her lap. Everyone there was dressed up, and for a moment he had an eerie feeling that he was back on the Coast. Then, looking around, he realized they were all Coastal citizens, staying in Des Moines for various reasons. He realized this was the Inland's market for museums, upscale dining, nice hotels, and entertainment.

After the show, they started walking back to his hotel. She held her raincoat folded over her arms.

"Thank you for going to the theater with me," she said.

"Why don't you go more often?" he asked. "You love it."

"Well, to be honest, I don't have anyone to go with. I have friends, of course, but they're not really into it."

"Who cares—you should just go by yourself. You'll meet someone there who also enjoys musicals and will go with you."

She smiled slightly at the thought of having a friend with whom she could go to musicals all the time. Then, she casually and instinctively lifted her shoulder inward, pulling her arm just out of reach of the hand of someone passing by who was hoping to feel Purebred skin.

Jenna's face had remained unchanged, and Chris realized she had not even noticed what she had done. He turned his head, following the young teen girl with his gaze as she passed by them. It made sense to him, now, why Jenna was so guarded, glancing about every so often and not allowing many into her life. He had never thought about what it might be like to grow up being different from those around you, to be seen more as an object or oddity than a person, and to meet looks of surprise that you were not as bad off as you were supposed to be, not because of anything you had done but simply because of who you were.

He put his arm around her shoulder and pulled her closer to him. "Let me take you to one on Broadway sometime."

She looked at him with surprise and excitement, but then her expression quickly changed back to normal. "I don't think New York City is my type of place. I'm not that big into crowds and lots of people."

He sensed that what she really meant was that it would be nearly impossible for her to get permission to travel to New York City, or anywhere on the Coasts for that matter.

They walked in silence for a minute or two, and then she asked, "Do you travel to New York often? For your work?"

"I've only been there a few times in the last five years or so." There were three targets he could think of that he had eliminated in New York City, but if he gave himself time, he probably could have remembered more.

They walked in silence some more and then arrived at his hotel. She put her raincoat back on and looked up at the looming clouds. They stood outside the door for a moment, looking at each other.

"Well," she said. She stood with her legs crossed at the ankles and with her hands clasped and relaxed down in front of her hips, holding her purse and the two umbrellas.

"Will you send me a message so I know you got home safely?" he asked.

"Yes," she said.

"Do you want to come up?" he asked, pointing to the hotel.

"No," she said and laughed.

"Okay," he said, also laughing. "You don't live under a bridge or anything, right? You have a real place to go?"

"Yes," she said assuredly, laughing again.

"Well, I just wanted to make sure I wasn't leaving you out on the street."

She nodded her head slightly, still smiling. "Thank you for your concern."

She was unaware of how concerned he really was. She did not know that his team had located an anarchist in her city.

He told the doorman that she needed a taxi before she could try walking home alone. When the taxi came, Chris gave the driver his card and opened the back door for Jenna. She gave him a quick hug and got in. While he was shutting the door for her, Chris reminded her to send him a message when she got home. The driver gave him his card back and pulled away. Chris followed the cab as much as he could with his eyes, trying to figure out exactly where it was headed. He stood on the sidewalk outside his hotel, debating whether or not to call his contacts to see where she lived and if they could get a satellite visual. *Walking to work can't be more than a mile, right?* he thought. But he did not want to treat her that way. He wanted to find out everything about her from her, not from his resources.

As he turned to go inside, he nearly bumped into the Mexican man. He stepped back and held his hand out, offering the Mexican man to go in ahead of him, and then watched the Mexican man walk toward the bar. As the door shut behind him, the downpour the clouds had been threatening to let out came down with the crashing sound of thunder.

5

At three o'clock the next morning, Chris went to the hotel where the final Robertson was staying. Though they had found him, Adam was still able to sufficiently hide from many of the surveillance tools they used. If Xiao wanted Chris to gather information, he had to get it in person, just as he had done for the rest of the family.

He walked nearly ten blocks before getting to the car Zaire had chosen for him. The car sat on the street every day from six o'clock in the evening to eight o'clock in the morning. Zaire chose the car because the owner of the vehicle kept a solid schedule and would not notice the car missing for a few hours in the night. When Chris reached the car, Zaire shut off the car's tracking device and Comm System, and Chris hacked into it to turn it on and drive it away.

He lurked in the shadows and avoided anyone's notice—walking around the area, around the hotel, in the lobby, and finally in Adam's hotel room. Adam Robertson slept soundly in the nearly empty room. He had a single suitcase and only a few things. Chris searched through them and found nothing of use.

There were no items that indicated his reason for being in Des Moines or how he was able to hide his identity and biometric signatures from Surveillance. Chris looked at Adam sleeping in the bed and knew that if there was anything in the room that would help him understand the final target, it was on his person or under the pillows or covers. Chris could not do that search without risking waking Adam, and while Chris would have gladly finished the mission in that moment, his orders were to wait and gather any information he could about plans Adam and Adele had in Des Moines. Once he was satisfied and knew he could do nothing else, he returned to his hotel and went back to sleep.

When he woke up again at six o'clock, he got ready for his day, doing his usual checks and exercises, including going for a quick run around the surrounding blocks, all the while recounting the case in his mind. After showering, shaving, and brushing his teeth, he put on jeans, a tee shirt, a jacket, and a baseball cap. He decided to wear casual Coastal attire because there was a huge possibility he was going to have to stay close to Adam, so he needed to wear clothes that would help him blend into as many different potential scenarios as possible. If he wore a suit, he would not be able to leave the Coastal District without drawing attention to himself; if he dressed like an Inlander, he would not be able to go to Coastal-exclusive locations, should Adam decide to go to any. To complete his look, he pulled a backpack out of his bag and put in it a digital notebook, his personal cell phone, a camera, and the novel he had started reading on the plane. In his pockets, he put his room key, his wallet, his temporary phone, and a transmitter.

The transmitter sent signals to an earbud that disappeared as he put it in his ear. The transmitter was not necessary for the earbud to work, but he could use it to amplify sounds in his environment, in general or for a specific target. It also acted as an additional way for him to stay connected to his team: it made him easy to locate because its position was continually tracked via satellite; his team could interfere with the signal and talk to him through the earbud; and when his voice said "ear base on," a microphone was activated and his voice was transmitted to his team until he said "ear base off." It was not the preferred method of communication for agents out in the field, but it was particularly useful if they were in trouble.

Finally, he strapped a knife around his ankle. Though strongly suggested by his superiors, he opted not to carry his firearm on a regular basis. Inserting the earbud and arming himself were always the last steps of his morning routine.

He pulled a small box out of his bag, opened it, and removed a card. On the front, there was a logo for Magna, a world-famous store in Texas that bought and sold surplus citizen-appropriate war gear. While doing research on the Robertsons, he had learned that the youngest of the family was a lover of war history and collected as much as he could from The War That Brought Order. As a result, he was often on the lookout for authentic items and collected antiques such as helmets or uniforms used by the soldiers. The card had the design of a gift card, and under the logo was a promise: "Present this with your purchase to receive a twenty percent discount." On the back was a barcode and fine print. *In* the card was a chip that could only be tracked by the device that activated it. When Adam disappeared, Chris had suggested to his boss to have the agency make the card as a potential way to track Adam, if he could get Adam to hold onto it. Chris put the card in a slot in the digital notebook he had put in his backpack. After signaling that it had been activated, he put the card in his jacket pocket and zipped his backpack closed.

He took a taxi to Adam's hotel and sat in the lobby, reading the novel he had put in his backpack and pretending to wait for someone. Just before nine o'clock, Adam Robertson entered the lobby. When Chris saw him, he stood up and pretended to answer his cell phone. "Hey, what's up…Oh, that's okay. I'm just going to hail a cab, and I'll meet you down there…No, I wasn't waiting long. Don't worry about it. I'll see you in a bit."

He went to the front desk and asked them to get a taxi for him, just as Adam Robertson was doing the same. Chris nodded to him politely and greeted him, per Coastal social custom. Typically, Chris did not allow those he was shadowing to ever see him, especially when he was just gathering information. This time, however, he wanted to stay close in case Adam was in Des Moines to carry out some brutal act that needed to be stopped immediately. In a Coastal city, it would have been obvious if he saw him everywhere he went. But unless Adam Robertson was going to a private residence, they would just look like two visitors in Des Moines staying at the same hotel and seeing the same local attractions. And if Adam Robertson was going to a private residence, hopefully he would take the bait and be easily tracked.

They both went outside and stood in the driveway in front of the hotel. Chris pulled out his camera and started taking pictures like a tourist documenting his trip, keeping watch of the target with his peripheral attention. Adam resembled his brother Talon Jr., but he was shorter and had a slenderer build compared to his brother. They both had the dark red hair and reddish hue to their skin tone that their father had. He was looking intently down at the ground and ran a hand through his hair, which was thick and wavy and fell just below his earlobes. It had been cut and styled recently and was not unkempt, but it was much longer than it had been the last time Chris had seen him when he was in Florida after Karen's death. Chris wondered if the change in appearance was an attempt to help him hide with Adele in Des Moines. He searched his memory for any changes Adele had made to her appearance, but he could think of none, further adding to his confusion about what their plans had been and how they had signaled to each other to meet. It occurred to Chris that she could have known he was following her, that Talon Jr. had been part of the conspiracy and had sent Chris to Des Moines on purpose, that this was all part of their plan and that Adam had set a trap for him. But it was hard for him to believe they would have made a plan that included Adele and Talon Jr. dying. Yet, there were so many unknowns when it came to the Robertsons, and Chris had long come to terms with how unpredictable they could be. As confusing as the Robertsons had sometimes been, their actions no longer surprised him, so he kept an open mind and remained alert to the potential threat Adam posed.

Adam was wearing a suit, in the typical Robertson style, and was relaxed. That he was not anxious or scared made him an easier target for Chris. If anything, he seemed distracted, and Chris knew that—like himself—Adam was assessing his situation. He looked like he was planning in his mind, thinking of what he had already done so far and what he still needed to do. Seeing Adam like this, clearly up to something, made Chris all the more eager to stay close to him and figure out why he was in Des Moines. It also made him equally eager to finish the mission to stop Adam from whatever he was scheming in his mind.

Chris thought about how in that moment of concentration, Adam would not likely be good at fighting back, though he would put up a fight. Chris had profiled him enough to know that Adam was not one to succumb to a threat. None of the Robertsons were. Though not apparent through the suit jacket, Chris suspected there was a gun underneath. He made note of his intuition to tell his boss later. How Adam Robertson was able to obtain, carry, and conceal a weapon without the detectors in every doorway going off was a job for Surveillance; Chris's job was to carry out the mission, even if someone was breaking the Ban on Weaponry law.

In his mind, he played out the actions it would take to overcome Adam and grab the firearm. Chris often did this as an exercise in vigilance to consider every option in any given scenario. He thought about the moves Adam would likely make in the counterattack and anticipated his weaknesses. Adam was smart, but not fast, and Chris thought about how easily he could take the gun and put a bullet through the base of Adam Robertson's skull.

Chris turned back to the hotel and took a picture of it.

The motion caught Adam's attention, and Adam smiled at him.

Chris returned it with his own smile and said, "For my kids. They always want to see where I go."

"Mine, too," Adam said. "I bring them with me when I can, but when I can't, they love seeing pictures. Wish I could take them everywhere with me."

"Same here," Chris replied.

When the first taxi came, they both started for it.

"I'm sorry, but I'm in a hurry," Chris said rudely, and before Adam Robertson could protest, Chris opened the car door, got inside, and told the driver to drive away quickly.

Adam Robertson noticed that in his haste to get in, something had fallen out of Chris's pocket. He was about to take it inside to the front desk when his taxi pulled up. He got in and, looking at the card, realized it was a discount card for Magna, a place he went regularly. He put the card in his wallet.

Chris told his taxi driver to go downtown and watched in the rearview mirror as Adam's taxi headed in the same direction. When they got downtown, Adam's taxi pulled over.

Chris told his driver to turn down the next street, and he got out. He saw a café nearby and decided to go there to set up.

So far, Chris had only been in the few blocks of Des Moines where Coastals would stay, but the café he chose now was outside of the Coastal District. Being downtown and still amongst middle-class Inlanders, he did not stick out too much, as it was not uncommon to see Coastals in this part of town. But he knew this was as far into Inland culture as he could go without changing his attire to look like an Inlander himself so he would not be noticed. There were no Coastals in suits in this part of town, but there were some dressed in casual attire, like himself. If they were not apparent from their clothes, which were not only of better quality but also featured such luxuries as pockets, their manners gave them away.

Chris went up to the counter and ordered tea. The woman taking his order did not look him in the eye or even say a single word. He noticed her jaw was clenched as she set his tea on the counter for him to pick up.

"Your bag," an officer said, stopping Chris before he sat down. Chris opened his bag, and the officer inspected it before walking away without saying anything or acknowledging Chris in any way.

Chris sat down at a table and opened up the notebook. Assuming Adam Robertson had the card with him, he was nearly ten blocks from the café where Chris sat. He quickly routed the signal so Zaire could track the card's location, too. From his office, Zaire could visualize the card's location from satellites. The program on which Chris was viewing Adam's real-time location recorded all activity such that the left half of the screen showed the card's location as a moving dot on a map, and the right side of the screen showed a list that was constantly updated with the time and coordinates of the card's location every time it moved. The coordinates would later be analyzed for behavioral profiling. These images were embedded, revealed only to the location of Chris's retinas. To other eyes, it was just a media site, showing the latest gossip and news stories.

His plan had been to simply set things up so that Zaire could access the card's data and so he could get a quick feel for what Adam was up to before observing him in person. However, Chris ended up sitting in the café for more than two hours and observing his target on his notebook because Adam did not stay in any one location for more than five minutes.

When he was able to, Chris got visual data from security cameras so he could see what Adam was doing. Adam was not dropping things off or picking things up. If anything, he was just walking around looking at everything, almost like a tourist just wandering around the city. If he had been planning on meeting Adele somewhere, or if he thought she would be in any particular location, it was not apparent from his actions.

But surely he's found out about her accident and knows she's not here, Chris thought to himself.

When his phone rang, he looked around him at the people in the café to get an idea of how to communicate to Zaire. Assuming correctly that nobody around him could speak Indonesian, he decided to use it as his code language.

Since the Great Redistribution following The War That Brought Order, the citizens of The Sectors were slowly morphing their languages into one Common Language. There were still twelve official languages in The Sectors, though it was expected that the Common Language would be the only official language within a generation.

Agents were required to be fluent in all twelve of the official languages and five additional extinct languages that had not survived The War. During The War, Indonesia, along with the majority of Southeast Asia and Oceania, had been made uninhabitable, and as a result, the people who lived there, along with their languages, were destroyed as well. Speaking Indonesian did not make Chris stand out, as it was not uncommon to hear languages other than the twelve official ones. People still spoke their native languages; the problem was finding someone who could understand them. To further homogenize the population and create a single race and society, the government continually redistributed citizens, as necessary for the greater good, and rarely upon request, though requests were usually denied. Additionally, every citizen was redistributed upon his or her eighteenth birthday.

"Are you watching this?" Chris asked Zaire, referring to the readout of the subject's location. He remained serious and focused on the screen.

"Yes, what is he doing?" Zaire resumed his half of the conversation in Indonesian as well. The line was secure, but they never took chances.

"The only thing I've come up with so far is that he's getting to know the city. Maybe she wasn't supposed to come now and this is a scouting trip. Or maybe he's just getting acquainted with the surrounding areas of where he's planning to do something. The obvious problem is that he's on the opposite side of the river as the government buildings. Maybe he's lost. Or maybe he already visited those buildings before I got here." As he spoke, he inconspicuously looked around to make sure that everybody was ignoring him and that nobody could understand him.

"You saw him this morning?" asked Zaire.

"He doesn't have a bag or anything with him. He did not appear to be meeting up with anybody."

"And he's still alone," Zaire added.

"There's something about his mannerisms that does not sit well with me. He has a sense of urgency about him that I don't like. He's not talking to anyone or really *doing* anything." It was the not knowing what Adam was up to or what his motives were for this odd behavior that Chris did not like. If he had some sense of Adam's plans, Chris could prepare to intercede, but the unpredictability of his actions were what made Adam particularly dangerous. "I'm going to give it another hour or so before I start following him myself. I've been waiting for him to stop somewhere so I could drop by and eavesdrop, but it's too inconvenient with his inconsistent movements."

"Don't get near him again until you're sure he's going to stay. It's not worth it if he catches you. He's the most vigilant of the Robertsons, from what our sources have told us. Let's just watch him for now. As odd as this behavior is, he has been doing it consistently for two hours." Zaire paused for a moment, and Chris could tell he was going to change the subject. "So, the theater last night?"

"Yeah, what about it?"

"Are you going to tell me Adam went to a ballet?"

"It was a musical, actually, and he wasn't there. I checked."

Zaire just waited.

"I met someone."

"*Met* someone. That sounds serious."

"It might be," Chris said. "Let's just say, if Xiao wants me to take the time to figure out why the target is here and longer to get rid of him, then I don't mind camping out in Des Moines for a while."

"Want to tell me about her?"

"No."

"What does she look like?"

"No."

"What does she do?"

"No."

"Come on, just her name?"

"I'm not letting you get the goods on her. I'm doing this the old-fashioned way. I'm going to find out everything about her from *her*."

"I should have looked for her last night," Zaire said, "but what was going on didn't occur to me until this morning. Come on, I won't tell you any of it. Just let me get a look at her file. You know, technically it's a matter of your security, so I have to. It's my job. And I'm kind of bored at the moment, anyway. I've exhausted everything about this Adam guy, and I have no other cases to work on, and you always cover your own bases. Come on, let me look her up."

"No." Chris had been calm throughout the whole conversation, watching the screen the whole time, always expressionless.

"It's only a matter of time." Zaire had also been watching the screen.

Adam Robertson had stopped somewhere for a full five minutes. They both went silent. Chris could hear Zaire tapping away on his keyboard, zooming in on the satellite image, viewing security camera footage, and double-checking Adam's location with other measures to make sure he had not just left the card somewhere. Chris did not have access to nearly as much surveillance data as Zaire did, but he also double-checked that Adam was still with the card. From the information Chris could get on his notebook, it appeared as though Adam was sitting down at a table in a restaurant.

They both glanced at the clock, and at the same time, they said, "Lunch."

Chris hung up the phone, packed up his stuff, and headed for the place where Adam was probably eating. He got out of his taxi two blocks from the restaurant.

"He's toward the back," Zaire said in his earbud. "There's an entrance from the street and an entrance from inside the building."

Chris went in the building first and saw that there were windows all around the restaurant. He saw his target, sitting alone. He entered the restaurant and asked for a table near the front, in the corner. Annoyed, the hostess honored his request. She rolled her eyes to a fellow worker, indicating she was tired of these Coastals who came here expecting the good manners and special treatment they were used to on the Coasts.

A waiter came to his table shortly after he sat down. "Nice bag," he said bitterly, referring to Chris's backpack, which was made of fine Coastal fabric and was not see-through. Inlanders were only allowed to carry clear bags and purses so the contents could easily be checked by officers at any time.

Without acknowledging the comment, Chris ordered something to eat. The restaurant was not crowded, but it was an even mix of visiting Coastals and resident middle-class Inlanders. Chris wondered if Adam purposefully chose Coastal-friendly locations or if there was another reason why he was spending so much time in this part of the city. He never looked directly at Adam Robertson but kept him in his peripheral vision. Adam appeared tired and looked like he was taking a break from whatever it was he had been doing that morning that required so much walking and observing. Chris pulled the book out of his backpack and read it while he waited for his food, keeping part of his attention on his target. Adam sat with his elbows on the table and rubbed his forehead with one of his hands. He looked exhausted, not just physically, but mentally, like he had thought of every possible option and was now grasping for any tiny clue he could have missed. Chris thought that it was possible, however unlikely, that Adam did not know Adele would not be coming to the city. Perhaps that was the reason he looked so contemplative. More likely, however, was that Adam knew he was now alone, so his deep look of concentration was probably from having to devise a new strategy by himself.

Chris's personal phone rang, and when he saw that the incoming call was from Jenna, he hesitated before answering. It was not that he thought she would distract him from watching Adam; he was too experienced to allow anything to distract him from a target. But there was something about dividing his attention between her and his work that made him feel guilty. Not sharing the truth of his profession with her made him feel deceitful, and he did not want to lie to her. At the same time, he liked himself when he was with her, and if he was serious about pursuing a relationship with her—or any relationship, ever—he would have to figure out how to do this sooner or later.

"Hello?" he answered.

"Hi," she said quickly. Her voice sounded distant, like she had given up and was about to hang up when he answered. "Sorry, you're not busy are you? I'm on break and just thought I'd see if you were around for lunch."

At the sound of her voice, he relaxed. He could feel the corners of his mouth pulling into a smile and was already happy he had decided to answer the call. "I wish I could, but, unfortunately, I'm booked all day."

"Oh," she said, "well, I'm glad I get to talk to you at least. But I really want to see you again."

He could feel her blushing as she said it and smiled to himself.

"I mean, before you leave," she added with slight bashfulness in her tone.

"Well, it looks like I'll be here a few more days, at least." He realized he was going to have to come up with some official date on which he was supposed to leave. He set his elbows on the table and looked, not out the window, but at the reflection of Adam Robertson in the opposite corner.

"Oh, well, I hope everything is okay with work, but I'll admit to being happy that you're stuck in the Inland a little longer."

"Me, too," he said.

"I think you're the first Coastal in history to ever say that."

He laughed and said, "That may be, but I also recall that you promised me a tour from a local, and that place last night didn't seem very *local* to me."

"Maybe you're tired of Coastals? Or just bored of steaks?" she teased.

"That's not possible. But if you have a favorite place, I'd love to get to know it firsthand."

"I do, in fact, but it's nothing special."

"Sounds like the perfect place."

His waiter came by and picked up his empty plate without saying anything, and Chris was grateful to be talking on the phone. It made him blend in and appear more like a visitor exploring the city than someone working. As soon as he felt it, his gratitude turned to guilt as he thought of Zaire's comment, reprimanding him for never seeing people as anything more than elements of a case. He dismissed the feeling and instead focused on being happy to get to talk with her, regardless of how it made him look to Adam Robertson or anyone else who may have noticed him.

"But I can't do it tonight because I have to get dinner with a coworker and some clients we're about to start working with."

"What are you doing tomorrow night?" he asked.

"Treating you to my favorite meal?"

"It's on me," he said, "as a thank-you for allowing me to avoid the less desirable places to eat in the city."

"I still owe you for yesterday's breakfast at the diner."

Had it really been less than forty-eight hours since they met? he thought to himself in disbelief. As little as they knew about each other, he already felt like he had known her a lifetime. "We'll see."

"No, I insist," she said. "Last night, I got you back for dinner Saturday night. Tomorrow, I get you back for breakfast yesterday morning."

"Fine. I'll play along. But I'm pretty sure my dinner last night was the price of your so-called fillet and breakfast combined."

She laughed but said, "It's not about cost. It's my privilege to take you to my favorite place. I'll pick you up at your hotel. We'll have to drive because it's not in the city. I'll get us a travel permit and call you tomorrow afternoon when I know a more definite time. When will you be done with your business?"

"I'll probably be available by five o'clock." He was certain Adam was not going to pull anything the following day. He did not look like a man who was in the middle of carrying out a previously planned action; instead, he looked like he was still in the planning phase of whatever he was up to.

"Okay, then I'll try to call by four o'clock to let you know."

"That sounds good."

"Are you getting to walk around a little bit?" she asked.

"Yeah, a bit."

"It's a nice day outside. I don't know where your business is, but if you have some downtime, you should try to go to the riverfront. It's not particularly gorgeous compared to the rivers I'm sure you've seen in other cities"—her remark made him want to laugh, and he tried to hide his smile. It didn't work, and he knew she could sense him grinning on the other end. With a smile in her tone, she finished, "but it's nice. Maybe before you leave, we can go to one of the lakes."

"I'd like that." He paused for a moment. "You know, Des Moines is not nearly as bad as you make it out to be."

"I know, but unfortunately there's really not much else to do here except eat." Not much else for *her* to do was the unspoken qualifier. "I find that I wish there were more exciting things to show you."

"You're enough." He forced himself to say it without thinking first, lest he talk himself out of it. "I'll see you tomorrow afternoon, then. Take care tonight."

"I will. If it's not too late, maybe I'll call you and drop by afterward?" she asked.

"Please do."

They said their goodbyes, and Chris was unable to take the look of satisfaction off his face. When Adam left, Chris stayed in the restaurant to watch his movements on the notebook, just long enough to see if Adam was going anywhere or if he was doing more of the same scouting as before. After fifteen minutes, Adam was still going into each place along a street and then turning to go down another street and do the same. Chris could not observe him in person without it being obvious that he was following him, so there would be no stalking that day.

Chris packed and zipped up his backpack and decided to go back to his hotel room to continue his monitoring there. On the way, he stopped at the riverfront. It was, as she had said, just a riverfront. Even though he did not see anything particularly interesting in stopping to look at the river, he pondered her mention of it. He realized that she was a lover of nature and especially water. Some people loved meadows and trees and were usually dreamers, and others loved mountains and forests and were usually serene, but it had been his experience that those who loved water were especially observant and perceptive.

*   *   *

By evening, Adam Robertson had systematically explored a large portion of the downtown area, excluding the Coastal District and the government buildings. With Adele gone and Adam alone in the city, Chris now assumed his actions were purely for reconnaissance. Adam returned to his hotel room and stayed there, and Chris remained in his hotel room, watching Adam's location on his notebook and messaging with Zaire about possible intentions and explanations for Adam's behavior.

Eventually, Zaire went home, and Chris set the notebook to his side and pulled out the novel he had put in his backpack. He kept the notebook in his peripheral vision so he could see if the location ever changed. In addition to the program that was keeping track of the card's location, Chris was also watching live feed from the security cameras in the elevators, in case Adam left the card in his hotel room. With the target remaining stationary, he allowed his mind to wander and thought about Jenna and the events of the weekend. Whether it was because he was still in mission-mode or because he knew no other way to recall memories, he started with their first meeting and thought about everything that had happened, all the way to watching her taxi leave just before the storm.

At that memory, he thought of the Mexican man. He had not seen him at all that day, so there was no longer cause for concern that he was following him, but Chris knew better than not to look up someone he saw coincidentally more than three times. He put the book down and picked up the notebook and accessed security footage from the hotel lobby from the previous evening. When he saw the Mexican man, he selected him in the image and ran it through a facial recognition program. The file that appeared was basic, and he knew he would have to ask Zaire to look more into it because what he could access on the notebook was not enough if they needed to actually look into this Mexican man or his history. As part of the results given by the program, it automatically found the real-time location of the Mexican man and showed the live video feed. Chris was about to skip the video and scroll down to review the Mexican man's file when a motion in the background of the image caught his attention.

Jenna was sitting in the lounge with three other women— one Inlander, who Chris assumed was her coworker, and two Coastals, who Chris assumed were the clients she had mentioned getting dinner with on the phone—and a male Inlander, who Chris could tell was not part of the group. He was paying special attention to Jenna, who seemed like she was being polite to him but largely trying to ignore him. The scenario made Chris laugh under his breath, but after a second, he felt guilty for watching. He turned off that program and pulled up the other program that was tracking Adam Robertson.

He had told Zaire he wanted to learn everything about Jenna from Jenna, so he had vowed to himself not to look her up or use any of their tools of surveillance on her. But there was something about the scene that bothered him. He tried to let it go, telling himself that it was due to his training and experience, which dictated that he look up everyone and know as much as possible about any person or situation that he could. Yet, he also knew from his training and experience that if his instinct told him something was not right, he had to pay attention to it. For someone in his line of work, not paying attention to such an instinctual warning could be a matter of life and death.

It's not hypocrisy if I look him *up and leave her file alone...*Chris thought. It was all he needed to convince himself that the action was justified.

He pulled the program back up and selected the male Inlander who was sitting next to her and ran his image through the program that brought up his file. At the top, as it had for the Mexican man, it showed the real-time footage from a surveillance camera in the lounge. Chris scrolled past it to review the man's file. Not a second later, Chris had set an alert to be sent to his phone if Adam Robertson moved and was already in the hallway, heading toward her location.

*　　*　　*

Jenna checked the time; it was too late to call Chris and stop by his hotel to see him that evening—at least, too late for how early it was in their relationship, or at least too early in the relationship for him. Maybe. She was not sure. It was one of the reasons why she had decided to let him take the lead in the physical aspect of their relationship. The other reason was because she knew she should not get into a relationship at all, with anyone, so if he decided this would go nowhere, then that would help her do the right thing and make that decision, too. In her previous life, she would have been much more forward, but she had also been more carefree and therefore more vulnerable back then, and those were two traits about herself that she had dropped when she was redistributed to Des Moines.

She was sitting with her coworker and their two clients in the lounge of the hotel where the clients were staying. Normally, she did not mind working late, but that was before she had someone to see. She had not been able to take her thoughts off Chris pretty much since the moment they met. Luckily, her job did not require much attention, especially at this point in the evening. The clients were two businesswomen from the West Coast of the Western Sector who owned a group of factories just outside the city. They were booking a large event at the museum's gallery to celebrate the business's success and planned on inviting all the local managers as well as their Coastal business partners. They had already discussed much of the details for the event over dinner and would finalize everything at the meeting the next day. Now, they were just getting to know each other and having a good time.

While her coworker was in charge of managing some of the details for the event, Jenna's boss usually put her at the forefront of these meetings. Even though she was a Purebred, she made customers comfortable, and clients felt at ease discussing their particular desires for their events with her. She was good at catering to the demands of Coastals while gently letting them know those demands could not be completely met but that they would do their best to make the events as Coastal-like as they could. Or, if clients were rude, she handled it gracefully, compromising and negotiating deals so the clients would still be pleased. She also had a sneaking suspicion that Coastals liked her because she did not overdo it in terms of sucking up to them and paying excessive attention to them. The upper-middle-class Inlanders who worked in the Coastal District often treated visiting Coastals that way, hoping for a recommendation that would go into their permanent file that might eventually lead to getting promoted to a Coast someday. Some Coastals loved that part of visiting the Inland, but in her experience, most of them were annoyed by it, if not made extremely uncomfortable by it, especially knowing they were expected to give something in return, be it a large tip or a compliment to a supervisor. Jenna made no such demands of her clients, or any Coastals who visited Des Moines; as long as everything was okay and going according to the plan, she was going nowhere. She wanted to keep it that way.

After an hour, the clients and her coworker had drunk three drinks each, had become much less formal with each other, and were largely ignoring her. Her coworker was doing most of the talking and had dominated the conversation, trying to get in good favor with them, no doubt so it would go in her permanent file so she could one day be promoted to a Coast. Truthfully, Jenna hoped her coworker would one day have that chance.

She continued to smile and nod and pretend to be part of the conversation between her coworker and the clients. It was not awkward or uncomfortable for her. Jenna was used to being an outsider. She took the opportunity to allow her mind to wander and think about Chris. She had not once felt like an outsider around him, perhaps because, like herself, he almost lived in both cultural worlds of Inlanders and Coastals and had to straddle the two as he lived in one location but had to interact with the culture of the other. Plus, he was a born Inlander, which meant he had worked his way up to whatever it was he did on the Coasts, and she could not help but love that about him.

She thought about Chris in business meetings and imagined he was probably not like the clients she usually met with. He had not treated her like an Inlander, let alone a Purebred Inlander. He had not asked the restaurant manager to move her. She was sure others around them had wanted to. For all she knew, they had asked but the manager declined the request because they thought she was with Chris.

Unlike many Coastal-born managers, he was probably nice to his employees. She was sure he was still firm and authoritative, as he had been with the bartender and server at the restaurant and when he asked for a taxi for her. It was just his personality. But he was not rude or arrogant about it like many Coastals were when they interacted with Inlanders. That was one thing about the Coastal-Inland structure that had always bothered her. Though Coastals were nicer in general, she hated how they treated each other with manners and respect but they did not extend the manners to Inlanders. Granted, it was the social custom, and it was not like they went out of their way to be rude, and they probably did it just because it was expected, but it was all just so fake. She could not help but see such conditional treatment of others as a weakness. It was one of the few things she appreciated about her upbringing and one of the very few things she kept when she was redistributed to Des Moines. She remembered one time, when she was a child, someone had said something to her mother that was disrespectful, and Jenna had lashed out and said something mean—she couldn't remember what. What she did remember was that instead of standing up for herself or for her child, her mother had chastised her for saying it, and when Jenna had said, "But that woman is rude," her mother had replied, "But we are not."

She had made an effort to change everything about herself when she was redistributed, but a strong code of conduct was one thing Jenna could not let go. It was, after all, one of the reasons she had ended up in Des Moines in the first place.

At the memory of her mother, she quickly pushed the thoughts out of her mind. It was an old life that, even after so many years, she was still trying to completely forget. She had done a good job of that; it was the first time she had thought of her mother in a long time.

As she pushed the memory aside, there was a sinking feeling in her stomach, a cross between shame and regret. She hated that she had to hide so much from Chris. He kept nothing from her, and it was not fair that she could not return the favor. More than that, though, was the novelty of the desire to tell him everything about herself. Over the years, she had mastered the art of apathy and keeping an emotional distance from everyone. But she could not help herself with him. She knew it the moment they started talking that she was in trouble with him; she knew she should have ignored him or left as soon as she had finished eating or found another place to eat. She knew better than to spend so much time with someone or to let anyone get so close. She knew better, and yet it was almost like he left her no choice.

He was kind, sincere, playful, funny, and entirely irresistible. That was another thing about Coastals: they were all so beautiful, but most of them were beautiful for show, either through genetic cosmetics their parents had bought when they designed their offspring or from cosmetic surgery. When they met, he had been wearing black pants and a light blue button-down shirt that softened his appearance, but even with the long sleeves, she could see how muscular he was. Normally, she would have feared being around such a strong man, but then he was so relaxed, and he was not at all forward—which she now understood to be naiveté, but at the time it had made her feel safe. Chris did not seem to care about how he looked, unlike typical Coastals. They all had beautiful bodies that fit the genetics their parents probably paid for or from regular sessions with a personal trainer, but his body had a look of purpose to it. He never did say what business he was in, and she wondered if it was construction or some kind of factory work that required manual labor, and for this she was even more impressed with him for moving up in the system because she was under the impression it was extremely difficult for citizens who had been assigned those Societal Roles to get promoted to Coastal status.

Another thing she could not help but love about him was that even with the confidence that came with being a Coastal, and even with as much fun as they'd had during that first night when they met, he had a shyness about him that was endearing, despite how in control and authoritative he was. He had clearly never struggled, not like she had, which gave him innocence, but it also gave him vulnerability. She could tell he had never had to face weakness before, just by the way he acted. He was used to things being easy for him—not that he was not a hard worker; his Inlander-turned-Coastal status proved that he was not spoiled or entitled. But she had learned to read people and act accordingly over the years, especially since being redistributed to Des Moines. Whatever he did, he had always been good at it. His success was a tribute to the accuracy of the system of rounds of testing and assignments to Societal Roles.

If she had to force herself to be honest, she knew she was scared—not of him, but of getting close to him and especially of letting him get close to her. She had not allowed herself to do that since she had been redistributed to Iowa. But now that she had gotten a tiny bit of the experience, she realized that maybe she was a little tired of being so cautious and so guarded. And it was so easy with him. For the first time since deciding to completely change her life and who she was, she wanted to give in.

He brought some of that back out of her, and she loved it. She did not know how much she had missed herself until she met him. Yes, she was scared out of her mind when she thought of what could happen and where this could go if she was not careful, but she was also tired of never feeling anything. The truth was, meeting him put her at a crossroads because now there was no way she could go back to the way she was living before, even if she never saw him again after his business in Des Moines was over. It was like she had closed up the possibility of ever loving again, of ever falling for anyone ever again, of ever getting close to anyone or letting them get close to her ever again. It was like she had shut that possibility into a room in her mind with a steel door protected by a dozen deadbolt locks, and in one evening he just tore the whole door off and flooded her with feelings and possibilities, and now that they were out, they could never get locked away again.

Even if she never saw him again, he taught her that maybe it was okay to let someone in. Maybe it was okay to trust someone. Maybe there was at least one person that she did not have to be so cautious around. Maybe this was a man she could truly and completely be with. Maybe she did not have to hide.

"Jenna, can you get us some more drinks? We're all out over here," one of the clients asked.

"Certainly," Jenna said with a smile. She got up and went to the bar.

As she was waiting for the drinks, a man approached and stood next to her.

When the bartender handed her a tray with three drinks on it, the man said, "Oh, I got this," and handed his card to the bartender.

"Actually, it's on the museum's tab," Jenna told the bartender.

"No, it's not," the man said.

Jenna insisted, "Yes, it is."

The man picked up the tray. "Where are you headed?"

Jenna sighed and walked away, and the man followed her, carrying the drinks.

She thanked him when he set the tray down, and the clients and her coworker shared a look as they took their drinks off the tray. Jenna quickly put their empty glasses on the tray and took it back to the bar, mainly just to get the man away from them. It worked, and he followed her.

She placed the tray with the empty glasses on the bar top. The bartender took it without thanking her, but she had not expected manners from a fellow Inlander.

"Can I get one for you?" the man asked her.

"No," she said. "I'm working, so I can't really talk."

The man looked back at the women to whom she had delivered the drinks. Then, he leaned in closer to her and whispered, "I don't think they'll mind."

Not wanting to look like she was abandoning them for a strange man, Jenna went back over to the area where her coworker and clients were sitting. The man followed and sat next to her.

She had become used to being targeted after she moved to Des Moines. It scared her at first, but it happened just often enough to almost be a normal part of her life now. The creeps always went for the Purebreds because they were not confident enough to go after Modified women and assumed Purebreds would be flattered that a Modified would be interested in them and could help them with their status in society.

He started talking with all four of them, but it was apparent to all present that he was paying a little too much attention to Jenna. Then, he made a not-so-subtle comment about her being the prettiest woman in the room and probably the whole city, and that was when she knew she had to get rid of him before the clients asked him to leave, which would have just made the situation more awkward.

"Excuse me," she said to the women she was sitting with. "I just need to use the restroom."

"Me, too," the man said.

She stood up, and he followed her to the host's station, where Jenna asked for the location of the nearest restroom.

"Behind that curtain over there is a hallway, and the restrooms are to the right," the young man told her.

Once they were in the hallway behind the curtain, Jenna quickened her pace and went directly into the women's room and instinctively put her back against the door when it closed.

After a moment, when nothing happened, she was grateful he was not aggressive enough to follow her in there.

She stared in the mirror for a few moments, trying to figure out the best way to shrug him off. She decided that he was probably standing right outside the door, so when she saw him, she could explain to him that she was in a business meeting, get his number from him, and promise to call him the next day. She took a deep breath, plan in mind, and opened the door.

He was not there. She waited a few seconds for him to come out of the men's room, but then she realized it might look like they had snuck away together, and she hated the idea of the clients thinking she was unprofessional.

She headed back to the lounge area, but when she pulled back the curtain to exit the hallway, she immediately spotted Chris. At first, she was elated at the sight of him, but her excitement was quickly replaced with shock and confusion as she realized he was talking with the very man she was trying to get rid of. Caught off guard, she stepped back behind the curtain, letting it fall so she could watch him through the small opening between the curtain and the doorway. They were roughly fifteen feet away from her, facing each other so that she was viewing their profiles. She could not stop herself from gazing at Chris, though he was only in jeans, a tee shirt, a jacket, and a baseball cap. He looked young in a hat, more playful and fun. He was relaxed, with his hands in his pockets. She liked seeing him in casual attire, though she imagined he would have looked good in anything. She smiled involuntarily as he laughed with the man, his eyes disappearing into his cheeks and his dimples deep and endearing. She watched the muscles in his back, shoulder, and arm, as he had patted the man on the shoulder. Then, Chris turned, and she thought he looked directly at her. Startled, she backed away from the curtain, retreating even farther into the hallway, not wanting him to see her. She watched them leave, and then she returned to her company.

Nobody seemed to notice that the man left, and she tried to act unaffected for the rest of the evening. She could not help but have feelings of pure exhilaration at having seen Chris from the outside, not interacting with him personally. But at the same time, she also could not help but wonder why Chris had been there and why he had left with the man who was interested in her. She was not sure if he had actually seen her watching him or if he had even known she was there in the first place, but the idea that he had somehow known she was there was unsettling. And if he had led that man away from her because he was jealous or possessive—well, if that was the case, then she did not know who was the bigger creep out of the two. As grateful as she was that the man was gone, it was absolutely chilling to think that Chris might be the bigger predator.

It could have been a coincidence. It probably was. Perhaps that man was one of Chris's Inlander employees. But they looked too friendly for that. Her instincts told her that something was not right about that encounter, as friendly as the two men had seemed, and that there was much more to Chris beyond his Coastal businessman appearance.

She decided to put the thoughts out of her mind for the rest of the evening and chose, instead, to focus on the clients and let them distract her. She would take him to dinner the next day, as planned, and be extra careful. She wanted this gut feeling about him to be wrong, and she wanted him to be the man she thought he was and who she had been daydreaming about all day. But if it was clear that he was lying to her or hiding something, then she would break it off. She prepared herself for the possibility that this had been a mistake and that all the feelings she had allowed herself to feel in the last forty-eight hours were false. Maybe she *would* go back to the way things were before she met him, staying cautious, not letting anyone get too close. Maybe he was not someone she could trust or completely be with. Maybe she had been wrong to let her guard down with him.

6

Tuesday morning, there was a message from Zaire saying he had a breakthrough in the case. Chris called him immediately, and Zaire told him more details on how complicated the anarchist group's relations had been. Neither had ever worked on a case so tangled up in contacts and resources. One source always led to another that opened up possibilities and connections to other crimes committed in the past. Zaire said it would not surprise him if the Robertson family had ties with all the Purebred extremist groups in the Western Sector, though Pure Star was only half the size of The Rite and only slightly smaller than Maximum. Other smaller groups surely existed—not just in the Western Sector but in other Sectors, too. But this Robertson family, in the name of Pure Star, had taken it upon themselves to take action against the government and even The Order itself.

"Do you think they could all be working together?" Chris asked Zaire. Up to this point, they had treated each group separately, since the groups made no apparent attempts at joining or helping each other. But now that he thought about it, one group's attacks or crimes never interfered with another group's. Viewed from this light, one might even see a pattern and coordination in their efforts.

"I think there's definitely an alliance between Pure Star, The Rite, and Maximum," Zaire said. "They could be planning an attack together. I have set up meetings all day that I hope will give me more information and leads into these alliances. You'll have to keep a sharp eye on the target."

Zaire was shuffling papers in the background, and Chris heard him turn to one of his computers and type something short.

Thinking beyond Purebred extremists, Chris asked, "Do you think that Pure Star or any of the other groups are allying with Mexico?"

There had been rumors since The War that Mexico was building an army and planning an attack on The Order. But they were always assumed to be rumors. With each passing year of peace between The Sectors and Mexico, the rumors carried less merit. But because Mexico had opted out of signing the Treaty of The Sectors, tension between Mexico and The Sectors remained. For this reason, inhabitants of Mexico were not allowed in The Sectors. As the only country and still-habitable region of the world that did not sign the Treaty of The Sectors following The War, Mexico was a lawless area of the world, lacking rules of order and surveillance. The government of Mexico did not keep track of its inhabitants, modify or advance their genomes, nor did they keep any order that was maintained in The Sectors such as redistribution and strict surveillance. They did not even have division between Coastal cities and Inland cities. As a result, few citizens of The Sectors ever tried to go to Mexico, but those who did seemed to disappear.

"If there's an alliance with Mexico, Adam would definitely be at the forefront. We know through his drug business that he has connections," Zaire answered.

"Alleged," Chris corrected him with a hint of sarcasm, mocking their boss.

Zaire chuckled and said, "Yes, alleged connections."

"There's a Mexican man I've seen several times here in Des Moines. I looked him up last night, and he checks out as a legitimate Sector citizen, but I'm limited with what I can get here. If Robertson connections have found out about me, he may be an ally tailing me. I'll send you his information."

"I'll let you know what I find out," said Zaire, and Chris heard him get up to leave before getting off the phone. He would have to fill him in on any details later. At first, it had not occurred to him that the Mexican man was related to the case, but with Zaire's suspicion of an alliance, he thought it was worth a second look.

After they hung up, he ordered breakfast to be delivered to his room and read through the logs that were recorded while he was sleeping. Adam Robertson had not moved the entire time. Realizing he was probably still asleep, Chris took a shower after eating and got ready for the day so he was prepared to leave at any moment. By nine o'clock, he was reading his book, half paying attention to it, half recalling all the details of the case. This had always been his way of letting subtle facts stay in his subconscious to be worked out and realized later when they surfaced in his consciousness. By noon, Adam Robertson had only moved around in his hotel room, and Chris had finished his book.

Since the previous evening, Adam had stayed in his hotel room. He had not made any phone calls, nor had he shown any indication he was leaving. Whatever was happening was happening in that room. Chris could not access the phone records securely, so he messaged Zaire, asking him to do it when he got a chance. From Zaire's office, he could access the hotel phone and any cell phone calls made to or from the building without any trace of having done so.

With his phone still set to alert him when Adam moved, Chris decided to go to a bookstore he had seen the previous day. It was just beyond the Coastal District but still in walking distance. As Chris left the familiar blocks he had walked with Jenna, the tension in the atmosphere increased. Even in the Coastal District, the air and attitude were more uptight and anxious than anywhere on the Coasts, but citizens looked at him more suspiciously here, and their clothes were noticeably ragged and worn. The officers walking among the citizens were constantly checking hands and bags. Chris also noticed that officers here carried a baton in addition to a firearm. At one corner was a group of riot police with helmets and shields.

Everyone walked swiftly and kept to themselves. Several people bumped into him without apologizing. One citizen tried to reach into one of Chris's pockets when he bumped into him, but Chris blocked his arm before he could do it. An officer saw the incident and immediately arrested the man, who argued, "He can afford to be robbed." The officer, without any acknowledgement to Chris, put the man in handcuffs. Chris kept walking without looking back. He heard the man say "Coastal scum" and spit on the sidewalk, earning him another citation from the officer.

He reached the bookstore, and an officer at the door pointed to a sign, which reminded citizens that no bags were allowed in the store, to keep their hands where the officers could see them, and specifically for Coastals to keep their hands out of their pockets. Chris nodded to the officer to acknowledge that he saw the sign and walked into the store. The clerk at the register did not acknowledge him, continuing to frown as she stared out the window. The store was small and had a rank smell to it of old water damage that had never completely been cleared away. There was only one other customer in the bookstore, a Coastal, and he looked nervous in the unfamiliar territory. He smiled at Chris and greeted him in the Coastal custom, grateful to see a fellow Coastal.

Chris probably had more books in his own house than were on the shelves in this bookstore. Education was strictly enforced in The Sectors, and everyone was taught reading and writing in the emerging Common Language. But books were strictly censored, and most Inlanders worked for most of their waking hours and thus did not have time to read. All the books in the store were in the Common Language. When he saw one he had not read before, he took it off the shelf. It was used, as all the books in the store were, but it did not look like it had ever been opened.

Chris took it to the counter, and the clerk scanned the book without looking at him or saying a word. She flipped through it and stopped at a page. It had a note in the margin written in a language she did not recognize. Chris saw that it was written in Spanish, but he did not have a chance to read it before she marked over it with a thick black marker and threw the book in the trash can. Still without meeting his eyes, she waved him away, indicating he needed to choose another book. He did, and this time she scanned it, flipped through it, took his card, charged him, and put the book on the counter for him to pick up—all without looking at him or speaking to him. He took the book and left without acknowledging her. The other Coastal in the store quickly got a book and caught up to Chris walking on the street, staying a few paces behind him. When they got back to the blocks where more Coastals were, the man said, "Have a good day," to Chris and walked away with ease. Chris got lunch to take back to his hotel room, and he resumed his position on watch.

At nearly three o'clock, he received a call from Zaire and Xiao.

"I think I know why he's in Iowa," said Zaire.

"What did you find out?" Chris asked.

"As Talon Jr. said, Adam has been betraying his family," Zaire said, "but not his cause against the government. The Robertsons have always stayed true to the Western Sector, adamant about returning it to the old North America. But Adam *has* been in business with inhabitants of Mexico."

"You finally found proof?" asked Chris.

"Yes, but he has also been in touch—I think via inhabitants of Mexico—with anarchist organizations in the Eastern and Central Sectors. His family just wanted America back, but he has sided with Mexico. I believe there is a sister group," Zaire continued, "a Mexican gang hiding in Iowa. Adam has helped smuggle inhabitants of Mexico into The Sectors. I doubt we're the only team after him."

Chris asked, "So, you think the sister Talon Jr. was referring to was actually a sister group, and hiding was referring to keeping the sister group hidden, and Talon Jr. didn't agree because the Robertsons stayed out of Mexico affairs? Do you think he's here to meet with someone?"

"No, I think he's just there to scope out the place," said Zaire. "That's what it looks like, anyway."

"Are you confident he has been alone this whole time?" asked Xiao.

"Yes," Chris said, "but I have not shadowed him closely. The times I've seen him for myself, he was alone."

"Every time I saw him on video, he was alone," Zaire reported. "I checked all phone records in the hotel, and none of them show any connection to Adam Robertson. Of all the cell phones used in the area in the last three days, only one was used to call numbers we know are connected to the Robertsons. I checked the records for that cell phone, and it's only been used to call people we already know about and are already watching. All the other phones are registered to legitimate people. There's no way he's contacting anyone without us noticing."

Their boss cut him short, saying, "Unless he's selectively using anti-tracking technology more advanced than our surveillance tools. Many of the Pure Star members that have been arrested since we began this mission were found with such devices. That he is still doing business with inhabitants of Mexico shows he has access to such technology."

They were all silent for a few moments.

"So, what should I do?" Chris finally asked.

"It's your call," Xiao said decidedly.

"We can wait around to see if anything comes up," Zaire started.

"Or we can prevent a meeting from ever happening," Chris finished.

"Whatever you do," Xiao advised, "be extra cautious that you are not falling into a trap. He knows someone is after him by now."

"I haven't been followed as far as I know. Zaire, am I clear?"

Zaire gave his report. "No retina patterns exist around you, and I've checked all flight and phone records, and you seem clear of any shadows. I seriously doubt we should be concerned, though. You're too good at what you do."

"He's right," Xiao said. "It's your call, Rockford."

"Zaire, I sent you the info on that Mexican man I told you about earlier. His movements do not sync with mine, but if he is connected to the Robertsons, or if he's tailing them, he may be onto me."

"Well, first of all," Zaire started, "the most dated recognition of him in Des Moines is two months ago, so he definitely didn't follow you there." Chris could hear clicking in the background as Zaire set more parameters on the search. "And there are no coincidental appearances of him with Adam Robertson. Not even close in time or space. I would conclude he has no connection whatsoever to the case. I'll go ahead and see what I can get on him, though."

"But in your spare time, Zaire," Xiao said. "Our first concern is Adam Robertson. If there is nothing connecting him directly to Chris or Adam, investigating his relation to Pure Star will have to wait. Other teams are surely investigating all potential ties to Mexico, but our mission is to eliminate the Robertson family."

Chris asked, "What if we had Adam Robertson arrested and questioned him?"

"It's too dangerous," Xiao said. "The group may do something drastic if he's in custody."

"And the Robertsons don't talk," Zaire added, "especially Adam Robertson."

"And there's really not much more we can get from him," Xiao added. "If he is meeting a contact anytime soon, simply getting rid of Adam Robertson will stop the deal from going down. We've already seen the effects of the absence of the rest of the family. All the plans have fallen through, many of the organization's lower members have been placed in Purebred Communities, and the gang has practically deteriorated." He paused. "It's your call. Do it now, or wait and see what you can find out."

"All right," Chris said and thought for a moment. "I'll decide tomorrow night at ten o'clock."

Setting a time to make decisions was something he had learned through experience. In training, he had learned how to best make decisions as quickly as possible, but when it came to something that had to be thought out, he found that setting a time was best. This way, he allowed his thoughts on the matter to rest, and when he recalled the debate with a fresh sense of recollection, only the really compelling arguments remained, allowing him to make a clearer decision.

"Zaire, can you watch Adam Robertson while I go on call for a while?" he asked.

Agents in the field went on call sometimes, when their duties were not immediate. Chris usually went on call when he was with his family, but Zaire and Xiao both knew he was not with family this time.

"I won't be in Des Moines, but I won't be far. It won't interfere with the mission."

"We know," Xiao said. "I'm going to check out. Keep me updated." He hung up his phone.

"It's not a problem," Zaire said. "Just send me a message when you want me to start watching, and I'll keep my schedule open this evening." Then, he added, "Have a good time with Jenna."

Chris sighed. "Really, Zaire?"

"Matter of security. I got an alert when she applied for a travel permit to a place just outside Des Moines city limits for one Jenna Macklemore and a Christopher Rockford. I never dreamed she'd be a Purebred. It took her nearly all day, calling and providing documentation and finally going down to the Travel Permit Office in person." It was all Zaire could do to not laugh out loud at the ridiculousness of the situation. "Really, Chris, you should have just told her you'd get the permit and have me put one on your notebook. Or you could have just told her you're in government and that it's not necessary for her to have a permit if you're with her. It's not very gentlemanly for you to make her go through all that trouble."

"I didn't know it was that complicated. I've never gotten a travel permit before," Chris said defensively.

"I'm just glad you took my advice, though I didn't think you were serious about going for the Purebreds."

A pang of guilt shot through Chris as he remembered joking around with Zaire. "I wasn't."

"No matter, you have to start somewhere."

Chris did not say anything in response. He did not know how to convey to Zaire that she was not just anyone to him.

"And if you're going to practice on someone, it might as well be a Purebred."

Chris's guilt turned to anger, first at his friend for regarding a woman he cared about as some insignificant category, and then at himself because he would have made the same comment, or at least agreed to it, just days before.

"Anyway, I'll hack her car remotely, so you don't have any issues."

"No, don't," Chris said urgently. "Only if it's necessary."

"Okay…" Zaire said slowly, like he did not agree with Chris's decision. "She checks out, by the way, but I won't tell you more if you don't want to know." Chris did not answer, and Zaire continued, knowing Chris would stop him if he did not want to hear it. "She's from Utah and was redistributed to Des Moines when she was eighteen. Apparently her talents as an artist put her on the radar, so she was recruited to the art museum when it opened there. She's twenty—"

"That's enough," Chris said. "I don't want to know any more. It's not fair to her if I already know everything about her."

"All right…"

"Did you look up Melinda when you met her?" Chris asked, referring to Zaire's wife.

"Every single detail. And that was before I met her in person. But you do what feels right. Every relationship is different."

Chris could tell someone had just stepped into Zaire's office, so they both hung up. Chris sat looking at his phone. He supposed it may have been possible that Jenna was somehow pulled out of a Purebred Community and was trained to be like a Coastal for her job at the museum. But it was extremely unlikely. The Purebred Community System was a cycle few were able to break. The only real way out was for a couple to get married, pass the exams and be given a Child License, and then not opt out of the genetic modifications for their children. Even then, they would only be redistributed to an Inland city. It would be up to the Modified children to find favor with the Department of Redistribution to make it to the Coasts. And Chris was sure she had grown up in a Coastal city.

Just then, Jenna called.

"Hi, I'm so sorry, but there's a delay. I got the travel permit, but I don't know when I'm going to be able to get off work today." She sounded disappointed.

"Is there anything I can do?"

"No, it's kind of a long story."

"I have time to hear it if you have time to tell it."

"Well, we have two new assistants who were going to stay late tonight to stuff envelopes for this gala we're throwing together, and they absolutely have to be mailed tomorrow. They were supposed to be mailed last week, actually, but the printing company that does our stationary could not get the invitations to us until today. We just got them, and there's a mistake, so I have to deal with the company, and then I guess I'll help the assistants figure something out." She sounded really down. "I really wanted to see you tonight. I'm so sorry."

"Then can I come there and help stuff envelopes?" Chris asked.

"Uh—" she made a noise as she started to say something but stopped herself. His offer to help do something so beneath him had truly surprised her. "Sure."

She gave him her location, and he sent Zaire a message: "Start now. I'll be back after 10pm." He quickly changed into nicer clothes, called the front desk to make sure a taxi was waiting for him outside, and got to her work within ten minutes. As he exited the taxi, he felt eyes on him and turned to see the Mexican man glancing at him as he turned the corner. For a second, Chris considered following him, but he knew Zaire was probably looking him up at that moment. It was best to get all the knowledge he could before seeking the Mexican man out himself.

When he arrived at Jenna's office, she was on the phone. She smiled brightly and waved to him, clearly surprised that he had gotten there so quickly. Jenna was talking to a woman at the printing company and put her on speakerphone just as the woman was saying she was going to check something and put her on hold.

"She's going to put a man on the phone," Chris said, pulling up a chair and sitting at the desk.

"What?"

"She has everything in front of her and is intimidated. She's going to find a man to put on the phone, even though he doesn't know any more than she does, except that you're in the right. What's the problem?"

Jenna handed him one of the invitations that had the incorrect part highlighted. At the bottom of the page, the phone number was missing a digit. "Why do you think that?" she asked as she handed him the paper.

"It's in her voice," was his response.

A moment later a man was on the phone. He asked her what the problem was, and as Jenna explained to him what she had already twice told the woman, Chris took a blank sheet of paper from the printer and wrote on it: "STALLING. He'll ask you to come down and discuss it in person so he has more time." Right after Jenna finished reading what Chris had written, the man on speakerphone suggested she bring him the paper they sent so they could discuss it in person. As he was saying it, she looked at Chris. He had a victorious look in his eyes. She gave him a questioning look, and he nodded toward the phone. She told the man she would be at the printing shop within ten minutes.

"Can I come?" Chris asked her when she got off the phone.

"You must. I'll need a mind reader." She hurriedly gathered her belongings and the box with the invitations. The assistants started to come with them, but Jenna told them to work on something else.

"I can handle him, if your boss doesn't mind me getting into your business," Chris said as he took the box from her hands.

"Thank you," she said, "but it's okay. I should be able to deal with this myself. I can't believe they are trying to charge us for reprinting these."

"I'll tag along, just in case, if that's okay."

They went to her car, and she drove to the printing company's location across the river. When they arrived, Chris took the box of misprinted invitations in with them. At the entrance was an area with a couple of tables where customers could place orders. Chris noticed that despite the few tables, there were no chairs anywhere, presumably to keep costs down. Behind the main counter, Chris could see the machines where they printed up the orders and kept their records. They looked too nice to belong to a locally owned business, and Chris wondered if the Coastal in charge had ever set foot in the building. The whole place looked like a warehouse, as if the company had moved right in without finishing the inside. The framework and all the pipes of the building were exposed, and the floor, walls, and ceiling were raw concrete. Upon their arrival, several employees in the front room straightened their posture when they saw Chris. The workers were surprised to see him, and some stared like they had never seen a Coastal before while some looked down like they were self-conscious. They all looked tired, but not because it was the end of the workday. It was a different kind of tired, the chronic tired look most Inlanders carried.

Jenna went directly to the man with whom she had spoken on the phone. He had the order form, which only showed the number of copies ordered. As he approached, Chris glanced at it from over her shoulder. At the sight of Chris the man straightened his posture. He looked angrily at them both, as if he had been tricked. He was expecting the Purebred Inlander to come alone, not with someone, and especially not with a Coastal. He took the sheet on which she had highlighted the mistake and went to the back.

Jenna sighed. Then, she looked at Chris as if expecting him to say something.

He looked back at her, puzzled.

"Well," she asked, "what's he going to do?"

Chris laughed. "Okay, well, I think he's going to come back with some nonsense about how you were supposed to proofread it carefully and that they were just supposed to print it."

She nodded, seeing that it made sense.

"Is there an original document that you sent to be printed?" Chris asked.

"It was an email." She pulled out a printed copy of what she had emailed to them. "This is the email, which tells them our order, and this is the attachment I sent with it, which is what we wanted printed."

Chris looked over the email. "You requested the stationary they have on file."

"Yes, we do all our official documents through them, so they have one on file for us."

When the man returned, he said she was supposed to have proofread the document carefully and that the agreement stated they were merely to print mass copies of the document she sent them.

Jenna told him there was nothing wrong with the part she had written and pointed to the phone number at the bottom. "The phone number was part of the stationary on file," she explained. "What I sent you was to go in the body. Somehow the stationary on file has been altered."

The man did not say anything while he thought of an excuse.

"Can we see the original agreement?" Chris asked.

The man and Jenna both looked at him.

"What agreement?" the man asked.

"The one she signed that says she was supposed to proofread this carefully and that she's responsible for any misspellings or other errors for the stationary on file."

The man's expression turned pale, and he got on the computer and searched the records. He turned the screen toward them. It was a scanned copy of a document she had signed three years earlier. The three of them looked at it carefully.

"Can you bring up the original letterhead that this agreement is referring to?" Chris asked.

The man quickly turned the screen so they could not see it anymore and pretended to search the records. Then, in a huff of anger, he left and went to the back.

After a few minutes, just when Jenna and Chris thought he may not return, he came back and pretended to search some more. When Chris cleared his throat, the man finally gave up. He gulped and nervously said, "It's not on file anymore."

"Why not?" both Jenna and Chris asked at the same time.

The man was silent.

"How long does it take to correct the mistake and reprint this many copies?" Chris asked, pointing to the original order form.

"We can have it done by the end of this week."

"No," said Jenna.

The man looked at her incredulously. "It's the best we can do," he insisted, offended she would have the audacity to protest. "We have many orders."

"Then I'd like to withdraw our order, and I'll take a complete refund."

The man smiled condescendingly.

"I'm sure it will be cheaper to just buy ink and paper and print these myself. It would also be faster and more reliable," she said, unaffected by the man's attitude toward her.

In contrast, the muscles in Chris's jaw and arms had involuntarily tightened.

The man looked at her with anger. He laughed and shook his head and was about to remark on the absurdity of her behavior and the implication that she could do anything about the situation. But then Chris caught the man's eye, and the anger turned to fear. So instead, he said, "It would take about fifteen minutes to correct it and program the machines to print them, and then it would take about two hours to get them all printed up and maybe an hour to look over them and make sure they look good and don't have any smudges on them. It might take more time if a machine runs out of ink or if something happens that we have to fix."

"Does that happen often?" Chris asked.

"It is more likely to happen with such a large order, but we do not expect it to happen, naturally."

"Naturally," Chris repeated.

"So I can come back in three hours?" Jenna asked.

"We close at five o'clock," the man said.

Chris looked around at the workers and the printers in the back and thought, *They may close at five, but they clearly work well into the evening.*

The man followed Chris's gaze to the printers and then looked back at them, addressing only Chris. "But we'll stay to finish this order tonight."

"Thank you," Jenna said to the man, who had stopped paying any attention to her. "I'll be back at—"

"Actually," Chris interrupted, "we have plans tonight."

"Well, so do I," said the man. Now, he acted like Jenna was not even there and had even stepped closer to Chris and turned his body toward him.

"No, you have a job to keep," Chris said.

Jenna looked at him with surprise.

Chris turned to her and added, "If it's okay with you." Then he looked back at the man, whose shocked expression was humorous to Chris. This man never dreamed he'd see a Coastal ask an Inlander, let alone a Purebred Inlander, for approval. "We're going to go eat. Her assistants are going to come here in an hour to start stuffing envelopes. Will there be correct documents printed by that time?"

"The first batch could be printed in forty minutes—*will* be printed in forty minutes," he corrected himself.

"Thank you," Chris said. "We're just going to leave this here." He put his hand on the box with the incorrect invitations.

"Yes, and this will be done at no extra charge," the man behind the counter humbly said to Chris.

Jenna thanked the man again, though he did not acknowledge her. She glanced around, unsure if she should be embarrassed, and felt slightly uneasy at having caused a scene.

"Maybe I should come here with the assistants to make sure he doesn't give them trouble," Jenna said when they got in her car.

"He won't give *them* trouble," Chris said, a little agitated. But then he changed his mood and added optimistically, "And they know your phone number, right?"

"Yes."

"Then, I think they can handle a game of spot the difference to keep their jobs. If they have any problems, they can call you and we'll come back."

She thought about it for a minute and debated calling her employer to ask for permission. But she was technically the supervisor of the assistants and therefore should have been allowed to tell them what to do.

"If you're really concerned, we can stay and do this all night. I won't complain as long as I'm with you," Chris relented.

She thought for a moment more and then said, "You're a bad influence."

She called the assistants and told them the plan. After they assured her they would not need her help, she thanked them and hung up.

"So where are we going?" Chris asked.

"It's about thirty-five minutes outside of town. It's nothing special, just a little family-owned place. The food is real and takes forever to make. The restaurant has been in the family for four generations."

"Sounds great. It's been a long time since I've had a home-cooked meal that I did not make myself."

"I'll have to have you over for dinner sometime." She blushed after saying it, mainly because she realized she had forgotten that he was only in town for a few days. "I suppose that sounds like an empty promise with you leaving so soon."

They sat in comfortable silence for the first lag of the car ride. Once they were out of the downtown area, she was pulled over for a random ID check, likely because her non-Modified retinas had set off an alert.

"Where are you from?" the officer asked as he took her ID.

"Is there a problem, officer?" Chris asked.

"Just a routine check," he said, not paying any attention to Chris and looking at Jenna's ID. "I don't like anything that looks suspicious. Is this your car?"

"Yes," she answered. Truthfully, she was surprised to have gotten so far without being pulled over already. With the retina scanners at every mile marker, the lack of Modified retinas in the driver's seat almost always set off alarms of suspicion, resulting in her being stopped for questioning.

"How?" the officer asked.

"I work at the art museum in Des Moines," Jenna said calmly. She was not nervous talking to the officer and handed him the travel permit she had obtained. "He is traveling with me."

"You look a lot younger than your age. Your parents must have—" He did not get to finish his rant before Chris interrupted him.

"A routine check means you need my ID, too, right?" Chris handed his ID to the officer, and as it was passed in front of Jenna's face, she noticed it was marked as government status.

The officer looked at Chris's ID and then back at him.

"Sorry, didn't see you in there. You two have a good night." He handed their IDs back to Chris and walked away.

When they reached the Des Moines Border Checkpoint, Jenna handed the officer her ID and travel documents. "These look forged," the officer said. "Park the car over there. You'll have to come with me while I get them checked out."

"They check out," Chris said as he handed his ID to the officer.

The officer looked at Chris's ID, handed it back to him, along with Jenna's ID and travel permit, and waved them through.

Jenna put the car in gear with a little more force than usual and continued on the road.

"Everything okay?" Chris asked.

"Yes." She realized she sounded agitated, so she softened and added, "I'm taking you out, remember?" When she looked into his eyes, she realized he was not going to let it go. "I just sometimes think it's ridiculous I can't live a normal life without being a suspect, like I should not have the privileges like everyone else, simply because my parents did not get government approval and incentives. It isn't so bad when I'm around you."

She sighed. "I like being with you, but it infuriates me that you validate me. I'm used to being ignored when I'm by myself or with Modified Inlanders. But when I'm with you, people see me as completely fine and normal. Like when we were in the Coastal District at the diner and the theater, as long as I was with you, I was almost treated like a Modified."

"Is that why you're with me?" he asked.

"No, of course not. I like being around you, regardless of your status. Though, that ID is like gold, and I wish I had one."

The comment made Chris laugh out loud. "It's one of the perks of turning your life over to the government."

"Well, thank you for your service," she said. "You didn't tell me you work for government." At the first sight of his ID, all her fears and doubts from the previous evening had subsided because it explained the mystery surrounding him.

"Yeah, sorry about that. Now, I wish I had told you so you wouldn't have to deal with all the travel permit stuff. Really, I didn't know it was such a hassle."

She gave him a flirtatious glance and said, "Welcome to civilian life." She took the next exit, and they soon pulled into the parking lot.

At the restaurant, the wait for a table was nearly an hour. "I forgot to tell you that it's also really crowded," Jenna remarked. "And they don't take reservations."

He looked around blankly. There were three government-approved antique shops next to the restaurant, but other than that, the only thing in sight was farmland.

"I don't know where all these people come from," she said in response to his look.

After putting her name on the list, they went into the nearby antique shops. Signs posted at the doors reminded customers to keep their hands where officers could see them and that bags were not allowed. Like everywhere else they went, Jenna was the only Purebred, but there were many employees and customers over forty years old. It was rare to see so many of the older generation, and Chris wondered if this part of Iowa was specifically set aside for them, like the town in Arizona where his parents were redistributed when they retired. It was obvious that the restaurant and antique stores were privately owned, and it impressed Chris that four businesses here could afford to stay in the family. After The War, all businesses were owned by The Order, except for those willing to pay the exorbitant taxes to remain privately owned and operated. Thus, privately owned businesses were typically owned by Coastals. Occasionally, someone in an apron would come into the shop and say a name, indicating that the table for that party was ready at the restaurant. Such an archaic system was an entirely new experience for Chris, but the informality of the system gave the place a homelike ambience, like everyone there was family.

They walked around the stores and talked about the different antiques, most of which were no older than forty years, and any antiques in the store that were pre-War were government approved. They pointed out things they liked or disliked. They joked about some of the advertisements and toys kids used to play with. His stomach growled occasionally, and they both apologized—he for the noisy stomach, she for making him wait so long to eat.

He pointed at a train set. "I had something like this when I was a kid. We still have it at my house in Idaho." It was not the first thing he had pointed out that reminded him of his house in Idaho.

"Your childhood home sounds like a fun place, like an old house with lots to explore."

"It's a good place for a child to explore. The house is not that old, but everything in the attic is."

"Oh, I loved exploring attics as a kid." She continued walking, and he followed her out the door. "But I didn't have one growing up."

"Really?" he asked, turning to her.

By now they were outside the restaurant sitting on a bench, waiting to be called. He could not stop himself from staring at her. She looked so beautiful in the light of the setting sun. And she had finally mentioned her childhood.

"That's too bad," he said.

She nodded her head and looked back at him. "I agree."

They sat looking at the sunset. Each was grateful that the silence was never awkward between them. Neither felt obligated to fill the empty space in conversation. They looked like they belonged in this cozy place, full of old friends and families that knew everything about each other. They did not stand out like two people who had only met just days before.

They were finally called into the restaurant, and after they ordered, she started a conversation that let him know what she had been thinking about during all that silence.

"Are you psychic?" she asked.

The question caught him off guard and caused him to laugh. "What?"

"Can you read minds? You always seem to know exactly what to say."

"I can read people—facial expressions, mannerisms. I notice what they wear and what they pay attention to."

She looked at him, searching, wondering if it could really be that simple. "Nothing else?"

"You're disappointed," he stated and took a sip of water. When she did not respond, he continued. "There's no magic. There are no voices." He looked around and then back at her. "Just years of experience, observing, guessing, and then probing to see if I was right."

"I guess there's not much else to it, but, for you, it seems too natural to just be guesswork."

"I won't deny my accuracy," he said without arrogance, "but it's not word-for-word consistent with the thoughts of people. Just an observation of the little things and then an assumption of the big things."

She sat there, somewhat amazed, wondering how someone could perfect such a skill. "Could you teach me?"

He gave her a half-smile in response. "I'll guide you, if you'd like, but it's really just something you jump into and teach yourself as you go along and get more acquainted with the art."

"Couldn't you say that about anything to be learned?"

"This is just like anything else you learn to do."

She sighed, realizing how right he was. The rarity of any skill was that so few actually put in the effort to do it. An expert was someone who was simply well practiced. Even being observant could be improved upon by mere practice.

"Give it a try," he continued, "and then just keep playing with it until it becomes second nature. It works for any kind of learning, really. Just repeat it until it sticks."

"Some things never stick," she asserted.

He sat up and leaned forward. "You just didn't repeat it enough," he said in a low, flirtatious voice.

She mirrored his position, sitting up and leaning forward. "If I could have repeated anything I was told in chemistry, it would have meant that I had learned it in the first place."

He laughed and relaxed again. "Not a chemist?"

"That's beside the point."

"The point?" He narrowed his expression, but continued smiling.

"How do you know everything about everyone?" She was smiling now, too, trying not to laugh.

"I just told you."

She thought for a moment, never breaking eye contact with him. "You played around with people until it stuck?"

"Basically," he said. Most of what he learned from someone in the moment was a reflex from something stirring in his subconscious, but it helped to have the extra resources his job gave him.

She shook her head, not believing him, but she was still smiling.

"Just guess," he said. "Sometimes you're right. Sometimes you're wrong. Eventually, you start to see patterns you can't describe or explain but that you feel. Let the feelings form, and learn to read and trust them."

"When did you start guessing?"

"In kindergarten," he started, and her eyes widened as she leaned back and laughed as he continued, "I decided to try to predict who would steal toys from other children. From there I started guessing what foods were in their lunchboxes. After that, I moved to strangers and different things about them."

She looked at him in wonder for a moment. Then, she said, "And now it's second nature." Her eyes were filled not with envy or fear but with respect and admiration. As far as she was concerned, he was not creepy or odd, as she had considered when she saw him the previous evening. Rather, he was unique, a hidden treasure never found because no one had bothered to look.

"No, but I'm right about enough that I can figure it out or get around what I'm missing." He did not mention that, on top of his own experience in trial and error, he had been taught extra techniques in his job training.

"So, you're just super perceptive."

"I guess so."

"So, what about me? What do you perceive about me?"

He thought for a moment about how to answer. He did not want to tell her that he could tell she was hiding something related to her life before Des Moines. He did not want to tell her that he knew how she felt about him and that the feelings were mutual. Nor did he want to tell her that he knew she did not want him to leave and that he was the first person she had really connected with in a long time. He wondered if she knew that she was the only person he had really connected with, ever.

"All right," he started, as though accepting a challenge. "I can perceive that you don't like deception. You are true to yourself and desire to be true to others." He saw a subtle change in her expression, one he would not have noticed without proper training. He could tell she was afraid he would go on to mention that she could not always be truthful to others, though he did not know why. "You're genuine, kind, and good natured. You like to interact with people, but you force yourself to be guarded. You're not shy or insecure, but you can come across that way. I think that's because you just want peaceful relations with everyone. You're happy, and you want others to be happy."

She started to smile.

"I'd go on, but the rest of it would just be my own feelings toward you," he added.

"I won't push you to tell me what they are," she said.

"If I've succeeded in my actions, you should already know them."

She blushed and said, "Same here."

Their food came, and after that, there was not a silent moment between them. They asked each other about what their favorite things were in different categories and what they would do in what-if and would-you-rather scenarios. At one point, he asked her what her dream job would be, and she said she'd love to teach art to children. It hurt Chris to hear her say that. He had been picked from adolescence to do a job, and he loved it. If he had ever been given the opportunity to choose a dream job, he was sure it would be to do exactly what he was already doing. But that the system had not assigned her to the job she really wanted and that she was not able to pursue her dream job bothered him beyond his own comprehension.

When dinner was over, he let her pay, understanding it was a point of pride for her.

"Thanks for dinner," he said as they walked to the car. "It was every bit as good as you said it would be."

"It's my favorite," she said, and they got in the car.

They drove in silence, and when she was pulled over, Chris gave the officer his ID. As he did so, he reached across her, using his other hand to put her hand with her ID and the travel permit down in her lap.

"Teaching her to drive?" the officer asked sarcastically as she took his ID. After glancing at it, she let them go without another word.

When the officer was out of sight, Jenna looked at Chris and just laughed.

On the way home, she received a call from the assistants that everything had been completed and that the envelopes were ready to be mailed. She thanked them and told them she would buy them lunch the next day.

"I'm sorry to have kept you out so late," she said to Chris as they approached his hotel.

"I'm not. It was a pleasure."

She started to ask when he was leaving but stopped herself. "Will I see you tomorrow?"

"I'll be here until tomorrow night at least, maybe longer, depending on how things go."

"As promised, I'll make you dinner, if you'd like."

"I'm not sure it can beat what I ate tonight, but you can try."

She snorted. "It won't be as good as what you ate tonight."

"Then I'll eat before I come over."

She laughed at his joke as she brought the car to a stop in front of the hotel entrance.

They were silent for a second, and then he said, "Thanks again for the lovely evening." Before Jenna could respond, he took her hand and kissed it. "Goodnight," he said and got out of the car.

When he got back to his hotel room, he called Zaire to relieve him of keeping watch. Zaire gave him a brief report that nothing had changed. Furthermore, Adam Robertson had made only one phone call that was to his house, leaving a simple message that he would call again. Zaire said he'd have to hear about the date another time because his wife wanted him to get home. Adam was asleep, and Chris set the alarm to go off if Adam made any moves. He was happy to have the time to himself so he could think of the events of the evening without any distractions.

*   *   *

Driving away, Jenna could not stop smiling the whole way home. She felt as giddy as a high school girl and just as foolish for it. She kept glancing at her hand where Chris had kissed her.

When she got to her townhouse, she went through the routine of checks she always did when she got home: she took a moment to assess her surroundings as she approached the front door, sensing if anything was amiss or out of the ordinary; once she was inside, she locked the door behind her and then started with the front entrance, checking all the potential hiding places she could think of and clearing the lower level until she reached the back door and looked outside as she checked and double-checked that the doors and windows were locked; then she went upstairs and checked it to make sure she was alone, unlocking her closet and checking it as well. There were not many places to hide in her townhouse, so the ritual never took more than a few minutes, but she always forced herself to do it, every time she came home, since she had been redistributed to Des Moines. Even after all these years and the hundreds of times that she had gone through the procedure, it still caused her heart rate to quicken, though she was much calmer about it now than she had been when she first started the practice.

When she finished checking the upstairs to make sure she was completely alone in the house, she looked out her bedroom window from a side angle so that anyone looking in would not be able to see her, and she checked to make sure nobody was outside. It was the last part of the routine, and when she saw only the familiar faces of two of her neighbors on a walk, she relaxed.

She turned on the TV in her bedroom, not to watch but to have on in the background while she got ready for bed. She did not normally have it on. She used to do that, when she first lived alone, just to have some noise in the background so she would not feel so lonely. But it had actually made her more anxious because she kept having to mute the sound so she could make sure she did not hear any unfamiliar noises in her house. For a while after that, she turned it on, but without sound and with subtitles. Then, eventually, she just quit turning it on altogether.

Tonight, however, she had it on because she wanted to hear the weather report for the next day. She was hoping they would predict nice weather so she could serve dinner outside. She disappeared into the bathroom, and when she returned to her room to get her sleeping clothes, she glanced at the television screen. Then she looked at it again, more closely, stopping mid-step. The mugshots of three sex offenders who had recently been released from prison were on the screen. Jenna felt all the blood drain from her face and a knot form in her stomach as her eyes widened in recognition of the man in the middle. He was the man at the hotel lounge from the previous evening.

She turned up the volume and paid close attention to what the news anchor was saying.

"According to law," the anchorwoman said, "we are unable to reveal the residential addresses of these convicts, but you may see them as they go from door to door to alert their neighbors. According to law, they have been sterilized, and according to the program, they have been rehabilitated. But citizens should continue to be cautious around these convicts. As always, if you feel your safety is compromised, call the authorities at the number on the screen."

She remembered seeing Chris talking to him, smiling and laughing with him even, and a sense of alarm rose within her as she thought of them being friends.

She replayed it again in her mind. Yes, Chris had been laughing with him, and then he patted him on the shoulder, and then they left together. And he *had* looked straight at her. She was sure of it, now.

But then she thought of his ID and that he worked for government. As she sat down on the bed, calmness spread throughout her as she realized Chris had simply diverted the man's attention, not threatening or making a scene, and safely led him away from her.

7

At work on Wednesday, Jenna was nervous about having Chris over. She knew she would not have been so nervous if she were not so attracted to him and if he were not a Coastal government employee. And she would not be so nervous if she had people over more often. Since being redistributed to Iowa, she had invited only two people over to her house, both coworkers. And she only considered a few people in Iowa to be her friends at all, and she had worked with each of them at one point. She had no idea if she even possessed everything someone was supposed to have when hosting dinner. She heard her mother's voice in her mind reprimanding her for not taking the day off to prepare the house for company. She shoved it out of her mind—that was an old life. Her mother did not even work, and Jenna was her own person. Chris would like her as she was, not as her mother would want her to be.

When the time to get off work finally came around, she called Chris to let him know she was on her way to his hotel to pick him up. It was not just that he was coming over for dinner that made her nervous. She knew that was not the only reason.

It was also because of the man she saw on the news the previous night. Even though she ultimately decided Chris was good, it still shook her when she remembered seeing the two of them standing together, even laughing together. Instinctively, she was not necessarily *afraid* of Chris, but she feared there was something about himself that he was hiding because he knew it would bother her.

They were at her house in less than five minutes—it *was* less than a mile from his hotel. As they pulled into the driveway, he asked, "Are you sure it's okay if I come over? We can go somewhere else."

"Yes, I'm sorry if I seem nervous. It's because I haven't entertained anyone in a long time." She put her hand on the door handle to get out, but then she paused. She put her hands in her lap, and, turning her body toward him, added, "But it's also because I have to ask you something."

"What's on your mind?" He shifted his body to face her.

"Did you know that guy?" She did not have to specify that she was referring to the man she had met at the bar and later saw on the news.

He nodded. "Yeah."

She sat completely still. Had she been wrong in her conclusion about him? She grew tense, unable to breathe, and considered the irony of the first man she brought to her house being the friend of a criminal.

He caught it. "No, I didn't know him," he corrected himself. "I knew of him." In a calm and reassuring voice, he said, "I make it my business to know when criminals are released from prison and are in the same location as I am." It was a mostly true statement. He knew the man was a convict recently released from prison, but Zaire or other team members on the case would be the ones looking out for nearby criminals.

Tentatively, she asked, "Did you know I was there?"

He met her eyes and nodded his head. "Yeah, I did."

She let out a long deep breath. She was not surprised, as she had all but convinced herself throughout the previous night that his reason for being there had been to get the man away from her. But she was not sure she wanted to know how it was that he knew she was there in the first place. She tried to reconcile in her mind the uneasiness that came with knowing he somehow checked on her whereabouts with the comfort and security that came with knowing what he had done to remedy the situation. But in her gut, she knew she trusted him.

She narrowed her eyes at him. "What is it that you do, exactly?" She knew it was an all but forbidden thing to ask a government employee, but she could not help herself.

Deciding he would not lie, he told her, "Well, I work in law enforcement."

She nodded her head. Then, she added, "But you're not an officer."

"No."

"So, do you work in intelligence?"

"Sort of, but it's not that easy. It's more on the side of *enforcement*." He held her gaze, trying to get a feel for how she was taking the news.

"So, you're like a detective?"

He looked away from her and shrugged. "Kind of," he said and then added, "when necessary." He looked back at her, still unsure of how she was taking it.

She understood that he was not going to tell her a straight answer. The government was a complete mystery to the general public. Things went on, decisions were made, and government made things happen, but the majority of it was shielded from civilians. She knew better than to ask more questions, knowing it was probably against the rules of his profession for him to talk about it.

Aside from his family, she was the only civilian who knew he was in government, and his family knew little of his life, only that at thirteen he had been recruited to join the special operations unit of government. But officially he was just recruited to "government," and "government" could mean anything, from foreign policy and spying in Mexico, to engineering and research, to being an officer.

As much as he wanted to keep his job from her, it encompassed so much of who he was. He wanted to share that with her, despite the official and unofficial rules. Since The War's end, no person in government ever revealed their specific job titles. It was a policy created to discourage and prevent corruption, and only officers and public officials shared their job titles with the public. Sure, people found out—sometimes it was inevitable. But it was in everybody's best interest to keep these things secret. For Chris, he knew it was in his family's best interest to keep them in the dark. But he did not want to keep Jenna in the dark. He did not like hiding so much of himself from her.

She nodded her head and said, "Well, all the same." Then, she looked directly into his eyes as she said, "Thank you. Not just for the other night but also just in general, for what you do. You help get rid of the bad guys."

He did not say anything at first, just holding her gaze, and then after a moment he said, "I *do* get rid of the bad guys."

She relaxed, thinking about how he calmly walked away with the convict. "Yes, thank you," she said again.

She had not caught his real meaning, and he decided to let it go for now. If she had been ready for such information, she would have received it in his words, but she did not. He wondered if he made the wrong choice in telling the truth. He had never told anyone this much about his job, as little as it was, and it occurred to him that without more detail others might suspect they were in danger.

"I was happy to do it," he said. "But I want you to know I only knew you were there because I was looking into something else, and I would not have interfered had he not been dangerous. I'm sorry I can't tell you more. But I don't want to scare you away. I promise I wasn't following you or stalking you."

"You don't scare me," she said. "If anything, this"—she motioned to the space between them, indicating their relationship—"is what scares me. This wasn't supposed to happen. But I'm glad it did." Then, she added, "I feel safe with you."

The remark took him by surprise. Nobody felt safe with him. It was his job that people would not feel safe with him. Aside from his family and the people he worked with, he was the last person people wanted to see or be around because he often *was* the last person people saw or were around.

"I know it's a weird thing to say," she continued, "but ever since we met, everything has just felt right when I'm with you. Usually, I'm so guarded and paranoid. I don't tell people about myself, and I never would have gotten in a car with someone or left Des Moines with anyone. But I feel safe with you, not only with my physical safety but also with who I am." She started to say something else, but she stopped herself.

"What else?" he asked.

"I understand if there are things you can't tell me about your job. It's okay. I trust you."

"I'm glad," he said. "You know you can always trust me."

She smiled warmly and opened her car door.

When they entered her townhouse, he asked, "Do you mind if I look around?"

"Sure. It's not much, and I'm not much of a decorator," she said as she went to the kitchen area.

The main floor of the townhouse was a completely open floor plan, such that the kitchen, dining, and living areas were all really one big room, separated by furniture. The layout was basic, as were all layouts in the Inland, and the structure, furniture, and carpet were of the cheapest quality, as were all things in the Inland. The stairs going up to the second floor were at the front of the house, right in front of the door. He imagined the upstairs was probably a similar floor plan with just a bedroom, closet, and bathroom. He had been in this style of townhouse before. The Inland cities were full of them: identical narrow living spaces, separated by thin walls, stacked side by side in rows and rows of buildings. These were the most common living quarters in the Inland. Those that moved up in society could be assigned to or pay extra for apartments in the Coastal District downtown or houses on the outskirts of the cities. Though still part of the working class that composed Inland society, these privileged citizens were usually managers.

He heard her pull out ingredients and pots and pans behind him as he looked around the room. She called to him and offered him a drink.

He looked around a little more, getting a general feel for the place, and then he walked over to the kitchen area and offered to help.

"No, thank you," she said. "There's not really anything to help with. It's not anything fantastic, just basic."

"As long as it tastes good," he joked.

"Well, we'll see."

She handed him a cup of water, and he leaned against the counter while she continued to prepare dinner.

"I like what you've done with the place," he said.

She rolled her eyes. "I know it's not much. Is this your first time in an Inland apartment?" she asked playfully.

He laughed and said, "No, actually, it's not. Remember, I grew up in Idaho."

They talked while she cooked, joking and laughing with each other.

She asked if working in government had any other perks aside from getting out of being pulled over, and he assured her that was the only one that made it worth it.

"Oh, come on, I'm sure it's satisfying protecting the general public."

"It is, now that I know you're a part of it."

She rolled her eyes and hit him with a dish towel.

She made fried chicken, mashed potatoes, cheese grits, and green beans. When he tried to sneak some bites, she pushed him away, and he grabbed her around the waist and hugged her.

When it was finally ready, she took off her apron and led him to the table on the patio outside. Like the front of the townhouses, the patios were all identical and formed a long line of small squares of concrete. There was a playground in the middle of the complex, and a few neighborhood kids were there playing. It was nice outside, so there were several people out on their patios, but Jenna's neighbors on either side were not out.

"Where did you learn to cook like this?" he asked as she handed him a plate. "You never did tell me where you are from. Georgia? South Carolina? Virginia?"

"You don't already know?" she joked, and he felt a tinge of guilt. He vowed not to look up anything about her or listen to anything Zaire had to say about her again.

He began to eat. "This is the best food I've ever had in my life."

"Thanks," she said matter-of-factly. "But I see through that compliment."

"No, seriously, even my mom's cooking isn't this good." He pulled her chair closer to his. "Granted, I'm a bit biased because you cooked it, and I got to watch."

"Mm-hmmm," she responded with emphasis on the first syllable, keeping her mouth closed since it was full. She dipped a spoon in the jar of honey and drizzled it over her chicken.

"Coastal Georgia?" he guessed.

She just looked at him, chewing her food with a flirtatious smirk. "You know I'm never going to tell you, now. Is this the first time you haven't already known something about someone?"

"Maybe," he said. "But, really, the food is simply wonderful. I wish we had been eating here the past few nights."

"Simple, it definitely is," she agreed. "I thought about making something extravagant, but I went with simple and homelike instead."

"Good choice." He took the jar of honey and looked at her curiously. "Is that any good?"

She shrugged. "I like it."

He put honey on a piece of chicken and took a bite. "Woah."

He swallowed his bite, and she laughed.

"Very sweet. But very good," he said.

"I'm glad you like it."

They ate in silence for a few minutes. He finished eating, and she offered him more, which he gladly accepted. She got up and went back inside. He looked out at his surroundings, at this typical Inland neighborhood. There was nothing special about it; he could have been in any Inland city in that moment. Yet, he felt more relaxed than he had in a long time, and he knew it was because he was there with her.

"Do you have to stay fit for your job?" she asked when she returned from the kitchen, handing him his plate.

"Do you think I eat too much?" he joked.

"No," she responded, playfully defensive. "You're just very…" She tried to think of the right word. "Athletic-looking."

He laughed. "I have physical tests I have to pass once a month."

"Once a month? I thought those exams were annual."

"I think they are for some jobs, for officers at least."

"Have you been working out while you're here? What do you do?" she asked curiously.

"I run nearly every day, when I have the chance. The hotel I'm at has a fitness room, so I use it. Regardless of where I am, my morning routine always consists of stretches, push-ups, pull-ups, and sit-ups."

"I wish I did that every day."

"You have a great body," he said, not lustfully but more as an objective observation.

"Do you do it for looks?" she asked playfully. "I would just like to be more fit."

"You're probably more in shape than you realize," he assured her.

"I belong to a gym, but I usually jog through the streets. There's a part of the city teeming with officers, and that's where I go. Most people avoid it, but I prefer to have them around. At first they were awful, but now they're used to me and leave me alone, so it's easier to just go there."

"Want to go for a jog tonight? Somewhere you're unwilling to venture alone?" he asked.

Her eyes lit up with excitement at the thought. There were many places she wanted to go. But she declined the offer by shaking her head. She did not want his last memory of her being one where she was sweating, barely able to keep up, and in baggy Inland sweatpants and an old tee shirt.

"You will see me again," he said, as if reading her thoughts.

"What?" She was caught off guard in her disastrous vision of jogging with him.

"I will leave when my business here is done, but then I'll see you again. I promise. We both know this"—he motioned to the space between them like she had done earlier in the car—"is not worth giving up when I leave."

She smiled and softly agreed, "No, it's not."

He picked up their empty plates and headed for the kitchen.

"No, let me get those," she said, taking the dishes from him. "Do you want to go to the park? Or we can stay here and watch a movie or play a game or whatever. What do you want to do?"

"Let's go to the park and stay outside while the weather is nice," he said, looking over at the playground nearby.

"No," she said, laughing. "Not like the playground. I mean a real park, with a lake."

"Oh, a *real* park. Will you jog around it with me?" he asked.

"It's a bit too big for that. But it's a clear night tonight with a full moon. I thought it would be nice to show you more of the outdoor life of Iowa. And I've never been there at night, but I've always wanted to go."

"Then, let's go."

They got in her car, and she drove to the lake nearby. By the time they got there, the sun was setting, and sparse clouds made shadows of everything in sight.

When they got out of the car, she took him down a path that led to a dock. They sat cross-legged on the dock, with their knees almost touching. They were facing each other, with the lake to one side and the woods to the other. He took her hands, and she let him examine them. Though subtle, one was different from the other. He examined it more closely and realized it had gone through reconstructive surgery. He closed his hands around hers, and they looked at the sky and the lake in silence for nearly an hour. By nighttime, patches of stars shone around the clouds, and the full moon cast a bright reflection on the lake. Only once did an officer approach them. Jenna did not even move a muscle, nor did she look away from the water while Chris showed the officer his ID and told her they were not to be disturbed again. They absorbed the air around them, enjoying the moments together.

Finally, she spoke. "You've been kind not to ask me so many questions. I know you're confused about how and why I ended up here, but I'll tell you, if you want to know."

"When you're ready," he said.

"I want to tell you more about myself."

He looked at her with expectation, but then his expression changed to one of understanding as she added, "But I can't."

"That's okay," he said.

"You don't understand." She was looking down at his hands now, exploring them with her fingertips. They were big and strong, fitting his build, but they were not rough or callused.

"I'm not told that often."

"I know, but this time you don't." She looked back up at him. "I can't even tell you why I can't tell you. I mean, I will eventually. But I'm surprised that I want to tell you at all. I've kept myself so guarded that I've never wanted to tell anyone where I come from. But with you..." She trailed off without finishing.

He looked down at her hands in his, looking at each one. "I want to find out everything about you. Even your hand." He kissed one of the subtle scars, and her eyes watered slightly as she realized he already knew she had undergone surgery. How much he must already know.

"I want you to get to know me," she said, "even if my body tells you before I do…*if you can be bothered with it*." As she said the last part, she grinned involuntarily.

They both laughed at the awkwardness of it all, and he felt embarrassed at her allusion.

"I can be bothered with it," he said. "I'll take whatever you'll give me." He kissed her other hand, and they laughed again.

She looked down at her hand, and he touched one of the scars.

"I can't believe you can see them," she said. "They told me the treatment would make them invisible."

"I've been well trained to pay attention to fine details," he said.

She took a deep breath. "I was on a road trip in Texas with my best friend, who was also a Purebred, and we were in a car accident. We borrowed my brother's car. He had hacked the car's Comm System to make it look like a Modified was driving so he would never get pulled over. But hacking the Comm System meant turning off all of the car's smart features, so it was not forced to stay under the speed limit, nor did it communicate with the other cars on the road. So, it didn't force-stop so we crashed into the other vehicle, which *had* force-stopped. We were only sixteen. My best friend died instantly, and I was in a coma for nearly a month. When I came out of it, I found out I had to have many surgeries." She started pointing to all the locations. "My cheekbone was shattered, and my nose was broken. My collarbone and shoulder were broken, along with my wrist and hand and a couple of ribs. And my legs were bruised, but they came out okay."

"Are you ever nervous driving?" he asked.

She shook her head. "I'm not afraid of cars, even after the accident."

"I've noticed that you are never nervous or afraid," he said, "except when you picked me up at the hotel earlier this evening."

"That was my inner child more than anything. My mother's criticism will always rule my life. She was a very good hostess and would be very disappointed in me tonight." Dramatically, and with her voice full of scandal, she said, "I served a Coastal government employee food on plain Inland dinnerware." She laughed. "It's stupid, isn't it?"

"No, we all have our anxieties and fears." He paused. "Mine is that I will scare you away."

"I told you, you don't scare me," she said. "I meant it when I said I feel safe with you. And you can feel safe with me."

He looped his fingers in between hers so their palms were touching. "Like you," he said, "I also have many things I can't tell you. But I do want to tell you. I've never had the desire to tell anyone about myself. It's so ingrained in my mind not to tell people, the thought never even occurs to me. But I don't want to hold anything back from you. One part of me has a strong pull to hide it from you, for fear of scaring you off. But the other part of me is being pulled to let you in. I know you said you understand that I can't tell you about my job, but I don't know if I can live like that. My job is my life. But I know you won't like it."

They looked into each other's eyes, fully understanding each other, each with a scary inside, encompassed by a steel outside with no entrance. But tonight they each discovered a chink in their own armor, for there was someone dangerously close to getting in. She put both of her hands around his. Then, she propped her elbows on her knees, and he mirrored her position. She rested her chin on their clasped hands, contemplating this situation she had gotten herself into.

"You know," she said, looking at the lake, "you can tell me anything. I will understand."

He kissed the top of her head. "I know."

She closed her eyes and tilted her face up toward his.

As he bent down, he caught sight of his watch. It was three minutes to ten o'clock, time to make a decision.

He could not do this, be with her while keeping his job a secret, not when he knew she so strongly objected to the information he was withholding. It felt too deceptive. And it wasn't fair to her.

Instead of kissing her lips, he kissed her cheek and then rested his forehead against hers.

8

They left the park just before midnight. Chris went back to his hotel and checked in with Zaire for any updates on the case. He tried not to think about her as he got ready to complete the mission. He tried to put out of his mind how incredible she looked in the moonlight with the reflection of the water on her face. He would not allow himself to remember the feeling of her soft hands in his. He would not let the regret of not kissing her impact the mission. He would not let himself linger on the reality that his decision to finish the mission that night was made because he just wanted it to be over, because he was ready to move on, because he wanted to stop thinking about the Robertsons and think about her instead. He would not be sloppy now simply because for the first time in his life he wished he did not do what he did, even if it had led to her. He would do this well, with the precision and perfection he was accustomed to.

He then realized that every quality about himself was the result of his job, and there was nothing to him outside of that. He was a rich Coastal because people assigned to his Societal

Role were given a large stipend, intelligent because he had been trained in logic, confident because he was good at what he did, physically fit because being able to run and fight were part of his job, and personable because gaining trust was key to missions. And while all these qualities, on the outside, may have seemed like all the features that made a person perfect, these were all qualities of his job. At the end of it all, he was still an assassin, and Jenna would not want to end each day with an executioner.

He knew she would understand if he never told her about his job because as a government employee he was not allowed to. But it wasn't that simple. If that were all it was, just him being in government, then maybe it would have been easier for him to do it. Maybe if that were the case, he could have treated her the way Zaire treated Melinda and not tell her anything. But what complicated matters was that he already knew how she felt about his job and how she would feel about him if she found out that his job was something she thought was an urban legend. He thought of how she had asked, *"Can you imagine what kind of person would take on that job and what that would do to someone?"* and he knew she would be disgusted with him if he told her what he did. She would end things immediately. Finding out that it was true, that there were people who had taken on that job and that he was one of them, would destroy any trust she had in him. He could not keep his job separate from his life because his job was his life. If he kept his job from her, there was nothing left of him to give.

He changed clothes and put on his dark, silent outfit.

He vowed to himself that this would be his last mission as an assassin, and he knew exactly how he was going to finish it. The plan was to get in the hotel room while Adam was sleeping, slit his throat, make it a clean cut, and get out. He knew it would be bad for business for the hotel. He knew they would have to investigate and that the case would never be closed because he would never be caught. He knew he could stage an accident or a suicide, but he wanted to send a message to all criminals that he won in the end. He wanted everyone to know the family had been tracked, hunted, and killed with purpose, and anyone following in their footsteps would meet the same fate. He may have been walking out of the business, but they did not know that. *I want every criminal to expect me to be out there, ready for them*, he thought to himself.

He grabbed two guns and three knives and put them in holsters in his clothes, each accessible from different positions he might end up in.

He left his hotel through the only entrance that did not have a working camera. *How could they let an entrance be without a camera?* he thought as he left. *Someone like Jenna could get in a situation in this spot, and no one would know because she does not have the easily tracked retinas of a Modified.*

He walked to the car he had used when he went to Adam's hotel before. As he walked, he remembered the man at the print shop, assuming his problem would go away because someone like Jenna would not be able to understand or do anything about the misprint. As he drove to Adam's hotel, Chris realized how tense he was. He was getting too emotional. He was not focusing on the mission. He wanted to be dramatic to make criminals think he was still out there getting rid of them after he left. But in truth, he was being dramatic because he wanted to do something, anything, to make Jenna's life better. He wanted to fix all the cameras in the city so she would be safe. He wanted to tell everyone that she was smart and interesting and creative and funny—not someone who should be treated the way that man at the print shop and the bartender the night they met and the officers on the road treated her. He exhaled forcefully at the thought of the memories.

That was not his job. That was not who he was. His job was to eliminate the Robertsons. Chris calmed himself down, taking slow, deep breaths. No, he did not have to glorify himself for the sake of scaring criminals out of their immorality. He could not be the best forever, and someone would come along to take his place. There would be other criminals, and there would be other agents to take care of them. He needed to do this right to ensure there would be no problems with this case.

He parked the car two blocks from the hotel where Adam Robertson was staying. Silently and without being seen, he snuck in the shadows to the hotel. As he was approaching the building, he felt a jolt of electric current in his left upper thigh. In situations where he could not make noise, his phone sent a shock rather than a sound or vibration.

He looked around to make sure nobody was in sight or earshot as he slid behind some bushes that lined the building next to the hotel. He checked the alert on his phone and saw that Adam Robertson was leaving his hotel room. He sent a message to Zaire and his boss. The three of them watched in anticipation. Chris stood just outside the circle of light from a nearby streetlamp with his back against the building. He turned on the transmitter in his pocket with the volume up so he could hear the hotel front door open. With one hand in his pocket controlling the volume of his earbud and the other hand holding his phone, he watched for Adam Robertson. He checked for signatures on his phone. Aside from himself and Adam Robertson, there was not another human outside for a ten-block radius.

At the same time, Zaire checked via satellite for any heat and infrared signatures of someone else nearby.

"No one else is in sight," Chris heard Zaire say in his earbud.

Then, he heard Adam Robertson coming closer. He silently sank to the ground, disappearing behind the bushes, as Adam came into view. Adam walked across the median that separated the parking lots of the building Chris was standing against and the hotel where he was staying.

"He's headed for the Comm Center," Chris messaged to the other two.

"Agreed" was the response they voiced to him through his earbud.

Zaire set up the equipment so the call could also be heard by their boss and Chris.

Chris took out another earbud. He held it to the corner of his phone until a dim red light flashed, showing that it was connected. He inserted the earbud into his empty ear. A message appeared on his phone: "Pak." Adam was calling his contact back home, an accomplice they already knew about.

Comm Centers contained all forms of communication—phone, video, email, text—but all were strictly monitored and recorded. Everyone knew that. Adam had to know it was the least secure line of communication, even with his anti-tracking device hooked up to it. It didn't make sense that he would use a public Communication Center instead of his phone, unless he needed a solid alibi for something going on at that moment that he had already set up or knew about.

The two did not talk about any plans or attacks. Adam asked how his family was, and Pak told him his son brought home good grades on his progress report.

"I can't find her," Adam finally said. "You're sure we have no more leads?"

"No," Pak answered. "Maybe it's time to move on to the next."

He must know about Adele by now, Chris thought. Yet, none of the conversations they had monitored while he was in Iowa indicated anyone had told him. Chris sent a message to his team: "He doesn't know about Adele and probably not about Talon Jr., either."

"No, he knows," Zaire said. "He has to."

"Your call, Chris, but I think Zaire's right," Xiao answered.

Chris sent a message back: "Going in."

Xiao closed his connection after the news that the mission was about to be completed. Zaire, not because he doubted Chris, stayed on watch as an extra precaution. Chris checked his surroundings, though he was fully aware there was no one around. Even the front desk of the hotel was empty. Adam looked around every so often, but for the most part he faced the video screen, with his back to Chris. Chris snuck along the side of the building as much as he could, but the Comm Center was out in the open under a streetlamp. He turned down the volume of the earbud and pulled out a gun.

He imagined the scenario in his mind, readying himself for any possible outcome. He thought of shooting Adam from his current location. But he knew that would not do because he wanted to be sure, using only one clean shot to finish the job, and to do that he would want to be closer. Plus, it was not the most silent option because the bullet would break the window of the Comm Center, and Chris knew it would be best if there was absolutely no noise.

He thought of another option: Zaire could cause a system failure, shutting off the Comm Center so Pak would not see him coming and so there would be no video recording. He envisioned sprinting, swiftly and without the faintest noise. Just before opening the door, Adam would turn around and point a gun at his chest. But before Adam could realize what was going on, Chris could grab the gun and drop it, along with his own, and wrap the anti-tracking cord around Adam's neck. With his own body, Chris would press Adam's body up against the wall of the Comm Center so he could not move. He would then tighten the cord so that it took as little time as possible for the last Robertson to die. Chris imagined the body loosening and dropping to the floor when Adam passed out. Chris would keep the cord tight, put a knee on Adam's shoulder and pull the cord upward. In his knee and his hands, he could almost feel the vibration of the vertebrae in the neck stretch and separate. He would check the pulse, keeping his hand pressed to Adam's neck for a full minute.

That was still not the most ideal scenario, though it would work, and it would send a message. But he preferred to leave deaths with obvious causes so the police would feel no need to investigate.

Chris thought of yet another plan. *If he doesn't have a gun—*

"Hi, dad." The sound of Adam's oldest son in his ear interrupted Chris's vision. He realized that in planning the attack, he had not paid any attention to the conversation on the phone. Adam's son sounded sleepy and had clearly been staying up waiting for the call. From his location, Chris could just make out the image of the child on the video screen in the Comm Center. "When are you coming home?" his son asked.

"I'll be home soon."

Chris detected the slightest tremble in Adam's voice that indicated he did not believe his own words.

"Is Uncle Paxton helping you with your homework?" Adam asked his son.

His son's voice perked up, and Chris could tell the boy was excited to talk with his father.

Chris's heart sank. Now was not the time, not in front of his son. "Not going in. Will later tonight," he messaged Zaire and turned off the receiver to give Adam privacy. Zaire was still listening to the conversation, as he had been the entire time, but it was not necessary for Chris to listen, too.

Chris waited, crouched behind the bushes, until Adam left the Comm Center and returned to the hotel. When Adam was gone, Chris said, "Ear base on," to turn on the microphone. "I need a pharmacy," he told Zaire.

"There's one three blocks from you," Zaire said in his earbud and gave him directions.

"Cover me," Chris told Zaire as he left and followed the directions.

Zaire paused the image on the security cameras before Chris came into view of the lenses so that he was never caught on any of them.

Chris broke into the pharmacy and walked through the aisles, grabbing items along the way. Ingredients in hand, he went back to the hotel where Adam Robertson was staying and waited in the lobby bathroom.

"I'll go in when he's asleep," he told Zaire.

Via satellite Zaire watched the signatures of Adam's brainwaves, and when he was securely in deep sleep, Zaire told Chris to go in.

Chris closed his connection with Zaire by saying "ear base off" before he left the lobby bathroom and went up to Adam's hotel room and snuck into it as he had done before. He quickly checked the room for new items but found none. He grabbed a cup that was next to the sink in the bathroom and mixed his ingredients. He soaked the mixture into paper towels.

He left the bathroom and approached Adam, who was deep in slumber. He was lying in the bed on his back, covered only up to his waist. His hands were folded on his chest.

Chris stood over him, taking in the rhythm of the man's breaths. *Why did you wait until now to call your son?* he asked the sleeping man, in his mind. *And in a brightly lit Comm Center? Why are you here?*

For a split second, he wondered if prolonging this would answer that question; maybe if he followed Adam tomorrow, Adam would lead him to his answer. But Chris had learned long ago in training that all questions worth answering could be answered in more ways than one, and it was also possible to follow Adam for the rest of his natural life and never get the answer at all.

No, it was time.

Adam inhaled a deep breath, almost snoring, and slowly let it out. When Chris was sure he had exhaled completely, he put the soaked paper towels over Adam's mouth and nose just before his next deep breath. Adam inhaled deeply. The dose was much stronger than necessary, but Chris wanted it to be quick. Adam did not have a chance to wake up or register what was going on before his heart went into cardiac arrest and stopped beating. Chris checked for Adam's pulse, holding his fingers there for a full minute. When he was sure he was dead, Chris went to the bathroom, pulled out fresh paper towels, and soaked them with water. He cleaned Adam's face of any trace of the drug. For a moment, he regarded Adam's lifeless face, haunted by his son's voice.

He snapped out of it, blinking and swallowing hard. He vowed he would sleep at least eight hours after this, attributing his weariness to fatigue and the final ending to the longest mission of his career.

He pulled out his phone and saw that Zaire had closed the connection. He searched the hotel room once more, this time in more detail. Like himself, Adam Robertson was accustomed to packing light when he traveled. Other than necessities and clothing, Chris found nothing that indicated the reason for coming to Iowa. There were no personal notes, no maps, no documents, no blueprints or statistics. He searched the suitcase for secret pockets. He opened every drawer and looked thoroughly through the closet and under the bed.

After searching the room, Chris pulled back the covers to search Adam. One single artifact was found in a pocket of the pants Adam was sleeping in. Chris picked up the small ceramic giraffe that fit easily into his palm and, unable to remain expressionless, furrowed his brow in confusion. *What the hell?* he thought to himself, examining the small figurine. It had obviously been professionally made but was painted by a child. On the underside of the animal were initials and an age.

He glanced around the hotel room. He set the figurine down and went through everything again. Finding nothing, he put everything back to the way it had been when he arrived. He took off his gloves and washed his face. He examined himself in the mirror to make sure he looked relatively normal. Glancing at his watch, he saw that it was almost three o'clock. He gathered the materials he brought with him, went back to the main room, took the giraffe, and snuck out of the hotel.

When he had returned the car and was back in his hotel room, he called his boss and Zaire.

"It's done," he said. They had long since abandoned greetings.

"Did you find anything?" Xiao asked.

Chris started to say something but stopped.

"What?" Xiao asked urgently.

"The only—and I mean *only*—thing in that hotel room was a giraffe," Chris said.

"A what?" Xiao and Zaire asked at the same time.

"A giraffe. It's a small figurine, no more than two inches in height, painted yellow with different colored polka dots all over it."

"What the hell?" It was the first time Chris had ever heard his boss use a confused tone. "It doesn't make any sense. You found *nothing* that could lead to a reason he was in Iowa?"

Chris offered the only explanation he could think of. "Maybe he was extra cautious because he knew it was impossible that he was not being followed. He had to know Adele wasn't meeting him here, if not from the night he arrived then surely by tonight. I'm telling you, this was the *only* thing in that hotel room. There was a suitcase, two suits, a few shirts, a toothbrush, a razor, socks, underwear, and this little giraffe. If there was a deal going down, it had to do with this artifact, or he already did his business."

"Where did this giraffe come from?" Xiao asked.

"He must have had it on him when I searched his hotel room before. I haven't seen it before tonight. I'm thinking it's most likely something his kid made at school and asked him to bring it with him. It says 'K. R. age 8' underneath."

"He doesn't have any children with those initials," said Zaire.

"His eldest sister's name was Karen. Maybe she made it as a child? It looks pretty old," offered Chris.

"It doesn't make sense that he would take it to Iowa with him," said Xiao.

Zaire offered another explanation. "Maybe he met with someone without us knowing it, and they gave it to him. He is a master at eluding Surveillance."

"Bring it in for analysis," Xiao said. "You checked his body?"

"As thoroughly as I could without a scanner," answered Chris.

"That's probably safe," Xiao said. "I'll have an agent watch the investigation, though I'm sure it will be seen simply as a heart attack in his sleep."

"Pak will probably come looking for Adam when he doesn't hear from him," said Chris.

Zaire agreed.

"The family will still get the message, especially since Pak will probably suspect murder, anyway," Xiao said. "But he won't go to the authorities. Still, I'll put some agents on media control to make sure this doesn't make the news for any reason." With that, their boss made it final. The case was nearly closed. "We'll see you in a few hours, Rockford."

"Yes, and," Chris began. He could feel Zaire's heightened interest. "I'm going to request some time off."

At first, his boss was speechless. Chris had never asked for time off. Then, he said, "Sure, Chris. In ten years, I'd say you've earned some time. For this last case alone, I'd give you extra time if you needed it. This is easily the most victorious case in our history."

"I'll finalize everything myself and personally check on this giraffe business," Zaire said.

"Get some sleep, both of you. We'll wrap up the case as soon as the giraffe is cleared." Their boss then hung up his phone.

"Time off?" Zaire asked.

"I think this will be my last mission as an assassin."

"It's time," Zaire said. "Chris, you may be the best assassin in the agency's history, but even you can't do it forever."

"I'm just going to see where this takes me."

"I'll let you know when a spot in my department opens," Zaire suggested.

"I'd rather file things, if that's okay."

They both laughed at the thought of Chris hunched over a computer and file cabinet for the rest of his life. "You would die of boredom. Sleep well. We'll catch up Friday morning over breakfast."

After they hung up their phones, Chris put the giraffe on his nightstand and got ready for bed. He turned out the lights and shut out all incoming morning light with the curtains.

Though he looked forward to uninterrupted sleep, he could not stop thinking about Jenna. He replayed his favorite memories of her, now that his mind was free to think whatever it wanted. He thought to himself how incredible it was that he had only just met her. Even sitting by the lake under the full moon seemed like it had not occurred only hours earlier.

A new feeling of lightness came over him. Upon completing other missions, he would begin mentally preparing for the next, but now he had nothing to think of except her, and he allowed himself to do that. He thought of how she so fully paid attention to each person, and he willed himself to follow her example and focused all of his attention on her as he fell asleep.

*   *   *

Hours later, he dreamed of being at the lake with her, holding her hands and kissing them, first the palms and then the backs. In the dream, she pulled away and walked into the water, disappearing forever. In the next dream, he was back at the Robertson mansion, approaching the back of the house through the gardens. Mrs. Robertson put her hand up and waved to him from the window, and Karen appeared before him, holding out her hands. He took them, as he had taken Jenna's, and started kissing them and then kissed Karen on the lips.

He woke then, not startled, as he often dreamed of his missions. Though the family was eliminated, he still had to finish this last piece, and doubtless his subconscious was helping him as it always did. No, the mission was not over, yet, and his attention must still be divided. He picked up the giraffe, hoping to help his mind figure out what he had not yet realized. He looked at the inscription, "K. R. age 8," set it back on the nightstand, and went back to sleep.

9

By noon on Thursday, Chris felt more relaxed and rested than he had in a long time. It was the strangest feeling in the world: For the first time in eight years, he did not have a target to think about or a mission to prepare for. And even though the case was not yet over, he knew once this last little mystery of the giraffe was figured out, he would be free of this mission and free of this Assignment. Had it always felt like such a burden? He thought he loved this job, but if that were the case, how was it that he now felt so light? How did he feel so much relief in the closure that came from the prospect of putting this era of his life behind him?

He checked his phone and saw a message from Zaire saying that his plane would leave at four o'clock that afternoon. Immediately, he sent a message to Jenna asking if she had any time to take a break that day. They agreed to meet at the riverfront park near where she worked an hour later.

He grinned when she responded, and the thought of seeing her sent a rush of excitement throughout him. As he performed his usual exercises and got ready for his day, he thought only of her. He was happy, really happy, just thinking of her. He thought about the previous evening, sitting with her at the lake, sharing pieces of themselves with each other, the light from the full moon shining through the clouds, the reflection on the water, the sound of the leaves rustling in the wind, the late summer night air around them, the knowledge that she could only be there at that time of night because of him. He knew he should have kissed her. He knew she had even expected it, but since their discussion on past relationships, she had taken to following his lead. He sensed it was partially because of his inexperience but mostly because she was breaking some sort of rule, self-imposed or otherwise.

He finished getting ready, putting his phone in his pocket and the earbud in his ear and strapping a knife around his ankle. Then, he packed his belongings into his duffel bag and glanced around the room. Everything was exactly as it had been when he arrived. There was not a trace of evidence that he had ever been there.

As he walked to the riverfront, he thought about the conversation ahead of him. He knew they were both at a decision point: if they decided to pursue this, there would be no turning back. He knew it would be difficult, if not impossible, not to tell her about what his Societal Role had been for the past eight years, but he would try. The previous night, he had not been sure if he could live the secretive life of his job—even if he switched departments and never assassinated anyone ever again—while being completely open and honest with her about everything else in his life. Now, he knew he would do whatever he had to, even if it meant hiding this enormous part of himself, if that was what it would take to be with her.

When he got to the riverfront park, she was waiting for him, and as soon as he saw her, he was filled with both excitement and fear. Though he had made up his mind, there was still the possibility that she would tell him not to come back. There was still the possibility that she had decided it would be better to use his leaving as an opportunity to end things between them.

"So," she said, looking at his bag. "I take it you're leaving today?"

He looked down at his bag, too, and then back at her. "Yeah, my plane leaves in a few hours."

"I'm sorry to see you go. I want you to know that these past few days have been—"

"Actually," he said, cutting her off, "I want to come back and see you." He set his bag down and stepped closer to her.

"That would be really nice." Though she tried to smile, there was sadness in her tone. He didn't know if it should give him hope because she would miss him or if he should prepare himself for her to break it off with him. "Will you call me sometime?" she asked. "Or would you mind if I called you? I'd like to stay in touch. I mean, until you get a chance to come back, at least."

He reached his hand out and brushed her hair away from her face and tucked it behind her ear. He held his hand there. "Actually, I was planning on returning tomorrow."

She raised her eyebrows. "Tomorrow?" All the sadness in her tone was replaced with excitement, and he knew she did not want to end things with him.

"Yeah, I already asked my boss about taking time off." He shrugged one shoulder. "He says I've earned it."

She laughed slightly, still looking into his eyes.

He moved his hand down below her ear, spreading his fingers behind her neck. She looked down at his lips.

He looked down at her lips, too, and then back into her eyes. "I'm sorry about last night."

She put her hands on his chest and watched them as she slid them up over his shoulders and looked back into his eyes as she wrapped her arms around his neck. "It's okay," she whispered.

"It's just that I'm not sure there's any turning back if we go through with this, regardless of what our secrets are."

"I know," she said. "But I can't go back to the way I was living before I met you."

"Me neither," he whispered.

"Are you sure about this?" she asked, and he knew she understood how difficult this decision was for him because it was just as difficult for her, too. She also had things she was not supposed to share with anyone but that she wanted to share with him.

"I am if you are."

In response, she nodded slightly, and he leaned down, gently pulling her closer to him as their lips met. Her embrace was tender, but her kiss held a passion he had not expected. She tightened her arms around his neck, bringing him closer to her, and he wrapped his other arm around her waist. He loved feeling all of her attention on him. He felt her smiling, and it sent lightning throughout his core and out through his limbs. He wanted to give himself to her, all of it: all the emptiness, all the attention, all the strength, all the secrets. She could handle it. He felt her so deeply now, he realized she could handle all of him. And he would tell her everything.

*　　　*　　　*

When he landed in Washington, D.C., Chris went straight to his boss's office, where Zaire and Xiao were waiting for him, and he showed them the giraffe.

"And there was *nothing* else in there?" his boss asked, examining the figurine.

Chris just shook his head.

"Check it for fingerprints, and do a complete chemical analysis." His boss handed the object to Zaire. "See if there is anything inside it." Then, he added, "Be *extremely* cautious. There are ways to put explosives and chemicals in that tiny object. He may have planted it. Even if he knew he would die doing it, Adam Robertson may have planned this all along, wanting to avenge his family's deaths. It's just the type of thing he would do."

"I'll run this straight over now. Hopefully, we'll have something in a few days," Zaire said to them both. Then, turning to Chris, he added, "Are you going to stick around?"

"I'm going to go home and get some rest, but I'll probably leave tomorrow afternoon to return to Des Moines." Chris turned and addressed his boss. "Is there somewhere I can stay?"

"We'll arrange a place for you. But the case isn't over until this giraffe is cleared," his boss answered.

"I'm going to talk to headquarters about switching departments tomorrow, too," Chris told them.

His boss nodded his head; he had expected Chris to make such a request.

Chris turned to Zaire. "Breakfast?"

"I have some time before a press conference at nine."

"All right, let's meet at seven?" Chris suggested.

Zaire nodded his head and said, "See you then," and started to leave. When he reached the door of their boss's office, he looked back at his friend. "And Chris," he called to him in a lighter tone, "your smile suits you."

*   *   *

At breakfast, he told Zaire as much as he could about her: how she made him laugh, how he felt like he had known her forever, how they instantly fit together, how they were slowly letting each other in.

As Chris talked, barely touching his food, Zaire listened in amusement with a suppressed smile on his face. When Chris finally paused to take his first bite, Zaire spoke. "So, did you sleep with her?"

When Chris only chuckled and took a drink of his tea without saying anything, Zaire asked, "Did you finally look her up?"

"No," Chris said. He took another sip of tea and looked around the restaurant, with its thick and soft tablecloths, clean and ironed to perfection; silverware made of silver instead of cheaper metals or plastic that looked like silver; porcelain plates instead of plastic that was made to look like fine dinnerware; tables made of authentic and real wood, not plastic made to look like wood; flooring that was natural stone, not vinyl designed to look like natural stone; and light fixtures made of crystal or real glass and not plastic. Jenna had taken him to the nicest restaurant in Des Moines, and it was not nearly as nice as the most casual restaurant on the Coasts.

"There's nothing interesting in her file, anyway," Zaire continued. "She seems pretty average."

"Maybe," Chris said. He looked around the restaurant again, this time looking at the people: their usual waitress, fellow agents, and other government employees. They all wore suits or casual attire made especially for them by tailors who took their measurements in clean and well-maintained boutiques, where they could sit on chairs and chaises made out of real wood and comfortable cushions while being served drinks and hors d'oeuvres as they picked out quality fabrics for clothes that would be delivered to their houses later. Even the staff's uniforms were made this way, unlike Inlanders, who wore pre-made monochromatic clothes made in vast quantities in sizes such as "small," "medium," and "large" that were arbitrarily determined to fit generic body types and that were never even altered. He looked back at Zaire and said, "But she's not very average to me."

Zaire laughed at him, and Chris glanced around the room one last time.

There were no Purebreds.

"Anyway," Zaire said, pulling out his notebook, while Chris did the same. Zaire continued, moving his fingers across the screen, "I checked up on that Mexican man you encountered." Zaire transferred some data to Chris's device and started summarizing his findings. "His name is Raul, and he's pretty clean. He's not actually from Mexico, but his parents are, and they moved here just before the Ban on Mexican Immigration. His mother must have been pregnant with him when they made the move because the Ban was implemented a month after they became Sector citizens, and he was born only a week later. So he actually is a Sector citizen. He was redistributed to Des Moines about two months ago and has been making regular patterns of movement ever since. He has a job downtown, and he rents an apartment with two other Inlanders."

"He wasn't staying at the same hotel I was?"

"No, I guess he just likes to eat there. His brother has an impressive background," Zaire said sarcastically as he scrolled through the list on his screen, "theft, armed robbery, gang activity, gang initiation practice, street fighting, and murder. A single unnamed witness identified him in a trial a few years ago, and he's been in prison ever since. According to my research, that witness is the only one that survived long enough to testify at trial. But if the witness is still alive, they won't be for long. These gangs never let anyone go. Your guy visited his brother every weekend until he was redistributed to Des Moines, and now his visits are every other weekend."

"But *he* wasn't in the gang."

"Nope. Odd, isn't it? Looks like everyone he knows is into gang rivalry. They all have rap sheets with either drug trafficking or street fighting." Zaire put his notebook away. "Really, they should be ashamed of themselves. It's not like Mexico looks so great right now, and these gangs are not helping, even if they are Sector citizens. They need to realize they represent their Mexican cousins and aunts and uncles and all the other inhabitants of Mexico."

Chris thought for a moment. "There's just something about him that doesn't sit well with me. Was I somehow involved in the case that put his brother in prison?"

"They've never had any run-in with our type. Their murders and fights are amongst each other, usually having to do with drug dealing or gang territory, and it can almost always be traced back to drug lords in Mexico." Zaire did not say it, but Chris knew his friend thought they should all be sent back to the chaos of Mexico rather than continuing to be a burden by occupying Sector prisons, whether or not they were legitimate Sector citizens.

"Well," Chris said as he raised his eyebrows and drank his tea. "I guess it was just a weird coincidence."

"I'll keep an eye on him while you're in Des Moines, but I doubt you have any connection to him." Zaire got up and put on his jacket. "Well, I have to head out and prepare for my press conference."

Chris stood up to leave with him.

Outside, Chris watched his friend walk away. Zaire's dark gray suit and light lavender shirt complemented his light brown skin and soft green eyes. He knew Zaire had chosen the outfit because it made him appear even more trustworthy than he already was and would therefore help him with his new Assignment in Public Relations. In that moment, he realized how odd the position was, for someone like Zaire to be in charge of relaying information to the general public when he was set so far apart from it. Zaire was his best friend, someone who would always be by his side, and Zaire was really good in Public Relations. But Zaire would never understand Jenna. Having never worked in the field and having grown up on the West Coast before being placed in Washington, D.C., Zaire had never been to the Inland. Chris tried to imagine Zaire in Des Moines and thought of the nervous Coastal he had seen in the bookstore. Zaire would never be afraid, but he had also never known a Purebred who was not from the Coasts, if he knew any Purebreds at all. He knew Zaire was being polite by not saying anything, keeping his thoughts about Purebreds to himself while he let Chris talk about Jenna. But Chris could read it in Zaire's face, the confusion, wondering how Chris could possibly think so highly of a Purebred, especially one that was an Inlander. He saw the look in Zaire's eyes. He saw that Zaire thought this was just a fling, that Chris would soon wake up and realize he could do so much better. Zaire was waiting for Chris to get this out of his system, thinking this thing with a Purebred Inlander could not be permanent and that Chris would eventually end up with a Modified Coastal.

If only Zaire met Jenna, Chris thought, *would he get it then?* Now that he thought about it, he was not sure Zaire had ever even met a Purebred. Or a Mexican.

Chris turned and started walking to the building next door, where his boss's office was. A young woman moved out of Chris's way before he bumped into her and smiled as she said, "Excuse me."

Chris stopped and looked at her. "No, I'm sorry," he said. "I wasn't paying attention."

She smiled back at him and lightly touched his arm as she said, reassuringly, "Don't worry about it." And then she continued walking.

He watched her walk away. She was gorgeous—not in the natural way Jenna was, but in the Modified way. Most Coastal Modifieds were stunning, but it was hard to appreciate unless they were standing near the older generation, the people who were bred and produced before modifications, or in comparison to a Purebred like Jenna, or in comparison to Inland Modifieds, whose parents did not have the extra money to pay for cosmetic genetic modifications. Especially on the Coasts, where families could afford the extra modifications to their preferences, babies were born with a specific skin color, eye color, and hair color. Eye shape, eyelash length, bone structure, height, general body type and build, hair thickness, lip fullness—all the genetic sequences for specific physical attributes were known and could be inserted to replace inherited genes. He wondered if Zaire and Melinda would design the baby they were in the process of getting a License to produce. Of course they would. For Coastals, that was half the fun of procreating.

He turned and kept walking.

Looking down, he saw the sidewalks he had walked for years. Unlike the sidewalks he and Jenna walked in Des Moines, these were flat, maintained, without cracks or flaws, just like the streets. Looking around, he saw the land and lawns were manicured and gardened. Every plant was healthy and bright and intentional, placed by artistic design, and there were no weeds or signs of dehydration or malnutrition. Except for trees and bushes that managed to grow and survive on their own, he did not remember seeing any plants at all in the Inland cities.

They were not planted intentionally, and he couldn't imagine anyone paying to maintain them, anyway.

When he looked down the road, he saw a police officer, the first he had seen all morning. The man was alone; there were no other officers in sight. No partner. No backup. No riot police, just in case. He was on a bicycle, but he was standing on it, one foot on a pedal and one foot on the street. He was talking with a fellow Coastal. They both started laughing, and Chris realized that in contrast to the officers in the Inland, this Coastal officer did not carry a baton, not in his hand nor on his belt. The two presumably ended their conversation, and the officer waved as he rode off, both of them still smiling.

He could see them down the road because there were so few people around to be in the way of his view. People walked freely with large bags and hands in their pockets, if they chose. Even he felt more relaxed without effort. What a difference it made to feel trusted and secure without fear of being unreasonably suspected. What a difference it made to not subconsciously be prepared to defend oneself or one's actions, either physically or verbally. What a difference the attitude of a society made.

He remembered the crowded streets of Des Moines and Jenna subtly bringing her shoulder inward to avoid the touch of a fellow Inlander, a Modified Inlander. *How did she live like that?* he wondered.

The truth was, he had wanted to ask her to come back to D.C. with him. He wanted to take her away from the Inland and free her from the life she seemed to be trapped in. But he knew it was not the time to ask such a thing of her. He had decided that in the time off he was about to take, he would figure out how to make it work. He would tell her about his job and try to convince her to stay with him. He would do whatever it took to ease any concerns she had. And then eventually, if it all worked out, he would ask her to live with him.

He entered the building and waved to a security guard standing in the distance as he approached the elevators. He entered the elevator and pressed the button for the floor of his boss's office. The buttons were bright, well lit and smooth, not dim or without any light or cracked like the ones in the hotel where he stayed in Des Moines. The elevator ride was smooth, without creaking like the elevators in Des Moines.

He reached his boss's office, and upon entering, Xiao indicated for him to shut the door behind him. Xiao tapped away at some buttons on his desk, and Chris knew he was making the room a digital dead zone. It was not as secure as the dead rooms in the basement of government buildings, where absolutely no signals, signatures, or communication could penetrate the walls, but this did give them the highest amount of privacy they could get. Xiao did this sometimes if they were going to talk about specific aspects of a case or if he just wanted to have a secure conversation with his agents.

Chris sat down across from Xiao.

"Chris," Xiao said, "thanks for coming in. Have you talked to headquarters about a new Assignment?"

"No, sir, I'm going to, right after this."

His boss pressed his lips together. Then, he asked, "What department would you like to be assigned to next?"

"I'm hoping for something more stationary, something with less travel and less fieldwork." Chris did not mention his reason to Xiao, but his boss had probably already guessed this had to do with Jenna.

"You know, Rockford," his boss started, "people have been watching you. The Presidents in particular have been asking about you. They are really impressed, and you have found much favor with them." Xiao's expression went from being serious to being more relaxed. He was proud of his protégé.

"I hope you took the credit for being such an excellent mentor."

"I did," Xiao said, happily, "but I didn't have to because they already knew how much I pushed you to be so successful." He got serious again. "What are your thoughts on Mexico?"

"What about it?"

"A disordered area of the world is definitely a threat to The Order. Even if they're not actively planning an attack, they may in the future, or a disease may make its way over here. By not having our surveillance and tracking systems, they are unable to stop their inhabitants from entering The Sectors and bringing drugs, crime, and disease with them. Simply keeping them out may not be enough. With your extensive experience in the Department of Anarchy Prevention, you would be of service on that front."

"Can we not work with them?" Chris asked. "When was the last time our Presidents talked with theirs?"

"Chris, this way of thinking—asking about working with Mexico instead of leaving their government out of the conversation—this is not how a typical agent thinks. You think of the big picture. That is how you are so successful in your missions and why you have remained in the Department of Anarchy Prevention for so long. You don't focus on just the target. You are able to focus on the target and all the variables and potential interacting factors and the overall status of the mission, all at the same time. That level of thinking is needed right now, and the Presidents have been looking for such talent."

"You mean in terms of Mexico?"

His boss nodded. "Yes, but if that does not interest you, there are other departments that could use your services, too."

He paused before continuing. "What would you think about that? Instead of switching to a new department as an agent, what if you transitioned into a boss position in Mexico Relations, instead?"

There it was. Not the actual official offer, but an actual official confirmation that Chris was being considered for a specific position as a boss. Outwardly, Chris remained professionally expressionless, per agency protocol and culture, but inwardly he was immensely satisfied at the very close and very real prospect of what would be by far his greatest achievement in life.

Chris nodded seriously and said, "I would like that, sir."

"The Order wants them to sign the Treaty and become part of The Sectors. It's been the plan all along, but now they are getting more serious about it." Xiao studied Chris for a moment and then said, "But you must understand that the boss position is not a settling-down, family-friendly job. It's much more demanding than being an agent. It's a round-the-clock position, where you have to be available, physically and mentally, at all hours of the day."

"Sounds like the last eight years of my life."

Xiao gave a rare smile and conceded, "That's true." Then, he returned to his normal serious self. "I know you're thinking long term with this woman you met in Des Moines. You cannot allow whatever happens in your personal life to ever affect what you do here. And the job—especially for a boss —*always* comes first."

It gave Chris hope that Xiao did not give him an ultimatum or tell him it was a bad idea to pursue a relationship with Jenna. Xiao could read people better than anyone. If he thought the relationship would not work, Xiao would have said so.

"Yes, sir."

Chris was about to say more to assure his boss of his competence but stopped when Xiao tapped a few buttons on his desk to disable the digital dead zone.

Xiao looked toward his office door as someone knocked on it. "Come in," he told the person on the other side.

An agent entered the room and handed Xiao the giraffe. "It's clear," she said. "All results are negative. It's nothing."

"Thank you," Xiao said and dismissed her.

Xiao set the giraffe aside. "I'll have this processed and put into the evidence archive storage."

Chris picked it up and looked at it more closely. "Can I hang onto this?"

With complete trust in Chris, Xiao asked, "What's on your mind?"

Chris turned the giraffe around in his hand, examining it. "I don't know."

Xiao leaned forward and asked, "What does your instinct tell you?"

Chris paused for a moment, contemplating but not having a clear picture in his mind of what his thoughts were. He shook his head slowly and then looked at his boss. "I just don't think this case is over, yet."

10

Chris was back in Des Moines by Friday afternoon.
Throughout the previous evening and while he was in his car on
the way to Des Moines, he thought of how he would tell her.
Chris had remained calm and expressionless, as usual, when he
spoke with Xiao, but he wondered if Xiao knew he wanted to
tell Jenna about his position in government, even though it was
not allowed. That Xiao had specifically reminded him that his
job and personal life had to remain separate led Chris to believe
it was at least possible Xiao suspected that he was thinking of
breaking the rule; at the same time, Chris had never asked for
time off before, so Xiao could have just been reminding him
that his emotions and personal life should never interfere with
the job and that as a boss he would never be allowed to take
time off. Chris was determined to do that, of course, to
continue to be the best in the agency without interference from
his relationship with Jenna. But he was also determined to share
with her the truth of what he had been for so long. He planned
to do it gradually, first by dropping hints, then by discussing the
possibility of such a Societal Role, and finally by proposing the

idea that maybe someone in that position would not be the monster she thought they would be. He would take the time for her to get used to the idea first, while showing her that he was not what she thought an assassin would be like. Then, when she was ready, he would tell her. By then it would not be such a shock, and she would know he was still who she had always known him to be.

And if his plan did not work? He did not want to think of how much that would hurt. If she chose to walk away upon finding out what he was, it would be immensely painful. He did not know if she would accept him when he told her the truth. He did know, however, that she was worth the risk.

He met with the manager of the apartment he would rent, which was located in the Coastal District downtown, just a block away from the hotel where he had stayed. The manager showed him the alarm codes to get into the parking garage, the building, and the apartment. It was an updated apartment, with a bedroom and a living room that opened up into the kitchen and dining area, but with the typical Inland cheapness, the look of luxury without the quality. Most of the things were made of plastic that was designed to look like the hardwood, tile, or natural stone one would find on the Coasts. The manager told Chris about the gym and laundry facilities and gave instructions for parking and using the appliances. Finally, just before she left, she swiped Chris's card to pay the rent for the entire month and handed him the keys. The meeting and walk-through ended around the time Jenna would have been getting off work, so as soon as the manager left, Chris locked up the apartment and walked to the art museum.

When she saw him, she greeted him with her usual warm smile, but she had a cautious air about her that he had not noticed since the night they met, which meant she was nervous about this, too. He took her hand as they walked back to his apartment.

"So, I was thinking, maybe tonight I can have you over to my place? I can make us dinner, and we can watch a movie or something. Or whatever you would like to do is fine with me, too."

"*Finally,*" she said sarcastically. She nudged him playfully as she said, "I've been waiting to see how you fare in the kitchen. I hope you brought back something good from the Coasts."

"Oh." He had not even thought about bringing something back for her.

She laughed. "It's okay. Actually, it's probably for the best because it would have just made me hate the food here and constantly think about what I'm missing."

"Or maybe I didn't because I wanted to entice you to come back to the Coast with me. We have great food, you know. You should come check it out sometime."

She did not respond at first. "Maybe," she said. Then, she lightly joked, "But I think you just forgot about me."

"The opposite, actually. But I was busy with work and getting ready to take time off and come here."

"I understand," she said and squeezed his hand.

They reached his apartment, and she set her purse on the kitchen countertop and took off her jacket. "This is nice."

"Yeah, it's not so bad," Chris said as he followed her into the kitchen area. As he took a step, the floor creaked. "What would you like for dinner?" He stepped down on the spot again, feeling for exactly where the noise was coming from. He started walking around the spot, checking for creaks in the floor. He had not yet done his own thorough inspection of the place.

She did not answer and instead just watched him. She was looking at him differently than before he left. He had originally attributed her change in attitude to anxiety because he was nervous. But now he realized she looked at him differently not because there was a potential permanence to him and their relationship—she wasn't looking for reasons this would not work. She was watching him as if searching for a man different than the one she had met a week ago.

He stopped, still looking at the floor. *She knows*.

"Chris?" she asked.

He quit checking the floor and focused on her, willing his thumping heart to calm down. "Yes, Jenna?"

"When you said you *do* get rid of the bad guys...?" She trailed off without finishing her question. "I just..." She shook her head. She had put it all together, and now she knew exactly what he was. She knew that he had come to Iowa with a criminal on his agenda and that he had assassinated that person. Now, she searched for the killer in him, a reason to leave and escape the presence of a murderer and flee back to the comfortable normalcy of her life before she met him. "I just didn't know people in your position actually exist."

"It's not exactly classified, but we tend to keep it secret."

"So...that guy?" she asked, referring to the creep she had met when she was with clients.

"No, not him."

He cautiously took a step toward her. She did not back away.

"Maybe it wasn't wise for me to tell you, but I couldn't *not* tell you." Softly, he said, "I don't want to keep anything from you."

She shrugged slightly, barely lifting one shoulder. "I did say that you could tell me anything, and I meant it. I still do. It's just that I've always assumed it was officers and detectives and officials and politicians, but maybe I always knew there was more to our government, spies and things they keep from the public for our safety. I just assumed it was out there somewhere"—she waved her hand in the air—"and not so close to home." She crossed her arms and sighed.

"I wanted to tell you, gradually, to allow time for you to adjust to the idea, but now that you know, we can talk about it, if you want to. But I understand if you want to leave and need some time to think about it alone."

"I've been thinking about it since you left. I guess I started putting all the pieces together after we got back from the lake. I was just so confused about how you knew about that convict that I saw on the news, and then I thought about what you said when I asked you about your job." She paused, and he stayed silent, not wanting to disrupt her thoughts. "Honestly, I still don't know what to think." Then, she stepped closer to him, and in a low whisper, she asked, "What do you think?"

He knew she was not asking him his opinion of his job, but rather, she was asking what his intuition was about her. "I think you wouldn't be here if you were going to run when you heard the answers to your questions. And I will answer them truthfully when you ask. You can always ask me anything, Jenna. I don't want you to ever feel uncomfortable around me."

She stood, arms still crossed, staring back at him like she had known him forever but was only seeing him in person for the first time.

"What I do is not a typical day job," he continued. "It's my life. I cannot leave it, not completely. I swore an oath of loyalty when I graduated from the academy, so I am legally bound to it forever, and, also, I don't break promises." He paused but continued looking at her, trying to figure out if she understood what he was saying. "I'm going to request that I no longer be assigned to the position of assassin, but you need to know that I can't turn down the order if that's what is asked of me."

At the mention of the word "assassin," at finally hearing it out loud, she froze. It was real.

She met his eyes and asked, "Does it change you? To just take someone's life like that?"

"I'm not heartless," he said, wanting to ease her concerns. "I mean, I don't feel emotionally connected to the cases, but I have not lost empathy or natural emotions. I'm not a murderer. I don't seek out people to kill for my own pleasure, nor am I any more likely to do that since taking on this job. If anything, I am more sympathetic toward the victims of the criminals I pursue. But I'm not particularly hostile toward those criminals. I won't allow myself to become like that." As he said it, he felt a pang of guilt as he thought about the other night, when he almost *had* allowed himself to get hostile.

"Are you ever afraid you'll turn on someone, like your friends?"

"No, of course not. I would never hurt anyone I love. But I should tell you that I have few friends. My best friends are my boss and a coworker and his wife. Otherwise, my life is rather solitary. I am mainly cautious because I love my family, and when I think of my niece and nephews, I don't want to become someone who is immune to the things I do."

"No, being immune to it would not be healthy," she agreed.

"It's not. And they try to prevent it in the workplace, mainly by assigning people who won't get too emotionally involved. And it's rare that anybody does this part of it for more than two years in a row. Those who get hostile or desensitized typically don't do as well of a job. The reason I keep getting assigned to this position is because I make sure I am just as cautious as I was the first time I ever carried out an assassination. If an agent becomes careless, the job becomes messy."

She cringed.

"I meant messy in the sense that mistakes would be made," he clarified.

"Like, you'd leave fingerprints."

"Fingerprints are not an issue. I always wear gloves, but I still wouldn't leave fingerprints." He held his hand out to her.

She took his hand in hers and closely examined the tips of his fingers.

"We burn them off."

She pulled her hands back suddenly, looking up at him as if his fingers were still on fire.

He laughed and held his hand back out to her. "It wasn't painful. It's just part of the training. They use lasers to do it."

She put her fingertips back on his, feeling the smoothness and then comparing it to the feeling on her own fingers. "What else is a result of the training?" she asked, more relaxed and curious now.

"Vigilance is a major part of it," he said as he leaned against the kitchen countertop. "Every time I walk into a room, I immediately know every exit. Usually, within a few minutes, I know most of the major points in the room. Major points would be"—he pointed to the part of the floor that had creaked—"places where the floor creaks when you step on it"—he pointed around the room to the table and kitchen counters—"positions of objects and people, materials of major structures like the wall or support beams or big glass objects. I know how to maneuver around the room in the most silent way possible. Shortly after that, I am fully aware of every person in the room, and I start profiling their personalities. It's like taking a quick snapshot of the layout. Then I refresh it as people move around or come and go. The majority of the training is constantly being aware of surroundings, even when one sense is missing, like being blindfolded or distracted by loud sounds.

The rest of the training is ensuring that no traces are left behind in the jobs that are done."

Putting her hands on the countertop behind her, she lifted herself up so she was sitting next to where he was standing. As she did so, she asked, "So, from the moment you stepped into the hotel restaurant where we met, you knew all that?"

"Estimated all of that." He turned so he was facing her, still leaning on the counter with one hand. "It's impossible to completely know anything."

As he said that, he thought about how little he really knew about her. He tried not to guess the big secret she admitted to having, how someone of her intellect and obvious Coastal upbringing could have ended up in the Inland. Yet, he could not deny his ability to read mannerisms and choices so well. She was very guarded. She kept a low profile. She made herself as inconspicuous as possible for someone in her position. Her apartment had few decorations, even though she herself was so expressive. She kept tabs on her surroundings, even though she did not have the level of training he had to be good at it. She talked little of her life before Des Moines, reducing herself to only the few years of her life there. It was clear that she had run from someone, and it was very apparent that this someone could have friends who would try to befriend her, making her very cautious to get to know people.

Yet she did not allow that fear to penetrate her everyday life or who she was at her core. She could dress down to get demoted to a lesser position at work to be less noticeable, but she did not. She could treat people with the same disdain with which they treated her, but she did not. She could keep her eyes down and be worn and tired like everyone else around her, but she did not. She refused to lose the parts of herself she wanted to keep, regardless of what it might cost her. Despite what Zaire may have found in her file about her being from Utah, she was not an Inlander. She did not belong there. She treated people equally, even when they did not return the favor. She was friendly and confident enough to look people in the eye when she spoke to them. But beyond the basic social interactions her job demanded, she lived alone.

She touched the side of his elbow as she said, "That's true," and the gesture brought him back from his thoughts. He watched her index finger trace down his forearm to the tip of his thumb on the counter.

"I'm sorry I didn't tell you sooner. I was afraid because of what you said at the restaurant before we saw the musical, about the type of person who would have this job." She looked up, and he met her eyes. "I had this plan, where I was going to show you what a great guy I am so that when I did finally tell you, you would know it's okay and not hate me for it."

"You already did that. I thought an"—she stumbled over the word—"assassin would be so different, but you proved me wrong. I know you probably weren't supposed to tell me, but I'm glad you did." She pulled lightly on the front of his shirt to bring him closer to her, and he leaned down as she kissed him softly, fully accepting him for who and what he was.

"Me, too," he said, and then he kissed her again.

"You know," she said, and he leaned back, "I was thinking that since you were able to get some time off and hang out here, maybe I could take some time off work, too."

"Really?"

"Yes, I actually talked with my boss today, and she said it would be okay."

"That's great," he said, delighted.

"I have to go in on Monday, and there's a gala at the museum on Friday evening, so I have to be there for that to help make sure everything goes smoothly. But otherwise, I'm free to take the rest of next week off."

"What do you want to do?" he asked. "Do you want to go somewhere and get away for a few days?"

"*Go somewhere?*" she repeated excitedly. "I hadn't even thought of that. But, yes, of course, I'd love to!" Except for areas just outside the Des Moines city limits, she had not left Des Moines since she had been redistributed there.

"All right, where do you want to go?"

She placed her hands on the counter beside her hips and let out a "hmm" as she looked up and thought about it for a moment. "How about Idaho?" she asked, looking back at him. "The way you talked about it made me homesick, even though I've never been there."

"Okay, since you have to be back on Monday, do you want to go on Tuesday? Or do you want to go tomorrow?"

"Tuesday, so we have more time," she said excitedly. "It's been years since I've gone on a trip." Then, remembering that reminded her of all the preparation required for traveling, and she sighed. "It's Friday afternoon."

"So?"

"I don't know if I'll be able to get a travel permit by Tuesday. The offices are closed until Monday, and for flights I think it takes a long time to get one." A long time for an Inlander to get one. An even longer time for a Purebred.

"You don't need one if you're with me," he reminded her.

"Oh, yes," she said, the excitement resuming in her voice. She nudged him playfully and added, "You have that magic government ID."

He laughed, a little embarrassed.

"So, do you just walk on the plane?"

"Basically," he confessed. "But it will be less of a hassle if we have permits so we don't have to explain ourselves." After a second, he added, "I'll get them for us."

"Good idea," she said.

"We can fly into Boise Tuesday morning, and then we can get a car and drive to the town where I grew up. It's gorgeous this time of year. There won't be any snow, yet, but the canyons are amazing at sunset, and there's a lot of hiking we could do."

"I think that sounds perfect."

"Me, too," he said and kissed her again. "Are you hungry?"

"You did promise to cook for me, didn't you?"

"Yeah, but we'll have to get the ingredients. I haven't had time to get anything, yet."

"Then, let's go," she said as she slid off the counter and took his hand.

They took the elevator to the parking garage, and he led her to his car. When she saw it, her eyes widened. It was not like any car she had seen before. She did not know anything about cars, but she knew luxury when she saw it. It confused her, though, because it seemed so out of place, even for a Coastal. Chris dressed like a rich Coastal and was well mannered like one, but he had never given any indication that he actually cared about looking like one.

"Where did you rent this car?" she asked. "I didn't think we had anything like this in the Inland."

"I drove it from D.C."

"You *drove* here? When did you leave?"

"A little after noon," he said, smiling in response to her confusion. "I took the tunnels."

"The tunnels?"

"They connect the Coasts underground." He pointed to metal plates on the side of the car. "Once in the tunnels, the magnetic force along the walls takes over. The car shuts off, and the Tunnel Operating System controls the speed and traffic of all the vehicles. It only took me three hours to get here." He opened the passenger door for her, and she got in.

When he was seated in the driver's seat, she pointed at the speedometer. "Does this thing really go 400 miles per hour, or is it just for the look?"

"Just for the look?" He laughed out loud. "Surely you know me well enough to know that everything I own has a practical purpose."

"So it's not chipped?" All civilian cars had a microchip that prevented the cars from physically surpassing the speed limit for the road they were on.

He shook his head and answered, "No." He turned the car on and started to drive to the store.

She looked around the inside. It was the most comfortable car she had ever been in, and he looked very comfortable driving it. The front panel had two screens, and there were many buttons and dials she had never seen before.

He watched her looking around. "We can test it out if you want to."

"Do you know how to drive it that fast?"

"Okay, now you're just insulting me."

"Won't you lose control? What if you hit another car? Or a tree or a person or something?"

"It's not like I went out and got this car to impress you, without having any idea of its capability. I've had it for years. And it's more like a company car than my own car."

"*This* is the car the government puts you in? Who do they expect you to go after?"

"It's not for chasing. It's for running."

"I don't follow."

"When I go after a target, I plan everything out carefully. It's a very meticulous job, actually. There's no high speed chase in my line of work. Now, if I'm in trouble for some reason and need to flee, that's where the car comes in. Though, admittedly,

I've never been in that situation, I do enjoy the occasional joyride for fun."

"So, you've driven at high speeds before."

"Yes." He looked at her again. They had reached the grocery store, and Inlanders walking by the car were staring at them. "Do you want to go for a spin?" he asked, ignoring the people around them.

"I'm thinking about it. I wonder if I would get dizzy."

"How fast have you gone before?"

"Maybe fifty miles per hour?"

He laughed, but he tried to conceal it by keeping his mouth closed.

It didn't work, and she started giggling, too.

"Just say the word, and I can show you."

"Let's just get groceries first," she said as she opened her car door.

When they returned from the store, he made dinner while she sat on the counter and talked with him. The drawers and cupboards were typical for the Inland, not shutting properly and getting stuck. He tried to play it off like he did not notice or like it did not bother him, but it only ended in her giggling, and then they would laugh at it together. He had not remembered things in the Inland being so cheaply made that they were nearly falling apart. But then, he had not lived in the Inland since being recruited for government, minus the breaks when he went back home. Moreover, his home was nothing like a typical Inland home. Coastals always complained when they had to go to the Inland for business or to stay for any amount of time. He had judged them before, feeling defensive of his childhood home and believing they were too snobby. But now he was beginning to take their side. He thought, *Have things gotten worse in the Inland, or am I the one that has changed?*

After dinner, Chris's phone rang. He went to the bedroom to take the call, and even though Jenna remained in the living room, he chose to converse in a language he knew she would not understand. Looking down at his phone, he saw that both Zaire and Xiao were on the conference call.

He sat on the corner of the bed as he answered, and one of the wooden slabs fell out beneath him. At the sound of it, Jenna appeared in the doorway asking if everything was okay, and when she saw what happened, she burst into laughter. He suppressed his own laughter and held up a hand, indicating the call. She whispered an apology and went back to the living room area and turned on the television to give him some privacy.

He took a deep breath to stop laughing and got serious. "Sorry," he apologized. "I'm here."

"As usual, your instincts were correct," Xiao said. "Zaire, tell him what was found."

Zaire reported, "In closing out the case, we've come across an article nearly twenty years old that features Talon Sr. It's a lengthy article, highlighting his business ventures, but buried in it is half a sentence that mentions his youngest daughter, Katherine, holding his hand while he was being interviewed."

"His youngest daughter Katherine? A typo?" Chris asked. "They thought Adele was named Katherine? Maybe his niece or a daughter of a friend?"

"We don't think so. The article says that at the time of the interview, Katherine was sitting between her father and her mother, Adele and Adam were sitting on another sofa nearby, and Karen and Talon Jr. were away at college. The way they describe it, Katherine sounds like a child much younger than Adele or Adam."

Chris sighed and stood up from the bed. "So there's another sibling." In Chris's tone, he revealed his relief.

Everything about Iowa was explained. He thought about what Talon Jr. had said about Adam going to Iowa for their sister and Adam saying he couldn't find her and the "K.R." on the giraffe. The giraffe must have belonged to her. Instinctively, he knew it.

"But as far as we know, there are no other records of her having ever been alive. They scratched everything."

Chris thought about this new piece of the case: she could be anywhere; she could be their most secretive and most dangerous ally. She could live purely in the shadows, someone who, on paper, did not exist and thus could not be found guilty of anything. But she was not infallible. Though they had clearly made every attempt to erase her existence, they had overlooked at least one piece of evidence.

"Or maybe she's dead?" Chris asked.

"No record of that either," their boss stated, though that was not conclusive. She could have been buried in an unmarked grave.

Zaire said, "We're working backwards, starting with recent legal and official documents, going back to the time when she would have been born. We're looking for signs of bribery, where government officials might have destroyed all evidence. I've written up petitions to give to other agencies and the military, presenting the case against Katherine Robertson and the importance of finding her."

Chris said, "I'll come back tonight and help the search."

"No, you can stay where you are," his boss said. "We'll need you to be ready to go wherever she is, which is likely in Iowa, if that's truly why Adam was there."

"I was planning on going to Idaho on Tuesday," Chris told them. Both Xiao and Zaire knew that was where Chris had grown up. "I can cancel the trip, though, or I can be back here with four hours' notice if I take my car."

His boss asked, "How long do you plan to stay in Idaho?"

"Just until Friday morning," Chris answered.

"From where I stand, finding her will take much longer than a week," Zaire said. "Not to mention, we have absolutely no evidence against her personally. Of course, I'll keep you updated with each piece of information I get, but we have no leads aside from this one sentence. They truly erased any sign of her."

"But Adam knew where she was," said Chris. "This must be what Talon Jr. was referring to when he talked about Adam being in Iowa. It just makes sense."

Xiao countered, "But he didn't know where she was. Otherwise, he would have led us to her. Adam met with no one while he was there."

Chris thought about how Adam had systematically gone down the streets, not staying anywhere for any amount of time, and knew Xiao was right. Adam had been searching for her on foot and in person because he had no other means of finding her. "But somehow he knew she was somewhere in Iowa."

"I'm trying to figure that out," Zaire said.

"Go ahead with your trip," their boss said to Chris. "We'll let you know if the plans change before then, but I don't anticipate that we'll be able to find anything. It took us this long to find this single piece of evidence."

"And there's not much she can do by herself," Zaire said. "If she were planning something, we'd already know about it, given all the intel we've cracked with this case."

"Or she's even more elusive than the rest of them, better at covering her tracks than even they were," Xiao argued. "I expect it will take us a while to find her. Be more alert, if possible. We'll call you with each update we have. Let us know if you come up with anything on your end."

"Will do," said Chris.

With that, they ended their call.

Chris waited a few moments before going back to Jenna, thinking about the case and how it was far from over. Though the agency's resources, skills, and intelligence were limitless, it had taken years to gather enough evidence against the Robertsons. It could take that long to find Katherine, too.

Chris went back into the living room and sat down on the couch next to Jenna.

"Is everything okay?"

"The case isn't closed yet, so I may have to bolt at any moment." Then, reassuringly, he added, "We're still okay to go to Idaho, but I may have to cancel it or cut it short if they call me back."

"You didn't…check, to be sure?" Jenna asked, confused.

"No, not like that. The one I came for in Iowa is gone, but he may have had an ally. But it could be weeks before they identify the location."

"Oh," she said.

"But, at this point there's nothing for me to do except wait."

"Okay," she said. "I guess I should start getting used to this sort of thing happening, right?"

He nodded. "I'm afraid so."

She shrugged. "That's okay. We can still enjoy the time we have." She moved over to sit closer to him, and he put his arm around her.

"Want to watch a movie?" he asked.

He pulled out the notebook the manager of the apartment had given him and started scrolling through the options. She chose one for them to rent. They stretched out on the couch and watched the movie, hand in hand, with her head on his chest and his arm around her. When the film was over, they both lay there in silence, neither wanting to move nor wanting her to go home, yet.

"How do you avoid getting pulled over?" she asked, thinking of his agency car.

"Have you seen the cars officers drive?"

"Yes, but they have magnets in them that force cars to stop if the car's Comm System does not force it to pull over and stop."

"They can't stop a car going that fast."

"They could call someone."

"The car is chipped so that any radar that detects it receives a signal letting them know it's a government car. I'm the only one who can activate the engine, so the car only runs as long as I'm in the driver's seat and my hands are on the wheel. Sometimes amateur cops don't believe the signal or they are unfamiliar with how it works—why they don't include this in their training, I don't understand, but that's how it is—and they usually give up after a few minutes of chasing and call it in, only to have the person they call tell them it's a government car." He sat up and looked at her. "Anything else?"

"I just don't see why you need it if only government agents can have them. Why would you need to run from them?"

"I wouldn't run from them. We're the only ones who are authorized to have these cars, but it doesn't mean that criminals don't get their hands on a few. Those are the people I would run from, *if* I got in a situation where I was in over my head, which is not likely to ever happen, especially after I transfer to a different department when this case is over." He continued to watch her, and when he saw she had no more questions, he asked, "Want to try it out?"

"It's very tempting."

"Now is the best time to do it. At night there are fewer cars, and Iowa has a lot of highways. But if you're weary because of the accident, I understand. I don't want to pressure you."

She took a deep breath. "Okay. Let's do it."

He turned off the television, and they went to the car.

"Okay, just let me know when you want me to slow down or stop, and it's no problem," he said as they got in. "If you feel like you're getting sick, close your eyes and take deep breaths." He started programming one of the screens. "This one shows me a map of all the surrounding objects. The car sends out a signal and calculates the location, velocity, and density of its surroundings." He programmed the other screen. "This one does a similar calculation, but from a satellite, as an extra precaution so we don't hit anything or anyone." The programs did their calculations, and different colored dots appeared on the black screens. "Dots are moving objects. Lines are stationary," he explained. "If I get too close to an object, or if one of these dots were to dart out in front of me suddenly, the car would automatically override my movements to avoid them, so don't worry about me hitting anything." He looked at her and smiled at her fascination. He zoomed out with one of the screens, and she saw that outside the city were few dots and lines. He scrolled around. "We'll take this road"—he pointed to the one going east—"because it has the least around it." He pressed a few more buttons. "These activate the signal that will be sent to officers to let them know I am not a criminal." He pressed a few more buttons, this time putting in a code. "And that ensures nobody bothers us."

"Bothers us?"

"There are microphones and speakers in here."

"Of course," she said. All cars had them, apparently even government cars.

"But now they're off, and we're alone." He put on gloves, started the engine, and put the car in gear.

She watched the screens and compared them to what she saw when she looked out the windows. "That's pretty cool."

"Go ahead and play around with them, if you'd like. The one on the bottom is satellite feed, so you can zoom in and out with it."

She touched the screen and moved the map around. "Why was that guy a green dot?"

"The colors don't mean much for us, but if I were looking for someone, I could put them on the map, and that person would be a red dot. The other colors usually indicate status, like government employees are green, officers are blue, and there are other colors for others, but general citizens are gray, along with animals or anything else that is moving." He did not show her the setting that revealed the identity of each person in range, though the software was capable of getting that information from Surveillance.

She watched the screen as the program performed the calculations. "This is insane."

He shifted into the next gear as they got on the highway. "Well, if it's too much, we can turn around."

"Nope, I'm ready." She leaned back in her seat and looked forward.

He looked at her and smiled to himself as he threw the car into another gear, and they were flying. He saw her chest elevate upward as she breathed in deeply, and he asked, "Are you all right?"

"Yes." She looked at the speedometer. They were going 120 miles per hour. She looked at the screen on the top, constantly calculating their surroundings. The screen on the bottom was still zoomed out, and she watched the moving dot that was their car moving among all the stationary objects. She looked outside and focused on a factory in the distance instead of the ground closer to her, which made her dizzy to look at.

She looked back at the speedometer, and now it said 180. She took another deep breath and held onto the door.

"Still okay?" He looked over at her and saw that she was smiling.

"Still okay." She looked at him. "I'm definitely beginning to feel a lot more trusting of you." She looked back out the window. "You have a lot of control."

He gave a half-smile, switching lanes and zooming past a car as they neared 220. "This officer up here is going to chase us."

"How many have we passed already?" she asked.

"Three."

They approached 250, and the officer's lights went on. She turned around quickly, trying to see the officer's car chase them, but it was out of sight in seconds. "Okay, I don't need to go faster. This is good."

"You sure?"

"I'm feeling a little queasy." She shut her eyes and took deep breaths. "I think it was the lights that did it. I feel totally disoriented."

"That's usual for the first time. It's better we did this at night."

He stayed at 175 when he realized it did not bother her. Now, he was just enjoying the drive.

After a while, Jenna looked at Chris. He was calm and unmoved by sudden changes or distractions when he drove, and it occurred to her that how someone drove was very much an indicator of how they lived.

Eventually, he slowed down and got off at an exit to turn around and go back to Des Moines. When he saw her looking at the sky, he glanced up, too. There was nothing around them, and the stars were bright and numerous.

"Want to stop for a bit?" he asked.

"Yes," she said, without looking at him.

He drove down the road, away from the highway, and pulled off to the side. They got out and looked up. "Wow," he said. "I've never seen this many stars in my life."

"They're beautiful, aren't they? I haven't been out this far to see them in…forever."

He looked at the sky in awe. "I can't believe this was above me this whole time and I never bothered to look."

"You're just new, that's all. You can't really see them near the cities because of the lights from the buildings and smog from the factories."

They moved to the top of the car, lying on their backs. They stayed there nearly an hour just staring, and then they started talking again. She pointed out constellations, the Milky Way, other galaxies, shooting stars, and satellites.

"Do you think humans will ever go out there?" she asked.

"Where, in space?"

"Yes."

"No."

"You'd think with all the technology we have today—I mean, even your car seems like it could go out there."

"Yeah, but what's the point? There's no reason to waste resources and send anyone out there. Satellites are the only things worth sending up. If there were a reason to go, we would have been there by now. The sky just isn't that useful to us." It's what they were taught in school, anyway. He pondered that for a moment. "How do you know so much about the stars?"

"I went camping a lot when I was young. My father showed me all of them and told me all the stories. You wouldn't believe what people used to think about the stars. They had whole religions devoted to them."

Chris did not know if that was true or just stories her father made up, but he looked at the stars with this new knowledge, and they seemed to change. People long ago looked at these same stars. "I can understand why they would. It's hard to think there isn't something bigger than us out there when you look at a sky like this."

They looked in silence for a few minutes more before she spoke again.

"My father believed humans went to the moon," she confessed.

Chris tried to hide his laughter, but then they both burst out laughing.

"Really?" he asked.

"Yes. He used to say there is a flag up there, the old American flag, and bootprints to prove it."

"Bootprints."

"No wind to blow them away."

Chris was silent for a minute, looking at the moon. "I'm sorry, but I have to say your father was nuts."

Jenna laughed. "I know. He was in love with the old America. He talked about it all the time."

Chris looked at her, alarmed. It was forbidden to talk about the time before The War, before the nation-states joined to become The Sectors.

Jenna looked back at him, unfazed. "He said people were free back then, to do whatever job they wanted, to live wherever they wanted, to marry whomever they wanted." She turned to look back up at the sky. "Can you imagine?"

He continued looking at her. Hesitantly, he asked, "Do you think he was telling the truth?"

"Maybe. He wasn't the only one who said that. My mother would sometimes slip up and say things, but my history professor talked the most."

"Your professor?" Chris asked, shocked. "You went to college?"

"Yes. But I couldn't finish before I was redistributed to Des Moines. I was planning on becoming an art teacher, but I loved history, too." She looked at Chris. "My history professor would always go on these rants, going on and on about how we are not free. I'm sure she was arrested for it, but she didn't care about the threat. She would say it was worth it for us to hear someone say it."

"We are free, though."

"Yes," she agreed unconvincingly.

"You don't think so?"

"I go back and forth about it in my mind, but I usually end up agreeing that we are better off now than how it was before The War," she said. "What about you?"

"We're safe," he said with strong conviction. "We don't have to worry. Everything is in order. Poverty and homelessness have been eliminated. Aside from Mexico, the world is one nation, divided into three Sectors. Continued redistribution ensures the flow of genetics and culture. We don't have to worry about war between countries or disputes among groups. Disease has been completely eradicated."

"But we can't travel to the other Sectors. We can't even travel outside of Des Moines, except in your government car, which may still be illegal," she protested.

"My boss would cover for us."

"I couldn't go alone."

"Where would you go?"

She looked up at the sky. "My father used to tell me of places he went when he was a boy, places across the ocean that are now in the Central Sector and places that are now uninhabitable. His family used to travel all the time, wherever they wanted to go, whenever they wanted to go, without any sort of permit or permission."

"Wasn't it dangerous?" Chris asked.

"It was worth the risk for them."

Chris had never heard anybody talk about the time before The War, let alone like this. "What happened to him? Wasn't your father arrested for talking about it?"

"I don't know," she said. "I haven't seen him or heard from him in a very long time."

"Maybe he fled to Mexico," Chris suggested. "The old America he described sounds just like Mexico is today."

"I doubt it," she said. "We grew up in the house his great-grandfather built. He would rather die than leave his home."

They stared up at the sky another few minutes in silence, and then she said, "Thank you for bringing me here. I certainly couldn't have come alone or with anyone else."

Chris looked at her and was overcome with a deep sense of appreciation. He had shared the secret of his job with her, and she showed him that she was a safe place for his secrets. Now she was speaking freely with him. Not only could she never have come out here alone or with anyone else, but she also could never have spoken as freely about these topics with anyone else. He wanted to show her that her secrets would find safety in him, too. "No," he said. "Thank *you* for showing *me*."

Chris looked back up at the stars, imagining Jenna with her father while he told her these stories. He did not know which was more discomforting: that her father talked about it that way or that he might have been telling the truth, that the world before The War was not as awful as they had been taught in school.

He thought of Jenna growing up in a house her great-great-grandfather had built. What was the world like when he built his house? And why would anyone ever want to regress back to it?

The world before The War, they were taught, was like modern-day Mexico: disorganized and full of crime, overpopulated without any tracking of people, no knowledge of where people were and what dangers could be around, violence and drugs rampant, poverty and homelessness and diseases, people without jobs and jobs to be done without people to do them, babies being born without permission or genetic modifications before systems and society were ready for them, people marrying and moving around at random. They were taught that Mexico was backwards like the old world, not progressive like The Sectors.

But to hear Jenna talk about the old America her father described without fear or disgust made him wonder if the world before The War—and modern-day Mexico, for that matter—was really as bad as they were taught.

Then, he thought about the conversation with Xiao, about a boss position opening up in regards to relations with Mexico. He wondered if maybe that was what he *would* like to do next. Maybe it was time to see for himself how Mexico was dealing with the state of the world. Maybe it was time to stop listening to what everyone was telling him about it and start seeing it for himself.

As he thought of his future life as a boss in the Department of Mexico Relations, he could not fathom it without Jenna. He imagined the rest of his life like this, living in the safe space that existed between the two of them, where they could explore the internal worlds of each other and openly ponder the external universe they lived in without fear or shame or embarrassment. He knew now was not the right time to ask her to come back to Washington, D.C., with him, not with how much he had put on her already that day, but he knew he would ask her at some point. Still looking at the sky, he found her hand and interlaced his fingers with hers.

11

As five o'clock grew nearer on Monday afternoon, Jenna grew increasingly excited about their trip to Idaho. She and Chris had spent a fabulous weekend together, and she could not wait to go on a trip with him. She was already packed and ready to go even though their plane was not scheduled to leave until the following morning.

She finished setting up everything necessary for her absence at work and was preparing to leave when a man appeared in the doorway of her office. As soon as she saw him, she felt all the blood drain from her face. She hoped she could at least talk to Chris again before being redistributed, if not have the chance to give him some sort of explanation.

"Good afternoon, Jenna," the man said as he walked into her office and shut the door.

Jenna took a deep breath and stood up to greet him, shaking his hand and offering for him to sit in the chair across from her. When she sat down, she held her hands in her lap to keep them from making nervous gestures while she asked, "Can I at least say goodbye to someone before we leave?"

"I'm not here to relocate you," her protection agent said. "I'm here to deliver news and discuss options. But you are not being relocated, not yet."

"Okay," she said and pulled out her phone. "Let me just send a message that I will be late." She sent Chris a message telling him she had to work late while the man sat down at her desk. She put her phone back in her purse and looked at the agent sitting across from her, giving him her full attention.

The man leaned forward and put his elbows on his knees. "It's not agency policy to keep our clients updated on any information regarding their previous lives. As you know, we discourage any contact or searching any aspect of your life from before you went into hiding. So we typically refrain from relating any information regarding former friends or family members so as not to tempt anyone to make contact."

Jenna nodded her head. She remembered all of this from her initial briefings with the Protection Agency.

"So," he continued, "this is not an invitation for you to break that rule."

Jenna nodded again and said, "I understand."

"But," he continued, "we do keep track of the major players in a person's life before they went into hiding, mainly people who might be a source of danger, who we track constantly. We also track close friends and family on a semiannual basis, to ensure there is no cause for concern for the clients in our protection."

Jenna nodded her head again, encouraging him to continue.

"Jenna," he said, "I am so sorry to tell you this, but in our most recent check for your family, we discovered that they are all deceased, your parents and your siblings, but not your in-laws or nieces and nephews."

Jenna did not move or breathe. It was the last thing she expected to hear from him. She slowly started to exhale. *My family?* she thought. She had not thought of her family in years. She had never expected to see or talk to her family again. She did not want to.

"We were not going to mention it, as the deaths were not connected—not to each other, nor to your case—but when your brother Adam died of a heart attack last week here in Des Moines—"

Jenna inhaled sharply, and her eyes grew wide.

"We decided we should ask you about it." The man's forehead was creased, and his eyes were concerned. "We were afraid he was here for you, to tell you, maybe, about your parents, sisters, and brother. He had no business here and used a false name to travel. But there was also no indication that he knew you were here. His hotel room and luggage were searched, and there was no indication of why he was even here at all. That's actually what concerned us, what made us decide to get in touch with you about it. Did he contact you, Jenna? If he was here for you, that means he found you somehow. And if he was able to find you, then others could, too."

Jenna shook her head. *A heart attack,* she thought. *He was too young to die that way.* She thought about how stressful his life and his business endeavors must have become for him to meet such a fate. "A heart attack," she said. Then, she asked, "Are you sure?"

The man opened his mouth to say something but looked visibly uncomfortable pointing out that her brother did not have the Modified genome that would have prevented such a death. Instead he just nodded. Then, seriously, he asked again, "Were you in contact with him?"

"No, he did not contact me," she said. "But I do think I should be relocated, just in case."

The man nodded in agreement. "Okay," he said. "We'll make arrangements immediately." He started to stand up.

"But," she said, and the man sat back down. "If it's okay, I'd like to wait until this weekend. I'll be safe until then, and I was actually going to contact the Protection Agency, anyway, to tell you I have plans to go to Idaho tomorrow and will be returning Friday morning."

"Yes," the agent said, "with Christopher Rockford."

Jenna relaxed at the sound of Chris's name, more content now, knowing her protection agent already knew about him.

"He got a travel permit for you both a few hours ago," the protection agent continued. "Do you feel like you will be okay with him?"

"Yes," Jenna said, and she was about to go on when the protection agent continued.

"As a businessman in the textile industry, he does a lot of traveling for work, but he checks out. We have no concern about him."

Jenna kept a straight face, careful not to let her confusion show, but she understood that the protection agent did not know who Chris was, that the branch of government Chris worked for must have been secret, even from other branches of government.

"He has no connection to you, your family, or your case," the man concluded. "But be careful, Jenna," he said. "When you relocate, it will mean breaking all ties with him as well."

He stood up to leave, and Jenna stood up, too.

"Is there anything else I can do for you?" he asked.

"No," Jenna said. "Thank you so much for coming and telling me."

"You come back Friday morning?"

"Yes, I'll be back by the afternoon. We are hosting a gala at the museum that I cannot miss."

The man nodded slowly. "Someone will contact you on Saturday, then. We can take care of your work, or you can tell your boss you are leaving, if you'd like."

"Thank you," Jenna said, and the man left her office.

She sat back down at the desk, thinking about Chris. She knew at this point she could no longer put off telling him more about herself, even though she had sworn to the Protection Agency she would never tell anyone about her life before going into hiding. She would be relocated, with or without him. He had been very patient with her guard, and she owed it to him to let it down completely.

12

When they arrived in Boise in the early afternoon, they did not stay to see the city, which was nearly identical to Des Moines, in the fashion of all Inland cities. Instead, they rented an Inland car and took a leisurely drive to the town where Chris had grown up. The two-hour drive was similar to the plane ride in that they did not talk very much, content to sit next to each other and enjoy the scenery.

Eventually, she broke the silence. "I've never seen mountains like that."

"Really?" He turned down the radio that neither was listening to.

"No, only hills." She continued looking at the mountain range, thinking about what it must have been like for Chris to grow up with this around him, what it must have been like to grow up in the Inland.

"If you're up for it, we can hike up one of them tomorrow."

"Really?" she asked with excitement.

"Yeah, the one I have in mind is kind of strenuous, but it's worth it. You feel like you're on top of the world when you're on a mountain."

"I can imagine," she said. "What else are we going to do while we're here?"

"I thought I'd just show you around where I grew up and maybe go kayaking or something. We don't have to, though. I come here all the time, so we can do whatever you want to do." He took her hand, and they were silent again while she stared out the window.

When they got closer to town, he turned to go to the waterfalls nearby.

"I didn't come here often as a kid, but it's too beautiful not to show you while we're here," he said as he pulled into the parking lot.

They got out of the car and went on a path to take a closer look. Away from the city, the air was fresh, and the falls were loud and as clear as the sky above. Jenna closed her eyes and listened to the water for a few minutes. She looked alive, relaxed, and even free. They stayed at the park for nearly half an hour before driving back into town, where he led her on the footpath out to the middle of the bridge that crossed the canyon.

"Not coming too close to the edge?" he teased, as she stood a few feet away and shook her head. It occurred to him that if she never saw canyons like this before, she may have never been out on a bridge like this before, either. It also confirmed his suspicion that she was not really from Utah.

"We could jump if you want," he said, looking at her mischievously. Then, he added, "Not right now, of course. We don't have any parachutes."

"And…why would we jump?" she asked.

"For fun," he said like it was obvious. He turned back to look down at the canyon.

"Oh," she said, still not coming to the edge. She tried to relax, but watching him lean over the railing sent a tingling sensation throughout her skin.

"This is a good place to do it, during the daytime, of course." He turned back to her. "Want to learn? I have all the equipment at my house."

"Well," she said, trying to be polite and not hurt his feelings, "no, not really."

He laughed and walked back to her. "You okay?" he asked as he took her hand and led her back to the car.

"Have you ever done it?" she asked him. Then, remembering what he just said, she added, "Or is there a different reason you have the materials at your house?" She was more relaxed now that they were walking toward solid ground. Holding his hand helped, too.

"I was fifteen the first time I did it. It wasn't so bad, but I rarely jump these days. My brother still does a jump every time he visits. He's the reason we still have the gear for it. He likes to do flips and tricks and stuff, but I find it kind of boring."

"Of course you do," she said.

They took a path that went under the bridge and to another park. He pointed in one direction. "That's where the falls are, but you can't see them from here." Then, he turned the other direction and pointed to a neighborhood on the opposite side of the canyon. "That's where my house is."

Even at a distance, she could see it was not like the rows of townhouses where she lived in Des Moines that had taken over all the Inland cities. She looked around in awe of the view.

"It's so beautiful here," she said. She looked around once more, seeing a view that was, for the first time in years, not Des Moines. She sat on a small boulder, and Chris sat next to her.

In silence, he watched her take it all in.

They went to the store for groceries, and when they got to his family's house, he made dinner for her before settling in. After they ate dinner, he got their bags from the car and showed her the room where she would sleep. They had not yet spent the night together, and he wanted her to be comfortable, so he chose the best room for her, which was at the opposite end of the house from his own room.

The house was entirely different from what she had expected, nothing like anything she had seen in Des Moines, much too big and too nice to be a typical Inland home. It was a ranch-style house with several wings. Unlike the house she had grown up in, this one was not nearly as big. Also unlike her own house growing up, there were framed printed pictures of his family everywhere. Evidence that they lived here was everywhere she looked. Though they were not nice frames, not the quality of the things she had grown up with on the Coast, she marveled that an Inland household could afford to maintain a house like this one. Her eyes darted from frame to frame. She was eager to see it all. Watching her, Chris remembered the walls of her townhouse, bare except for a few cheap pieces of printed art.

Chris put her bags in the room where she would stay and left her, shutting the door behind him so she could get ready for bed in privacy. The room was large with a bed and a sitting area. It reminded her of her own room growing up.

She took a few minutes to look at the pictures that were on the dresser. Chris's parents were younger than hers, both with black hair and dark brown eyes, like Chris and his brother. She picked up one of the photos and looked at it more closely. Chris must have taken the candid picture because he was not in it. In the photo, his parents and his brother were laughing so hard that their eyes were forced shut by their wide smiles. His father had dark skin, so much so that in this photo with its terrible lighting all she could see were his teeth and the outline of his clothes. His mother was a light-skinned Asian woman with big teeth that made her smile naturally contagious. Chris got his eyes, dimples, and charming smile from her, but he got his tall broad build from his father. Chris's skin was darker than his brother's but not nearly as dark as their father's. Chris's brother, who was shorter than Chris, resembled their mother more and had softer features than Chris did, but even his skin was not as light as hers. Though features of their parents were uniquely present in each of the two boys, they looked so much like each other that their relation was undeniable.

For one fleeting moment, Jenna wondered what Chris and his brother might have looked like, had their parents been able to afford the cosmetic modifications the wealthier class chose when having children. Though she herself was not opposed to genetic modifications that contributed to health and well-being, the cosmetics of it baffled her the most when she thought about the parents of her Modified Coastal classmates and friends growing up. Some of her friends did not resemble their parents in the slightest bit. Would their parents have loved them as much if they had not designed them so? She remembered her first day in the Inland, how seeing so many parents with children who resembled themselves, even though they were Modified, had warmed her heart.

She examined Chris's brother in the photograph she was holding and in others on the dresser. He appeared to be the more outgoing and less guarded of the two. Just from the way he posed in the photos, she could tell he was friendly and outspoken, probably someone people instantly looked at when he walked into a room. Older siblings had that quality about them, she thought, recalling her own eldest sister Karen. And she thought again about how, like herself, Chris was so different from his family. His parents and brother seemed so much more relaxed and less serious.

She put the photo back on the dresser and realized she was smiling. Smiling without meaning to was another thing Chris had brought back into her life.

The bathroom was rich, with real marble—not vinyl flooring—and she marveled at Chris's parents being able to pull that off. They must have made themselves invaluable to the Coastals they worked for to be allowed to have such flooring. She took her time showering, allowing the steam to warm her body and fill her lungs. When she was done, she wrapped a towel around herself, and even it felt warm around her. This whole house did.

She sat at the vanity to brush her hair and moisturize her face. Though not nearly as nice as the things she had grown up with, it had been years since she had been surrounded by such luxury. She felt at home.

She looked around the room, at the floors and at the intricately carved wooden dresser and bed frame. She looked back at herself in the mirror, looking deeply into her own eyes. Then, she nodded in agreement to her reflection as if it had given her an order, pulled out the case for her contacts, filled it with solution, and removed them from her eyes and put them away.

When she came out of her room, she heard him in the kitchen.

"Would you like some hot cocoa?" he asked, stirring liquid chocolate in a saucepan. He was facing away from her.

"*That?*" she asked, pointing to it excitedly.

"I'll add milk in a minute," he said, as if she had been worried.

"I'll take mine without." She hugged him from behind, putting her arms around his waist and looking around his shoulder at the steaming beverage.

"I know it looks delicious as it is, but the milk tones it down."

"That's what I'm afraid of," she said and walked to the table and sat down, watching him.

He poured some for her and added milk to his. Then, he brought the cups over to where she sat, and he saw her eyes. "Whoa."

"I know you already know I wear contacts."

"You have the most beautiful eyes I've ever seen."

"Sure," she said matter-of-factly.

"No, really. They're bright dark blue. They look like the ocean on Rhode Island's coast. I'm sorry you cover them up." He looked at her more closely and saw the light, nearly orange freckles on her face and arms, not hidden by makeup. "I take it you naturally have red hair."

"More of an auburn color, darker in the winter than in the summer."

He sat down next to her. "I wish I could see it."

"You know, my nanny used to make us homemade hot chocolate all the time." She blew gently on the drink to cool it down.

"This is my mom's recipe. I grew up on it," he said, patting his stomach.

She rolled her eyes at his implication that he had any fat on his body. "My mom would never make hot chocolate. She never made anything, actually."

"Not a good cook?"

"And she was pretty clumsy, to be honest. The kitchen just wasn't her thing. Actually, not much was. She was just kind of a gorgeous socialite type that came from old money and married old money and didn't work and didn't raise her own kids and didn't have any hobbies except shopping and gossiping and hosting lavish parties."

"Sounds like she was a busy woman."

Jenna saw through his attempt to make it sound wonderful. "No, don't be polite. I hardly ever saw her. I was much closer to my father, but he was never around, either. He was a businessman and was always away on trips." She blew some more on her hot chocolate.

"So you were closest to your nanny?"

"In a way, I guess. I was really close to my best friend's mom, to be honest. She was sweet and kind and caring and accepting. She loved everybody. I never heard her say anything bad about anyone, not even my family. She and my best friend were the two most beautiful women I've ever known." She blew gently once more, careful not to blow any of the liquid over the side of the cup. "They were a Purebred family, too, but they were far less grudging about the law than my family. It wasn't that my friend's mom supported The Ban. She just never let anything interfere with her own happiness. I admired her and wanted to be just like her when I grew up."

"Are you?" he asked intently.

She laughed lightly. "I hope so. I'm at least nothing like *my* family. They were not so accepting. They hated Modifieds, but I think that was just because they didn't know any who were as rich as they were. They viewed Modifieds as weak and dependent on the government and unwilling to stand up for themselves."

"Is that why you went to Iowa, to get away from them?" Chris asked, knowing it was finally the time that he would know for himself why she was in Des Moines and where she had come from.

"No, actually." She paused and took a deep breath. "I am going to tell you this, but you have to understand that I justify myself telling you this because you work for the government and because I feel safe with you."

"I'll keep your secret," he said.

"I'm not supposed to tell *anyone* this."

He nodded.

"Anyway," she continued, "I know you suspected that I was in hiding, and I am. I wasn't working late last night. I was meeting with my protection agent. He made a surprise visit and told me I'm going to be relocated soon, as early as Saturday." She looked him in the eyes. "I know I'm not supposed to, but I want to stay in contact with you after I relocate, if it's possible."

Chris nodded his head. "We'll make it work. Why are you in Protection?"

She took another deep breath. "It happened when I was twenty years old, during my third year at college. One night—I lived with my boyfriend at the time—a group of guys broke into our apartment while we were sleeping. They were part of some Mexican gang or something, and they targeted my boyfriend for some reason." She put her hands up in defense. "I promise he was not into any shady business or anything. I don't know why they targeted him, but for some reason they did." She put her hands back around her cup of hot chocolate. "My boyfriend got up and told them to leave, and one of the guys shot him in the head, point-blank, right in front of me. Then, another one shot me."

She pulled her shirt down over her freckled shoulder to show him the scar. He stood up and examined it, like a physician would, while she continued talking.

"My boyfriend died instantly. I was sitting up in the bed when I was shot."

He looked back at her, replacing the neckline of her shirt back over her shoulder, and sat down.

"They assumed I was dead, too, and left. In actuality, I passed out, and I guess our neighbors called the police. The next thing I remember is waking up in the hospital. When the detectives interviewed me, they told me I would have to testify, but for my own safety, they suggested that I join the Protection Program and go into hiding after the testimony. So, I told them everything, and I testified against the guys that did it, and then I became Jenna Macklemore from Iowa." She paused before adding, "Actually, my official file says I'm from Utah and that I was redistributed to Des Moines after high school."

He did not bother asking her what her name used to be, knowing it was unwise for her to ever say it out loud, lest she become desensitized to saying it. He knew all too well from his extensive training that habits could save or kill a person. For her own safety, he hoped she had long forgotten her old name.

"I'm so sorry," he said.

She shrugged and took a sip of her hot chocolate. "Wow. This is amazing."

"Thanks," he said, and then he asked, "Was it hard?"

"To testify? No, they killed the man I loved. I was mad, and I wanted justice. I didn't care that I had to drop everything and go somewhere and be someone else. He was all I had, so when he was gone, so was I."

"It wasn't hard, though, to leave your family like that? Once you're in the Program, you can never contact them again."

"I was already estranged from them by that time. After I woke up from the coma in Texas after the car accident, I never went back home. But my family paid for all the surgeries, I know." She paused and then added, "I never even thanked them." Her voice cracked as she said the last sentence, and tears sprang to her eyes. She quickly blinked them away. She had never had any intention of returning to them, but as she spoke, she realized that now it was not even an option.

Chris reached out and took her hand.

"I never got along with my family, and they always hated me for not conforming to their ideals. For someone else, it would have been hard not to go back, I guess, but I had never felt any attachment to them. I just wasn't like them. It *was* hard, however, when I thought about my best friend's mother, who I always pretended was my own mother. I always thought I'd go back and see her someday. That was very difficult, knowing I would never be able to see her again, to never be able to talk to her about the accident, nor mourn the loss of her daughter with her. It's the one thing I wish I had done before going into Protection, to let her know that I'm okay."

Chris stayed silent, allowing her to collect her thoughts, not wanting to interrupt her memories.

She sighed. "So, that's how I ended up in Iowa," she said, finally.

"That's fascinating," he said. "I don't think I could ever do something that courageous."

"I assure you, it wasn't courageous. Courageous would have been to take the gun that was under the nightstand and shoot them before they escaped."

"You had a gun?" Chris asked. "How?"

She shrugged. "It wasn't mine. It was my boyfriend's gun. He had connections with Mexico. Maybe those connections had something to do with why the gang came after him." She thought for a moment. "Maybe that's why he had a gun, because he knew they might come after him. He wasn't a Modified, but he wasn't really a Purebred, either. His family had escaped the old South America before it was destroyed and had immigrated before the Ban on Mexican Immigration." She took another sip of her drink. "Anyway, I should have shot them.

Now, they're in prison and could possibly get out on parole someday."

"No, it was good that you passed out. If you shot them, they would have known you were still alive and would have made sure you died. Passing out probably saved your life." Then, as an afterthought he added, "And if you want, I can make sure they *never* get out. I could make sure they die in prison."

She smiled and laughed lightly, knowing he was joking. Then, she remembered his job, and for a fleeting moment, she allowed herself to seriously consider the option and the idea that he could make this problem disappear. "No, that's okay," she decided. "It wouldn't be right."

He sat there staring at her, unsure if he had ever admired or respected anyone as much as he admired and respected her in that moment.

Then, he said, "I still think it was courageous of you to testify against them. I could never do that if it meant breaking all ties. I am way too attached to my family for that sort of thing."

She looked around the house at all the pictures and personal touches. "You seem like you had a much different upbringing than I had."

He nodded in agreement.

She yawned and then said, "Sorry, I guess I'm tired."

"No, that's okay. It's late, and we should get some sleep for the hike tomorrow."

They got up, and Chris took their empty cups to the sink. *A Mexican gang*, he thought. Then, he remembered what Zaire had said about a single unnamed witness.

He went to his bag and pulled out his notebook and pulled up the photo of Raul, the Mexican man he had seen in Des Moines.

"Jenna?" he called to her as he walked down the hallway to her room.

She stopped at her door and turned around to face him.

"This isn't one of the gang members, is it?" he asked, handing her the notebook.

She froze, and he caught the notebook when it fell out of her hand. "Where did you get that?"

"Was he there?" His voice was strong but not harsh, just enough to have alarm without fear.

"No, but he looks almost exactly like the man who shot me. Why do you have that?"

"Come in here. Sit down." He led her to the bed so she could sit. Her face was pale, and she looked like she was about to faint. He said, "Take some deep breaths. Do you want some water?"

"No, I'm okay," she said and took two deep breaths as he had suggested. Then, calmer now, she again asked, "Why do you have that?"

"When I saw him coincidentally more than three times in Des Moines, I looked him up. Actually"—he looked down—"that's the real reason I looked up that other guy, the one at the hotel where you had your business meeting."

He ran Raul's face on a program, and a map with a flashing dot appeared on the screen. He tapped on it with his finger, and a real-time video started streaming from the location on the map.

"It's a security camera from the street. See, he's there." He pointed to a Mexican man walking on the sidewalk, and the program zoomed in on Raul's face. As he walked out of view from that camera, the screen changed to another one nearby that had the closest image of him, this time on someone's cell phone. "It's tracking him now." The screen changed again as the Mexican man kept walking. "When I thought he might be following me, I looked up his real-time data and saw you in the lounge talking to that other man." He laughed to himself, somewhat embarrassed. "So, naturally, I had to look *him* up to see what my competition was. When I saw that he was dangerous, I had to get him away from you."

He thought for a minute. "I looked him up, just as a precaution, but I knew he wasn't following me because I only saw him when I was with you."

He was talking objectively, but a knot formed in the pit of her stomach as she realized what he was saying.

"First, the bar the night I arrived, then the diner, then the steakhouse." He turned to face her. "But I didn't see him when I went out by myself before our date, nor when I was walking around the city by myself the next day." He turned to look straight ahead again. "But he was at the lounge that night, where you were. I can't believe I didn't put it together. I can't believe I get paid to stalk—" Turning back to her, he stopped mid-sentence when he saw the fear on her face as she stared at him with bewilderment.

"He's following me?" She whispered it, barely able to get the words out. "How did I not see him? I've always been so cautious. I—"

"It's okay," he said, trying to soothe her. "It's going to be okay. Look"—he pointed to the screen on the notebook—"he's still in Des Moines."

"But what if there are others?"

Chris got up, and Jenna followed him as he made sure the doors around the house were locked. He got another notebook from his bag and got his phone. She followed him to a closet in the center of the house. He pulled off a piece of the wall to reveal a metal box. With a wire cord, he connected his notebook to the box.

"Is that—?" she started to ask, pointing at the wire. They were illegal, banned and confiscated before she was born. She had seen them, but she never thought an Inland house occupied by law-abiding citizens like his parents, with a son who worked in government no less, would have them.

"It's for extra security measures," he said. "To ensure I have enough power."

She sat down next to him, and he showed her the notebook. He started setting it, swiping in codes and switching programs.

"I'm going to set it up so that it signals an alarm if anyone comes within a fifty foot radius of my phone."

"How will it know if someone comes close?"

He hesitated, unsure if he should tell her. Having worked in Surveillance, he knew that while the street cameras and retina scanners were well known to the public, much of the rest of the surveillance measures were entirely unknown to the general population. There were even measures he did not know about, he was sure, since he no longer worked in the Department of Surveillance. "In training, we were taught that after The War, the population was a 'manageable size.' "

She stared blankly at him, not knowing what he was talking about.

He continued, "They set up a system so that people are tracked, and now we do this with retina scans on roadways and at every doorway, as you know. But there are also heat signatures from satellites and drones, paired with gait and facial recognition software to track people with cameras. When I showed you the Mexican man on the security camera, it used facial recognition software so that we could visualize his location as more than just a dot on a map." He paused to make sure she understood. Then, he continued, "So, what this program does, basically, is to alert the satellite of my phone's position and create a sphere of space around its signal so that if any biometric signatures, other than ours, come within the fifty foot radius, an alarm automatically sounds."

She sat for a moment, thinking and processing what he had just told her. "It tracks *everybody* at *all times*?"

He nodded, not understanding the surprise in her voice. Everybody knew they were tracked. People did not mind as long as they were doing nothing wrong. People did not mind as long as it would catch criminals, especially the criminals his department went after.

"And you're okay with that?" she asked.

He wondered if she was joking. "Of course. It's to protect the citizens."

"Is it tracking our signatures now?"

"No. Mine are prevented from being accessed. It's a precaution so I am not detected by people who might be able to hack into the data. You can never be too cautious. Yours are a bit complicated, not just because you don't have the easily tracked genetically modified retina patterns but also because you are in Protection. The Protection Agency usually keeps the data of their clients in-house. That is, for the ones they protect, the signal only goes to them and is blocked from being accessed, even from other government agencies. But your signatures may be picked up by my satellites if the Protection Agency expects you to be in Des Moines and opens your signatures to be tracked so they can find you more efficiently."

"They know I'm in Idaho. I told my protection agent when he told me I might be in danger."

Chris held his phone up. "I have to set it so our signatures do not trigger the alarm. Mine are already in the program, but I need to enter yours manually since I can't access them from the Protection Agency's satellite."

She nodded in agreement, overwhelmed with the information he was giving her but reassured by her trust in him.

He told her to look into a point on his phone, and he scanned her retina. Then, he did the other eye. He held the phone next to his notebook, and a red light on each device flashed, indicating they were synced. He held the phone up again to perform a more general scan of her features, enough so the program could easily identify her with the satellite he was using.

As he did the scan and set more parameters for the program on his notebook, she said, "I feel so stupid. How did I not see him? How long has he been following me?"

"Not long enough for you to be in danger. The Protection Agency keeps track of these things, too. They know how often you come in contact with people, and they have programs that recognize patterns. If he got too close to your home or work too often, they would have relocated you already. It's just a coincidence that I found out now." He had finished setting up the alarm by this point and was crouching next to her.

"Come here," he said and pulled her close to him and kissed the top of her head. For an instant, he was angry with the Protection Agency for not telling her about Raul, for he was sure that was why she was going to be relocated. He considered why they would keep such information from her when it could help her be more cautious. But maybe they did not want to scare her. Or maybe they really did not know about him, and it was just a routine change in location for extra precaution. Thinking of how they may not have known about him—or any others—made him angry at himself. He should have caught this. He decided he would ask Zaire to check signature patterns when they got back, to see if he could find any more people related to the gang that might have been following her. If they were coordinating their efforts, then they could plan a way to take revenge without triggering the Protection Agency's algorithms and alarms. "You should definitely relocate," he said into her ear.

"Come on," he said, standing up. He held his hand out to her, and she took it as he helped her stand. "The alarm is set. No one will get to you now. Let's try to rest."

She looked down the hallway toward her room and then back at Chris. "Will you stay with me tonight?" Then, she quickly added, "I know this house is secure, but…" She trailed off, not wanting to admit she did not actually trust any of the technology he had just shown her, at least not as much as she trusted his physical proximity.

He stayed serious. "Of course."

He went to her room with her, bringing his phone with him. He lay on his back and put his arm around her when she put her head on his chest. He swallowed hard, trying to focus on sleep, and not her body touching his. Looking up into the darkness, he said, "We can still talk if you're too awake now. I know that's a lot to take in."

"I just feel like such an idiot," she said.

He lightly stroked the top of her head. "You shouldn't." Chris thought about all the times he had seen Raul and added, "Now that I think about it, every time I saw him, your back was turned or he was well hidden from your view."

"Ugh." She made a noise of disgust. "That's so creepy to think about."

"Then, please never remember how good I am at being invisible."

His comment made her laugh. "Okay, I'll try not to."

Smiling in response to her laughter, he moved his hand and started rubbing her back.

"I have a confession to make," she said.

"Okay."

"I was going to ask you to stay in my room tonight, anyway." She rolled onto her stomach so she could face him, resting her head on one hand and draping her other arm across his chest. "But I chickened out when you put my bag in this room and yours in the room that is the farthest away from this one."

He laughed lightly, like he had been caught in the act of something embarrassing. She involuntarily glanced down at his stomach when she felt his muscles tighten under her arm as he shifted his shoulders back and propped himself up on his elbows.

"This is the nicest room, and...honestly, I didn't know what to do."

She pressed her lips together and stifled a laugh, which only resulted in him smiling at the awkwardness and her giggling.

"It's okay," she said as she rolled back on her side and nestled up to him. "We can just sleep, if that is all you want to do."

When he did not move or respond, she propped herself up on her side so she could again face him.

His eyes had adjusted to the darkness of the room, and he gently stroked the strands of her hair that were brushing against his arm. He looked back into her eyes and said, "It's not all I want to do."

13

When Jenna woke early Wednesday morning, Chris had already packed up the car and was making breakfast for them. She had expected to wake up with a feeling of regret for having told him so much about herself, for sharing secrets that she had vowed never to tell anyone. She expected to feel sick from learning she'd been followed for so long. But instead, she just felt safer around him, physically and, more importantly, emotionally. Now he knew her, and she was not hiding anything from him. And he was hiding nothing from her. He acted like it was the most normal thing in the world for her to have gone into hiding. And why not? He was always hiding.

They left after breakfast, and after an hour of driving, Chris pulled over and parked on the side of the road. He got two backpacks from the back of the car and handed her the lighter one.

"Is this too heavy?" he asked.

She put it on and said, "Not at all."

"It's about ten miles roundtrip," he continued. "It's a pretty steep hike with no official trail. We don't have to go all the way to the top, but I promise it's worth it if we do."

"Then let's do it," she said as she tightened the straps of the backpack.

They started up the mountain at a slight incline. After nearly two hours, they reached a small lake. Jenna stared at it, marveling that she could see straight to the bottom, despite the reflection of the mountains around them.

Watching her, Chris sat on a boulder and pulled out a couple bottles of waters. She looked up and around her and then at him. He held a bottle of water out to her, and she took it as she thanked him and sat next to him.

They sat in silence, she taking it all in, he not wanting to disrupt her thoughts.

After another hour of hiking, the path became dramatically steeper, and their breaks became more frequent. She was breathing heavily, as the incline got steeper with each increase in elevation, but she was smiling.

They eventually got to the top of the mountain, and Chris led her around the last of the boulders and watched her as they stepped into the clearing, where the view was no longer obscured and the vast mountain range stretched out before them. She stopped and stood in awe for a few minutes, staring at the expansive beauty. There had been snippets of the view through the trees on the way up, but she had never seen anything like this before. It was wondrous, almost too much for her to comprehend.

She continued walking, and to one side, she could see more mountains. To another side, she could see a valley and a river. It was the most magnificent scenery she had ever seen in her life.

Chris took his backpack off and set it on the ground. He walked over to her and pulled at the straps of the backpack that she was wearing, and she let him take it off of her. Instead of setting it next to his, he held it and continued to stand next to her and look around at the scenery with her.

"You grew up with *this*," she said, pausing to stretch her hands out toward the mountains, "all around you."

He took a deep breath, inhaling the familiar air of the trees and damp soil, and nodded his head slowly as he exhaled and smiled back at her with pride.

She laughed, and a broad grin slowly appeared on her face. "This is breathtaking."

"I can't believe you've never been to the mountains before. You know these aren't even the mountains Coastals talk about when they refer to their ski holidays and vacations."

"No, I'm sure these are awful by comparison." She looked out again at the vast expanse, the rawness of it all, the emptiness filled with so many new and exciting and unfamiliar details to be explored. "I can't imagine what it must have been like to grow up here." She looked back at him. He did not look as stunned as she. "Does it no longer have an effect on you? Did it ever?"

"Did the ocean lose its effect on you? Did it ever have an effect on you?"

She pushed him away playfully, and he caught her hand and held it. They looked into each other's eyes, and she said, "Tell me more about it. How did your parents end up here? And what was it like growing up in this small town in the Inland?"

"I've told you," he said.

"No, you haven't. Not really. Not now that I'm here and can imagine it."

He shrugged. "It was...Inland," he began. "My parents were both redistributed to Boise after The War, and they met and got married there. My father moved up in the company he worked for, and when the Coastal owner decided to move part of the business out here, he chose my father to manage it."

He led her over to a fallen tree that was not too close to the edge of the cliff. They sat down, and he continued, "My father has a way with Coastal businessmen. He's a nice guy and a reliable worker. As the manager, he got a nice house and a decent stipend, and I think that's when he and my mother decided to apply for the Child License for my brother and me." He stopped and looked at her.

"And?" she asked. "What was it like growing up in the Inland?"

"I don't know how to answer that," he said. "It was…what it was. What was it like growing up on the Coast?"

She made a sound of defeat. "I mean"—she stretched her arms out toward the mountains—"what was it like having parents who worked, I mean *really* worked? My mom did not work. My father was a businessman, but he didn't really work in the sense of leaving the house and coming back at the same time every day. Most of the time he worked from home when he was in town. It was just a matter of conference calls."

Chris regarded her, thinking of her as a child. He imagined her in one of the huge Coastal houses. He imagined her playing in some room tucked away upstairs with her nanny while her mother socialized with other wealthy housewives downstairs and her father worked in an office somewhere else in the house making his important business decisions. He knew it must have been a huge house because only the wealthiest of Coastals could afford to own private businesses. But he did not want to ask her any questions about her childhood, not now that he knew she was in Protection and that it was better for her to cement a habit of never talking about her life before Des Moines.

He compared his imagined world of her upbringing to his own and looked back out into the distance. "My father went to work every morning around seven and came home around seven. When I was very young, my mother dropped me and my brother off at school and then went to work. Then, she would pick us up and take us home and start making dinner while we did our homework. Then, my father would come home. After dinner, my brother and I would play in the neighborhood with other kids or in our house. When I was thirteen and chosen in the first round for government, I moved to the West Coast for my training, but I still went home for the school breaks. My brother was not chosen, so he stayed here until he graduated from high school." He looked over at Jenna, who had been watching him the whole time. "You'd have to ask him what it was like to spend those years in the Inland."

"But wasn't that weird?" she asked. "To go from the Coast to the Inland so often?"

"It was. I mean, it was hard because of the cultural differences. I had a hard time relating to my brother. And I was not allowed to talk about any of my training, which was expected for government."

"Did they resent you? For being moved to the Coast?"

Chris shook his head. "No, my parents were proud, and my brother and I worked through it."

"How?"

"Through building," he answered.

"Building?"

"Yeah, through manual labor. My father managed part of a construction business. The branch he managed built cabinets and countertops and doors and furniture and pretty much anything else that would be installed in Coastal houses. Custom orders from Coastal clients." He nudged her with his shoulder. "Maybe he built something in the house you grew up in."

She laughed and shook her head. "Probably not."

"You'd be surprised," he said. "It was a quality over quantity type of business."

"Well, if it was anything like what I saw in your house, then I believe you."

"Actually, it was exactly like what you saw in my house," he said.

She looked sharply at him.

"I told you my father is impressive. When there was excess that was just going to be thrown away—wood especially, or cabinets and shelves Coastals returned or decided they no longer wanted—the company let my father have them, and we installed them in our house. We would usually have to alter them so the size was correct, and we added a lot of our own artistic carvings. That was my father's favorite part of the job, carving all the stupid little designs into everything. But it was good work and required just enough attention to keep our minds occupied and just enough teamwork to make us help each other. I think that was his way of forcing me and my brother to work together and stay close, to remind us that we were family. That was all we did when I was home, and later when my brother went to college and came back on his breaks. We altered and installed the cabinets and shelves and dressers and pretty much everything that's in the house as it is now."

Jenna looked at him with impressed shock. "You built everything in your house."

"Pretty much," Chris said, a little pride seeping into his expression.

"Wow," Jenna said, turning to look at the mountains. Then, she looked back at him. "I was wondering how such a house was in the Inland."

They both laughed.

"So," she continued, "maybe your upbringing was not so different from mine after all."

"Oh, no," he said, "I'm sure it was."

She nodded and said, "It probably was." Then, she added, "You know now I'm going to go back to the kitchen cabinets and that dresser in my room and study all those intricate carvings with a whole new perspective. I mean, before I was just confused, but now that I know it's your handiwork—"

"Oh, the best of it is in the library," he said.

"The *library?*"

"Yeah, it took us about four years from start to finish—I mean, working only on breaks means you don't get a lot done in any one stretch. Looking back, I can't believe my mother put up with that much construction going on all the time. I'm pretty sure since I was around eight years old, there was at least one part of the house she could not live in."

"I think your mother is my hero."

"I think you two would get along. My father built the library for her. It was not originally part of the house, but he had a bunch of his friends help him add on to the house to make it, and then we filled it with the shelves and tables and everything else."

"Why haven't I seen this library?"

Chris looked away, embarrassed at realizing he had not even shown her the whole house. "We'll check it out when we get back."

She pushed him away and said, "Now I see the rude Inlander, the real Chris."

"No," he said, embarrassed. "I'm sorry. I wasn't thinking."

"It's okay," she said. "A lot happened last night to distract us."

He nodded and checked his phone as he remembered the alarm. It was still set.

They sat in silence a few minutes before Jenna said, "I grew up in a huge house that was also under construction most of the time, but you would never know because there was plenty of house to live in without ever going near the room that was being remodeled or worked on in any way. Since birth, all of my clothes were made uniquely for me." She looked down at her shirt, a mass-produced, solid-colored, basic shirt. "Definitely not like these clothes. My schooling would best be described as a group of tutors—not like these huge schools you find in the Inland. My class size was only thirty, and we were taught in groups of two or three, but I still did not fit in with them." She sighed. "The thing about being a Coastal Purebred is that you don't fit in anywhere. You're too rich to fit in with the *real* Purebreds, the ones who live in the Purebred Communities, but you're too Purebred to fit in on the Coasts. I didn't have the sharp and beautiful features my Modified classmates had. I wasn't supposed to be there."

"But…" Chris started to say something but then fell silent.

She shook her head. "I resented my parents for it. Everywhere I looked, I saw people who were not like me—except for my best friend, of course. Maybe that's why we were so close, because we were living in a bubble nobody else could understand. I mean, there were Coastal Modifieds who tried, but it didn't help that my family was so hostile and so vocal about being adamantly against the modifications. I don't know if they knew—or maybe they didn't care—how it affected me growing up. How people looked at me. How people talked about me. How people made assumptions about me because I was their daughter."

Chris thought about Clara Fontanne at the ball and what she had said to him about not worrying about her, that she could look after herself because she had done so her whole life. He thought about how powerful her parents were and what growing up for her might have been like, to be considered inherently less than those around her in contrast with her father being one of the most powerful men in Washington, D.C. It had made her bold and confident, but it also made her carry herself in an unassuming manner. Like Jenna, Clara had learned how best to avoid confrontation. She had learned how to not draw more attention to her situation by humbling herself first.

At the thought, he felt immediately ashamed for making the comparison, that for all his contacts and missions, he knew but one other Coastal Purebred, and he was using that one other Purebred, that one other person, as an insight into what Jenna was talking about. But he could have no idea what she was talking about, not truly. He knew nothing of Jenna's life, after all. She looked back at him, then, breaking his trance, and he blinked and looked away.

He asked, a little tentatively, "Did your parents ever tell you why they opted out of the modifications?"

She did not answer immediately, and Chris felt ashamed for asking. But just when he was about to apologize, she answered, and he could tell by the way she said it that her hesitation had not been because the question was of personal offense to her but because the answer might be of personal offense to him.

"They did not trust the new government," she said and then pressed her lips together and looked into his confused eyes. "They believed in science and progress and curing disease with the new genetic editing tools, but they did not believe that was all the government was doing."

When Chris did not respond, she shifted her position so it was easier to face him, and he did the same.

She elaborated, saying, "They figured that if the government knew the function of every gene, combined with all the advances in gene editing, then it was likely that scientists knew not just how to fix a gene so it would cure a genetic disorder or prevent disease but also how to fix it so the new human could be whatever was desired."

"But Coastals do that when they design—" he started, but she shook her head, stopping him mid-sentence.

"No, I mean my parents thought the new government wanted to *make* humans that would fit a society they created. They reasoned that scientists could build soldiers, modifying them so they would have superior strength and senses and would also lack emotional reasoning and resistance to authority. Then, they could release them back to their parents, and when the new humans came of age, the government could pluck them back out of society and use them for the purpose they originally planned for them."

There was an awkward silence shared between them as they each realized she very well may have just described his own life.

She shook her head frantically and waved her hand, "No, that's not what I meant to say. I mean, that's what they believed, and that's what they told me, but I don't think that's what the government is actually doing. It was one of the biggest reasons I never got along with them. My parents also thought this applied to other professions, too, that people could be designed for a purpose in society: doctors, cleaners, factory workers, presidents of companies, accountants, teachers, everything. While people called us Purebreds, 'purpose-bred' was what they called Modifieds."

Chris exhaled and looked out to the mountains.

"Chris," she said, touching his shoulder, "I don't think—"

He looked at her with a reassuring smile. "I don't lack emotions or emotional reasoning, if that's what concerns you."

She sighed with relief that what she said had not offended him. "I know you have feelings."

"I've just been extremely well trained to focus and stay objective. But that's only for missions."

"Well, I know that. But I always had different beliefs than my parents. I think it was also pride that caused them to opt out. The government incentives for modifications offended them, I think. And for all their talk of conspiracies and agendas, they thought their genes needed no help and that what they were given was good enough."

She continued, "My parents loved science and nature and were naturalists. They believed in biology and the process of evolution, naturally, without the help of humans, who have relatively little experience when it comes to this sort of thing compared to Mother Nature. They thought the world was millions of years old and that life had been around for hundreds of thousands of years and had gotten along just fine without one of its myriad species meddling in the process." She turned back to look at the mountains. "You can imagine how *that* went when I brought it up in class." She laughed. "I was just repeating what I heard at the dinner table, but you learn early on in school to keep your mouth shut when you are different from everybody else. I think I was five or six when I talked about evolution and the world being so old, and all the other kids laughed at me. Our tutor was polite about it, though, and brushed it off by saying we could discuss that when we learned about science when we were older. She, at least, was one of the nice ones. You could tell most of them were only nice to the Purebred kids because of our influential parents. But they were just nice. Nothing more."

"I'm sorry," he said. "I wish things hadn't been that way for you."

"I used to wish that, too. But I don't know if that's how I feel, anymore." She looked at him. "I think it's why I can understand you and your position. You aren't what you seem. And neither am I. We have both been forced to know ourselves in light of how others see us."

They looked at each other, understanding their own likeness in each other's eyes. She did understand him. She understood what it was like to hide a portion of herself. He leaned in and kissed her, and she put her hand up to the base of his jaw as she kissed him back.

He pulled back and looked into her eyes. "But I don't just hate that it was that way when you grew up. I hate the way it is now. I see the way people treat you." He shook his head, almost in disbelief of what he had witnessed and in more disbelief and shame that he had just stood there while it happened. "Who are Inlanders to judge?"

With her hand still on his face, she shrugged. She looked down at his lips again and then back into his eyes. "They are frustrated with their position in life and rarely encounter Purebreds. So when they finally see someone lower on the social ladder than themselves, they jump at the opportunity to make themselves feel better."

He shook his head in disgust, but she stopped it with her hand and said, "We all have to play the cards we're dealt."

She kissed him again and then turned so that her back was to him and she was facing the setting sun. She leaned back against his chest, and he shifted into a more comfortable position so that he was facing the same direction as she. She put her feet up on the fallen tree and stretched out her legs.

He wrapped his arms tightly around her, knowing he was doing it more to reassure himself than to reassure her that she was loved, that she was wanted, that there was someone in the world who treated her with respect. He kissed the top of her head and said, "You do belong, you know."

"Hmm?" She turned her head to the side to glance back at him and then turned it back toward the sun.

"You said growing up that you didn't belong with the Purebreds because you were too Coastal but that you also didn't belong with the Coastals because you were too Purebred. But you do belong. With me, like this. We both belong when we're together."

She nodded and put her hands on his.

They watched the sun as it began its descent toward the horizon.

After several minutes, in a low, serious voice, he said into her ear, "Come back to D.C. with me."

Slowly, she sat up and turned around to look at him.

"Your protection agent will probably relocate you on Saturday, anyway. If I can pull some strings to get you relocated to Washington, D.C., would you do it?"

She nodded slowly and smiled as she said, "Yes," even though she had promised her protection agent that she would break all ties with Chris. She trusted him, and the Protection Agency would have to trust him, too. She turned back around, resuming her position of leaning against him once more, and they watched the shadows around them shift with the slow motion of the setting sun.

*　　　*　　　*

She fell asleep on the way back to his house, and when she got out of the car and started walking, her muscles were already sore from the hike. She laughed at herself, but he just picked her up and carried her to bed.

"But the library," she mumbled into his shoulder, with her eyes still closed from exhaustion.

"Tomorrow," Chris said. "I'll show it to you tomorrow. You'll have more energy. It will be better that way." He took her to her room, and she fell back asleep, still in her clothes.

His phone rang, and he answered it in a whisper.

"Do you have that giraffe with you?" Zaire asked.

"Yeah, of course," said Chris.

"I have an idea, but I need access to your signatures."

Chris went to the closet where his notebook was still plugged into the wall. He programmed it, allowing Zaire to access his heat signature but not Jenna's.

"Okay," Zaire said. "Now, hold the giraffe."

Chris went to his room and got the giraffe out of his suitcase.

"Okay, put it in your pocket and walk around," Zaire said.

Chris did so and walked to the library, closing the doors behind him so the sound of his conversation would not wake Jenna.

"Aha," said Zaire. "It's a block."

"It is?" Chris asked, pulling it out of his pocket and looking at it more closely.

"It has an anti-tracking device inside it," Zaire explained. "It blocks signatures. He was wearing it the entire time. That's why we couldn't see him before we planted the tracking card."

Chris walked to a window and examined it more closely by the moonlight.

"It's an old version, made before the Surveillance Project started. That's why our tracking card overrode the signal."

Chris set the giraffe on a shelf. "And now?" he asked.

"Your heat signature just returned," Zaire confirmed.

"Hmmm," murmured Chris.

"Chris?" Zaire asked. "Everything okay?"

"Yeah, why?"

"I've never heard you 'hmmm' before," Zaire said with a snort.

"Oh," Chris said, embarrassed. "I guess it's a habit I've picked up from Jenna. Anyway, any more news about the case?"

Zaire stopped laughing at Chris and changed his tone so it was more serious and professional. "I've ruled out military, checked with all the Purebred Communities, and all the other obvious options. She's either dead, in Mexico, or in Protection. But now that I've confirmed the giraffe is a block, she's probably wearing a block, too. That will make her impossible to find, since we have no base signatures to look for. But, I have a meeting with the Protection Agency tomorrow afternoon. If she's not there, we'll close the case on our end and pass it off to a team in Mexico Relations. Then it would be their case and up to them to reach out to Mexican officials to find her. After that, we're out of options."

"Sounds like a good plan," said Chris.

He heard Jenna stirring in her room.

"Anything else?" he asked Zaire.

"No, I'll call tomorrow after I've talked with Protection."

"All right," Chris said and ended the call.

Zaire would have the information Chris needed by the time he arrived in Des Moines on Friday. They had dealt with targets who had made their way into Protection before, and though it was complicated, it was a system Zaire knew how to navigate. If she was in their system, he would find her. Otherwise, the case would be closed.

He picked the giraffe back up and looked at it closely, thinking of the block inside. He would take it back with him and give it to the appropriate department so they could examine and study it. Their tests should have detected it.

Chris looked out the window of the library. The lines and crevices of the canyon outside the window were barely visible in the dark, but he knew them well. He traced the familiar paths of cracks and jagged edges with his gaze. He turned his attention from the case to Jenna. He would talk with her protection agent, and they would start the process of relocating her to Washington, D.C. He would also alert them to Raul's actions in case they really did not know about him.

He sighed and turned to go to bed. As he did so, a picture on the bookshelf caught his attention. He set the giraffe down and picked up the framed picture.

It was a photograph of his parents that he must have looked at over a thousand times in his life. It was his mother's favorite picture of her and Chris's father because it was the first picture ever taken of just the two of them, without anybody else in it. The photo had been taken almost a year after they had each been redistributed to Boise. They were at a picnic hosted by a mutual friend shortly after they met but before they had started dating. His father had his arm around his mother's shoulders, and they were smiling. They were younger than he was now, maybe even Jenna's age, and he saw, really noticing for the first time, that they did not have the scar that Modifieds had. Of course they did not, for they were born before modifications were implemented and in areas of the world where it was not practiced. But they were *non*-Modifieds. Like Jenna. But not like Jenna. They were not shunned from society like she was, for they had a legitimate excuse for not being Modified. "Purebred" was a distasteful term reserved only for children of parents who opted out of the practice after The War. But even if his culture denied it, Chris could not: his parents *were* non-Modifieds.

As he thought about their lack of the Modified scar, he thought of Raul. He also did not have the scar. In fact, the whole population of Mexico lacked the scar. But inhabitants of Mexico were not referred to as Purebreds, either, because genetic modification practices were not performed anywhere in Mexico. But they, too, were *non*-Modifieds. A whole region of the world composed of non-Modifieds. Like it was before The War.

He wondered about what it must have been like for his parents growing up in such a different world than his and to have Modified children when they themselves were not Modified. He thought about how he and his brother had always been treated as "better" by his parents, as if they were superior, and how there had always been an unspoken assumption that they were going to have a better life than his parents had growing up simply because of the way things were now. But they never actually talked about what it was like transitioning from the world they had grown up in to the world of the present.

He looked closer at the photograph, examining the young faces of the people who would later become his parents and for the first time found himself wondering what it was like for them to have to adjust to life after The War. As law-abiding citizens, they never talked about their lives before being redistributed to Boise. But he could see it in their faces. Yes, they were smiling in the photo, just as they had always been every time he looked at it over the years. And yes, even in the simple pose, one could see the chemistry between them. But now, looking at them not as his parents but as two individuals in a photograph, as viewed and analyzed by a skilled and highly trained profiler, he *saw* them: they were scared; they were in unfamiliar territory; they were still figuring life out, sorting out everything, and learning to settle into this new world. They were two completely unrelated people who would have never met if things had not turned out the way they did. But they had found each other. Like Jenna and himself, his parents had each found someone they could trust and confide in and find a home in, and for that, they were immensely happy.

14

The next morning, Chris did not immediately get up, as he usually did every morning. He checked his phone for messages, and when he saw there were no updates, he decided to lie there and enjoy the morning. He pushed all thoughts of the Robertson case out of his mind and focused only on the woman next to him. They were in no rush. She lay in his arms, and he loved feeling her body next to his, smelling her hair and feeling her breathing. He stroked her hair, letting the sensation of each strand linger on his fingertips. He thought about how solitary her life had become in the past few years and how the fear of accidentally revealing who she was through old mannerisms, stories, and habits had affected her. He knew all about the programs, seminars, and training that individuals in the Protection Program had to go through. They were practically brainwashed into never even thinking about their lives and who they were before they joined the Program. Even targets he had gone after who had joined the Program seemed like completely different people than who they were before they joined, when they had been criminals and anarchists. But she would not have to do that anymore. She would not have to pretend or hide, not with him. She could truly be herself with him. He would show her she could do that. And together they would show the world that a relationship such as theirs was not only possible but that it could thrive through truth and acceptance.

She stirred and looked up at him.

"Good morning," he said.

"You're still here," she said as she sat up to stretch.

Free of the fear of waking her, he also stretched out his limbs.

She groaned and started massaging her legs. "I guess I'm more out of shape than I realized," she said, laughing at herself. She stood up, and the soreness of her muscles was amplified as one of her legs gave out beneath her. She stood up straight, trying to correct her gait without further embarrassment.

"Take a bath," he suggested. "You'll feel a lot better. I'll make us breakfast." He got up, and she started to watch the muscles of his upper body as he put on a shirt, and then she looked away, blushing slightly.

He left, shutting the door behind him, and she went to the bathroom and started running the water for a bath. She considered asking him to join her, but then she thought better of it. He was still so shy around her, still holding back so much. But she could not blame him, given the secret life he had grown so accustomed to and having been trained so well not to reveal anything about himself to anyone. She felt honored that he trusted her. She knew she was one of the few people outside of his agency who knew what his position in government was, maybe the only person outside of his family. But she wanted him to know he did not have to hide from her. She wanted to be there for him, to be someone he felt he could share himself with completely.

Sitting in the hot water, relaxing, she realized she had not done this in years. Even without thinking about it, showering was done swiftly to decrease the odds that she would be caught off guard and vulnerable. She realized she often subconsciously made herself ready to leave at any moment. She liked having someone in the house who could keep watch while she relaxed.

She looked at the bathroom around her. It was not as flawless as one would be on the Coasts, but oh how she missed living like this. The bathtub in her townhouse in Des Moines was not even big enough to sit in. She sunk down into the water so that her entire body was submerged up to her neck and closed her eyes.

She started thinking about what life would be like after this weekend. If they were able to pull it off, she would move to Washington, D.C. She would go back to the Coast.

She thought about her life growing up on the Coast, shoving aside all the warnings and advice given to her when she joined the Program, the tips to help her so she would not slip up—not painting, lest anyone recognize her style, not talking of life before Des Moines, lest she accidentally reveal some detail about who she really was, not talking about her deceased boyfriend or her siblings or her upbringing. But how could she forget? It was true that she had forgotten a lot of it, for years of forcing those thoughts out of her mind as soon as they surfaced caused those memories to die out, but how could she truly give up where she had come from and who she was? She had not minded it when she joined the Program, the chance to finally and officially be someone else, to not have to be so ashamed of her family and the choices her parents had made for her. But now she wondered how good that was to do, truly. She would not be who she was without that life.

She imagined an apartment in D.C., made possible by Chris's connections, and she imagined she would do this every single night—with Chris. She did not care that it was a big move to make so early in a relationship. She was tired of being so cautious, of only having a few friends, of not really being anyone or really being with anyone, of only going through the motions of life. She wanted to *live*. With Chris. She did not care what the Program said about breaking all ties when she relocated. He brought something into her life that she did not even know was possible. She felt calm and relaxed and strong when she was with him, not strong in the sense that she could do anything, but strong in the sense that she was solid, that she meant something to someone, that she mattered.

She eventually got out of the bath and dried herself with a towel. She saw a robe hanging on a hook on the door and slipped it on, too tired to put on makeup or real clothes. She decided it was another act of rebellion to the life of constantly being ready to flee that she had been living since joining the Program.

"I hope it's okay that I borrowed this," she said as she entered the kitchen and sat at the table.

Chris turned to look at her, and when he saw her, with his mouth still open as he stared, a piece of omelet fell off the spatula and onto the kitchen floor. While grabbing a kitchen towel with his free hand, he put the spatula back in the pan. "Uh, yeah, it's fine," he said, wiping up the egg off the tile floor.

She suppressed a laugh and looked away.

He finished making breakfast and brought it over to the table where they ate. After breakfast, they moved to the living room, which was in the middle of the back of the house with windows that faced the canyon. They sat on the couch, and she chose a seat so that she could see the view out the window. She pulled her hair back with her hands so that it draped over her right shoulder. She had not put her contacts back in since taking them out the night she arrived, and with the natural light through the windows, her dark blue eyes were bright and enthralling. He was absolutely mesmerized by them. Her skin, bare after the bath and raw without makeup, was freckled, more so in some spots than others. It took all his strength not to kiss the freckles on her neck and collarbones. He forced himself to look away before he kissed the smooth part of her face where most of their generation had a scar from the *in utero* modification surgery.

"It's so beautiful here," she said, looking at the canyon out the window.

He also looked out the window and then looked back at her. "How long has it been since you were relocated to Des Moines?" he asked, and then he quickly added, "Never mind, please don't answer that," remembering it would be better for her not to think of those things.

"Since I graduated high school and was redistributed from Utah," she said teasingly.

"Correct," he agreed.

"Is this nothing to Washington, D.C.?" she asked, pointing at the view.

He looked out the window and then back at her. "It's amazing, but in a different way than this is." He stood up and walked over to the window to get a better view. "I've been fortunate to grow up here and then live on the Coasts, but D.C. is so different, even from where I trained on the West Coast. It's clean, and the people are friendly, and there are street lights everywhere, and they're on all the time. There are never blackouts, planned or accidental, like there are in the Inland. The air is almost as clean as it is in the mountains. The food is to die for. And, of course, I love the water, but you've seen that before," he teased, looking back at her.

She stood up and walked over to the window, too. "I do love the ocean. But my small town didn't have all these lights and buildings you're talking about."

"I've traveled to many Coastal cities and small towns, but I do think D.C. is my favorite. Each Coastal city has its own personality. They're not like the Inland cities that are all the same. Sometimes when I do a job in one Inland city, I forget where I am because they're all the same—granted, I'm not usually there long enough to really find out. Des Moines was the longest job I've ever had in the Inland."

"What does your family think about all this assassin business?"

"They know what I do is secret, but they don't know exactly what I do."

"Can you not talk about your job at all?" she asked, surprised that not even they knew about his position in government.

"A little bit," he said. "Obviously there is much I can't talk about because it's classified."

They looked out at the canyon in silence. Then, playfully, she nudged him and asked, "Is there an assassin's creed?" After he responded with a confused look, she explained further. "You know, some tenets or something, rules that if broken would outcast you from the assassin society."

He laughed and looked down. The question had caught him by surprise. He shook his head, not sure what to think of her question. "No, not from my employers, anyway. Basically, the government identifies a criminal, and if bringing public justice will do more harm than good and put more people in danger, then—"

"They send you in, and justice is brought to the criminal quietly and anonymously," she finished.

"Someone like me. I'm not the only one who does this," he said.

"What if someone rats you out?"

"That's unlikely. It's bad policy to talk about someone else's business. Also, each only knows their own business, and, even of my own business, I know only enough to do my part of the job. And there are things only I know. This way, the only way to know the whole case would be to question everybody involved, and it's impossible to know all who are involved. I don't even know who else is on the case most of the time, except for myself and my boss for the mission."

"Can you talk about your," she paused, looking around, trying to find the right word, "cases?"

"What do you want to know?"

"I don't know. What is it like, how many have you done, how often do you have to do it… Those types of things."

"Well, when I switch departments, I'll work on several cases at a time, but my schedule will be more routine than it is now. For now, I usually work on one case at a time, and they're usually swift, except for this last one. I can't honestly tell you how many I've done, not off the top of my head. I could probably sit here and bore you while I count them up from memory, but it wouldn't be exact. It's better to forget them than to risk being able to talk about them." He looked off to the side, thinking about his career. "And honestly, I've been doing it so long that I'm not sure what it's like *not* to do this. I started out my first two years doing surveillance stuff, but it was so boring. It was like watching other people live their lives instead of living my own."

"But are you nervous? Do you ever fear that they are a step ahead of you and you'll get caught? What about the police?" Then, after a pause, she added, "Sorry, I don't mean to bombard you with questions."

"It's okay. I'm glad you're asking so many questions. It means you took me seriously when I told you I didn't want to keep anything from you. I've had great training, so I'm never nervous. Anxiety will often mess up a job. In a way, you always prepare yourself for their next possible move. You have to exhaust all the possibilities in your mind and always have a backup plan. That's where not being nervous comes in handy. If you're calm, you can usually just do the job and be done with it with no problems—or at least that's how I am." He paused. "And the police are no problem. Sometimes I do have to break the law to get a job done—just minor things, though—but my boss makes sure nothing comes of it. It's rare that the police ever get involved, though. I'm good at covering my tracks. I think that's why I've been doing this for so long and have not been told to switch departments. Usually, agents change departments every two years. But I've been told I'm in high demand." He said it objectively, without pride or arrogance. He was good at his job, for better or for worse, and it was just a fact to him.

"So are you immune from the law? Can you be arrested for anything?"

"No, I'm too valuable as an agent, but, I still keep a low profile. If anything happened, I'd get bailed out. But I would never do anything illegal, anyway, not unless it was directly related to the case. And if it's required to solve a case, it's not considered illegal."

"So, is it like a secret government?" She wanted to know more about this life Chris had been assigned to. It felt parallel, in a way, to her own life these last few years, even though he lived in secrecy for entirely different reasons.

"It's more like a secret branch of the government, still governed by the Presidents. But the laws are adjusted for how we go after the criminals. At some point, a criminal no longer has a right to trial by jury."

"Really?" She stopped herself. "Sorry, I just have a hard time with that, I guess." She contemplated Chris's position and this secret branch of government. Finally, she asked, "What do you mean? What kind of crime is so bad it is kept from the public?"

"Well," Chris started, "the department I work for, the Department of Anarchy Prevention, probably has the highest number of cases where agents like myself are involved. These anti-government groups have leaders, and if we publicly go after them, their groups will do more attacks and cause more deaths and destruction. So, we get rid of them secretly, and then there is no uproar. And that's where I come in."

"So, the one you went after in Des Moines?" she asked. "He was an anarchist?"

Chris nodded.

"And he has a partner you just found out about before we came here." She shuddered. "His partner could do something soon, then. You have to find him."

Chris nodded. Then, he added, "*Her*, actually. It's his sister. We went after his whole family."

"His whole family?" she asked, surprised, but then she composed herself. "Sorry," she said. "You may have to be patient with me. I had no idea about any of this—in my own city, even—and it's all really new. But I want you to be able to talk about these things with me, if you want to."

"It's okay," he said. "I mean, I'm not supposed to talk about the specifics, of course."

"I understand, but you can't keep this all to yourself. It can't be healthy."

"It's not. We have sessions with our bosses to keep it in check, but I've also had extensive training in managing it. I may have had a similar reaction as you're having when I first entered the academy, but that was so long ago I can't remember anymore."

She walked back to the couch, sat down, and asked, "But it doesn't bother you, now, to go after families?" She looked heartbroken.

"Not children," he clarified, following and sitting next to her. "These are all adults who know what they're doing and have been planning it for a long time. They're not brainwashed children, but I'm sure some would argue they were probably brainwashed as children. But they're not children anymore. They know how to take responsibility for their actions, and that's what we hold them to."

"Oh," she said, surprised. "Sorry, I guess when you said family, I started thinking of all these pictures in your house"— she turned to a picture on the end table next to her and pointed to it—"and conjured up an image of happy innocent children." She picked up the photo. It was a picture of Chris's brother and his kids. Then, she set it back down and looked at Chris. "So," she said, "anarchy as a family business. That's rough."

"They started an anarchist group about five years ago, and we kept tabs on it all along, but it just grew bigger and bigger and rapidly got out of control. We traced it back to this family operation, and now it has started to dwindle. You know how anarchy has decreased drastically in the last year?"

She nodded. The weekly news of anarchist statistics had been unavoidable.

"This particular family is not responsible for all of the crimes, obviously, but they were a major part of one of the bigger groups. Their contacts were phenomenal, and their resources were limitless. In the past two years alone, their combined activities killed more than a hundred people and injured hundreds more. They became unpredictable, and we just couldn't keep up with them."

"You let them keep going until it got out of hand? How could you let it get that far? Why didn't you do it sooner?"

"They were terrible, but we have rules. We can't kill just anybody. It took a long time to find the source, and then we had to have sufficient evidence. When we were finally able to put all the pieces together and had enough evidence to show that all the crimes in question could be traced back to this family, we still had to come up with every possible idea before being convinced that this was the only way to stop them. If we did it publicly, their group would have revolted even more against the government. The family organized the attacks, but they were not the ones who actually carried out the crimes. So, if we brought them to public trial, there would have been an uproar. Their group was too big for us to take that risk."

"I can see how something like that would abrogate rights for a fair trial, but wouldn't doing it publicly just make it more likely that it would stop? Because people would know about the group and try to stop them?"

"What if people tried to punish them, and then we have to go after the people who committed crimes against the criminals in the name of justice?"

"That would be mayhem," she agreed. Then, she added, "You seem more like a hero than a murderer."

"Heroes save lives. They don't wait until people have died to prevent more deaths." He looked intently into her eyes and said, softly, "But I'm not a murderer. I'm not a hitman someone can hire to get rid of somebody who annoys them. I'm good at being an assassin. It's an art I have been trained in and excel at. I know it's a hard job to explain and that it's probably hard for you to understand, but I want this to work. That's why I'm answering all your questions. That's also why I'm switching departments as soon as this case is finished. I don't want you to have to struggle with this."

She reached out and grabbed his hands in both of hers, shifting her position so she faced him, careful to keep the robe from slipping and revealing too much. "Don't worry about me," she said. "I can handle it. I don't want you to feel like you have to protect me from your job or ever feel like you can't talk to me about it."

He adjusted his hands so they were holding hers and kissed the top of each one. Then, he said, "Let's start with one thing at a time. There's a lot more where that came from."

She looked back at him, knowing he had barely scratched the surface of information regarding his job, and she agreed, saying, "It's a deal. One thing at a time."

With her hands still in the grip of his, she set her hands down. He glanced at his hands in her lap and then back up at her, swallowing hard, but she was looking out the window, with her head turned away from him.

She sighed and looked around. "So, when do I finally get a tour of this place?"

"Right now," he said.

He stood up, and she stood up with him, still holding one of his hands. He led her out of the room and showed her the rest of the house. There were four bedrooms in total, the kitchen where they ate, the living room, and an entertainment room in the middle of the house, which, he told her, was originally a dining room before they converted it when his brother started high school.

As they walked down the hallway, she continued looking at the pictures on the walls and in the bedrooms. "There are pictures all over this house. I love looking at them. Everybody always looks so happy." She stopped in front of one of his brother and a woman. "Is she his wife?"

"Yeah," Chris said and then pointed to another photo and added, "and these are their kids."

"They're beautiful. Your whole family is beautiful," she added as she continued walking and looking at the other photos.

They reached the end of a small hallway, and Chris stood in front of two wooden doors. "And this," he said, sliding open the double doors, "is the library."

Jenna gasped as she stood, gaping at one of the most beautiful rooms she had ever entered. The room faced the canyon and jutted out from the rest of the house. There were built-in shelves lining all six walls from the floor to the ceiling. All the wood was dark cherry oak, giving the whole room a warm and old feeling. To her right, in one corner, there was a large fireplace with a sitting area in front of it. On each of the three walls that overlooked the canyon, there was a gap in the shelves for a large bay window with cushions to sit on. In the center of the room was a table, and next to it were two couches and three other huge comfortable chairs, all facing each other to form a square.

Jenna turned to him with a look of surprise and approval. "This room is gorgeous."

"It's kind of our masterpiece. We spent the longest time making sure the floors and shelves were perfect when we built it, and we had to wait for the materials to make sure we had enough that would match and still look good together."

Jenna could see a small dent on the side of the shelf to her right and knew that was how Chris's family was able to have it. Her mother certainly would have sent it back to the company if it had been delivered to her in such condition. But they were still nice shelves, and Chris's father had done a good job in hiding the flaws.

Chris continued, "My mother designed the room herself. We built it for her, actually, because she's the one who loves to read so much. You should see their house in Arizona. She has stacks of books everywhere. It drives my father crazy. I'm convinced that's why he built this room, so she would have a place to properly store all her books."

"Have you read them all?" she asked.

"No, but I've read most of them, or my mother read them to us. She used to do that while we worked. These are just her favorite books that she likes to keep here for when she visits. She put all of her favorite pictures in here, too."

In front of the books on the shelves, scattered around the room, were pictures in frames and various other statues or trinkets. Jenna started on the left and decided to work her way around the room, looking at all the books and pictures and artifacts. The majority of the books were in the Common Language, but there were older books in two other languages, as well. Jenna supposed they were his parents' native languages, and it made her happy to see they had kept them.

As she kept walking, she could not help but recall the library in the house she had grown up in. It was vastly bigger than this room with staircases and ladders, full of books from long before The War that generations of family members had added over the years. It did not contain a single book written in the approved Common Language. And Jenna would not have been surprised if it did not contain a single legal book in its entire collection. She remembered some of the titles and some of the discussions her family had about them. What she would give to go back to that library now, having lived outside of that world and realizing how she had taken for granted that every book in the house where she grew up was pre-War, banned and utterly unobtainable today. She never thought the time would come when she would wish to go back. Technically, she still did not. Not *really*.

She continued walking, looking at more books and pictures and little figurines and the carvings carefully designed into the bookshelves, and she knew she still did not want to go back to that house. This house, even with all its legal books and lack of history, was warm and kind.

As she walked, she shamelessly allowed herself to think of her family, despite what the agency told her about forgetting it all. What would they think of this library? What would they think of Chris and her relationship with him? She could already see Hawk sizing him up and telling her it was just a phase—not just because he was a Modified but also disgust at him being a born Inlander. At least a born Inlander redistributed to the Coast was better than a born Coastal redistributed to the Inland. She smiled to herself as she imagined Karen and Adele holding their hands out for a handshake with pinched and forced smiles. They were polite, she would give them that, but it would be hard for them. Adam would have accepted him, though. She and Adam had always been close. She was much younger than her siblings. Karen and Hawk had been born before The Ban and were not really considered Purebreds, not in the true sense. They were so defensive about it—not defensive about their own birth years but defensive about that of their siblings. They always went out of their way to let everybody know their family existed *before* The Ban on Pure Breeding.

But as she continued on to the next bookshelf—with its pictures and homemade crafts by Chris and his brother when they were young and new ones made by the grandkids—she could not help but think of how eerily accurate her parents' conspiracies of surveillance had been. When Chris showed her that Mexican man walking on the sidewalk, she felt like they had foretold the future. It was so easy for Chris not only to locate him but to even visualize him *in real time*. Just as they had predicted. She thought they were crazy at the time, that they were paranoid and uneducated fools. But now, she wondered about their theories. She wished she could remember more of what they told her, and her professor and her boyfriend. But she had forgotten so much of it, having forced those thoughts and memories out of her mind for so long. Now, she wished she had written it all down.

She continued walking and saw a book she read for a class in high school. Karen had told her to skip it. She thought of more memories, then, memories of a family she had lost long ago but that she could now truly never return to. She did not miss them, but she could no longer blame them for being the way they were. And she could no longer blame herself for *not* being the way they were. She forgave herself, then, in the library, for the resentment and shame she felt toward them growing up. And she forgave herself for trying to run away from it, knowing she could never truly be anyone other than who she was. *No one should be made to feel ashamed of their genetic history,* she thought. *We cannot be blamed for the ancestries we come from or for the families that raised us or for the choices our parents made, for we are, none of us, born into lives of our own choosing. It is only our own actions for which we can take the credit, for better or for worse.*

And that she had climbed out of the life she was born into, that she had veered off the default path fate had set before her—that was something to be proud of. She was not sure her siblings could have said the same.

As she forgave herself and released the shame of her attachments with them, a burden was lifted, and she felt lighter and finally free, more like herself than she ever had before.

She thought of her siblings' arguments with her teachers in a different light now. They had always been defensive and protective of her, even though she was more forgiving of her classmates and tutors than they were. Back then, she only saw that her siblings made her life harder, that they made her even more different than she already was. But now, she saw that they always had her back, that they regarded her as one of their own and treated her as if she were not the defiant and rebellious sister she was. They were loyal that way. They were fierce. They would never let anybody treat her like a second-class citizen.

But they were gone now. All of them.

As she continued walking, she felt a queasy feeling creep into her stomach that she could not explain.

Something was *off.*

But her mind could not yet identify it.

She felt a sinking feeling in her stomach as she remembered what her protection agent had said about their deaths. They were *each* gone. Each a coincidence. An accident. Without any trace of foul play.

She reached the end of the second wall and looked out the first bay window at the canyon. It was afternoon, now. They had slept in and enjoyed a leisurely morning, and tomorrow they would go back to Des Moines. She did not want to leave this place, and yet, the prospect of moving to Washington, D.C., and being with Chris was so exciting.

She continued walking, and she thought about what he had said about switching departments. She wondered how willing the agency would be to allow him to change his position. *He was in high demand, after all,* she thought. *He never leaves a trace.*

With that thought, she froze.

No, she thought. *No,* she assured herself.

She started walking again, scanning books and photos and artifacts her eyes were settling on but that her mind was not thinking about. She began to breathe slowly and deeply, thinking of how impossible it was. Her family, gone, coincidentally when viewed from the outside, but strategically if viewed from the inside. *And most recently, Adam, from a heart attack in Des Moines last week,* she thought, remembering her conversation on Monday. And then, thinking of her conversation with Chris that day: *An ally. A sister.*

Just when she was ready to convince herself it was all a crazy coincidence, that the two conversations were not linked at all, she stopped and stood motionless, her face expressionless, her hands still holding her elbows; she could not even breathe. For in front of her, nearly perfectly at eye level, was a small ceramic giraffe painted yellow with different colored polka dots all around it.

She remembered painting it with her nanny, so excited about her new toy. When it was glazed and baked, her mother gave it back to her, telling her a story about the giraffe and how it was her new friend and would protect her, saying, *"You can play with it, Katie, but keep it with you at all times. You must keep it on you, not just in your bag, but in your pocket or in your hand."*

She knew what it was. Her siblings were much older than she was and had blocks of their own that looked more like things adults would carry with them. They had created this block specifically for a child, so it would not be suspicious, and created a story for her so she would be careful not to lose it or break it or give it away.

Then, when Jenna went to Texas, she had purposefully left the giraffe at home, a sign she was leaving for good and never returning, a sign she was leaving her family and their conspiracies behind. She wondered if the block would still work—if it was the block from her childhood memory. *It was not that unique of a design,* she told herself. *It was a generic ceramic figurine that was produced en masse for kids everywhere,* she thought to herself, reassuring herself that there was no cause for panic.

But she had to check.

She knelt down, pretending to look at a photo on a shelf below, and she glanced up to see the underside of the giraffe. She felt all the blood drain from her face and terror creep into her heart when she saw the "K. R. age 8" that she herself had painted so many years and lifetimes before.

She looked down at the photo in front of her. Then, she looked back up at it again.

She started breathing heavily, putting it all together. He had gone after each member of her family, and now he had brought her out here. He could dispose of her body in the canyon. Nobody would know. He said so himself, that his boss would cover for him if anything went wrong.

She looked down again, thinking, planning. Chris was by the door, but she could figure out a way past him. She felt tears form in her eyes. She blinked them away. She had to keep herself together. She had to be calm.

She took deep breaths and started to plan. There were picture frames all over this room. She could smash one and stab him with the broken glass. She reached out and touched the frame in front of her. Plastic. *Cheap Inland crap*, she cursed in her mind. Looking around, she realized some of them did not even have plastic covers.

A knife, she thought. There were knives in the kitchen. They were dull, but they would work. She could run there, disable him, and then run to her room and call her protection agent. That would never work. Even if she got to the knives, he would easily overtake her.

Maybe she could run to a neighboring house. The houses were not as close as in the new Inland neighborhoods, but there were houses all around. Who was she kidding? Her legs were sore from the hike, and he was still in perfect condition. He probably had some Modified genes that gave him superior abilities to run fast, anyway.

But none of those plans would work because he was leaning against the doorframe, and she first had to get out of that room. She had to distract him somehow, to separate herself from him. Then, she could lock herself in her room and call for help. She could send him away. Maybe she could ask him to get something from the store. He was already dressed, and she could say she was still sore and wanted to rest. She could ask him for lotions or other things that would soothe her aching muscles. *Yes*, she thought, *that could work.*

She forced herself to stand up and had to put her hand on the shelf to steady herself. She forced her eyes to look at a picture next to the figurine, rather than at the giraffe. It was a picture of his parents, just the two of them, and they looked so young. And innocent.

But I'm innocent, she thought. *I must be wrong. I'm being paranoid.* He was not after her. He could *not* be after her. There was no reason for him to come after her. *But then why does he have that block?* she asked herself. She heard her mother's voice in her mind telling her, *Because he is at the end of the line, Katie, and now he has brought the last family member to Idaho to finish his job.* She felt like such a fool. She had let her guard down. He had torn it down, somehow, in his deceptive ways. Was that not his job?

She inhaled deeply as she turned around, ready to feign fatigue and sore muscles. But as soon as she turned around, she gasped as she saw him standing directly behind her, not a foot away.

"Sorry," he said. "I didn't mean to startle you."

She nearly screamed, but when she looked into his eyes, she saw not a killer but the kind, compassionate, safe Chris she had come to know and love.

He stroked the side of her face, and her heart melted as she realized he had no idea whatsoever. The thought that she could be the one his team was looking for had not once crossed his mind. She scanned his face and looked at his lips as they formed a slight smile, and she knew in her heart that he would never hurt her. She relaxed in the knowledge that this was all a misunderstanding, and she started to smile, too.

"I love you," he whispered softly.

He was sincere. He loved her, and she knew she loved him. If she could, she would not go back and change anything. She did not regret anything that had happened. He came into her life and reminded her of what it was like to live, to love someone, to have fun and to just be happy with someone.

She knew she would have to tell him. In the best case scenario, she would be wrong, and they would laugh about her mistake. But she had to tell him her theory, that she may be the sister his team was looking for. She would explain to him that she was innocent, and they would figure this out together. More than anything, though, she could not deny that she was so profoundly in love with him.

"I love you," he repeated with more conviction. He pulled her in, and his kiss was so soft and so full.

She kissed him back, sincerely and passionately, and surrendered herself to her love for him.

*　　　*　　　*

Hours later, after they had spent the rest of the day in each other's arms and after they had gone to sleep, Chris awoke, opening his eyes to stare up at the ceiling. He felt her bare body against his, her head on his arm, her hand on his chest. He looked down at her hand, over at her shoulder and then her neck and her face and her cheeks and her closed eyes and her hair. Then, he looked back at her hand on his chest. He picked her hand up, examined it more closely, and set it back down on his chest, still holding it as he forced himself back to sleep.

*   *   *

In the morning, they packed up their things and got ready to leave. She noticed that even though he was extra attentive to her, he hardly looked at her, either because he had turned shy from the intimacy of their trip or because he was taking in the last glimpses of his home before leaving it again. After breakfast, they put their bags in the trunk, and she stayed in the car while he went back in the house to check everything and lock up.

He retrieved his notebooks, checked the rooms, and then he went to the library. It wasn't like him to absentmindedly put a piece of evidence down and forget about it. He was mad at himself for it, but that was what had happened. Before putting the giraffe in his pocket to take back to the agency's labs, he examined it one more time. He was looking at the figurine, but he was thinking about a revelation that had awoken him in the middle of the night. He had focused on all the hands: Mr. Robertson's, as he drank at the bar where Chris served him his poisoned drink; Mrs. Robertson's, as she reached for a gun on a nearby table in her bathroom; Karen's, as she came toward him with rage; Adele's, as she chopped fruit at her kitchen counter; Talon Jr.'s, as he gripped the side of the balcony to steady himself before his fall; Adam's, as they rested on his chest, rising and falling with his sleeping breaths. And Katherine's, one made subtly different than the other from reconstructive surgery following a car accident. In the end, it was her hands that had given her away.

He put the figurine in his pocket, locked up the house, and got in the car to start their trip back to Des Moines.

15

Since his revelation, he did not look at her hands. He would not allow himself to look at her at all, except her eyes, which were brown with contacts, because every time he looked at her he saw pieces of her family in the features untouched by surgeries after the crash, familiar features he had studied for months in the members of her family. The spacing of her eyes in relation to each other and her cheekbones were the same as Karen's and her mother's. She, Adele, and Adam had chins similar to their father's. She, Adam, and Talon Jr. had inherited their mother's slim neck. The freckles on her shoulders were not unlike the freckles he saw on the shirtless Talon Jr. who swayed on the balcony. The way she rested her hands on her lap, reserved and without slouching, was a trait she was taught as a child. Her mother, Karen, and Adele all sat that way, too. No wonder she had seemed so familiar to him at the bar when he first saw her.

He wanted to escape to another world, where he could examine every inch of her body with the infatuation that had consumed him in the ignorance of her true identity. But he could not. His mind would not let him see Jenna when his eyes took in the familiar features before him. He would not think of it, pushing it out of his mind as much as possible and forcing his thoughts to focus on other things, things completely unrelated to the Robertson case: his brother, his parents, what projects he wanted to pursue on his house, what he would get his parents for their upcoming wedding anniversary, what he would get the kids for their birthdays.

There was always the possibility that he was wrong.

They arrived in Iowa, and he drove her home and waited in her living room while she got ready for work. Then, he drove her to the museum.

"Chris," she started. Her hand was on the door handle.

He looked back at her, directly in the eyes. Her expression was one of innocence, and his expression was soft.

"There's something else I need to tell you, maybe tonight when this is over?" She waved her hand toward the museum, where people were setting up for the gala. He tried not to picture Talon Jr. on the balcony when he waved his hand in the air as he spoke of his brother.

"Of course. Are you sure you don't want me to come with you?"

"No, I'm okay. There are lots of people here. I'm sure I'll be fine, especially now that I know what to look out for." She was referring to Raul, whom she now knew to be following her. But she really wanted to talk about Chris's current case.

They kissed, and she got out of the car. He watched her go in and pulled out his phone. He set it to alert him of Raul's every move and to sound an alarm if he got within one hundred feet of the museum.

He sat for a few more minutes, putting off what he knew he had to do. Then, he went to her house, broke in, turned off the alarm with a universal silencing code only his agency used, and started going through every square inch, praying for evidence of either her innocence or his error in judgment.

He took note of everything. From the few decorations she chose and where she placed them, he could infer her interests and personality and could get to know the part of her that existed before Iowa. He opened every drawer and cabinet. He checked under rugs and cushions. He searched for secret compartments, anything he could find. When he had thoroughly searched the downstairs, he went upstairs and started in the bathroom, even checking the toilet bowl and tank for hidden objects. He checked under the bed and under the mattress. Finally, he reached a locked closet. He pulled out a lock pick and opened it with ease.

He first looked through the clothes. As he backed away, something caught his eye from the corner of the top shelf. He reached up and pulled down a small box. He opened the box just enough to peek at the contents. His breathing was still steady, but his mind was trying to stop his hands from opening it further. He opened the box completely, and there was a letter and two pictures inside. One was of her in her teens with a guy. Chris could only assume he was the boyfriend whose death had caused her to go into hiding. The other picture was of five people sitting on the front steps of the porch of a house. It was a close-up, so it looked general, but he knew he had seen that house before. He looked intently, not at the people, but at the porch, the steps, the columns, the door. He searched his mind for movies or TV shows he had seen where he probably saw a similar porch. He wanted it to be a generic porch, not one he knew from memory.

He put the photograph in his pocket, replaced the box, shut the closet door, and locked it. As he left the house, he checked that everything was the same as when he had entered, even turning the alarm back on before exiting. He got back in his car and drove to his apartment.

He parked his car, pulled out the photo, and looked at it, this time forcing himself to look at the faces, one by one, able to call them each by name: Karen, Talon Jr., Adele, Adam, and Katherine. In the photo, Karen and Talon Jr. were in their early twenties, Adele and Adam were in their late teens, and she looked to be about five years old. Her hair was light red in the picture. He imagined her running around the huge yard and the huge house. He wondered if they ever called her "Kate" or "Katie" or "Kathy." Or if she just went by "Katherine." As he got out of the car, he put the picture back in his pocket.

As he walked to his apartment, he pulled out his phone to check on Raul's whereabouts. He approached his apartment door, preparing for the conversation that was surely on the other side, and opened it.

Chris turned toward the dining area as he shut the door and saw his boss coming toward him.

"I found the third daughter," Chris said, holding up the picture.

"I'm removing you from the case," Xiao said, now standing before him. They looked each other squarely in the eyes. "Or you can resign."

"She's not like them," Chris said in a low whisper.

"She's one of them, Rockford. She's a Robertson," Xiao insisted. "She was raised by them, brainwashed by them, and their agendas are deeply rooted in who she is as a person."

"She ran away from them long ago. She went into Protection to get away from something completely unrelated to them."

"Yes, she dated a man who was randomly shot by some Mexican gang. Are you sure she did not kill him herself and point the finger so that those men were sent to prison? Are you certain she was not in contact with her family when it happened? Are you positive that she broke off contact when she went into the Protection Program? Do you *know* that Adam Robertson did not warn her and that she did not spot you first, seduce you, and manipulate you into being on her side?" His boss's tone was getting intense.

But Chris remained silent.

"No, you don't, because no matter how good you are at reading people, you do not have one hundred percent confidence that she is not one step ahead of you. Nor do you know who else she is in communication with. It's not bad to have someone in Witness Protection in your anarchist organization. They're practically invisible as far as Surveillance is concerned."

Chris still stayed silent.

Finally, his boss said, "You know what has to be done."

"Don't take me off the case," Chris said with a tone that made it both a demand and a request. "I'll talk to her, and I'll do it myself if I find she's one of them."

His boss leaned back and tilted up his chin as he took a deep breath. After a few moments, he had made his decision. "I have a meeting with President Anders tomorrow. I'll talk to her about the case and see what she thinks. But on Monday, it must be resolved." Xiao then went on to tell Chris everything they knew about Katherine Robertson, though they could only get information about her life after she was redistributed to Iowa under Protection—everything else had been destroyed. But it was news to Chris that the protection agent she had talked with on Monday *had* told her why they were going to relocate her, and it had nothing to do with the Mexican gang that put her into hiding. He had told her about her family's deaths and the possibility that her brother had been in Des Moines looking for her.

His belief in her innocence, then, began to falter, as he thought more about the strategy from his boss's point of view: Adam kept contact with her and told her about what was happening; together they identified Chris; she found him at the hotel restaurant and feigned innocence to get him on her side.

But if that were really true, he thought, *then Adam would still be alive today.* If she really were a step ahead of him, they would have figured out a way to prevent his death, as well. *Unless she was willing to sacrifice her brother to make herself look truly innocent.* She had never spoken particularly well of her family.

Chris shook off the idea. He could not reconcile this target his boss laid out before him with the woman he had fallen in love with. He had until Monday to figure it out. Three days. Three days was a lifetime for Chris when it came to such a task. He was not ignorant of the risk Xiao was taking, and he nodded as he gave his boss an apologetic and grateful look. Xiao put a hand on Chris's shoulder and held it there a few seconds before leaving without another word exchanged between them.

16

At the gala, Jenna was busy making sure everything was going according to plan, but in her mind she was devising a way to tell Chris about their predicament. She had been thinking about it all day.

She thought more about what he told her about the case, how the family had killed hundreds in their activities. She remembered how sick she felt at the thought of such a family, and thinking about it again, knowing that family might be her own, was absolutely nauseating. She thought about her family, what she could remember of each of them, and she could positively believe that they had turned into the family he had described. They had always cheated and stolen from Modifieds, not regarding them as real human beings. They had always had a way with people, so much so that many fell at their feet and followed them. She remembered how, growing up, she always hoped she would not have that power over people.

She had to be the one to tell him. It was the only way. She rehearsed various scenes in her head, over and over. She had to think of the right words to say, the scenario that would end with him believing in her innocence.

What she did not know was that Chris was sitting at the table in the dining area of his apartment, staring at a picture he got from her closet, and also trying to figure out how to have the same conversation. He tried to find the right words to gently tell her what he had done, while maintaining her trust. He did not want to frighten her, nor did he want to be deceived by her if she really was like the rest of her family, as Xiao had suggested. He could not believe that she was in contact with them all this time, that she was truly duplicitous. More than anything, he just wanted to know the truth.

When the gala was wrapping up and she was no longer needed, Jenna sent Chris a message that she was ready to go home. When she got in his car, she opened her mouth to talk, but with his free hand, and without looking away from the road, Chris put his index finger up and shook his head, signaling to her to stay quiet. He did not drive in the direction of her townhouse. He drove to the courthouse three blocks away. He parked the car on the street and got out. Jenna remained seated, unsure of what to do. He opened her door and motioned for her to follow him. She did so, and he used his ID to gain access first to the building, then to the stairwell, then out of the stairwell two floors below, and finally into a room with a metal door. It looked like an interrogation room, but, looking around, Jenna saw no chairs, no table, no two-way mirror, no camera, and no microphone. The emptiness of the air between them slowly filled her and sank to the pit of her stomach.

She heard the door shut, and Chris was standing directly behind her.

He pulled out his phone and walked around as he scanned the room for devices as an extra precaution. The room was completely dead, void of all signals.

"Now, we can talk," he said in a low voice.

"Okay." She took a deep breath to begin her story, but he beat her to it.

"Monday evening," he began, "your protection agent approached you and informed you that the members of your family were all dead and that your brother Adam was here in Des Moines when he died last week."

She tensed up, and her breaths became shallow.

"Jenna." His voice softened. "I didn't know. I came to Iowa with one family member left. We didn't even know about you. I would have never gotten involved if—" He broke off abruptly. He did not mean it, and she knew it. They were both glad they had happened to each other and did not regret it. "Jenna, please," he said as he walked toward her. "Katherine. Give me something, anything concrete that proves you have not been involved since the attacks started five years ago. I *must* have hard evidence, proof that you are not using the Protection Program as a cover to secretly conspire with anarchists."

She closed her eyes and relaxed as she exhaled in relief.

It gave her away.

He took a step closer to her. He stood tall over her, ominous and stone cold. "You knew." His voice was dark and low. There was no happiness or relief in what he said. He was furious. "You knew about me this whole time."

"No"—she snapped her eyes open, her breathing turning quick and panicked—"you don't understand." She looked up at him, alarmed by the tone of his voice. His eyes had no glint, no water, no smile. They looked like spheres of living tissue, with no soul behind them. She had never seen him like this and realized she had evoked the detached soldier he was trained to be. Her eyes welled with tears at the sight of him. She looked at him desperately and shook her head. "Chris, please, you don't understand."

He stepped closer to her again, his body inches from hers. She tried to back away, but he caught her shoulders. She could tell he was not using much strength, but she could not move, as much as she tried to shrink away from him. "Why do you bother feeling guilty?" he whispered in a low, deep voice, trying not to sound hurt.

"No, you don't understand."

He was breathing slowly, trying not to lose patience, hope, or trust. He did not want to believe it, but his boss's argument was looking more plausible than ever. When he completely let out a slow exhale, he asked, challenging her, "What don't I understand?"

She inhaled deeply, trying to gather her thoughts and choose her words carefully. "Yes, I knew." She closed her eyes as she wiped away her tears, breathed in again, and looked back up at him. "But I have only known since yesterday. My protection agent told me about my family, and then you told me about your case. I still hadn't put it together, but then I saw the giraffe." She tried to move again, but his hands had turned to stone, though his grip was not so tight as to hurt her. "Please, Chris."

He was unmoved. He looked into each of her eyes, searching. Finally, he said, "I don't believe you."

"You have to believe me," she pleaded. "You have to understand. I am not like my family. Please." She was sounding desperate, so she closed her eyes and breathed deeply through her nose to calm down.

He intensified his gaze. "I brought you here because I was convinced that you did not know, that you felt about me the same way I feel about you. *I* had no idea, but *you*—" He released her from his grip. "Why did you do all of this?" he asked. "Why didn't you just run? You are obviously good at hiding."

She backed away as far as she could, and her back hit a wall. Instantly, she regretted it as he started walking toward her. "No, I just found out. Please, you must believe me. I didn't know."

"You didn't know?" He was angry. "You weren't warned by your family's numerous connections, by your brother who came here to visit you, though your location was supposed to be a secret? You didn't spot me instantly at the bar and target me? You didn't draw me in and make me fall in love with you so I wouldn't kill you? You didn't manipulate me and become the one person in my life I have ever truly trusted to be my real self with for the purpose of saving your own life?"

He was passionate now, less cold, and it gave her hope. He had not completely shut her out, yet.

She put her hands up in defense and said in a soft whisper, "No, I really didn't know." Then, when he did not respond, she said in a stronger voice, "*You're* the predator, not me. Everything *I* told you is true. They told me never to tell anyone anything about my life before I went into hiding, but you were the *one* person I have ever trusted enough to let all my guards down, and you're the *one* person I should never have trusted in the first place. This is *your* elaborate way of finishing your last target. You saw on one of your many tracking devices that I was headed to the hotel restaurant. You sat at the only place with one empty seat next to it, so I would have to sit next to you. *You* charmed *your* way into *my* life. You brag about your years of training and experience in profiling people. You brag about how you're so good at covering your own tracks that nobody ever has to cover for you. You knew exactly what you were doing."

She had never actually thought of all these points until she said them out loud. Hearing them now, she was so scared she thought she would faint or vomit or both. But, though she was shaking with fear, she was innocent, and she would stand by that truth.

"Then why did you sleep with me?" As he shouted his question, unable to conceal the hurt and anger and betrayal he felt, he banged the side of his fist on the sheet metal wall, sending an echo throughout the room. In the instant after it, he broke his gaze into her eyes to look at the wall where his fist had hit it, and she saw this break in eye contact was also a break in his assurance that she was guilty.

I'm just as confused as you are, she wanted to say, but she was silent, too terrified to speak. Then, she gave up and, in a whisper, said, "Because I love you, Chris."

She was looking him in the eyes, like prey that first notices the predator. She could only stare at him, unable to cry or breathe or speak or look away. And she saw that he stared back at her with the same fight-or-flight decision before him. Half of her wanted to flee, knowing he may snap into the fight part, but the other half wanted to hold him and tell him everything would be okay, that she had not been using him, that she had not been playing him all along.

"You're good," he said finally, complimenting her acting.

She started shaking her head in protest. "No, I'm not lying to you. I'm telling the truth."

"Perhaps I have met my match," he said as he stepped back away from her. He swallowed hard, and despite how relaxed the rest of his body appeared, she saw that his jaw muscles were tight and tense. "My boss is taking me off the case, and someone will replace me. I'll be sure to warn them of your tactics."

He went to the door and held it open.

She started breathing again as a sinking feeling seeped down her core. She looked around at the nothingness of the room that surrounded her, feeling as though she were looking around the inside of her own heart. Then she looked at the door, panic-stricken, and briskly walked out, trying not to cry. He led her back up to the street. When they left the building, he continued walking away from her, not turning around. Without looking at her and with only that cold, blank, soulless look in his eyes, he got in his car and left.

"Thank you," she whispered to him as he drove away, for she knew if he were going to kill her, that room was where he would have done it. She knew he was hurt, that he thought she had betrayed him this entire time, and knowing he was completely lost to her made her want to cry. She was not even scared anymore. She did not even care if he thought she was guilty anymore. She just wanted him to know that her feelings for him were true, that she did love him. But as he drove away from her, he drove away from the mission, and she knew she had little time before his replacement would come for her.

17

The roaring engine was almost as loud as Chris's breathing as he got on the highway headed east. He wouldn't bother with the tunnels tonight. He wanted to drive. His breaths were deep and fast, and every muscle in his body was tense. He had almost finished the mission in that room. She had known. Adam had warned her. Maybe she had given him the giraffe while he was in Des Moines. She was every bit as manipulative as the rest of her family. There was logic enough to justify finishing her. But he knew better than to finish a target with such emotion. His boss was right. He was too emotionally involved.

But there was another reason, aside from professionalism, that he did not finish her in that room: he knew better than to go against his own physiology and instincts. He focused on a single moment of memory: when his hand hit the wall, it left a mark of sweat. He could feel traces of sweat from his hands soaking into his gloves, even now as he was driving. His body knew something his mind had not yet realized. And he would not do anything until he found out what it was.

Intimidation and interrogation were never hard for him. Neither was remaining expressionless and emotionless. But hiding his feelings and trying to intimidate the truth out of her had been the hardest thing he had ever done. He had been blindsided before, but it never made him as unsteady as he was now. Either she was as good as the rest of her family, or something was not right about what had just happened.

He could not tell if this was actually true, that there was something terribly wrong, or if he just wanted it to be true. His breathing intensified as he thought about the relief on her face. She had known going into that room exactly what he was going to say. He didn't know which emotion he felt most strongly: anger, hurt, or shame.

He forced himself to take slower and deeper breaths to calm down. He had to focus. He had to think clearly.

He went over the events of the last two weeks in his mind, all the way up to the interrogation in the dead room.

Right now, he knew he could not trust her, not with all the points his boss had made about her manipulating him; nor could he trust that his boss was correct, given all the points she had made from her point of view. But he could trust his instincts. He was not some designed assassin who blindly obeyed authority. He was a trained profiler. His gut feeling, which he had not only lived with his entire life but that he had also trained and perfected over years of experience with targets and cases, was something he knew he could trust. He was calm, now, and he focused on his intuition, what he *felt* was correct, and his instincts told him she was innocent, that she was telling the truth.

He outran two more police cars when it finally dawned on him what was wrong. He remembered Zaire on the phone saying, *"We have absolutely no evidence against her personally."* Chris had never been given a target without first being handed all the evidence, all the proof that the target must be taken care of, evidence against the target and evidence that Chris's profession was the only possible solution.

And when he had awoken with the realization and examined her hand, shoulder, and face, had he not forced himself to go back to sleep to embrace denial? Hadn't he avoided looking at her all day to avoid coming out of denial? Didn't that also tell him something, that he did not immediately see her as a target upon realizing who she was?

He thought about how scared she was, how there was a Mexican man stalking her, and how stupid he was to think that this was some elaborate scheme to evade him. If she were smart enough to fool him into not killing her, she would have been smart enough to flee to Mexico and disappear there. It was certainly less risky and required a lot less effort. He thought of how she stood her ground, not wavering an inch in her declaration that she was innocent. His own self-doubt, thinking that she could trick him, nearly got her killed.

He turned the car around and drove even faster back into town. He drove to her townhouse, but her car was not there. He pulled out his notebook and looked for her signatures, manually since they were not on file for the agency but stored in his computer. She was driving on the highway, headed south.

He transferred the data to his car's tracking system and used it to watch her location. Her car stopped, and he drove faster.

As he approached, he saw that she had been pulled over. She was standing outside of her car. The officer, in a more than rough manner, was pushing her against her car and putting handcuffs on her wrists behind her. Chris pulled up behind the patrol vehicle and got out without a sound.

"Where did you steal this car?" the officer demanded. He looked like a teenager fresh out of training.

Jenna was calm in her response. "I work downtown at the art museum. I live in a townhouse, and this is my car. If you just check my ID in my purse. Please look at it."

"I don't believe in Purebreds living outside the Communities! I'll take you to the precinct, and we'll sort this out! If you don't have a place in a Community, I'll get you one!" He was leaning into her and shouting into her ear, his body pressed up against hers.

Chris grabbed the man's shoulders and pulled him off of her.

Completely surprised, the officer pulled out his gun and pointed it at Chris.

Chris put his hands in the air. "Please, sir, if I may just reach for my ID. She is under my jurisdiction, not yours."

"We can settle that when I take her back to the precinct. That's the protocol," the officer said.

"Please," Chris said as he motioned with one hand, "I'm going to reach into my pocket and get my ID."

"No, go back to your car, or I will shoot," the officer said, narrowing his eyes at Chris.

Chris could tell it was the officer's first time aiming a gun at someone. He was hesitant and unsure of what to do. Chris wondered if it was the officer's first night alone on the job.

Chris did not move. "If you don't put your gun down, I will be forced to take action."

The officer lifted the gun higher, and Chris kicked it out of his hand and up in the air and caught it. He pointed it at the officer as he said, "Let her go."

The officer called for backup as he positioned Jenna in front of him.

Infuriated by the officer's actions, Chris gently but swiftly pulled Jenna away from the officer and punched him in the face. The officer lifted his arm to fight back, but Chris caught it and put the gun to the man's head. "Call off your backup," he commanded.

The officer talked into his radio and canceled the call for backup.

"Now, uncuff her."

With shaky hands, the officer fumbled with the keys as he tried to unlock the handcuffs from Jenna's wrists. When the officer dropped the keys, Chris picked them up and, annoyed, shouldered the man out of his way and unlocked the handcuffs himself. He shoved them into the officer's hands.

Chris pulled out his ID and showed it to the officer. "I am taking her into my custody. I'm taking the gun, too, as an extra precaution. You'll get another one when you return to your workstation, along with an explanation. Now leave us."

The officer hesitated and then sprinted to his car and drove off.

They faced each other, and she looked at him, unsure if she should have been happy or afraid to see him.

With his eyes still on hers, he tucked the gun into the waist of his pants and said, "It felt really good to punch that guy."

She broke into a smile and started to laugh. Her eyes were still teary.

He grinned slightly and said, "I should have been doing that all along. I certainly wanted to—the officer that carded you at the bar, the officers that pulled you over when you took me to dinner—"

Still smiling, she shook her head and hugged him, burying her head in his chest.

"Oh, and that guy at the print shop. I really should have punched him."

He felt her hot tears soak through his shirt. He wrapped his arms around her, kissed the top of her head, and said, "I'm so sorry."

She sniffled and wiped her tears as she leaned back. "I really do love you," she said. "I wasn't just saying that to—"

"I know," he said. "I love you, too. Can you forgive me?"

She nodded and kissed him.

Then, he said, "We should leave. The officer probably called for backup while he was leaving. Is there anything in your car you need?"

"It's just the suitcase I took to Idaho."

He opened her car and got the suitcase, and she got her purse. Then, they got in his car, and he started to drive away.

"Do you need anything from your house?"

"No," she said.

He pressed a button on his steering wheel, and a woman's voice answered. "Good evening, Agent Rockford, how can I serve you?"

"There's a confused officer in Des Moines. He was near the south border, but now he is headed back to his workstation. I have his gun and the citizen he was arresting. The citizen's car is still parked on the street."

"Yes, sir, I'll take care of it right away," she said. "Is there anything else I can do for you?"

"I won't be returning to my apartment in Des Moines."

"Yes, sir, I'll have them send your things and notify the landlord. Is there anything else I can do for you?"

"I'm turning off the comms. I'll be in the tunnels headed back to headquarters, if anyone needs me."

"I'll put you on emergency notice only," she said. "Is there anything else I can do for you, Agent Rockford?"

"No, thank you," he said, and he switched off the communication system.

He turned to Jenna. "This way we won't be disturbed unless it's urgent."

"Chris, I'm so sorry I didn't tell you last night when I realized what was going on. I should have. I just wanted more time to think about it and how to say it. I really wasn't sure I was even right, but—"

"No," he said. "There's no reason you would think anybody except the Mexican gang is after you because you are innocent. I know that because I trust my instincts and because I trust you." He looked at her. "Do you trust me?"

She looked back at him. "You're the only one I trust."

"I'm sorry about your family, Jenna. I know you were not close to them, but I'm sorry this happened to you." He held his hand out to her, and she took it. "I'm going to get to the bottom of this," he continued. "My boss gave me until Monday before another team takes over. I'll talk with him tomorrow and convince him to close the case. There is no reason for them to go after you."

"And if they disagree with you?" she dared to ask.

"Then we'll figure something out from there," he said. "Together."

They entered the underground tunnels, and he set the destination to the exit near his house. The Tunnel Operating System took over, and the car shut off and lifted as the magnetic force propelled them toward the Coast.

18

Upon exiting the tunnels almost three hours later, they emerged on the streets of Washington, D.C. Jenna's eyes were as wide as her smile as she looked at the beautiful buildings, the clean streets, and the bright lights. No expense was spared on the Coasts. The city was not crowded, and the few people walking out on the street, even after the midnight hour, were having fun, without being questioned by officers. The buildings were huge and artistic, each one with its own unique charm—not like in the Inland, where all the buildings were hastily built with the same rectangular shape, the same color, and the same floor plan.

Chris drove to his house and pulled into the garage. Jenna got out, stretching her limbs as she did so. He took her suitcase out of the trunk and walked to the door of his house.

As the door opened, the lights on the other side switched on, and Jenna saw that they were in a basement. Along the wall, there were computer monitors that came to life as they walked in. Chris set her bag down and put a code into the first monitor. The screen then showed a blueprint that Jenna could only assume was the house they were in. It showed their heat signatures in the basement and had a few notes, updating Chris on any events that had occurred while he was away. He touched a few of the rooms and more icons, and the lights in the stairway came on.

"Just locking the garage, turning on the lights, and adjusting the temperature," he explained. He touched the figure of her on the screen and put in an additional code. "Now, it will never record your information."

"And yours?" she asked out of curiosity.

"It never does. And no one can access our data while we're here, not the Mexican gang, not the Protection Agency, no one." Then, after a pause, he added, "Well, maybe my friend Zaire, but he wouldn't."

"What about the Protection Agency? Won't they notice I'm missing?"

"I had Zaire set up a decoy signal for you, so they think you're still in Des Moines right now. We'll keep it that way until they contact you tomorrow. Hopefully by then we'll have all this sorted out."

She looked around her at the basement. It was so silent, the kind of silence that only occurs after an unnoticed sound has stopped. She had never realized how much ambient noise surrounded her or how much she subconsciously knew about the possibility of eavesdroppers, whether they were hackers or spies or her own government. It was surreal, this feeling of true invisibility, not even the possibility of being watched or heard or tracked. She could do anything in this house, and no one would know about it.

He looked at her as their figures on the screen behind him disappeared, and he relaxed, truly, for the first time since they left Idaho. "Come on, I'll show you around."

When they walked through the door at the top of the stairs, they entered a completely different atmosphere, like it was a different house altogether. It was warm and comfortable and inviting. It was well decorated and full of personality.

She stopped and stood still, staring around her. "*This* is where you live?" she asked with excitement and disbelief. "It's…" She had to think a minute for the right word.

"Not what you expected?"

"I guess it is, considering you would have to pretend to be normal when you have visitors."

"Visitors?" he asked. "Who?"

"Well, you must have people over sometimes."

He shook his head. "This is for my family. They stay here when they visit, and the decorating was all my mother's doing."

Jenna started walking around, looking at everything. Being in this house felt like having Chris's life wrapped around her. It may have been decorated by his mother, but it had pieces of him everywhere. She imagined him spending his downtime here, if he had any. She imagined him spending time with his family here. She imagined his niece and nephews coming to visit and completely taking over the whole house, making it busy with excitement.

"This is the kitchen, obviously," he said, gesturing about the room they were in. He walked her through the dining room to the living room, which was wall-to-wall with bookshelves. She thought it was fitting that there was a picture of him with his mother near the entrance, as this room had obviously been inspired by her. He pointed to a door. "That's another staircase that leads downstairs to an apartment. It's where my parents stay when they visit." They went to the main entry hall at the front entrance of the house. Across from the living room was a formal sitting room filled with more bookshelves. He pointed to another door down the hallway behind the stairs. "And that's a bedroom I stay in when my brother and his kids visit." He turned to her. "When they're here, they all stay upstairs." He led her up the stairs and down the hallway. "This is the room my brother and his wife stay in," he said as they passed a room. Then, he pointed to three other rooms. "His kids stay in those rooms."

"Which one is your room?" she asked. "I mean the one you normally sleep in."

He opened a door and led her up another flight of stairs that led to the third floor, which had a living room, a single bedroom and a bathroom. She walked across the entryway and stood at the door to the bedroom. He encouraged her to go in by lightly nudging her on the back. "Go on. Look around."

She went in, and then she turned to him. "This feels really weird."

"What does?"

"You're just watching," she said.

"Well, maybe I want to see what you find interesting."

"Okay…I'll let you know if I think anything is intriguing."

The truth was that the room, but nothing in it, was very intriguing. It was dark, with the single window covered by dark curtains, and the walls were bare. There was no television, no books, just lots of space. The bed was large but had only two pillows. The sheets and comforter were black. She turned back to him. "There's not much to explore."

He shrugged. "It's peace to me."

She looked around again, this time with his mindset. Yes, for someone who was always on guard, constantly vigilant and aware of his surroundings, continually planning the next move—this room was very peaceful. It was simple. She imagined him coming here for refuge when he needed to clear his mind. The room had a fitting calmness to it. Had it been anyone else's room, she would have thought they were boring or that they possessed no depth, but it was the opposite with Chris. With such a complex and demanding job as his, he would want some place simple and empty where he could rest, some place that would not get in his mind like the rest of his life.

"We can stay in a different room, if you want to. I know this one seems a bit creepy compared to the rest of the house. But you're the first one to come in it except for me."

She turned to face him. "Not even your family?"

He shook his head.

"No, I like it. It is very peaceful. I can feel myself relax in this room. Everything is clear and makes sense here."

They were both exhausted from the evening. She put on her nightclothes and got into his bed with him as naturally as if she did it every night.

*   *   *

Hours later, Jenna woke up to an empty room. She walked around the house, searching for Chris. When she could not find him, she decided to sit at the kitchen table and wait. He came through the door to the basement, his shirt soaked with sweat.

"I thought I heard you moving around. Do you want anything for breakfast?" he asked as he opened the refrigerator. "Actually...I don't have any breakfast food. I usually eat breakfast out."

"Just some milk will be fine," she said, seeing that he had a gallon of milk.

He opened it and smelled it. "It's old." He started pouring it down the sink. "Sorry, I didn't expect to be here, so I don't really have anything to eat. We'll have to go shopping. I'll take a shower and be ready soon."

"Okay," she said, and they went upstairs and got ready.

They left his house and walked to a café nearby for breakfast. People nodded and greeted them, but even with all their politeness, they could not hide their surprise at seeing her.

She and Chris both pretended not to notice, and it occurred to Chris that she could be the first Inlander some of these Coastals had ever seen.

On the way home, she stopped at a bench and sat down, watching the people as they walked by, and Chris sat next to her. It was so different from Des Moines. There were hardly any officers. Nobody was being carded, even the Purebreds, rare as they were. People were polite and treated each other equally. People here had energy and free time to enjoy their Saturday, not worn down and fatigued from work and trying to make ends meet. Everyone dressed well, in clothes that had more quality than what was sold in the Inland, and the clothes also looked so new compared to what Inlanders wore.

People could not help but stare at her, even if for only a second before they remembered their manners. And she could not help but feel embarrassed when people looked at her, a Purebred dressed in such plain Inland clothes. The two Purebreds she had seen were rich enough to not only live outside of the Communities but also to live on the Coast. It showed in their appearance, not just in their clothing but in their hair and skin and the way they carried themselves. It only reminded her of what an outsider she really was—a Purebred Inlander was almost as rare as her naturally blue eyes and red hair.

Runners were weaving in and out of trees and people. Teenagers were playing soccer in the open grass. Kids were running while frantic parents chased them. She envied them of their ignorance.

"I have a plan for what I'm going to say to my boss, but if it doesn't work, go to the Protection Agency and go back into hiding," Chris said.

Startled, Jenna looked at him in surprise. "What do you mean?"

"Just in case," he said in a calm voice. "If it doesn't work, go to Protection, and tell them your case has been compromised. You aren't on a watch list, yet, so they won't have any suspicions about deleting Jenna Macklemore and creating a new file for you. Go along with them until they leave you, and then try to get away as soon as you can. You won't be able to travel, but if you can stay under the radar for at least a day or two, I'll come find you. The new team won't have as hard of a time accessing your file since we have already opened it, but accessing real-time data from the Protection Agency is more difficult. It should at least buy us enough time for me to meet up with you, and then we'll flee together."

"*We?*" she asked. "Where will we go?"

"Yes, *we*," he assured her, almost sounding hurt. "We're in this together, remember? If it comes to it, I'll disobey direct orders, come find you, and we'll flee to Mexico."

"That's where I was planning to go yesterday," she confessed. "But I didn't get very far."

"I'll convince my boss to close the case, and we won't have to flee, but I wanted to let you know I have a backup plan." In truth, he did not feel as assured as he sounded. Xiao was so adamant about eliminating her as a precaution, like she was merely collateral damage as far as the agency was concerned. He would convince Xiao, though, to close the case because of her innocence. He would convince Xiao that she had absolutely nothing to do with the crimes.

"I already knew you had a backup plan, Chris," she said, looking at him. "I told you I trust you, and I always will."

He could tell she was still worried about it—and with reason. He took her hand in his and said, "You're not alone in this. I'll never leave you, as long as you'll have me."

"You would really disobey direct orders, go rogue, and we would somehow get to Mexico, a completely unknown foreign place with no idea of how to even get there—for me?"

"Yeah," he said, again sounding hurt that she would even question it. "I don't think you understand: I can't live without you now."

His seriousness made her laugh, but he knew it was because she was nervous. "Yes, you could."

"Could you live without me?" he asked seriously.

"I could if it meant you would be okay."

"*You're* worried about *me?*"

"I may not be privy to the inner workings of the government, but I'm pretty sure there would be severe consequences for you if you went rogue and took my side on this when they told you not to. And given your skill set and the knowledge you have, I'm guessing they will stop at nothing to prevent you from doing that. It's too much of a risk for them."

"Then I'll just have to make sure we don't have to flee. I'm confident we won't have to. But if we do, we'll make it."

"I would turn myself in, then, because I could not live with myself knowing I put you at risk or in danger of them going after you."

"Look," he said in a low, serious voice, "I'm very good at what I do. I know I sound arrogant right now, but you don't know just how many missions I've done and how many different types of situations I've been in, and I have always come out of them invisible and flawless. Yes, I had help from the agency's resources, but I also did a lot on my own, and you pick up a few things from eight years of living in the shadows and hiding in plain sight and being a chameleon to blend into surroundings and getting along with all sorts of people. Plus, it also means I know the agency's resources and, more importantly, their limitations. Trust me, if you're with me, fleeing will not be a risk."

She thought for a moment, and he knew he had convinced her of how passionately he cared for her. "Are you saying what I think you're saying?"

"That I want to spend the rest of my life with you? Yeah, I am saying that. I realize now I should have just come out and said that to begin with because you're not as perceptive as I am"—she smiled and rolled her eyes, which caused him to smile—"but I am very perceptive, and I already know you feel the same way."

She looked into his eyes and said seriously, "I do feel the same way."

He kissed her, and she put one hand up to his jaw as she kissed him back. When they pulled apart, a few people in close proximity were glancing at them with less courtesy than before, appalled, not by the public display of affection but by the audacity of a Coastal in such a relationship with an Inlander. Bringing her here was one thing, but for a Coastal to act in such a way with an Inlander in a public park was downright offensive to some.

A child walking by their bench stopped and stared at Jenna. His father quickly ushered him away with an apology. Jenna laughed involuntarily.

It embarrassed Chris that she was being treated this way, even on the Coast, but at least it was just because of her clothing and at least people were not too rude about it. "Come on," Chris said, standing up and offering her his hand. "Let's get you some new clothes."

*   *   *

When Chris arrived at his boss's office later that day, Zaire was standing in the hallway, waiting for him.

"I'm so sorry about this," Zaire said. "You know, if you ever need to talk about it or if there is ever anything I can do to help you through this, I'm here for you."

Chris was genuinely touched by how much his friend cared for him, but Zaire still didn't get it. He still could not understand how Chris could be so emotionally attached to someone like Jenna that he would challenge the orders given to him.

He put a hand on Zaire's shoulder and said, "Thanks, man."

"Chris, I'm serious," Zaire said, clearly thinking Chris was in denial. "Xiao is going to put a new agent on the case in your place. It's out of your hands now."

"I'm going to convince Xiao to close the case. There's no evidence against her."

"Look, I know you feel strongly about her and that this is difficult, but your duties are to this agency and to The Order."

With his hand still on Zaire's shoulder, Chris thought about what Zaire had said, about how he thought they already had an epidemic on their hands just by having so many Purebreds in The Sectors, even if confined to the Purebred Communities. He had agreed with him back then.

"I know," Chris assured him. "That's why I know it's the right thing to do."

Zaire sighed, and Chris knew he did not agree. "Call me when it's done, okay?"

"I will," Chris said. He patted Zaire's shoulder, and Zaire turned to go back to his office.

Chris knocked on Xiao's door.

"Come in," he heard Xiao say from the other side.

Xiao was sitting at his desk, looking over documents. He held out a hand, motioning for Chris to sit down in the chair across from him.

As Chris walked in, a woman who had been facing the window turned to greet him.

"President Anders," Xiao said, "this is Agent Christopher Rockford."

Chris bowed to President Anders and then looked at his boss, having thought his meeting with Xiao was going to be private and that Xiao would talk with President Anders before meeting with him.

As if reading Chris's thoughts, Xiao said, "President Anders wanted to talk with you, and when I told her I was meeting with you directly after meeting with her, she asked if she could stay. And I agreed."

Chris knew Anders and Xiao had a history. They had both been original founders of the agency and had been integral in the creation of the current system of government after The War. They were not just two people who had worked together for so many years; they were also close friends. If Chris had any chance at pleading his case, this was it.

"Agent Rockford, it's a pleasure to get to speak with you," President Anders said.

"The pleasure is mine," Chris responded.

They both sat down in chairs opposite of Xiao.

As he did so, Chris regarded his boss like he had when he met him fifteen years beforehand, but this time, he saw his mentor through the eyes of an adult. Xiao was much older than Chris, at least by forty years, but he had many wrinkles, even for his age. He was shorter than Chris, too, and he had a smaller build, but he was not skinny. Even at his age, Xiao was still swift and strong. Xiao had dark brown skin with sparse darker moles sprinkled across his face. His smooth and thick black hair was graying, but not balding, and his dark brown eyes had dark blue circles outlining the irises. Like all of their generation, Xiao and Anders did not have the scar of a Modified. None of the bosses or Presidents possessed the Modified scar. For a brief instant, Chris thought about what the Robertsons—what Jenna's family—thought about the non-Modified members of government designing the society they would control.

He quickly shoved the thought out of his mind.

President Anders turned to Chris and said, "The Council of Presidents has long since known of your talents and has watched your successes with enthusiasm. Agent Rockford," Anders continued, "the Council has also decided to open an additional boss position in the Department of Mexico Relations, which we invite you to occupy immediately. Your skills and quick thinking, knowledge and expertise, and extensive success record more than recommend you for the position. It is a waste of time to wait for a position to open."

Chris looked at Xiao and then back at Anders. "I thought this meeting was to discuss the case of Katherine Robertson."

"I will discuss her case with the Council at our next meeting," Anders replied.

Xiao added, "We do not want to take any risks with this mission. There is too much risk that the specifics of this case will reach the public. Katherine Robertson knows too much, and she could become a problem."

"That's not how we operate," Chris said calmly.

"We fear," Anders started, "that if any members of Pure Star knew she was alive, they may come back bigger and stronger, undoing all of the work we have fought so hard to accomplish."

"You know she's innocent, and we have no evidence against her," Chris stated. "We took out six of the biggest masterminds in anarchy. We have factual, hard evidence against them. Taking them out has been the best move in anarchy prevention since The War, and there's nothing else we gain from taking her out."

Xiao argued, "Even if she does not want to lead a group of anarchists, who she is and what she represents would still be out there. A group could turn her into a name, a cause they would stand behind, and they would make her the face of that cause, with or without her consent."

Chris argued, "If anything, pursuing her puts The Order at risk. How many people on this case know there is no evidence against this target? That's the risk the Presidents should be considering. If we eliminate her and people find out we had no case against her, we're done—not just us, but the whole branch of government we answer to. We can't just go out and remove someone because they could cause something to happen in the future."

"Taking out the six Robertsons has been tremendously helpful, Agent Rockford, and for this we extend our gratitude to you," Anders said, and turning to Xiao, she added, "and your team."

Xiao nodded to her in acknowledgement of the compliment.

"But the agenda of The Order is not complete until there is one race, one society, one manageable people," Anders continued, addressing Chris. "That is the true goal here, and that is what I will focus on when I bring up the matter with the other Presidents. Can I tell them that you have accepted the promotion and will take on the job as a boss?"

But instead of answering her question, Chris asked her, "What will you tell them about the Robertson case?"

Anders's expression remained neutral as she said, "I've been thinking about it, and while it is risky to keep her alive, if she had considerable cosmetic surgery and a new identity and placement in a Purebred Community—"

As Anders spoke, Chris realized his arguments for closing the case while keeping Jenna alive had not persuaded them. He thought of how calmly Jenna had defended herself to the officers who accused her of being a criminal just for existing, how she had stood up for herself to the man in the print shop, and how she had even stood up to him in the dead room when he accused her of being involved. She had stood firm and strong on the foundation of the truth.

He drew upon that strength and said, "No."

Both Anders and Xiao looked at him abruptly.

Then, Chris asked, "What if she stays hidden here, in Washington, D.C., as a Coastal citizen, and I'll be held accountable for her?"

"Are you trying to negotiate with me, Agent Rockford?" Anders asked him with a stern tone of authority that made her question sound more like a challenge.

"No, Madam President," Chris answered obediently.

"You want to draw out this case so it lasts longer," said Anders sharply.

"No, I want to close it, but if I'm wrong, then she will be close by and easily stopped."

"Would you turn down the offer to become a boss if the Presidents refuse these terms?" she asked, her tone back to neutral and her question sounding more like a statement.

"No," Chris answered.

Anders and Xiao exchanged a look, and then she turned back to Chris and said, "The Council meeting is in an hour. I will inform them of your offer to personally see to the containment of Katherine Robertson, and I will relay to them your points on how this is the best outcome for the case and is in the best interest of World Order." She stood up, and Chris and Xiao stood up as well. Then, she turned to Xiao. "I will send word of the outcome when the meeting is over."

Xiao and Chris bowed to her as she left, and once she was gone, Chris also started to leave.

"Rockford," Xiao said, "you will take the position of a boss in the Department of Mexico Relations, won't you? Even if the Presidents do not agree to your remaining with Katherine Robertson?"

"Jenna," Chris said. "She has not been Katherine for a long time."

Xiao did not say anything for a few moments, noting that Chris did not answer his question. "Jenna will need a new identity," he finally said. "I will call you when I hear from Anders regarding the outcome. If the Presidents agree to it, we'll close this case, and you can take Jenna to the Protection Agency to get her new identity as soon as possible." He did not comment on what would happen if the Presidents did not agree. Chris suspected Xiao already knew what Chris's decision would be in that scenario.

"Thank you, sir," Chris said, and then he left.

*   *   *

Waiting for the elevator, Chris caught sight of his reflection in the elevator doors. His scar was prominent in the light of the hallway, and he touched it, wondering what it really meant. He would be the first Modified boss. And he wondered what that meant, too.

He thought about Washington, D.C., the city he loved so dearly. The possibilities here were endless. Children growing up in this city would have more than he could have ever hoped for during his own childhood, not just in terms of physical possessions and surroundings but also in choices and opportunities. Even as a Purebred, Jenna had more growing up on the Coast than he had growing up in the Inland.

The Coastal-Inland system looked good on paper. It was orderly and neat, but it was not really efficient. If every child at birth had the opportunities of a Modified child born on a Coast, the exponential progress made in the world would have been phenomenal. It was not fair that Purebreds and Inlanders had the cards stacked against them. And someone born as a Purebred Inlander was utterly doomed.

He understood, now, how the Robertsons were against The Order, how they saw that the way society was set up would ultimately not work. It may have benefited the greater good, but it did nothing for the individuals that made up the society. They could have left it alone, continuing to live carefree lives, set apart by their wealth. The system did not really affect them. At least not yet. Instead, they chose to voice their opinion and fight for their cause.

But their voice was not heard because breaking the law had not been the right way to most effectively bring about the changes they wanted. They had thought it was the only way they could finally get noticed and be taken seriously, but in the end it had not worked. Ultimately, they had been powerless in the face of The Order.

He thought about how Xiao and Anders had so easily brushed aside his concern for Jenna. They did not regard her as a person, only as part of a case, a small piece of society, a mere matter to be dealt with. Prior to meeting Jenna, he might have agreed with them.

It was frustrating that they did not understand or see things the way he did. The world did not look the same to him, anymore. Now, it was full of disparities. With all its order and surveillance and rules, he saw that it was still crazy, disordered, unfair, and painful. But he also saw that we can create a smaller world with the people we choose to surround us, and that smaller world can be one that is safe and free, one that does make sense. Chris could not change the world, not completely, not the way he wanted to, but he could change himself and thus the smaller world that existed in his relationships with others. And perhaps the people in his life, inspired by him, would each choose to do the same, and then all the people in *their* lives, and so on, and so forth. And by changing all the smaller worlds, the entire world would be transformed.

19

When Chris got home, he found Jenna in the living room, reading a book.

"Which one did you choose?" he asked.

"History of the New World Order," she said, showing it to him. "I've already found several specifics my history professor would dispute. How was the meeting?"

"I think it was okay," he said, sitting next to her and putting her legs over his lap.

Then, he decided to tell her everything that was said at the meeting, including every detail.

"Now, we just wait," he said when he had finished. He turned and reached behind him to get a book.

"I haven't been this nervous since waiting to find out where I would be redistributed after testifying."

"How did you handle it?" he asked.

"I sketched. Drawing and painting used to always calm me down, but I had to stop when I went into Protection. They said if anyone knew my distinctive style, they might recognize it and trace it back to me." She held up the book. "So, I figured I'd try to distract myself with reading, instead."

"It's going to work out," he assured her.

After a few moments of them both looking at their books but neither of them reading, he said, "You know, you're stuck with me now, whether you like it or not."

"No," she said. "If they say 'no' to this plan, I'm not letting you come with me."

"I'm a trained professional. I'll find you."

"You didn't the first time," she joked, trying to lighten the mood.

He laughed lightly and said, "Ouch," which caused her to laugh. "That was because I did not even know you were there to find, and technically I did find you, even when I did not know to look for you."

"No, no, no," she argued playfully, but he could tell she was just trying to cover up being nervous. "Remember? You even said so in that room yesterday—"

"Oh," he groaned, "don't mention that room."

"You said *I* found *you*. I saw you at the bar and approached you."

"Fine, you're a better stalker than I am," he said, playing along.

She laughed nervously and said, "Of course you had to make it sound like a bad thing."

He took her hand. "Seriously," he said, "they'll agree to the plan. They have no evidence against you, and there's none to be found." He shifted so he was facing her more directly. "Look, I know you don't believe it, but I really am the best at what I do, and I've worked really hard for this promotion, and, quite frankly, I deserve it."

"Why don't you think I believe that?"

"Because look at you. You're so nervous."

"There's a possibility they are going to call you and tell you I have to be killed, if not by you then by someone else. Yes, that makes me nervous. And it has nothing to do with you or how good you are or how much they want you."

"And I'm telling you that you don't have to be nervous because they're going to go along with the plan, and even if they don't, then you have nothing to be afraid of because I am going to personally make sure nothing happens to you. Ever."

"That is not as reassuring as you think it is."

"Why not?"

"Because I don't want to flee," she confessed.

He smiled. "You want to stay."

"Yes." She moved closer to him and said, "I like waking up with you, and I love the idea of coming home and knowing you would be here. I don't want to leave you."

"I love you," he said.

She said, "I love you, too," but he could tell she was still worried.

She looked around nervously and asked, "But shouldn't we be preparing to flee, though, just in case?"

He squeezed her hand, trying to calm her, and insisted, "We won't have to flee."

"But—"

"They're going to agree with the plan."

"But how do you *know*?"

"I just do. Something about the way the meeting went, how they were so receptive to the idea. They didn't seem surprised by it when I brought it up. I suspect that's because Xiao already knew how I feel about you, that I felt this way last week, even. He probably knew I would want this, even before I did. You think I'm super perceptive? He's the one who trained me."

"Maybe they just wanted to placate you."

"No, it wasn't like that. That wasn't the feeling in the room. I've argued with Xiao before about how to pursue a target and how to continue a case, but this interaction was different. And President Anders did not reprimand me like I would have expected her to, for not blindly obeying her orders. I think it's because they already see me as a boss. I think that's what it will be like when I am one: instead of just taking whatever orders are given to me, I will be part of the conversation that decides what those orders will be for others. I think, in a way, this was a test to confirm their decision to make me a boss."

"But she said she was going to discuss it with all the Presidents. What if they don't agree?"

"There's no evidence against you. If it ever got out that the government went after an innocent civilian just because her family committed a crime that she was not a part of and did not even know about—that's a scandal they want to avoid."

"I think they could cover it up pretty easily."

"But what's easier: treating an innocent civilian like a criminal when there is absolutely no evidence against her and fabricating a story and creating evidence and reasons to do it to sufficiently cover it up, or monitor her closely just in case? It's not worth it for them to continue to pursue you as a target when I have laid out an easy alternative for them."

She looked down, seemingly convinced. "That's a good point. And I trust you." Then, looking back up at him, she continued, "I really do. I know if you feel like they will go along with your plan, then you're probably right. But I'm still nervous about it."

Chris got up and went around the room opening drawers.

"What are you doing?" she asked.

He found what he was looking for and pulled out a small paper notebook and a pen. He sat down next to her again and held them out to her.

She looked at them, not taking them at first.

Chris said, "Regardless of their decision, you're not going back into Protection after this."

She took the notebook and pen from him and began to draw. It was difficult after so many years of forcing herself not to and having it so cemented in her mind to resist the urge. Chris shifted his position and pulled her closer to him so that she was leaning back against him with one of his arms around her. She turned the page and tried again, embracing the distraction and unable to deny how good it felt. After several more attempts, the lines started flowing more freely, and she drew the view in front of her of the doorway to the living room and the front entrance of the house. Chris opened the book he had gotten from the shelf and started to read.

They sat comfortably like that, she sketching and he reading, until his phone rang. Chris stood up, and Jenna watched him as he walked to the kitchen for privacy, conversing in a language she did not understand.

"The Presidents agreed to your terms," Xiao said. "You are promoted to boss, and as a boss, you are personally responsible for Katherine Robertson."

"Jenna Macklemore," Chris corrected him.

"Well, whatever her new identity is. An office will be set up for you at headquarters. Come by my office Monday morning, and I'll brief you on your new duties and first conference. We have a conference with the Presidents and the other bosses across The Sectors every morning at ten."

"Yes, sir," said Chris.

"I will close the Robertson case. They want all records of her destroyed, what we have and what the Department of Protection has. She is to take on a new identity, effective immediately. An agent has already been briefed and is there now, waiting for you both. Take tomorrow off. You will receive your first case as a boss Monday afternoon."

"Yes, sir," said Chris.

They hung up, and he returned to the living room.

Jenna stood up as she braced herself for the news, but she could see in his eyes that there was no need to worry. She smiled and exhaled in relief as she wrapped her arms around him.

As he embraced her, he whispered in her ear, "You can get your own place, if you want to, but I'd love it if you stayed here."

She released him and took his hands in hers, looking down at their hands as if taking time to think about it, but she had already made up her mind. She lifted one of his hands and kissed it before looking back into his eyes and saying, "You know I want to stay."

"Good," he said with a big smile, unable to contain his joy. He pulled her close to him and kissed her, slowly, enjoying all the sensations coursing throughout him. He could feel her smiling as they kissed, and he knew they were both filled not just with relief but also with exhilaration for this new beginning and their new life together.

They pulled away, and he gazed into her eyes, which were brown because of her contacts. He brushed his fingers through her dyed brown hair and said, "Promise me you will fill these walls with your paintings. And wear what you want to wear. Buy the books you want to read. Take out your contacts, and quit dyeing your hair, if you want to. There is no need for hiding or secrecy in this house."

"It's a deal," she said and kissed him again. Then, she asked, "So what's next? How do we do this?"

"First, we have to go to the Protection Agency office. They're closing your case, and with it your identity as Jenna

Macklemore. I was thinking," he said excitedly, "with a new identity, you will get a new Societal Role, so we can suggest one for you teaching art. They'll get you enrolled in college, and you can go back to school next semester."

Her eyes widened. "Just like that? Are you sure?"

"Yeah, it's all part of your new identity." As he started to lead her toward the front door to leave, he asked, "What will your new name be?"

"Hmmm," she hummed. "I've always liked the name Cameron."

"And what about Rockford?"

With a big grin she said, "I could get used to that."

"Cameron," he started.

"Oh, please," she interrupted, "Call me Cam."

"Cam?" he asked.

"Yes, Chris?"

"Tell me more about your family and your professor and your boyfriend who had connections with Mexico. I want to know what they had to say about this world we live in."

20

A month later, Cam and Chris were in the kitchen, preparing to have Zaire and Melinda over for dinner. In the month that she had lived on the Coast, Cam got to experiment with so many more ingredients than were available in the Inland. She was excited to share some of her newest creations with them.

Chris and Cam were still getting to know each other and getting used to living together, which was perfectly normal for newlyweds in The Sectors. It would take some time to settle in, but for now they just basked in the euphoria of their new life.

He was still getting used to being a boss and working in an office. He had not left Washington, D.C., in a month, the longest time he had stayed in the city in eight years. It would have felt weird, he supposed, if not for the excitement of coming home to Cam every day, learning to live with someone, getting to know someone so intimately, and getting to know himself as a married man.

She would not start classes until January, and, in addition to exploring the city and experimenting in the kitchen, she had taken up painting to pass the time. She had painted all her life, except while in Des Moines. It came back to her naturally, as if she had never stopped, and one of her larger pieces now hung in the dining room at Chris's insistence.

Cam was checking and double-checking everything, setting the table, and making sure the living room was clean.

"Everything's perfect," Chris assured her when she came back in the kitchen to check on the bread. Then, he whispered in her ear, "Your mother will never know if it isn't."

She turned her head and kissed him on the cheek. "I still want it to be perfect. For me."

"I have to tell you," Chris said, stopping her to make sure he had her full attention. "Zaire's wife Melinda doesn't know anything—not about you, me, or even what Zaire does for a living, only that he and I work for the government."

"Don't worry," she said. "I'm good at keeping secrets."

Zaire and Melinda came over, and the four of them spent the evening eating and laughing. Cam was flawless at conversation, keeping it neutral and not at all letting on that she knew anything about Chris's or Zaire's Societal Roles. When Melinda asked Cam about her life, she told the truth, that she had grown up on the Coast in Florida, that she met Chris when he was on a trip for work, and that she was recently redistributed to Washington, D.C., upon their decision to marry. She was studying to be an art teacher and would resume classes in the spring semester. Zaire was also flawless, not at all letting on that he knew anything about Cam's previous lives as Jenna or Katherine. The evening came to a close, and Zaire and Melinda went to their car, which Cam recognized as a government car capable of exceeding the speed limit and navigating the tunnels.

From their car, Zaire yelled to Chris, "Breakfast tomorrow?"

"See you at seven," Chris yelled back.

Chris and Cam waved from the front door as Zaire and Melinda drove away.

As they closed the door, their guards came down, and they were truly themselves again. They had gotten good at that over the month, putting on an appearance around others and then returning to who they really were when they were alone.

Cam sighed as she picked up her sketchbook and a pencil and went to the sofa. Chris got a book off the shelf and sat next to her.

"Are you okay?" he asked her.

"Yes," she said, "just still trying to get used to it all. How does Zaire do it? Melinda is truly clueless about his work."

"I have no idea. He's really good at what he does."

"I guess he can talk about his work all he wants to when he's *at* work. Maybe for him it's a nice break to come home and be completely detached from his job," she suggested.

"No," Chris said. "He's never detached from his job, but maybe it is a nice break when he's with her."

"It's quite the opposite for me, isn't it? Out there, I can only talk about a few careful specifics of my life, but with you I am free to be me completely. It's too bad they don't have that."

Chris took her hand in his and, after kissing it, said, "I know exactly how you feel."

It *was* too bad that Zaire and Melinda did not understand the safe world of no secrets or shame or guilt that existed between Chris and Cam Rockford. Zaire supported Chris and openly accepted Cam into their company, but he still did not truly understand Chris's decision to marry Katherine/Jenna/Cam the Purebred. But that was okay. He was watching them and paying attention. He was beginning to see it, and that was a start. That was enough for now.

Author's Note

I hope you have enjoyed this story that touches on the possibilities of how technology can influence society. I originally wrote this book as a "starter novel," something that was just for fun and was supposed to help me learn how to write a novel in the first place. Whether this book actually accomplished that goal is certainly debatable, but I did learn much while writing it.

The first thing I learned was that the book tells the author the story. I have heard many authors say this, and now I have learned first-hand that it is true. I did not set out to write a thriller or a suspense novel, but after several people read it, I found that those were the shelves they placed this book on when they added it to their lists of books on Goodreads. So, in that way, the book told me it was a suspenseful thriller. I did not really set out to write a love story, either, despite the two main characters falling in love. Rather, I wanted to write a story about how meeting a single person can change someone's internal world and the way they see things and think about the environment and society around them. But some readers enjoyed this book as a true love story, which told me that maybe it was one. Finally, when I wrote this book, I wrote it as a stand-alone novel, but after so many people asked me when the sequel would be available, I figured it was the book's way of telling me that it was part of a series. This revised edition of the book reflects this lesson, as I made it more of a romantic thriller than it was in its original form.

One of the biggest lessons I learned from writing this book is that you cannot assume the reader will interpret what you wrote in the way you meant for it to be interpreted. When I wrote this, I assumed that since Purebreds are like modern-day (i.e., circa 2018) people, then they have to take medicines and get vaccines as we do, rather than having the genetic defenses against disease that the Modifieds have. I assumed the reader would also make that assumption. However, shortly after this came out, measles outbreaks across the United States dominated news headlines, and I found out that many of the readers thought Jenna came from a family of anti-vaxxers. I would like to clarify that here: "Purebreds" represent an "old-school" mentality of the future, which translates to our modern-day medicine. It did not occur to me at the time of writing this that people would assume that because her parents opted out of giving her the genetic defenses against disease that it also meant they would opt out of giving her *any* defenses against disease. That is not the case. She is like us: she has to get physicals and checkups and vaccines and take vitamins; Modifieds do not have to do any of those things because they have built-in defenses in their genes.

(As a side note, in this book, parents who get government approval to procreate have their children genetically modified and therefore get benefits from the government; those who do not get the approval and who do not get their children genetically modified do not get the government benefits. I think some readers thought only rich people in the book could afford to get their children modified, but it is the other way around: not getting their kids genetically modified is supposed to make them poor because they cannot afford to take care of their children because the government will not pay for them. It is a policy to encourage citizens to get their children genetically modified. The modifications that are purely cosmetic are the ones that only rich Coastals can afford because those are at a cost to the parents and are separate from the government-funded health genetic modifications. Please forgive me if that was not clear.)

Finally, I learned that I cannot predict the future. One of the reasons I chose a setting of pro- vs. anti-genetic editing was because prejudice is a highly emotional issue, and when it comes to highly emotional issues, everybody is already set in their ways. This means that to talk about it and be the person who brings it up will almost always be perceived as 100% offensive. I don't mean that the person bringing it up is offending anyone; I mean it in the sense that whoever brings it up is automatically perceived as being on the offense so this puts the other person immediately on the defense: their defenses go up, and they prepare themselves for an attack. There is so much preaching and shaming in these discussions that people will automatically assume whoever is talking about it is going to say, "You're wrong. The way you see things is wrong. What you think is wrong. How you feel is wrong. You are a bad and obnoxious person, and I am on a mission to fix you." NOBODY wants to be on the receiving end of that conversation!

Therefore, to talk about something like prejudice, I needed it to be objective enough that nobody would be emotionally attached to the point where they would feel like I was attacking or preaching at them personally. To do that, I needed a situation where characters could be categorized as being one identity or another without being any identities that exist in today's world. This way, readers would not automatically fit into the book's world as they are right now. I had to do this so the reader could see the situation objectively and therefore see how prejudice can affect a society in an objective way.

However, my plan did not completely work. (This is the part where I learned I cannot predict the future.) Shortly after I shared this book with others, a scientist in China claimed that a woman gave birth to twins that he had genetically edited when they were embryos. (If you are unfamiliar with this news story, type something like "China CRISPR babies" into your favorite search engine.) This posed a problem for my quest to be objective and have science fiction that was completely fiction. I did think that genetically edited embryos were an inevitability of the future, but I thought that future was much more distant than it apparently was. I do believe the mass genome editing of the Modifieds in this book is still in the very distant future, as there is still much to figure out for the technology. But the use of this as a fictitious example may not work for being something in which people are not emotionally involved, as more humans are born with genetic modifications and as non-modified people become more aware of all the genetically modified people around them. For that reason, I sincerely hope that as this becomes a less detached issue for society, we will remember to focus on each person as a whole (which encompasses all of their chosen and unchosen identities, the combination of which makes them and their views unique and therefore valuable) and not reduce them to a single identity or category—especially when it is one they did not choose for themselves, such as genetic background.

Overall, I hope this story helped to illuminate the implications of how prejudice can harm and even cripple society and how we must stay vigilant to ensure the right technology does not get into the wrong hands.

Thank you,

Kellyn Thompson
June 12, 2019

Acknowledgements

I would first like to thank my editor. Thank you for helping me clarify what I was trying to say, for your important suggestions, and for all your hours and effort. I could not have done this without you.

I would also like to thank IngramSpark for providing a platform for authors to publish. It is truly great to live in a time when a piece of work can be delivered to an audience with such ease and in such a widespread way.

About the Author

Kellyn Thompson is the author of the *Unexpected Inlander* series, which addresses prejudice in a world where human genetic modifications are required by law, where class is strictly regulated, and where equity is controlled by the government. In addition to writing fiction and thinking about how technology can influence society, she loves psychology, cuddling with cats and dogs, and going on walks. She lives with her husband and cats in the Pacific Northwest.

For more information about the author and to read deleted scenes from the *Unexpected Inlander* Series, visit
https://kellynthompson.com

preview of

The Modified Blueprint

1

"What's next on the agenda?" one of the Presidents asked.

The Secretary answered, "Christopher Rockford has submitted a request for a new mission."

The Secretary was just a voice, but the twelve Presidents were on screens. The two Presidents in the conference room, including President Anders, looked at Chris. The other bosses who resided in Washington, D.C., including his former boss and current mentor, Xiao, were also in the room, and they also looked toward their newest colleague.

"Rockford, you have the floor," President Anders said.

His image appeared on the screen reserved for the speaker. It was only his fourth time speaking at a conference, though they occurred every morning. It was customary for the Presidents to meet with the bosses of the agency across The Sectors to be personally briefed on major progressions and changes in missions. Those residing in Washington, D.C., met in a conference room at the DC Headquarters, while bosses and Presidents at other headquarters across The Sectors did the same. There were two headquarters in each of the three Sectors, with two Presidents residing at each. The other headquarters of the Western Sector was located in Vancouver, B.C. The purpose of the conferences was to promote a partial transparency, a way for the bosses to know they were accountable to the Presidents and also to each other. But full disclosure of any given mission was known only to the Presidents and to the boss assigned to that case.

For just over eight months, Chris had been a boss in the Department of Mexico Relations, commonly referred to as the DMR. It was supposed to be a branch dedicated to pursuing peaceful communications between The Sectors and the mysterious government that had refused to sign the Treaty of The Sectors following The War That Brought Order. For forty-one years, Mexico had kept its doors completely shut to The Sectors and the twelve Presidents that reigned over them. Over the years since The War's end, rumors that Mexico was planning an attack or takeover had come and gone, but no substantial evidence was ever uncovered. By far the biggest threat from Mexico and its refusal to be part of The Sectors was the potential for disease and a pandemic that could end humanity. It was the hope of the agency that a peaceful relationship between the two superpowers would prevent such extinction.

But establishing such a relationship was proving to be more difficult than Chris could have imagined. They were reluctant to send spies, as the agency had done years before, because no team of spies that successfully got into Mexico had ever returned to The Sectors, nor could they be communicated with once they got beyond the border. The wall surrounding the entire country was more than concrete: it blocked signals from getting in or out. The Presidents had told Chris they hoped he could eventually train a team to not just get beyond the wall but also to find those previously sent in who had apparently disappeared and bring them back. But that seemed far off in the distant future. Chris still did not even know how to contact anyone in Mexico. But he knew there was a way. There had to be. The illegal drug trade that made it possible for drugs created in Mexico to be sold in The Sectors suggested illicit communication between Sector citizens and inhabitants of Mexico. Yet, when his teams tried to follow this lead, they could not figure out how the perpetrators were carrying out the business.

So, the plan for the DMR was restructured, and the Presidents suggested that his teams first understand Mexico before reaching out to establish a protocol for communication. His agents talked with former inhabitants of Mexico, few as there were, and searched for any information they could gather.

It was in gathering that information that he found out about the Cipher.

Chris turned to the camera as he began to speak. "Recently, one of my teams uncovered some chatter referring to something that appears to be called the 'Cipher' by underground communications. What this so-called Cipher is, how it relates to Mexico, and what they want with it is what I would like to find out. My current teams are at full capacity and have neither the time nor the resources to pursue this. I would like to open a new mission dedicated to locating the Cipher, if it exists, and figure out why Mexico would want it."

"The Cipher," one of the Presidents in the Central Sector said. "Is there nothing else you can tell us about it?"

Chris answered, "We know it is for sale on the black market and that it has something to do with The Sectors and could possibly contain sensitive information. I suspect it's a digital document that contains some sort of code or code-breaking device, but we have been unable to confirm that suspicion. One of my agents found a message encrypted within a document. She believes she has traced it to one of the Purebred Communities."

"But you don't know what sort of code the Cipher is referring to or what kind of code it could break or translate," another President clarified.

"No, not at this time," Chris answered.

Just as a President from the Eastern Sector was about to speak, President Anders looked at Chris and said, "The Secretary will put it on the agenda for our closed meeting. After the Presidents discuss it, I'll let you know what we decide."

"Thank you, Madam President," Chris said, and his image disappeared from the screen reserved for speakers.

The Secretary moved on to the next item on his list.

After the conference, Chris returned to his office to check in with his teams. He was working with twenty-two agents in total, fifteen on one mission and seven on another. He was still learning how to manage projects and other people. As an agent, he had been assigned to the position of assassin for hundreds of missions, but only one at a time. He was focused and intuitive and also good at reading people, but delegating and trusting that his agents out in the field were capable of what they were doing was a skill he was still developing. He suspected that this was the reason the Presidents had not entrusted him with the entire plan for the DMR or how they were going to pursue a relationship with Mexico. They told him who the leaders were, but from what he could tell, Mexico's government and hierarchy was much more complex than that of The Sectors and perhaps more complicated than even the Presidents realized. He told Xiao as much, but he was waiting until he had a better idea of what Mexico's system of government was before briefing the Presidents on his suspicions. Either way, Mexico was a fortress even he could not hack into, and Chris had not been prepared for that.

He was still sitting at his desk when President Anders entered. She shut the door behind her and pointed to the privacy button on his desk as she sat in a chair. He switched it on, activating the blocking devices that lined the floor, walls, and ceiling, as he stood to greet her with a bow. The blocking devices prevented eavesdroppers from overhearing a conversation and jammed recording devices. Though the agency buildings were secure, the extra measure of privacy was used in cases of extreme caution.

He walked over to the sitting area and sat in a chair next to her. When he made the decision to request opening a new mission for pursuing the Cipher, he had expected a simple "yes" or "no." But after President Anders cut the discussion short at the conference, he knew there would be a more in-depth meeting to follow if they granted his request. Her sitting down made him optimistic that the discussion had been in his favor.

"As I'm sure you realize," she started, "your request has been discussed, and the Presidents agree that this is a mission worth opening."

Chris nodded formally without expression.

"We also agreed," she continued, "that you can spearhead the mission."

Chris nodded again, more slowly this time, hiding his contentment for a third mission. It meant he was doing well in his new position and that they trusted him with more.

"However," she added with emphasis, "I must impress upon you the importance of this mission. If this Cipher you think your team has heard of is what we think it is, then it is invaluable to The Order, and we must get it at all costs. It will not be enough to simply find it. We must find all of it, and any copies that also exist, and destroy it completely. I want this mission to take priority above your others. Do you understand that, Rockford." As usual, though she asked a question, there was no intonation in her voice. Anders was a commander, so even her questions came out as commands.

"Yes, of course," Chris answered seriously.

When Anders was satisfied that he understood how important this conversation was, she said, "Okay. Now, tell me *everything* you already know about the Cipher. How did your agent find out about it and what did your agent learn."

"She was looking into some digital documents she collected in gathering information about Mexico and how the line of communication could be opened. Per protocol, she ran the file through a program that scans for viruses, watermarks, tags—"

"Yes, I'm familiar with the protocol, Rockford. Go on."

"It detected a quantum encryption that revealed some chatter. She decrypted as much as she could, but it appeared to be part of a larger message or several messages. It was incomplete, but based on what she did find, it seems there is a file called 'Cipher' and that there is a deal to sell it to Mexico. The furthest she was able to track it was to a Purebred Community in Montana."

"The encryption said the Cipher itself is in Montana," Anders asked in her way that sounded like a demand.

"It's unclear if the Cipher is in Montana or if something related to it is in Montana. I believe it was the only location mentioned in the pieces of the message that she was able to find. But she believes it meant something is there, maybe the Cipher."

"And," Anders asked.

"That's all," Chris stated.

"It said nothing about what the Cipher actually is or what it decodes," Anders clarified.

"No, Madam President."

Anders pulled out her notebook, so Chris took his out as well. She projected her screen up on the wall and spoke while files transferred to Chris's notebook. "What you are looking at are two genetic codes that took years to sort out and understand. They are now commonly known as The Original Human Genome and The Modified Human Genome. They are the results of countless hours of manpower and finances to research and insert the necessary sequences for generating self-editing defense mechanisms for any new infections and superbugs, along with corrections for deleterious mutations and other improvements for genetic superiority and for curing all the genetic diseases that used to plague our world."

Anders looked him in the eyes, and Chris could see in the seriousness of her expression that he now held one of the most classified documents in their government. *This* was ultimately what The War had been fought over, when it came down to it. *This* was what separated two groups of people around the world: those who were for curing disease through genetic modifications, maintained by a governing entity that ensured natural mutations and evolving processes were controlled—and those who were against it, willing to surrender to nature and the chaos that ruled the world before The War That Brought Order.

He nodded and said, "I understand."

She turned back to the projection on the wall and pulled up a portion of one of the codes. "This is the Modified genome, the blueprint that every new human born into The Sectors is modeled after."

Every new approved *human*, Chris corrected her in his thoughts.

She pulled up a list of documents. "These are the mandatory modifications. Most of them will have been passed down by Modified parents, but they have to be checked for accuracy." She pulled up another list. "And these are the cosmetic modifications parents can choose from when designing their offspring prior to conception."

Chris knew about the process for having children but had become more familiar with it since his best friend, Zaire, and Zaire's wife, Melinda, had received a Child License six months earlier. Since the government paid for all citizens to take birth control pills, unplanned pregnancies were rare and usually aborted. The official protocol for procreation was for a married couple to apply for and be granted a Child License, and then the pregnant mother would undergo a procedure so the embryo's genome could be Modified. The mandatory modifications, as well as the surgery itself, were paid for by the government, but for an additional cost, cosmetic modifications could be added to the list of edits, as well. But only Coastal families could afford those. Being Inlanders, his parents could not afford cosmetic changes, so, like most Inlanders, Chris and his brother looked like his parents. The offspring of Coastals, however, bore little resemblance to their parents, and from what Zaire told him, Chris expected Zaire's child to look nothing like Zaire or Melinda, either.

In addition to the mandatory modifications and the surgical procedure to edit the embryo's genome, the government also paid for necessary child costs such as food, clothes, schooling, and school supplies. Those who did not earn approval to procreate by going through the process of getting a Child License, and thus whose children were not Modified, had to pay these expenses out of pocket. Without the government benefits, only Coastal families could afford to forego the Child License process, though it was rare for anyone to do so. Occasionally, even Inlanders would try to bear the cost of having a child without getting approval first. The Ban on Pure Breeding, the mandate that required the genetic modifications, was instigated at the end of The War forty-one years beforehand. And, though rare, the children who were born since The Ban on Pure Breeding was implemented but without the mandatory genetic modifications were referred to as Purebreds. The Purebreds were largely disregarded from society and often not considered real citizens. Though Chris had always been aware of them, it was only in the last year that he had been forced to ponder the philosophy of such a process, first as part of a mission for the agency and then more seriously upon marrying one.

Anders closed all the files, switched off the projection so the wall was back to looking like a solid surface, and shifted her body so she was facing Chris. "We believe the Cipher your team has detected may be a document that reveals information about the modifications, what the sequences are, where they are inserted or deleted, how they work, and what they change. If Mexico is negotiating with anarchists to obtain this document, it may be because they are starting to realize how good the modifications are and how they do improve our world. However, we believe they want it so they can build bacterial strains or viruses that the modifications cannot defend."

"But—" Chris started.

"But I just told you the modifications would protect against anything. It does not mean they are foolproof. That is why we genotype and correct every new human embryo of parents who have been approved for the Child License and why we contain the Purebred populations in Purebred Communities." Then, she added, "For the most part," referring to the exceptions, including Chris's wife. Had it been up to her, all Purebreds would have resided in the Communities.

She continued, "That is why all Purebreds undergo mandatory physical examinations every six months and why every illness is carefully documented in their hospitals. We are always on the lookout for potential epidemics. Biowarfare is Mexico's best angle at taking over the world, if that is what they want to do. It's why we stopped allowing their inhabitants to enter The Sectors and why we continue to keep them out. Anything could come from that country and cause another pandemic, and it is our responsibility to keep Sector citizens safe."

"We only know of one Cipher, but the team I assemble will also search for other copies," Chris assured her. "I also plan on monitoring the cameras and microphones of the Purebred Communities and searching the database of recorded internet activity, chat rooms, phone conversations, and video chats with updated keywords, based on the information we gather."

"I assume you are going to request that your friend Zaire be on this team."

Chris and Zaire had worked on many missions together, more than was typical for any two agents, but those cases had always been when they were both in the same department, first when they both worked in the Department of Surveillance and then when they were both in the Department of Anarchy Prevention.

"I would like to, but he still has over a year left in his Assignment in Public Relations," Chris answered. Agents spent two years in a department before being transferred for their next Department Assignment.

"This mission supersedes rules, Rockford," Anders said quickly, and Chris detected a hint of frustration in her tone. "He is the best codebreaker we have. If they are sharing it digitally, he can find it."

"I can ask him if he has time," Chris offered.

"He has time. I'm having him transferred to the DMR and put on your new team. Another agent can take over his current caseload."

As an agent in the Department of Anarchy Prevention, Chris had been the only exception to the two-year rule, an exception the Presidents allowed because he was so valuable as an agent in the field. That she was now making an exception to cut Zaire's two-year Assignment short meant this case was paramount.

"You're a good asset to the agency, Rockford. You were our best field agent, and you are proving to be a good boss. But you should know you are under careful watch. Each move you make is under scrutiny. I trust you because Xiao vouches for you, but I cannot say the other Presidents are so willing to take his word for it. You're still new at being in charge of missions, you're our first Modified boss, and even I am not thrilled that you are personally monitoring a member of a notorious elite anarchist family by living with her."

"I am married to someone who happens to be the daughter of two anarchist masterminds," he corrected her. "She has many times denounced them and tried to separate herself from that part of her life. She was never really one of them."

"Still," Anders insisted, "she could have much influence on you. And that fact does not escape us."

"I understand," he said with obedience.

"You are loyal, Rockford. That is how you have achieved so much success in your missions and how you have risen to this position. And that fact, also, does not escape us."

She did not smile, but, inwardly, Chris delighted in the praise. It was rare for any of the Presidents to say anything good about their subordinates.

She stood, and so Chris also stood and bowed to her just before she left, leaving his office door open. He returned to his desk and switched off the privacy setting, and the gentle hum that muffled any signal eavesdroppers might try to pick up softened to make the room completely quiet.

*   *   *

Nearly an hour later, Zaire arrived and knocked lightly on the door to Chris's office. "Boss Rockford," he said with mock formality as he walked in.

"Agent Melnyk," Chris said and motioned to the chair across from his desk. "Have a seat." Chris had seen Zaire at breakfast—they ate breakfast together at the agency's restaurant nearly every morning—but they had not worked on a case together since Chris had been promoted.

"I can't say I was surprised they transferred me," Zaire said as he sat down.

"No?"

"I knew you couldn't survive without me."

"Apparently not," Chris agreed. "I need you to crack an encryption and find some history on a document for me."

"You got it," Zaire said without hesitation. "Send it on over. I'll get started on it right away." Zaire pulled out his notebook and waited for Chris. He asked no questions, knowing it was not his place as an agent. Agents knew little about the cases they worked on because they only knew what was necessary for carrying out their part of the mission. It was a precaution set up by the agency so that no agent knew too much about any case and to ensure complete secrecy.

Chris pulled up the document and sent it to Zaire's notebook. "The message was encrypted in this file," he explained. "We need to find the item it refers to."

Zaire started programming on his notebook, but after a moment, he said, "I'll have to get back to my desk to work on this. I can't hack it on here." He looked at Chris and, with a competitive smirk, asked, "Did you already try to hack it?"

"I'm too busy."

"I'm sure you are," Zaire said with a hint of sarcasm.

"The agent who found it traced it to a Purebred Community, so I need you to write a petition for access to the Purebred Community database and search for any information about the whereabouts of whatever this item is. For now, we can look for keywords like 'cipher' and 'Mexico' and 'code', but obviously we'll need more information."

Zaire nodded. "All right."

Chris added, "Once you have access to the database, look for unusual behavioral patterns and anything that might indicate a network of individuals communicating. Then, once you identify groups, figure out what they are talking about and go from there. See if you can narrow it down to suspicious activity that can give us more keywords to search."

"Approach it from both angles. I can do that."

"Will you need help?"

"Nah, I got this," Zaire said with a smile. "I'll find this thing in no time." As Zaire stood up, he asked, "Anything else?"

Chris shook his head.

Zaire hesitated, looked at the doorway, and then turned back to Chris. He leaned in, placing a hand on the desk, and whispered, "I know this mission is a big deal because my time in Public Relations was cut short for it. But can I ask why this case is in Mexico Relations? This sounds more like Anarchy Prevention."

"Right now it's just a lead," Chris said, unsure of how he felt about Zaire asking for more information. As a boss, he probably would not be so open with an agent, but Zaire was his best friend. This change in job status was new territory for their friendship.

Recognizing that he may have crossed a line, Zaire said, "Right. Sorry, I was just curious." He turned to leave. But, unable to resist, he turned back toward Chris, leaned over again and asked, "What would Mexico want with the Purebreds?"

Chris hesitated, thinking of how he should handle this breach of protocol. On the one hand, it was not Zaire's place to ask; on the other hand, maybe he needed more information to find more keywords.

"Sorry," Zaire said, again. He stood up straight and left, giving Chris a final nod at the door before leaving.

After Zaire had gone, Chris continued to look at the doorway. He considered calling Zaire back into his office to give him more information. He was his best friend, after all; he felt like, at the very least, he owed him the small courtesy of offering his personal opinion or speculation. But the truth was, Chris had been asking himself that question ever since his agent brought the document to his attention, and he had not been able to come up with a single idea as to why the Cipher would be in a Purebred Community or how they could have any contact with Mexico.

CPSIA information can be obtained
at www.ICGtesting.com
Printed in the USA
LVHW052054261020
669863LV00017B/279